# SECRETS AND LIES

DREDA SAY MITCHELL

Love and Hate Series Book 3

Print ISBN 978-1-0685091-5-5

Editing and formatting: https://studioenp.com
Additional Editing: Lily and Christine Dunlop
Cover design: Mitchell and Joseph Ltd/ Book Brush
Cover Photographers: Iniraswork, Eyecan and Feedough

# Praise for Dreda Say Mitchell & Ryan Carter

'As good as it gets.' **Lee Child**

'Great book by a great girl.' **Martina Cole**

'A truly original voice.' **Peter James**

'A fast-paced thriller that will keep you guessing until the very last page.' **Paula Hawkins**

'Sharply observed and a moving story of conflicting loyalties and unfinished business.' ***Guardian***

'Zippy, twisty plot…a bevy of memorable supporting goodies and baddies.' ***Sunday Times***

'Thrilling.' ***Sunday Express*** **Books of the Year**

'Awesome tale from a talented writer.' ***Sun***

'Fast paced and full of twists and turns.' ***Crime Scene Magazine***

# Free Novella

## Join Our Exclusive Book Club

If you haven't already, plunge into the gangland world where the Steele and Watson Crime Family Drama started.

**DANGEROUS**

A LOVE & HATE SERIES PREQUEL

**Fate throws them together. The streets try to tear them apart.**

Bertram Watson, aka Brother Bertie, newly arrived from Jamaica, finds himself on the run in London's gritty streets. Jimmy Steele, son of a feared gangster, is bleeding out in a warehouse after a botched heist. Their paths cross in a twist of fate that will change their lives forever.

As Bertie's Jamaican street smarts clash with Jimmy's East End savvy, they form an unlikely alliance. But with rival gangs closing in and dangerous secrets coming to light, their newfound friendship is put to the ultimate test.

In this thrilling novella, loyalties are tested, blood is spilled, and love is pushed to its limits in the unforgiving world of London's underworld.

Visit www.dredamitchell.com

# Prologue

The East End Docklands
1974

Freezing water slapped him awake.

Blackness. The stench of river mud. Moonlight catching ripples of the Thames below. His wrists burned from ropes cutting into flesh, ankles bound with brutal efficiency. A filthy rag jammed between his teeth, the taste of grease and grime flooding his mouth.

He writhed on cold stone, panic surging through every fibre. Twisting his head, he spotted where he lay – ancient steps descending into murky water, notorious throughout London's underworld.

The Executioner's Steps.

His terror-filled gaze shot upwards. A coarse noose hung from a rusted iron davit jutting from the wall – once used for hauling cargo, now readied for human freight.

*God almighty! No!*

He thrashed madly, desperate sounds muffled behind the foul gag. Cold air bit into his skin, yet sweat drenched his shirt, plastering it to his trembling body.

The soft scuff of leather on stone froze him mid-struggle.

Shapes emerged from the darkness. Four silhouettes materialised in thin moonlight, faceless and silent. Watching.

The shortest figure approached, bending beside him. A hand ripped the gag away, tearing his lips.

Blood trickled down his chin. 'Please,' he begged, dignity abandoned. 'This isn't right!'

No response. Only cold, merciless silence.

The tallest shadow stepped forward, seizing him. He fought with animal desperation, kicking uselessly against the iron grip. His captor dragged him towards the waiting noose.

Rough hemp scratched his neck, tightening. His lungs burned, struggling for air before the drop even came.

'Please don't—'

A brutal shove.

The rope snapped taut.

# Chapter One

The East End
1974
Months Earlier

Jimmy 'Southpaw' Steele was on the warpath. His gleaming black Bentley Corniche screeched to a halt outside the derelict Victorian house, tyres spitting gravel down the run-down street near Brick Lane. The handcrafted luxury motor stood out like a brass monkey's bollocks, exactly how thirty-three-year-old Jimmy wanted it. Let every two-bob tosser see who was coming.

The man who was well on his way to becoming the gangland boss of the East End.

Jimmy commanded maximum respect. Everyone called him Southpaw or Mister Southpaw these days, a nod to his boxing champion past with a lethal left hook that had flattened plenty of faces on canvas. His fighting days, in the ring at least, were behind him now, but his reputation had only grown more fearsome.

Stepping from the car, he cut an imposing figure. Burgundy three-piece suit with wide lapels, expensive material stretched across broad boxer's shoulders. His cream shirt sported an extravagant collar framing his squared-jaw face. Not pretty-boy handsome but a proper bloke's features, hardened by years of dishing out punishment. Dark hair, longer than his fighting days, was styled back from his forehead. Thick sideburns ran along the side of his face. A gold sovereign ring glinted on a meaty finger, matched by the heavy gold bracelet circling his wrist.

Everything about him screamed the modern breed of East End gangster.

His silver-grey eyes, once warm when he smiled at his beloved Mini, were dead cold now. Five years without his adored wife had turned him into someone people sometimes crossed the street to avoid. Not that he'd ever harm an innocent – Jimmy Steele had principles, lines he wouldn't cross. But those who stepped on his toes? God help their miserable souls.

'Bloody hippie twats,' he snarled, slamming the heavy car door hard enough to rattle windows down the street.

The three-storey house stood battered and neglected, its front scarred with garish handwritten banners proclaiming: 'Housing for All' and 'Property is Theft'. Jimmy's property, to be exact. Part of his growing empire. East London real estate was dirt cheap, ripe for the picking for a man with vision and readies. The economic chaos meant opportunity for those with cash to splash.

Bloody squatters. Taking liberties in other people's property. No respect for sod all these days. The council should round the lot of them up and dump them in the Thames. But since they wouldn't, Jimmy would have to sort it himself.

Squatting was at epidemic proportions. Empty buildings filled with long-haired wasters who thought they could live for free. Not in Jimmy's buildings. Not on his bleedin' watch. He'd rather torch the gaff and watch it burn before his eyes than let these poxy freeloaders get their mitts on what was rightfully his.

He booted the door with force that splintered the lock and nearly tore it off its hinges. Jimmy's massive frame filled the doorway. His large fists clenched and unclenched, muscles rippling beneath his clothing.

The stench hit him first, unwashed bodies, patchouli oil, and cannabis smoke.

A figure stirred on the dusty floor of what had once been a respectable parlour. Classic hippie type in a ratty Afghan coat, patched jeans, hair longer than most birds Jimmy knew. The guy's eyes widened when they clocked Jimmy's murderous expression.

'This ain't a bloody hotel, you prat.' Jimmy grabbed him by his flowing locks and hauled him upright with one meaty paw.

The hippie yelped and flailed, feet barely touching the floor.

'We've got rights, man! Squatter's rights!' he protested, voice breaking with terror.

Jimmy let out a laugh that would've frozen the Thames in August. 'Rights? In my sodding building? The only right you've got is to decide whether you walk out that door or crawl out on your belly because you've got broken legs!'

He dragged the man to the door and tossed him onto the pavement, sending him sprawling. His pathetic possessions followed. Manky sleeping bag, guitar with broken strings, dog-eared copy of some political bollocks.

'Darken this door again and they'll be scraping what's left of you off the pavement with a toothbrush! Now sling your peace-lovin' hook before I redecorate this street with your guts!'

The squatter scrambled to gather his belongings, eyes darting between Jimmy and the safety of the street. 'This is fascism, man. The people—'

'The people can pay soddin' rent!' Jimmy bellowed. 'I see your mug round these parts again, I'll turn you into yesterday's news. That's not a threat, that's a promise of you being put six feet under.'

The man didn't need telling twice. He grabbed his gear and legged it, bare feet slapping against the pavement.

Jimmy turned back to the house, ears pricked for any other unwelcome guests. Ground floor appeared empty. He secured the broken door; mental note to call his builder tomorrow. He stomped up the stairs, checking each room methodically, booting in doors rather than turning handles.

He'd nearly concluded the place was clear when he heard it, groaning and rhythmic creaking from the back bedroom. Unmistakable sounds.

*You've gotta be fucking me sideways!*

Jimmy pushed the door open with his foot, hard enough to crack the plaster behind it.

A couple writhed on a stained mattress, so engrossed they hadn't heard the commotion downstairs. The woman straddled her partner, head thrown back, tits bouncing for England with each movement. The man beneath spotted Jimmy first, eyes widening but showing no fear.

'Want to join us, friend?' He beckoned with a grin, hands still gripping the woman's hips.

The woman turned, fixing Jimmy with a sultry smile and come-hither flash of eyes. 'Plenty of room,' she purred, deliberately arching her back to thrust her thrupenny bits towards him. She had to be high, pupils the size of pennies.

'You what?' Jimmy stared, momentarily thrown.

Her body was gorgeous, firm and inviting breasts, flat tummy, shapely thighs. He waited for his cock to stir, desperate to feel anything. Physical attraction. Lust. The simplest human response.

Nothing. His heart lay dead since his cherished Mini – God rest her pure soul – had passed. Five long years of emptiness.

Jimmy hadn't been a monk. He'd had women, plenty throwing themselves at him because of who he was, what he represented. But the truth was he went through the motions, found physical release, but his heart remained untouched. Some people said since his missus had died, he was a right cold bastard. They weren't bloody wrong.

A choking sadness descended, heavy and suffocating, followed swiftly by familiar fury that Mini had been taken too young. Twenty-seven. His Mini, with her fierce loyalty and wicked laugh.

The familiar ache spread through his chest, squeezing his lungs tight. His throat closed until he could barely swallow. The grief hit him in waves, stealing his breath when he least expected it. Some mornings he woke reaching for her, the phantom scent of her perfume in his nostrils.

'Out.' The word emerged as a rumbling growl from deep in his chest. 'Get your shit and fuck off before I chuck you both through the fucking window.'

His lethal expression must have penetrated their drug-induced haze. The smile slid from the woman's face in record time. Her partner pushed her off and groped for his clothes.

'No need to be hostile, man,' the bloke muttered and yanked on his trousers.

'I'll show you bloody hostile if you're not gone in ten seconds,' Jimmy snarled, advancing a step.

They dressed with frantic speed, the woman eyeing him with undisguised terror now. Good. Fear was useful. Fear kept people in line.

They were out in less than a minute.

Jimmy walked through the rooms again, this time with his business eye, noting potential. High ceilings. Original features under the grime. The place had good bones. With the right renovations, he could triple his investment. Another piece in his growing empire.

Descending the stairs, Jimmy considered that this was his life now. Empire building, both legit and under the table. Looking after his kids. Surviving each day without Mini. And if he felt nothing inside himself most days, so be it. Feeling nothing was better than feeling the pain.

The next step in Jimmy moving upwards was to expand his empire. Property in the East End was all well and good, but the real fortune was Up West. Mayfair, Belgravia, Chelsea. Places where the rich cunts lived. Jimmy had his eye on a new business acquaintance who could potentially get the ball rolling. He'd already dipped his toe in the water with the guy and liked where it was going. That's why he'd set up a new meeting with Jack Blacklock. Everyone called him Dash. Funny thing was, he was also the nephew of the same man, Lord somebody or other, whose family had owned the docks in Sugar Cane Wharf, where Jimmy still lived and had grown from a weed to a man. Of course, the docks were an East End memory now, long dead.

Dash came from the branch of the wealthy family who lived in Jamaica.

*Jamaica.*

Jimmy wished he hadn't thought of that word because it made him remember… He shook his head. There was no time for looking back on a past friendship long dead, only looking forward.

He pushed through the broken door into the grey afternoon light. Time to—

'Jimmy?'

The voice stopped him dead. He spun round. A thin figure emerged from the shadows beside the building, clutching two plastic bags and what appeared to be a cat. The woman was hollow-cheeked, her once-platinum hair now dull and stringy. She wore a threadbare coat that had seen better decades, haunted eyes staring from her gaunt face.

'Auntie Chrissie?' Jimmy couldn't believe his eyes. 'Bloody Ada, what's happened to you?'

His dad's sister had once been a proper knockout. A bombshell straight out of a 1950s mag. Platinum-blonde hair, hourglass figure that could stop traffic, always dressed to the nines. Men used to break their necks just to catch a glimpse of her parading down the street. She was also a real handful, usually up to her neck in trouble, a Steele to the core.

This wasn't that woman. This was a broken shadow, all sharp edges and frightened glances.

'I was just…' She shifted the bags nervously, and Jimmy caught sight of the cat's yellow eyes, which glared fiercely at him with undisguised hostility.

'Christ, Chrissie, when did we last see you?' Concern pushed him towards her. 'You need help? Money? A place to stay?'

But she was already backing away, shaking her head frantically. 'No, no, I can't… I've got to go.'

'Wait!' Jimmy called, but she was already belting down the street with the desperate haste of someone running from more than just family.

Jimmy watched her disappear around the corner, a chill settling in his stomach that had nothing to do with the weather. His glamorous aunt, reduced to a bag lady with a manky cat.

What nightmare had shattered Chrissie Steele?

# Chapter Two

Chrissie ran like the wind. She didn't stop until she reached Commercial Street between Spitalfields and Petticoat Lane. Even at this early hour, the working girls were already out, strutting their stuff along the pavement. A couple of them eyed her with professional interest before clocking her outfit. Not competition, then. Just another dried-up bird trying to survive.

The bitter wind cut through Chrissie's thin coat, slicing right to her bones while she clutched Tel, full name Tequila, her prized cat against her body. The tabby's claws dug into her bony arms, but she barely felt the sting. Nothing compared to the crushing ache in her chest, the shame burning her cheeks red raw.

Her previous landlord had booted her out like yesterday's rubbish.

His cruel laughter still rang in her ears: 'Three weeks behind, love. Time to sling your hook.'

She'd tried to explain about the nightmares, the sleepless nights when twisted memories crawled out of dark corners. Tried to tell him how the booze was the only thing keeping her from going completely barking mad. But all he'd seen was a skint woman with empty pockets and dead eyes.

*Story of my bloody life. More screwed than a Soho professional, me.*

Chrissie stumbled to a halt outside the stone steps that led down to the underground public lav on Commercial Street, right outside Christ Church Spitalfields. The Victorian brick entrance was stained with decades of London grime, but it had running water and mirrors.

Tel meowed pitifully while she descended the grimy steps. The underground space opened up before her, all old-style tiles and flickering electric bulbs. The original Victorian fittings were still there: white porcelain sinks with brass taps, mirrors in ornate frames, and cubicles with heavy wooden doors.

At one of the mirrors, a bleached blonde in a tight red dress was touching up her lippy. Although she couldn't have been more than twenty, her gaze already held the hard glint of someone who'd seen too much too young. She glanced at Chrissie in the reflection, taking in the sunken cheeks.

'Rough night, babes?' the blonde asked, her voice surprisingly gentle.

Chrissie managed a bitter scoff. 'Rough year, more like.'

The woman nodded, understanding passing between them. She capped her lipstick and gathered up her handbag. 'Take care of yourself. These streets eat girls alive.'

With that, she clicked up the steps on her stiletto heels, leaving Chrissie alone.

'Right then, Tel.' Chrissie set the scrawny cat down gently. 'Let's see what we're working with.'

She caught sight of herself in the mirror and nearly gasped. Blimey, where had all her flesh gone? Her sharp cheekbones jutted out, and her once-adored hair hung in rats' tails around her face. The famous Chrissie Steele curves had done a proper runner, leaving behind a scarecrow in a dirty dress.

*Christ, I've seen better-looking corpses at the morgue.*

*This ain't you. This ain't the girl who had half of London eating out of her palm and the other half queuing up for seconds.*

She turned on the brass taps, grateful when actual hot water spluttered out. Cupping her trembling palms, she splashed her face, scrubbing away the grime and dried tears. The water ran grey down the drain.

From her battered handbag, she pulled out a quarter-bottle of gin. Her last precious drops. The harsh liquid burned her throat, but it steadied her limbs. Stopped the trembling, just for a moment.

She rummaged deeper in the bag, finding her compact and lipstick. The slap was cheap shit from Woolworth's, nothing compared to the Revlon and Max Factor she'd once worn. But it would have to do, wouldn't it? Beggars can't be choosers and all that bollocks.

She dabbed concealer under her bloodshot eyes, trying to hide the purple shadows that spoke of too many sleepless nights. The lipstick was Red Velvet, bold and defiant. She traced her lips carefully, watching while some colour returned to her pale face. A bit of mascara to brighten her dull eyes. Some powder to smooth out the worst of the damage.

*That's better. That's more like it.*

But the moment she stared at her reflection again, everything shifted. The electric bulbs seemed to dim, and suddenly she wasn't staring at a forty-five-year-old woman. She was fifteen again, standing in front of another mirror in another place, trying to fix herself after…

*No. Not now. Not bloody now.*

Her hands shook while the memory dragged her under. She could feel *his* demanding grip, hear *his* sickening snigger while he…

*Help me,* the girl in the mirror mouthed. *Why won't anyone help me?*

'Shut up!' Chrissie screamed, her voice bouncing off the tiled walls. 'Shut up, shut up. SHUT THE CUNTY-FUCK UP!'

Her clenched fist connected with the mirror before she could stop herself. Glass exploded in jagged fragments, and sharp pain shot up her arm. Blood welled from her cut skin, dripping into the sink.

The shock of it snapped her back to the present. She was gasping, her chest heaving. Tel was cowering, fur standing on end.

*Bloody hell. Lost it again, didn't you? Off your trolley, you are. Proper mental.*

She glanced down at her bleeding hand, then at the shattered mirror. Most of the glass had fallen into the sink, but one shard had landed on the edge, sharp and about four inches long.

Without thinking, she picked it up, feeling its heft in her palm. It was the kind of thing that could solve problems. The kind of thing that could force people to pay attention.

*Or force them to pay.*

She wrapped the shard carefully in her handkerchief and slipped it into her coat pocket. Then she gathered up Tequila, who purred despite everything, her loyal friend never judging, never abandoning.

Twenty minutes later, she stood outside a neat terraced house in Bethnal Green, her hair brushed, her makeup perfect, appearing every inch the old Chrissie Steele. Well, almost every inch. The door opened to reveal Malcolm Hennessy. He sold insurance during the day and collected rare books in his spare time. A proper gent, his neighbours would say. Salt of the earth.

He'd provide a place for her to sleep.

His pudgy face lit up when he spotted her; his hungry eyes lingered on her now-pert breasts, and his pink tongue darted across his lips.

*About as subtle as a fart in a telephone box.*

'Christine,' he leered, his voice thick with barely concealed hunger. 'What a lovely surprise.'

She smiled, the same devastating smile that had once brought men to their knees. 'You all right, Mal. I was wondering... could I come in? I find myself in a bit of a situation.'

He stepped aside immediately, practically pulling her through the door. 'Of course, my dear. Anything for you.'

The moment she crossed the threshold, Tel hissed softly. Smart cat. Animals always knew, didn't they? They could smell the wrongness that lurked beneath all that respectable codswallop.

The door closed behind them with a soft click. The shard of broken glass seemed to pulse in her pocket, sharp and ready and waiting for its moment to shine.

# Chapter Three

'You what?' Bertram Watson, better known round these parts as Brother Bertie, exclaimed. He couldn't believe what he was hearing.

'You heard me right the first time, Bertie,' Todd Saunders, the building site foreman, answered sympathetically. The man's shoulders sagged, and his tired eyes couldn't meet Brother Bertie's astonished stare. 'There's no work for you. Christ, I wish it wasn't this way, mate. It's this bloody Three-Day Week malarkey the government's dumped on us. We can only get leccy for three days now. Can't keep the site running without power.'

Brother Bertie had swapped his criminal crown for a wedding ring, and most days he reckoned it was the best trade he'd ever made. At thirty-two, the man who'd once been Jimmy Southpaw's right-hand now clocked in at building sites across East London, his famous pork pie hat the only reminder of wilder times. That million-quid smile still worked its magic, but these days it was reserved for Sin and their boy, Isaac, lovingly called Izzy, not for charming his way out of trouble.

Don't mistake his legitimate turn for going soft, though. He might've chosen love over criminal loyalty, family over the firm, and walked away from easy money to build something real, but cross his wife or threaten his boy, and you'd discover that going straight didn't mean going weak.

'Three-Day Week?' Brother Bertie's words came out strangled. 'What the hell's that then?'

He knew fully well what it was. The whole damn country did. From January first, businesses could only operate three consecutive days weekly. Essential services got exemptions, but building sites? They were expendable.

Todd filled in the gaps anyway. 'Government's rationing electricity, innit? Coal miners are on strike, power stations running low. These Westminster tosspots have got the whole country by the nuts.' He looked ready to spit in disgust. 'I'd keep you on in a heartbeat if I could, Bertie. You're one of the good ones. But I can't magic electricity out of thin air, can I?'

*Bloodfire!*

Brother Bertie gripped the concrete mixer to steady himself. The colour drained from his face, leaving him ashen beneath his brown skin. Sweat broke out across his forehead despite the freezing wind.

'I got a wife and young 'un,' he managed, voice barely audible. 'Izzy's poorly again with his chest. Without a wage, how the hell am I going to pay the heating bill? My boy can't live in a cold flat.'

Todd shrugged helplessly. 'You know the rule. Last in, first out. That's how it goes. Wish to Christ it was different.'

The cold wind whipped across the site, cutting through Brother Bertie's donkey jacket and chilling him to the bone. His pride lay shattered. Each day on this job had proved he'd truly left the criminal world behind, that Bertram Watson could provide for his family without breaking heads or bending the law.

Now some pussy politicians had pulled the rug from under every working man in Britain.

He trudged towards the site's gates, legs heavy, each step dragging him deeper into despair. Bitter memories of easier times crept into his thoughts. The adrenaline rush of a job with Jimmy, the electric thrill of danger, pockets heavy with quick money after a successful heist. A reluctant grin tugged at his lips, remembering the wild nights, the brotherhood, the respect that came with being Jimmy Steele's blood brother.

He quickly shook off the dangerous nostalgia. He'd given all that up for something better. Sin's warm body beside him every night, Isaac's gurgling laughter, the simple satisfaction of honest work. He wouldn't trade his legitimate life for all the criminal glory in London.

The real question gnawed at his guts now: How was he going to tell Sin that her husband, the man who'd promised to provide and protect, had lost his job?

***

Brother Bertie stood in the doorway of their kitchen, watching Sin making the finishing touches to dinner. Her chestnut hair caught the light from the window, falling in big bouncy layers that feathered perfectly around her face, glossy and styled with the professional skill she'd never lost from her hairdressing days.

Thirty-one-year-old Cynthia 'Sin' Watson had traded her swinging sixties style for motherhood and marriage, but she'd lost none of her fierce spirit. She'd given up dreams of magazine covers and Paris catwalks for something better: a love that burned steady instead of wild.

She'd chosen her estranged brother's former best friend over her own blood, walked away from everything she'd known for this council maisonette on the Isle of Dogs.

Four-year-old Izzy sat at their little Formica table, carefully arranging his toy cars in perfect lines, his tongue poking out in concentration. The lad had Brother Bertie's warm brown eyes but Sin's stubborn chin, and right now he appeared completely absorbed in his important work.

'Daddy!' Izzy spotted him and scrambled down from his chair, launching himself into his father's arms.

Brother Bertie caught his son, lifting him high before settling him against his chest. 'There's my big man.' He lovingly pressed his face into Izzy's soft curls. 'What you been up to then, eh?'

'Me and Mummy made your dinner!' Izzy announced proudly. 'And I helped stir!'

'Did you now?' Brother Bertie caught Sin's eye over Izzy's head, and she grinned back at him, flour still dusting her dark jumper.

'He's been a proper Galloping Gourmet today.' Sin wiped her palms on her apron. 'Nearly had the whole kitchen decorated with cheese sauce.'

Settling his son back at the table, Bertie moved to his wife, sliding his arms around her waist from behind. Sighing, she leaned back into him, and for a moment his disaster at work faded. This was home. This was everything.

'Smells incredible, darling.' He inhaled her familiar scent: soap and warmth and something indefinably Sin. 'You didn't have to go to all this trouble.'

Sin turned in his arms, her lips curving into a tender smile. 'You've been working so hard lately. Thought you deserved something special.'

The words formed in his throat. *Just tell her. Tell her now.*

'Sin, I need to—'

But she was already back to facing the stove, stirring the sauce with practiced movements, humming softly under her breath. So content. So trusting. How could he shatter this peace with his failure?

*Tell her you've only gone and lost your job. Tell her you can't provide for your family.*

His mouth opened. Closed. The confession died on his lips.

Guilt tore him up. While she'd been here creating this perfect domestic scene, he'd been getting sacked like some useless tosser. While she'd been cooking his favourite meal, he'd been walking home with his tail between his legs. The shame burned through every cell in his body.

His gaze wandered to the kitchen table, where Sin's worn leather Bible sat beside the salt and pepper. The sight of it sent familiar irritation through him. Every day that book seemed more prominent, and every day Sin seemed to drift further into the arms of the Catholic church.

Sin caught the direction of his stare, and her chin lifted slightly. 'Sister Bernadette asked when we're going to have Izzy baptised. We should have done this when he was a baby.'

Brother Bertie's jaw tightened instantly. They'd been down this road before. 'He's fine the way he is.

Don't need some priest splashing water on him to make him holy.'

'Bertie...'

'Our boy's perfect without any church messing about with him.'

Sin's eyes flashed dangerously, but before she could respond, Brother Bertie stepped closer and cupped her face in his palms. His expression softened completely.

'Listen to me, sweet ting,' he said, his smooth Jamaican lilt wrapping around the words. 'Izzy's got all the blessings he needs right here between us. He's got parents who love him, a home full of warmth, and more goodness in his little finger than most people manage in a lifetime. What more could any god want?'

Sin's fuming wavered; she was caught off guard by his sudden tenderness. 'You always do this.'

'Do what?' He feigned total innocence, but that cheeky gleam in his eyes was a dead giveaway.

'Turn on that charm when you want to avoid a proper conversation.'

'Is it working?'

Despite herself, Sin's mouth twitched. 'Maybe. But only because I'll never stop loving you.'

Later, they stepped out together onto their back balcony with its commanding view of the Thames. Brother Bertie pulled his beloved wife close, never able to get enough of her.

'Do you ever regret it, Bertie? Giving up so much for this life with me?' she asked.

He shifted her so she could see the honesty on his face. 'Sin Watson, you listen to me. I'd rather punch a thousand clocks and change a thousand nappies than go back to that life without you. You understand me?'

The irony of his words cut deep. Here he was, talking about punching clocks when he didn't even have a clock to punch anymore.

She melted into him then, all soft curves and warm skin. When his mouth found hers, she responded with the same desperate hunger that had first drawn them together. Her lips parted under his, sweet and eager, while her fingers tangled in the hair at the nape of his neck. The kiss deepened, years of marriage doing nothing to dim the fire between them. When they finally broke apart, both were breathing hard, foreheads pressed together in the gathering dusk.

'I love you, Bertram Watson,' she whispered on his lips.

'And I love you back, Mrs Watson. More than life itself.'

So if he loved her so much, why couldn't he find the courage to tell her the truth?

From inside came a sudden, harsh coughing fit that made both parents freeze.

'Izzy!' A frantic Sin was already moving towards the sound.

Brother Bertie's chest constricted. *Not again. Please, not again.*

They rushed inside to find their small son doubled over at the kitchen table, his body racked with violent coughs that seemed too big for his tiny frame. His face was flushed, eyes watering, and each breath rattled with the sound of fluid.

'Come here, baby,' Sin said, her voice steady despite the panic Brother Bertie could see in her eyes. She gathered Izzy into her arms, rubbing his back in slow, soothing circles. 'It's all right, sweetheart. Mummy's here.'

Brother Bertie quickly got his medicine and then watched helplessly as his son struggled for breath. This was agony. Pure, undiluted agony. His little boy, his precious son, suffering. He'd faced down hardened criminals without flinching, but watching his child in pain reduced him to nothing.

Izzy's coughing finally subsided after they prepared a steam bath.

'Better now?' Sin asked softly. She smoothed Izzy's curls back from his damp forehead.

Izzy nodded weakly, leaning against his mother's shoulder. 'Sorry, Mummy.'

'Nothing to be sorry for, my brave boy,' she murmured then kissed the top of his head.

Brother Bertie knelt beside them, placing a gentle hand on his son's back. The boy felt so slight, so fragile. How could someone so dinky carry such a heavy burden?

'We'll need to call the doctor in the morning,' Sin said quietly. She met Brother Bertie's troubled gaze over Izzy's head. 'And we're due for his monthly visit to the private clinic next week. The specialist wants to try a new treatment, but it's not available on the NHS.'

Suddenly, the walls were closing in on him. More medical expenses. More money they didn't have. More bills he couldn't pay because he didn't have a bleedin' job anymore.

'How much?' he forced himself to ask, though he dreaded the answer.

The figure she quoted rocked him. She might as well have said ten grand. Brother Bertie nodded, forcing his expression to remain calm even as his world crumbled around him. 'Whatever he needs. We'll find the money.'

*How, eh? How are you gwan find that money?*

Over a million people out of work. How was he supposed to compete against those odds? What chance did he have of finding another job when the whole country was falling apart?

Sin's sharp eyes missed nothing. 'Everything all right? You seem tense.'

*Tell her!* his conscience screamed. *She deserves to know!*

'Just tired.' He ruthlessly slashed down the voice in his head. 'The gaffer let us finish early since the weather turned nasty. Everything's cool.'

But nothing was cool. How long could he keep this secret before his family life came crashing down around their ears?

If Brother Bertie had known what was coming for his family, he would have held on to this moment forever. Sin's trust, Izzy's innocent need for his father's protection, the simple illusion that love could conquer all.

But he didn't know. And by the time he did, it would be too late.

# Chapter Four

'It's an almighty disgrace, Councillor Steele!'

Mrs Dorothea Chesterton's voice rang with righteous indignation, her brown patent handbag with its gold clasp clutched to her ample bosom, her lips thin and tight above the knot of nylon headscarf beneath her chin. 'That establishment on the corner of Fisherman's Lane is nothing but a knocking shop! Tarts hanging out like whores' washing at all hours, punters skulking about in flash cars. They're turning Sugar Cane Wharf into a red-light district!'

Her gaze rounded on the gathering. 'As our national chairman of the Clean Up Britain campaign, Oliver Harrington MP always says, "We must reclaim our streets from the merchants of vice who prey upon our communities."'

Danny Steele leaned forward at the head of the horseshoe-shaped table, nodding in agreement.

'Dorothea,' he oozed with an intimate tone that carried warmth throughout the sparsely filled Town Hall chamber. 'You don't mind me calling you that, do you? I feel we know each other so well after all these months. Especially as you are also the esteemed leader of the local chapter of the Clean Up Britain organisation.'

Her cheeks flushed pink with pleasure at his attention. Just as Danny suspected it would. He still had the ole loverboy charm in spades, was his considered opinion, despite being in his mid-fifties.

Councillor Danny Steele, that's what the brass nameplate on his office door read these days. He'd traded his docker's credentials for a council badge, but that wicked grin and the jagged scar slicing through his cheek still had the ladies swooning. The grey threading through his dark hair gave him a distinguished appearance that played well with the voters, and that silver tongue of his could talk up for his community just the way he had back in the day for dockers to the management.

He cut a leaner figure now than in his younger days, all Savile Row suits and polished shoes. He'd mastered the art of public service. Shaking hands with church ladies on Sunday, cutting ribbons at community centres, kissing chubby-cheeked babies, spouting off about law and order up at the Town Hall with the passion of a born-again saint. The men respected him, the ladies adored him, and the local press couldn't get enough of the former docker who'd pulled himself up by his bootstraps.

'Course, not everyone was buying what Councillor Steele was selling. Whispers still followed him through the corridors of power, murmurs from old-timers in the local boozers who'd tap their noses knowingly when his name cropped up. They reckoned you could take the man out of the docks, but you couldn't take the docks out of the man, know what I mean?

Old man Fitzgerald struggled to his feet, his walking stick striking the floor. Danny bestowed his full attention on him. 'Mr Fitzgerald, before you start, how did young Joey get on in the under-fifteens match last Saturday? I've been dying to hear.'

The old man's grumpy expression softened immediately at the mention of his grandson. One of the things folks loved about Councillor Steele, he remembered everyone and asked after them.

'Scored two goals! Thanks for asking. But about this brass house business.' His voice hardened again. 'We've been complaining about that place for months. Nothing's been done.'

Danny rose from his chair slowly, his imposing frame and magnetic charisma commanding attention. 'I give you my word that this council will not stand idly by while merchants of vice pollute our streets.' His intent gaze swept all those present, each in turn so none would doubt the fierceness of his promise. 'These bloodsuckers think they can operate with impunity, but they're about to learn different.'

'I will personally ensure that this establishment is investigated thoroughly.' His tone rose with biblical fervour. 'If laws are being broken, if vulnerable women are being exploited, then by God, we'll shut it down ourselves!'

The crowd erupted in applause. Dorothea Chesterton swallowed hard, clearly moved by Danny's passionate declaration.

'This is a disgrace that demands immediate action!' he thundered. 'I'll shut it down personally if that's what it takes to protect our community!'

The chamber doors burst open with a violent crash that silenced the applause instantly. A young woman wavered in the entrance and then stumbled in, her flame-red hair dishevelled. One strap of her short black dress was torn and hanging loose, her makeup smeared across her stunning face. Her torn stockings revealed scraped knees.

The gathering gasped collectively.

The woman's green-eyed gaze swept the room desperately before locking directly on to Danny's face with laser intensity.

'Help me,' she moaned. Her pleading, desperate stare never wavered from him. 'Please!'

Mr Fitzgerald's tone cut through the shocked silence with smug satisfaction. 'I've seen her… at that house.'

'Good Lord,' Danny breathed, his tone thick with horror. 'This poor soul… she's clearly been victimised by the very establishment we've been discussing.'

He moved quickly around the table. 'This unfortunate woman is living proof of the wickedness that plagues our streets.'

He reached out to steady her with gentle hands, declaring, 'This poor fallen soul has clearly suffered at the hands of those who would exploit the vulnerable for profit.' His arm wrapped protectively about her waist. 'Fear not, my dear. You're safe now. I'll personally see to your care.'

Dorothea Chesterton was practically weeping with admiration. 'Oh, Councillor Steele, you're a true Christian gentleman!'

'Indeed I am, Dorothea,' Danny replied solemnly. 'Now, if you'll excuse me, I must tend to this poor victim. Involve the police.'

Gently, he guided the young woman towards his office.

Danny's office was a testament to his success. Mahogany desk, leather chairs, framed photographs of him with local and national dignitaries.

The moment the door clicked shut, Danny's compassionate mask dissolved completely. He spun the woman around roughly, his fingers digging into her shoulders while his expression contorted with fury.

Danny growled, all trace of the caring councillor gone, 'What the fuck are you doing here?'

***

Danny snapped her hard to his body, his hot breath growling in her face, 'You never ever come here. That's the rules.'

Instead of being scared, she huffed, tossing her bright hair defiantly. 'Rules? You want to tell that bunch of la-di-da ponces that their money doesn't buy them the right to rough me or the girls up.'

If those concerned citizens wanted to find the pimp who owned the brothel they were complaining about, they needn't have searched very hard. He was amongst them all the time. Danny ran that knocking shop and plenty more besides. In fact, many called the mystery man who ran an empire of vice from the East End to the West End, The King of Porn.

It was a bloody masterpiece of deception, really. By day, Councillor Danny Steele fought tirelessly against the very establishments he owned by night. His respectable role gave him perfect cover – who would suspect the moral crusader denouncing sleaze of being its biggest peddler? He used council meetings to identify which areas had less police attention, presented himself as fighting sin while actually controlling it. His community outreach let him scout new locations and corrupt the right officials. The councillor role gave him insider information on police raids, advance warning that kept his operations one step ahead of the law.

Without warning, he crushed his mouth to hers in a brutal kiss that tasted of power and possession. When he pulled away, his eyes were dark with lust and fury.

Scarlett Fox had been his mistress for two years now. More than that, she was the outward face of his sleazy business empire, the red-haired temptress who could make even the most respectable gentlemen forget their wedding vows and moral principles.

Standing barely five feet two inches, with that fiery hair cut in the latest shag style and green eyes that could melt steel or freeze blood depending on her mood, Scarlett was everyman's fantasy and nightmare rolled into one. She could purr like a kitten then transform into a spitting wildcat in the space of a heartbeat.

Danny was fucking mad for her, and he knew it made him weak. Who would've thought Danny Steele would have his head turned by a piece of crackling like that? But Christ, she made him feel like a randy teenager again, all desperate hands and racing pulse whenever she sashayed into a room. The woman was pure sexual dynamite in a package designed to destroy men's common sense.

'These special parties you're putting on for your wealthier clients at the house in Belgravia,' Scarlett complained. She dabbed at her split lip with the back of her hand. 'Some of those toffs are getting well out of hand. They think their money buys them the right to treat us like punching bags.'

Danny's face darkened, and he grabbed her chin roughly between his thumb and forefinger. 'Listen here, you gorgeous little slag. I'm running this show, not you. You do what you're paid to do and keep your mouth shut about the rest.'

But Scarlett wasn't finished. She pressed herself on him, her hands sliding down his chest with practiced seduction. 'You know what would solve all our problems?' she purred and fluttered her eyelashes with mock innocence. 'Put that wife of yours into the nuthouse.'

Danny's stomach turned cold at the mention of Iris, his brain-damaged wife who stared at him with those blank, stupid eyes every morning. 'All in good time,' he muttered, trying to push the image away.

Scarlett's lower lip jutted into a petulant pout. 'But you promised I'd become Mrs Danny Steele. I'm getting tired of being your dirty little secret.'

Danny's control snapped. He slammed her back onto his mahogany desk. His hands were all over her; one yanked up her dress while the other fumbled desperately with his belt. 'You want to see how much I fucking want you?' he grunted into her neck. 'This is what you do to me, you little tease.'

She gasped and arched into him, her nails digging into his shoulders. 'Danny, you animal…'

He pushed her legs apart and drove into her hard, the desk scraping over the office floor with each brutal thrust. Scarlett's head fell back, her mouth opening in a silent cry of pleasure and pain.

'One of these days, Danny,' she moaned breathlessly in his ear, her voice barely a whisper, 'something really bad's going to happen at one of those kinky parties. Mark my words.'

# Chapter Five

'Plastic is fantastic!' Jemima, the Tupperware saleswoman announced with dramatic flair, her crimson-painted lips stretching into a dazzling smile. 'Say it with me, ladies. After three. One, two, three—'

'Plastic is fantastic!' All the gathered women in Gertie's prized private parlour chanted together, their words bouncing off the walnut radiogram and the 3D painting of the Last Supper that dominated the front wall.

Gertie Watson beamed with glowing pride from her position beside the settee suite, still pristine in the plastic covering it had been delivered in.

At forty-five, Gertie remained a force to be reckoned with, though you'd never know it from her kind manner. Built stout and strong from years of hard graft, she commanded respect. Her traditional red, gold, and green head wrap didn't have a fold out of place, and her deep-brown eyes held the kind of wisdom that came from surviving life's worst blows and still finding reasons to wake up each morning and smile.

She was Brother Bertie's God-fearing older sister, though she was the only soul alive who still called him Bertram, a privilege she guarded fiercely. Five years had passed since the brutal attack that had nearly killed her, and while her body had mended, the wound to her arm had left her with persistent aches that flared when rain was coming. The arthritis served as a constant reminder of how quickly violence could shatter a peaceful life.

This room was her sacred territory, the front parlour of her Whitechapel boarding house that nobody, and she meant nobody, was allowed to enter without her express permission. Every surface shone with fresh polish, every crocheted doily and ornamental knick-knack was perfectly positioned. She'd been saving for months to throw her first Tupperware party, and by God's grace it was turning out to be a proper triumph.

All the important women in her life were present.

Sin sat perched on the edge of an armchair, her brother's wife scrubbed up beautiful for the occasion in a smart navy dress that hugged the slim lines of her body just right. Gertie had to admit, that despite her initial reservations about the marriage, she had grown very fond of Sin over the years. The girl had a good heart and was the best mother to Gertie's adored nephew, Izzy.

*Still…* she couldn't shake the niggling doubts that maybe, just maybe, Sin and Bertram weren't a match made in heaven. That perhaps there was another path meant for her headstrong brother. But who was she to question God's plan? Gertie pushed the disloyal notion aside. Bertram had made his choice, and things were working out well for him and his new family.

Nora Baxter, known to one and all as Ruddy, sprawled across half the settee, her beehive hairdo defying gravity and good sense in equal measure. That woman never did anything by halves. Today she'd squeezed her skinny frame into a psychedelic mini-dress that would make a rainbow weep with envy, the swirling patterns of orange, pink and purple practically burning everyone's retinas. Her white go-go boots stretched up to her knobbly knees, and she clutched a glass brimming with Brother Bertie's infamous Lord Have Mercy Rum Punch.

'This stuff's got more kick than a Millwall supporter,' Ruddy cackled into her drink, earning disapproving stares from some of the other women, who attended Gertie's Pentecostal church. They wore their Sunday best pressed to perfection, every hair in place beneath their finest hats.

Lady Prudence was positioned near Ruddy, looking completely out of her element but loving every minute of it. Here was proper aristocracy, slumming it in Whitechapel, a million miles from her posh Grosvenor Square mansion. Ruddy worked as her housekeeper, but the two had become thick as thieves, an unlikely friendship that defied every social boundary in the book.

This was what Tupperware parties were all about. Women only, no men allowed to spoil the fun with their grunting and moaning. A proper ladies' do where they could have a good ole natter without some bloke telling them to pipe down or accusing them of wittering on about nothing. Here, they could speak their minds, share a laugh, and say what they really thought without getting the usual 'women's talk' rolled eyes from their old men.

'Now then,' Jemima continued, her words carrying the confident authority of a woman who'd flogged more plastic containers than anyone in East London. 'Who among you brave souls is ready... for the BURP?'

Arching her brows, she swept her arm toward the table laden with sparkling containers in harvest gold, avocado green, and sunshine yellow.

The women exchanged confused glances, murmuring amongst themselves.

'Burp?' someone hesitantly questioned.

Planting her palms firmly on her hips, Gertie's gaze flashed with killer disapproval. 'Anyone burp in my parlour will get a lick from my pot spoon 'round their bad-mannered head!'

Jemima let out a tinkle of laughter and then purred, 'Oh, you're in for a treat. This is where modern science meets your kitchen cupboard. Where innovation meets your daily grind.'

She selected a medium-sized container and filled it with water from Gertie's best porcelain jug, then positioned the lid on top of the container. 'Now watch very carefully, because what you're about to witness will change your domestic lives forever. Press down on the centre button while sealing the edges... and...'

*BURP!*

The container made a perfect little sound as the air escaped, creating an airtight seal.

'Bloody Nora!' Ruddy exclaimed, nearly launching her rum punch across the parlour. 'It actually burped! It's got better manners than most blokes I know!'

Lady Pru clapped her fingers together in pure delight. 'How absolutely marvellous! It's revolutionary!'

'Better than revolutionary, your ladyship,' Jemima beamed, clearly chuffed to have titled gentry in her audience. 'It's the future! Now feast your eyes on this.'

She turned the sealed container completely upside down and held it high above the table.

The parlour held its collective breath.

Not a single drop leaked.

Jemima triumphantly added, 'Air locked out, freshness locked in.'

Sin's expression lit up with enthusiasm. 'Think of all the food I could save! Izzy's always leaving his sandwiches half-eaten, but with these...'

'Exactly!' Jemima seized on her interest. 'The Wonder Bowl range starts at...' The price she quoted produced groans of disappointment, but she did not let that deter her. 'But think of all the money you will save preserving foods for longer.'

'My grocery bill's doubled since this Three-Day Week nonsense started,' Sin lamented.

Ruddy interjected, waving her glass. 'That lot in Parliament couldn't run a piss up in a brewery. How can you run a proper country when the lights keep going out every five seconds? Mind you, at least these Tupperware beauties will keep our food fresh during the blackouts. They're so bleeding clever they probably work by candlelight!'

Gertie found herself only half listening, fretfully glancing at the window. Where was Hyacinth? Her church sister had promised faithfully to be here by half past two, and it was nearly four now. That woman was never late for anything, punctuality was next to godliness in her book.

'Everything all right, Gertie?' Sin noticed her distraction.

'Just wondering where Hyacinth got to. She was so excited about today, been talking about it all week.' Gertie forced a smile. 'Probably got held up at work, that's all.'

Jemima's enticing manner drew them both back to her pitch. 'Right then, who wants to try the famous burp test for themselves?'

'Come on then, Lady P,' Ruddy encouraged, her speech slightly slurred. 'Live dangerously for once in your pampered life!'

'I couldn't possibly... what if I break it?' Lady Pru's words quavered with genuine terror.

Leaning forward, Sin placed her steady fingers over Lady Pru's. 'You won't break it, love, because—'

'PLASTIC IS FANTASTIC!' the entire assembly erupted in unison, the church women clapping their palms in rhythm.

Pressing down tentatively on the container's lid, Lady Pru squeaked with pure delight when it obliged with a perfect burp. Her features transformed with wonder.

'I did it! Did you see? I made it burp!' She beamed at everyone in the gathering.

The saleswoman slid effortlessly into the next stage of her demonstration. 'Right then, dear souls! Time for our special game: Write An Honest Advert To Sell Your Husband!'

Nearly choking on her drink, Ruddy's features lit up with wicked glee. 'Now you're talking my language!'

Producing paper and pencils from her seemingly bottomless case, Jemima explained, 'The rules are simple. Describe your man as if you were flogging him in the newspaper. Be brutally honest! The funniest entry wins a free Tupperware Cereal Bowl!'

The women seized their papers with fervent enthusiasm, their heads bent in concentration.

'Time's up!' Jemima announced after five minutes of furious scribbling and muffled giggles. Rubbing her palms together, she surveyed the group. 'Who's brave enough to go first?'

Features flushed with rum punch courage, Ruddy volunteered, 'For sale: one boyfriend, barely used and slightly shop-soiled. Comes with motorcycle, leather jacket, and wandering eye. Good with his fingers but rubbish with promises. Eats like a horse, farts like one too. Warning: may contain more hot air than substance. Offers considered, but don't hold your bleedin' breath!'

Scandalous laughter erupted, even the church women covering their mouths to hide their amusement.

Bouncing to her feet with infectious enthusiasm, Sin waved her paper in the air. 'For sale: one husband, excellent condition despite heavy use. Jamaican model, built for comfort and reliability. Features include: devastating smile, porkpie hat, and ability to charm birds from trees. Comes with mysterious past and heart of pure gold. Warning: highly addictive, may cause permanent happiness. Not for sale at any price!'

The tender way she spoke, her whole countenance glowing with genuine love, made Gertie's being swell with emotion. That woman adored her Bertram something fierce.

Just then, the parlour door exploded open.

Every head snapped toward the sound, conversations dying instantly.

Hyacinth Marshall stood in the doorway, her body heaving with ragged breaths. 'Gertie... my daughter...' Her words came out in broken gasps. 'My Araminta is missing.'

# Chapter Six

'The police think I'm making it up and won't help me find my daughter.'

Hyacinth's choking revelation cut through the remnants of what had been such a joyful afternoon. Empty teacups bearing lipstick traces dotted Gertie's kitchen table, alongside crumpled papers from the husband-selling game and a forgotten Party Susan still gleaming under the overhead light. The other women had offered to stay when Hyacinth burst into the parlour with her devastating news, their faces clouded with concern and solidarity. But Gertie had gently thanked them and sent them on their way. She knew her church sister well enough to understand that private grief required private comfort.

Now they sat alone in the kitchen, Hyacinth's fingers clutching an embroidered cotton handkerchief, delicate blue flowers beautifully stitched that had earned her a reputation for exquisite needlework throughout Whitechapel. The fabric grew damp from constant dabbing at her red-rimmed eyes.

Gertie reached across the table, her palm covering Hyacinth's restless hands. The gentle pressure carried decades of hard-won wisdom.

'Tell me everything, Sister Hyacinth, from the beginning.' Gertie's brown eyes sharpened with protective concern. The term 'Sister' rolled naturally off her tongue. Not blood relation, but the deep bond shared by women who attended the same Pentecostal church every Saturday.

Hyacinth's shoulders shook beneath her winter coat. 'My Araminta was meant to arrive from Trinidad two weeks ago! I saved every penny, worked three jobs to pay her passage from Port of Spain.' Her agitation rose with her ragged breaths. 'She wrote me that she had employment lined up, respectable lodgings arranged with a church family. She promised to contact me the moment she was settled.'

Her lips pressed together in a tight line. 'I never heard from her.'

Oh Lord! Gertie's chest tightened with intense worry. Young women didn't just vanish from their families without explanation, especially not ambitious daughters with clear plans and devoted mothers counting the days until their arrival.

Reaching for the teapot, Gertie felt the familiar ritual of hospitality offering comfort where words fell short. The slight stiffness in her left arm sent a twinge through her shoulder - rain was coming tonight, she could feel it in her bones. She poured steaming tea into Pyrex glass cups.

'What did the police say exactly?'

Hyacinth's face drained of hope, her reply coming bitter and sharp. 'They barely glanced at her photograph. Said women from *the islands* change their minds all the time about staying in England. That maybe she'd found herself a man. A man! Made my girl sound like a woman of the night!' Her composure shattered completely, fresh tears spilling down her cheeks. 'They dismissed me like I was dirt beneath their shoe. Couldn't be bothered to take a mother's concerns seriously.'

Gertie's stern gaze darkened. She'd witnessed similar treatment from authorities who dismissed their community's worries with casual indifference. It made her blood boil, though she kept her rage dampened down. Flying off the handle and getting angry wouldn't help her friend.

'Show me Araminta's picture,' Gertie said quietly.

Hyacinth fumbled in her worn leather handbag, extracting a studio portrait. The young woman in the picture possessed striking beauty, high cheekbones, intelligent eyes, and a confident smile that spoke of dreams and determination. She wore a crisp white blouse and had styled her hair in the latest fashion.

'She's beautiful,' Gertie murmured, studying the image. 'How old?'

'Nineteen this past Christmas. Worked in an office back home.' Hyacinth's tone swelled with maternal pride. 'She had it all planned out. Proper references, skills, ambition. Said London was going to be her fresh start.'

The love in her manner made Gertie's soul ache. How many mothers had sacrificed everything to give their children opportunities they'd never had? That's what mothers did – ensured their children's needs always came first.

Running the boarding house had taught Gertie to read people, to sense when stories didn't add up. A young woman with clear plans and regular correspondence didn't simply vanish without reason. Especially not when she'd worked so hard to reach England in the first place.

'Araminta wouldn't just disappear.' Hyacinth planted her fists on the table to underscore her words. 'She wrote religiously every week from Trinidad. Told me about every job interview, every preparation she was doing. She even sent me a photograph of the dress she bought for her first day of work.'

Gertie leaned forward, her brown eyes holding Hyacinth's desperate gaze. 'I believe you completely. A mother knows when evil has touched her child.

It's instinct, stronger than anything those police could understand.'

The relief that flooded Hyacinth's features was painful to witness. She sagged in her chair, tension finally releasing from her rigid shoulders.

'Thank you. Everyone else thinks I'm being dramatic. Even Pastor Williams suggested I pray for patience and trust in the Lord's plan.' A visible shudder ran through her. 'But this feeling in my bones won't go away. Something terrible has happened to my Araminta.'

Gertie studied her friend's ravaged face, choosing her words with deliberate care. 'Give it another week or so. Sometimes letters get delayed, or maybe she's moved lodgings and hasn't had the opportunity to write.' She paused, letting hope flicker in Hyacinth's tired eyes. 'But if you don't hear anything soon, I know where we can go for proper help. There's an organisation called Mini's Place. They specialise in supporting young women and families who've fallen through the cracks. Real professionals who actually care about getting results.'

Hyacinth straightened in her chair, hope flaming bright in the emotional darkness surrounding her. 'You'd come with me?'

Gertie reached across to squeeze her friend's trembling hand. Her grip carried all the solidarity their shared community had built over years of supporting each other through hardship. 'Of course.

We take care of our own, Sister Hyacinth. Always have, always will.'

But even while she offered comfort, that newspaper fragment from last week's *Evening Tribune* nagged at her memory. Buried on page six between advertisements for furniture sales and job listings:

**YOUNG CARIBBEAN WOMAN FOUND DEAD IN THAMES.**

The brief article had mentioned the woman's family couldn't understand why she'd left her lodgings without warning. Found floating near Wapping Old Stairs, no identification, no explanation.

Gertie's blood chilled while pieces formed a horrifying pattern in her mind. What if someone was deliberately targeting young Caribbean women fresh off the boats from home? Vulnerable daughters with dreams and ambitions, women whose families were thousands of miles away and whose disappearances would barely register with indifferent authorities?

The thought sent ice through her veins, but she kept her expression carefully neutral. No point terrifying Hyacinth further until she knew more.

That unnamed dread had been gnawing at her peace for weeks now, a restless feeling that trouble was brewing somewhere close to home. It had also unearthed memories she'd long tried to bury, shameful secrets from her own past that she'd sooner take to her grave than let her baby brother discover. Truths that, if brought to light, could shatter the respect she'd painstakingly built in this community, the trust that vulnerable souls placed in her strong hands and generous heart.

That's why Gertie was no stranger to darkness. She had learned long ago that when evil came hunting, you either fought back or became its next victim. And that was precisely why she was going to fight tooth and nail to uncover the truth about what had happened to Hyacinth's daughter.

# Chapter Seven

Jimmy stalked into The Ruby Lounge like he owned the place. Because he fucking did.

The thump of David Bowie's, 'Rebel Rebel' shook the place. Blokes strutted their stuff in platform shoes and bell bottoms while women shimmied in sequins and hot pants, wearing tops that were a mash up of paisley and Indian prints.

'Mister Southpaw!' The cry went up near the bar, and faces turned.

Nods of respect followed him through the crowd.

Tino, the barman, spotted him coming. 'Evening, Mister Southpaw.'

'You said we've got a problem.' Jimmy wasn't here to hang around.

The barman dropped his voice for their ears only. 'A shifty-eyed little toerag working your club without permission. Been at it all week.' Tino snorted. 'He's in the gents. Thinks he's being proper subtle about it. Cocky as they come. Brown jacket, skinny legs. Name of Matt.'

Without another word, Jimmy prowled towards the toilet. The crowd parted for him; nobody wanted to be caught in The Southpaw's way when he wore that expression that said he was about to tear someone's fucking head off.

Jimmy pushed open the door just as some skinny runt in a brown jacket with ridiculous wide lapels was handing something to a young man.

'Fuck,' the buyer gasped, spotting Jimmy.

Matt, the dealer, whirled around, shoving whatever he was holding into his pocket.

'Out,' Jimmy growled at the buyer, who didn't need telling twice and bolted past him without a second glance.

The twat who had been caught bang to rights in Jimmy's establishment tried to tough it out with a smile. 'Mister Steele. Nice place you got here.'

Jimmy's answer was to calmy close the door behind him. The fluorescent light buzzed overhead, turning Matt's face a sickly green.

'You know who I am.'

''Course. Everyone knows The Southpaw.' Matt's eyes darted towards the cubicles. Empty.

'Then you know this is my place.'

'Just using the facilities, ain't I?'

Jimmy moved faster than Matt could track. His left hook slammed into the wall beside Matt's head, cracking the tile and sending ceramic shards scattering across the sink.

'Let's try again.' Jimmy's voice remained conversational. 'You've been selling in my club without my permission.'

Matt appeared on the verge of pissing himself. 'Listen, Mister Southpaw—'

'Empty your pockets. Now.'

When Matt hesitated, Jimmy grabbed him by the throat. 'I won't ask again.'

Matt fumbled in his pockets, pulling out a wad of notes and three small plastic bags of white powder.

Jimmy knocked them from his hand. The bags hit the floor, one splitting open. White powder scattered across the dark tiles and, Jimmy noted with cold fury, across the bottom of his trousers and shoes.

'Fucking coke?' Jimmy was furious. 'You're pushing this white shit in my club?'

'It's just business—'

Jimmy slammed him into the wall, knocking the air from his lungs. 'Not on my turf, it isn't.' He pressed his forearm on Matt's windpipe. 'Who's your supplier?'

'Can't say,' Matt choked out. 'He'd have my bollocks for earrings.'

Jimmy increased the pressure until Matt's face turned purple. 'What you should be worried about is what I'll do to you right now.'

Matt's eyes bulged. His hands scrabbled uselessly at Jimmy's arm.

'Last chance. Who's supplying you?'

Jimmy eased the pressure just enough to let Matt gasp: 'Can't... he'll kill me.'

'And what do you think I'm going to do?' Jimmy yanked Matt forward by his shirt collar, then slammed him back on the wall again. Matt's head smacked the tile. 'Think I'm some soft cunt you can fuck with?'

Blood trickled from the back of Matt's head, staining his collar. 'Please—'

Jimmy dragged Matt towards the door and hauled him through the corridor. The music seemed to dim when they emerged into the main club. Conversations died. Faces turned. Nobody moved to help.

'Tino,' Jimmy called to the barman. 'Got a problem needs sorting.'

Tino and another lad hurried over, falling in behind Jimmy while he frogmarched Matt towards the back exit.

Jimmy booted open the fire door. The night air hit them cold. He hurled Matt down the metal steps into the alley. Matt tumbled, screeching in pain. He thumped into the wet concrete, landing in a puddle beside the overflowing bins.

'Hold him,' Jimmy ordered, then removed his jacket and proceeded to roll up his shirtsleeves with chilling slowness.

'Now then.' Jimmy stood over Matt, flexing his fists. 'Let's try this one more time.'

'No—' Matt's protest was cut short by a sharp punch connecting with his stomach. He doubled over, retching.

'Wrong answer.'

Jimmy followed with a straight right to Matt's jaw that would have dropped him if he wasn't being held upright.

'Who's supplying this shit?'

Matt gasped, blood and spittle dripping down his chin. 'New player. Connected. That's all I know.'

Jimmy grabbed Matt's hair, jerking his head back. 'Nobody's connected enough to sell that poison on my turf without consequences. Not to my people.'

'Dunno his name,' Matt blubbered. 'I won't come back. Swear on my mum's life.'

Jimmy studied the pathetic figure before him. 'You've got five seconds to disappear. If I ever see your ugly mug again on my manor, they'll be using you as bait on the Thames.'

Matt ran for his life towards the end of the alley.

Jimmy pulled a handkerchief from his pocket and wiped blood from his hands. 'Tino, good work tonight. There'll be something extra for you both.'

The barmen nodded their thanks, relief visible on their faces.

Jimmy's fury ebbed.

Alone in the dark, he looked down at the traces of white powder still clinging to his trousers. Cocaine. Some new player thought they could move in on his territory.

This was the part of the job most people never understood. The constant vigilance. The need to stamp out every small fire before it became a bloody inferno. Being the Face wasn't about flash motors and birds hanging off your arm. It was about respect. And respect in the East End came from fear as much as admiration.

Let one worthless, scumbag ponce get away with selling gear on your patch, next thing you know, everyone's at it. Then the filth come sniffing around, and your legitimate businesses suffer. Before long, you're up to your brass balls in trouble, and some other hungry bastard is sniffing around your turf like a starving dog eyeing a juicy bone.

The punters in his club needed to see what happened to those who took liberties. The whispers would spread through the East End faster than clap in a knocking shop. The Southpaw doesn't allow drugs on his patch. The Southpaw protects his own.

That's what separated him from the other firms. Jimmy wasn't just another thug with a few heavies. He looked after his people. They paid for his protection, and in return, he kept the worst elements away. No smack. No cocaine. Nothing that destroyed families from the inside out.

It wasn't like Jimmy was some bleedin' choirboy. He'd done things that would make a priest's hair curl. But a man needed a code to live by in this world. Without it, you were just another animal waiting to be put down.

And this new player, whoever this gobshite was, needed to learn that lesson quick-sharp. Nobody moved in on Jimmy Southpaw's territory without permission. Nobody undermined his authority. Not if they wanted to keep breathing London air.

# Chapter Eight

The corridors of power in Sugar Cane Wharf Town Hall stretched before Jimmy, in all of its Victorian faded grandeur and pomp.

Danny knew how to climb the ladder, Jimmy had to give his old man credit for that. From major league criminal known as the King of The Docks to respected councillor, quite the transformation. However, loose lips were whispering about his father's seedier, behind closed doors activities. High-class parties, expensive girls, powerful men with sick appetites. Each to their own, but flesh peddling left a bitter taste in Jimmy's mouth.

The nameplate on the heavy door read 'Councillor D. Steele' in gold lettering. Jimmy knocked, two sharp raps.

'Come.'

One word carrying decades of authority.

Jimmy entered Danny's domain, immediately clocking the show of dominance in his positioning. The old bastard sat behind an imposing Victorian desk, fountain pen poised over official documents like some kind of municipal king. His grey suit was expensive but conservative, styling that spoke of respectability and tradition. His hair was slicked back with Brilliantine.

The last five years had carved a chasm between them wider than the Thames. Jimmy had thrown himself into building his operation, brick by bloody brick, while Danny had played the political game – glad-handing, speechifying, trading favours in committee rooms. Two different worlds, two different kinds of influence. Jimmy had always been suspicious of politicians, slippery fuckers the lot of them, smiling while they shafting you in the back. Having his old man turn into one left a sour taste that wouldn't wash away.

'Son.' Danny didn't raise his head from his paperwork, the calculated snub designed to remind Jimmy who was really in charge. At least, in his dad's eyes.

The dismissive tone would have cut deep once. Now it just confirmed what Jimmy already knew about Danny's petty nature.

Jimmy remained standing, hands clasped loosely behind his back. No fidgeting, no nervous energy. Just patient confidence while Danny performed his little theatre.

*Let him have his moment. Play king of the castle. Soon enough, he'll suss whose really top dog around here.*

Danny finally set down his fountain pen with deliberate care and slowly raised his head to meet his son's gaze. 'Drink?' The offer came with an offhand gesture toward the crystal decanter.

'I'm driving.'

A sardonic smile twisted Danny's mouth. ''Course you are. That your Bentley outside? Very flash. Very... showy for a man who should know better.'

The cheap shot bounced off Jimmy without leaving a mark. Time was when his father's disapproval could gut him to ribbons. Now? Jimmy saw it for what it was – just jealousy dressed up as concern.

Jimmy shifted his stance slightly, the movement casual but controlled. 'I need planning permission for the Stepney warehouse conversion.'

'Planning permission.' Danny leaned into his leather chair and thoroughly considered his son. 'That's what brings my successful boy crawling back to daddy?'

*Here we go,* Jimmy thought. *The great Danny Steele, testing for weakness where none exists.*

'Residential units. High-end market.' Jimmy kept his voice level, professional. No desperation to give his father ammunition.

Danny's eyes narrowed, studying Jimmy's face intently. Searching for the cracks, the weaknesses, the same anxious need that had once driven Jimmy to his knees begging him for money to buy a house.

*You won't find it, old man. Those days are dead and buried.*

'These things take time,' Danny began, playing the big man. 'Proper channels. Committee approval.' He spread his hands in mock helplessness. 'Red tape's a right bastard when you're not in the inner circle.'

His dad's attempts to make him feel worthless were about as obvious as a turd in a punch bowl.

Jimmy nodded once, all emotion wiped from his face. 'Fair enough.'

The response clearly rattled Danny, surprise flickering across his features.

He expected me to dance to his tune, Jimmy observed with cold satisfaction. Still thinks I'm that desperate young pup who needed daddy's approval to breathe.

'Of course,' Danny continued, trying to claw back the upper hand. 'if it was urgent...'

'It's not.' Jimmy buttoned his jacket with unhurried movements. 'Councillor Price will fast-track the application through his committee tomorrow. Should have approval by Friday.'

Danny's features hardened, the respectable mask slipping to reveal the vicious control freak beneath. 'Price' he scoffed. 'You went to that spineless cunt behind my back.'

'I came to you first.' Jimmy never took his eyes off his dad. 'Family comes first. Your words, not mine.'

'But you had another option ready.' Danny was clearly outraged by the turn of events.

Jimmy met Danny's blazing stare without flinching. 'I always have options now. You taught me that too. Never depend on anyone who might let you down.'

His dig found its target and the colour of Danny's cheeks rose high and red. 'Price is weak as piss. Gambling debts crawling out of his arse. Someone owns that pathetic wanker.'

'Yeah, I know. Me.' Danny's face went ash-white. Jimmy calmly continued. 'Bought his debts six months ago. Good business. He's more accommodating than a Soho brass these days.'

Danny let out a cold smile, his voice even tighter. Controlled. 'Building your property business, buying politicians like they're second-hand motors? You think you're the dog's bollocks.'

'I think I'm careful.' Jimmy remained relaxed but alert. 'And grateful for the education you gave me about control. That respect gets earned, not demanded. That loyalty works both ways. That the people closest to you will shaft you quicker than anyone.'

Danny's composure finally snapped. He bared his teeth. 'After everything I've bloody done for you ---'

Jimmy cut him off clean. 'You did plenty. Made me exactly who I am today. A man who doesn't beg for scraps from anyone's table.'

With that, he headed to the door, then paused with his hand on the brass handle. 'Give Mum my love. Tell her I'll bring the kids round Sunday.'

Outside, Jimmy climbed into his Bentley and sat for a moment. The disappointment he felt at his dad's treatment of him was there but manageable. Not the crushing blow it would have been years back.

Because since his wife had been taken from him, he'd hung onto the memory of how his dad had gone all out to try to deny Mini her dream house. She'd done everything in her power to make sure he stood on his own two feet. Became an upstanding, independent man. If she could see him now, running his little kingdom, she'd be chuffed to bits. He'd built something proper solid, hadn't he? Something that was his and his alone. No begging bowl. No bowing and scraping to that conniving bastard he called Dad.

Jimmy started the engine and pulled away, the memory of his dead wife's beaming smile warming him more than any victory over Danny ever could.

# Chapter Nine

Jimmy sat in the elegant Georgian front room, a heavy leather bag resting beside his chair, listening to Jack 'Dash' Blacklock bang on about London property like he was delivering the bloody gospel itself.

Dash was the kind of flash git who could sweet talk his way into the Tower of London and have the guards helping him carry out the Crown Jewels. Standing tall with flowing dark hair that kept flopping across his forehead in a way that made women swoon, he flashed the kind of devilish grin that had sensible ladies forgetting their own names. His light jacket hung open over a cream silk shirt, the top three buttons undone to reveal a triangle of tanned chest and a thick gold chain with what seemed like a family crest medallion that caught the afternoon light.

They'd called him Dash since he was a nipper because he lived life at breakneck speed. A white Jamaican born into the island's wealthy set, Dash had inherited both worlds and the morals of neither. The tropical heat had burned wild ambition into his blood that no amount of breeding could tame.

Jimmy noticed how Dash's accent shifted when he got excited, harder Jamaican rhythms creeping through like a hidden identity slipping past his polished exterior. Those piercing blue eyes could switch from warm charm to cunning calculation between one blink and the next.

Right now, though, he was all charm and hustle, sweeping his hand around the spacious room with its high ceilings and ornate cornicing. 'Check this out, Jimmy baby. Pure class, solid bones, just crying out for the right touch, you dig?'

Biting the inside of his cheek, Jimmy fought back a smirk. His head spun trying to keep up with the geezer. It was like watching three different people trapped in one body. One minute he was all 'Frightfully sorry, old chap, but I'm rather keen to discuss the particulars of our venture.' The next all hip-groovy, 'Right on, brother! This deal's gonna be outta sight, you dig it?' And then purebred Jamaican, 'Irie, my youth! Tings between us is blessed and highly favoured.'

But Jimmy couldn't deny he liked the flash bastard. He reminded him of himself – hungry, had plans, willing to take risks. While other young toffs were living off Daddy's money, Dash was out here making moves, building something real.

Dash leaned forward until his elbows rested on his knees, his eyes gleaming with barely contained anticipation. 'Jimmy, my man,' he said, voice dropping to a conspiratorial purr, 'you ready to make some serious bread? This property game's about to get heavy, and I mean stone beautiful heavy.'

The house was a real stunner, Jimmy had to admit. Four storeys of Georgian elegance in the heart of Bloomsbury, the kind of address that screamed respectability. Original features everywhere – marble fireplaces, intricate plasterwork, sash windows that flooded the rooms with natural light. The sort of place Mini would have loved, would have filled with her warmth and laughter. His gut twisted at the thought, grief ambushing him when he least expected it.

'Me and you have already invested in other properties,' Dash continued, drumming his long fingers on his thigh.

Jimmy nodded – true enough, but most of those were derelict warehouses. He'd been buying up docklands property for years, snapping up buildings for next to nothing.

'The Three-Day Week chaos has created some spectacular opportunities, man,' Dash carried on, his tongue darting out to wet his lips. 'Property prices hit rock bottom because everyone's panicking like headless chickens. Smart cats like us?' His perfect white teeth gleamed in the afternoon light. 'We buy when others are practically giving away their assets.'

Jimmy forced himself to concentrate. This was important, expanding his empire beyond the usual East End rackets and warehouses. The Steele family had always been players, but Jimmy wanted to be a proper empire-builder. Legitimate business feeding the illegitimate, clean money washing the dirty, respectability masking the power underneath.

Dash's eyes gleamed. 'Six months to transform this beauty into two luxury apartments.'

Apartments?

'Apart… apartments?' Jimmy scowled, the unfamiliar word feeling strange in his mouth. He tried it again, slower. The sound was flash, expensive, foreign. He quite liked it. 'You mean flats?'

Dash's mouth curved into a knowing smile. 'Ah, my friend, you're thinking too small again.' Spreading his arms wide as if embracing an invisible audience, he continued, '"Flat" sounds flat, doesn't it? Common as muck. But "apartment" – now that's far out, exclusive, like the finest American luxury. The future belongs to apartments, Jimmy. You get me?'

Feeling himself drawn into the scheme, Jimmy straightened in his chair. 'You really think London's ready for that kind of change?'

Standing and striding to the window with practiced showmanship, Dash swept his hair back with a casual flick of his wrist. 'London's going crazy for it, man. All these professional cats, City workers, people with real dough who want something groovy. Not some grotty pad with a shared bog down the hall.'

As if on cue, a woman appeared from the back of the house. Middle-aged, respectable-looking in her brown coat and sensible shoes, the sort of woman you'd trust with your life savings without thinking twice.

Dash turned in her direction, his charm cranking up another notch. 'Beautiful timing. Jimmy, meet Mary. She's our current tenant, keeping the place together while we sort out our conversion plans.'

Mary beamed at them both, her lined face crinkling with apparent sincerity. 'Oh, Mr Blacklock's been an absolute angel, he has. Given me work and a roof over my head during these trying times. I don't know what I'd have done without his kindness.'

Resting his long fingers lightly on Mary's shoulder, Dash nodded with graciousness. 'Mary's been totally invaluable. Makes sure no squatters move in, keeps everything cool. We'll be sad to lose her when the work starts, won't we, love?'

Mary clasped her hands together, her eyes bright. 'It's been a privilege. Such a gorgeous house, it deserves to be something special again. Oooo, it'll be magnificent when you gentlemen are finished with it.'

Jimmy surveyed the room again, mind racing with possibilities. Together with his existing operations, this could be the foundation of something massive. Property empire by day, criminal network by night. A sweet as a nut set up, the perfect bloody racket.

Noting Jimmy's intent expression, Dash prowled closer, lowering his voice to a confidential murmur. 'But I need capital, Jimmy. Serious money to move fast before others catch on to the goldmine we've discovered.'

The moment had arrived. Knowing it was decision time, Jimmy's attention shifted to the leather bag that had sat silently throughout their meeting. He opened it and stared down at the neat bundles of twenty-pound notes wrapped in elastic bands. More money than most people saw in a lifetime.

Dash went completely still, his piercing gaze fixed on the bag.

Plucking one of the bundles from the bag, Jimmy tossed it lightly in his grasp. 'Is this enough to secure this house and get my foot in the door of the West End?'

Dash could barely contain his excitement. A muscle in his jaw twitched as pure greed flickered across his features. 'More than enough, Jimmy, my bro.'

Jimmy closed the bag with a decisive snap and extended it towards Dash, who took it with a super bright smile. 'Don't let me down. I'm trusting you with serious money here.'

Dash's smile stretched wide, a strand of hair falling over his brow. 'You won't regret this. By Christmas, we'll own half of London, you dig?'

***

The moment Jimmy's Bentley disappeared around the corner, Mary's entire demeanour transformed. The sweet, grateful tenant vanished in a heartbeat, replaced by a hard-faced bitch with vindictive eyes and a mouth that could strip paint off walls.

'Time to get back to business,' she reminded him soullessly.

Dash's own transformation proved just as dramatic. The groovy charmer evaporated, leaving something cold and menacing behind those blue eyes.

Resting Jimmy's bag on the mantelpiece with reverent care, he displayed it proudly, a hunter with his prized kill. He rolled his shoulders. 'How are our guests settling in?'

Mary fished keys from her coat pocket, her face contorting into a sneer. 'Getting restless. Been asking questions, making demands. The new one especially. Thinks she's the fucking Queen of Sheba.'

They walked towards the back of the house, past the elegant rooms Jimmy had admired, towards a door that led to the basement stairs. Mary unlocked it, and immediately the smell hit them. Unwashed bodies, fear, and desperation mingled with the natural damp stone.

The basement was hell. What had once been a proper cellar had become a makeshift prison. Thin mattresses on the freezing stone floor, chains bolted to the walls, a bucket in the corner that served purposes no decent mind could contemplate. The single bare bulb cast sickly yellow light over everything.

Six young women huddled in the dim light, their expressions pure terror. They ranged in age from barely eighteen to perhaps twenty-five, all bearing the exhausted, haunted features of people who'd travelled far only to find nightmare instead of hope.

Dash pulled out a vial, tipped some coke onto the back of his hand and snorted, long and deep. He didn't move until he felt the burn at the back of his tongue. Now he stood ready to survey the real purpose he needed property.

'Ladies. Hope you've been keeping it together down here.'

One of the women, a beautiful girl with dark skin who hadn't yet been completely broken, lifted her chin, defiant. 'My name is Araminta Marshall. I came from Trinidad to work, not to be kept prisoner. Let me go to my mother, and I'll keep my mouth shut about all this.'

Cursing a storm, Mary advanced on her with vicious intent. She loomed over the girl, who did not flinch, her hand raised. Before she could strike, Dash seized her wrist in an iron grip.

His fingers dug into Mary's flesh until she winced.

He spoke, his quiet authority chilling the room. 'No damage to the face. Don't forget the house this prime piece will be going to has customers who don't want to stare at spoilt goods.'

But Mary wasn't finished. Savage and efficient, she grabbed a handful of Araminta's thick black hair and yanked viciously, forcing the girl's head back at a painful angle.

Bringing her face inches from Araminta's, Mary snarled, her breath hot and rancid. 'Listen here, you uppity little cow. You ain't in Trinidad now. You're in my world, and in my world, you do what you're bloody told.'

Araminta's defiance crumbled into desperate pleading, tears streaming down her cheeks. 'My mother will be expecting me to write. If you let me go, I swear on all that is holy I won't tell anyone about this place.'

His eyes gone flat and cold, Dash studied her, his interest detached. Then that charming smile returned, made more terrifying by its apparent warmth.

He stepped closer to Araminta. His medallion glinted in the sickly light when he ran a finger down her cheek, carving his malice into her flesh.

'Tonight you learn your place in the food chain, darling,' he bit out, all pretence of easy-going hipness gone. 'And trust me when I say, you're nothing but meat.'

# Chapter Ten

The gagged, naked woman hung suspended from the ceiling in the house in Belgravia, her wrists bound by silk ropes that cut into flesh already raw. Sweat trickled down her shuddering body, catching the harsh lights that illuminated the makeshift stage. The assembled men watched in bestial silence, some licking their lips, their faces pumped with sleazy excitement, eyes glazed with lust and coke.

'Gentlemen!' announced the master of ceremonies, a lanky man with slicked-back hair, decked out in a purple crushed-velvet suit. 'The evening's special entertainment.'

Three masked figures emerged from behind heavy curtains, carrying riding crops and other implements that made several audience members shift in their seats with lecherous appetites. Soon the sound of leather brutally striking bare flesh echoed through the room, followed by muffled cries of pain.

Danny Steele stood at the back, a glass of his trademark Caribbean rum in hand, observing the most exclusive part of his kingdom with arrogant satisfaction. The men who came to the house that touted itself as an exclusive membership club weren't the usual ordinary punters gawking and getting a hard-on at the show. No, these were men of influence, power, and staggering wealth. Politicians, tycoons, high-ranking church members. All of them paying through the nose for what his exclusive establishment provided.

Danny caught Scarlett's eyes across the smoky room. She was a vision of orchestrated perfection, every detail designed to ensnare. In her role of hostess, she ensured these men of money came back.

Her flame-red hair had been teased and sculpted into a dramatic bouffant, hairpieces woven seamlessly through her natural locks, creating cascading curls that tumbled over her left shoulder in a waterfall of fire. The whole magnificent construction was shellacked with enough lacquer to survive a hurricane, not a strand daring to move out of place.

Her green eyes were rimmed with thick kohl and framed by false eyelashes so dramatic they cast shadows on her cheekbones. Her gold silk halter dress clung to every curve of her dainty figure, the colour making her red hair positively incandescent. Cut daringly low at the back but maintaining an air of expensive sophistication at the front, it hit just above her knees to show off legs encased in the finest sheer stockings.

When she returned his stare, her glossed lips curved with just the right mixture of invitation and mystery. She was his prize exhibit – always – the perfect hostess to make his distinguished guests feel like kings while their moral compasses spun wildly off course.

On strappy gold heels, she sashayed over to him, her diamond drop earrings catching the light.

'Everyone behaving themselves?' he asked. Danny wanted to crush her possessively to him, his greedy hands roaming all over her body.

'The bubbly's flowing, the marching powder's disappearing, and our guests are going doolally over the merchandise.' She glanced down the corridor. 'That Bishop from across the river is in the Blue Room with two of the Swedish girls, just the way you instructed.'

Danny grunted with delight. That familiar rush of power pulsed through him watching these supposed pillars of society reduced to their basest needs under his roof. They might look down their snobby noses at an East End lad during daylight, but here, in the dark, he was their fucking master.

'Lord Xander said he was bringing someone special tonight,' he said to her. 'Has he put in an appearance yet?'

Lightly shaking her head, Scarlett ran a polished nail down the front of his expensive shirt. 'But I've got everything prepared. Including that black girl you wanted kept separate.' Frowning, she pursed her lips and told him emphatically, 'She's a fighter, that one. Took three of us to get her ready. Although, I still think you're making a big-time error getting girls supplied through that particular route.'

Before Danny could respond, a crash echoed nearby. One of the younger hostesses had dropped a tray of crystal glasses, the shards glittering across the marble floor of the main salon. The girl, dressed in a sheer negligee that left nothing to the imagination, stood frozen in horror.

Without warning, Scarlett's demeanour switched in a heartbeat. The seductive puss vanished, her beautiful face twisting with an ugly rage that would make a hardened gangster think twice about crossing her. Her eyes went cold as a grave, her mouth a vicious slash across her face. This wasn't some dolly bird now, this was a proper dangerous piece of work.

'For fuck's sake!' she hissed, already marching towards the damage. 'That's the second time this week.'

'Sorry about that, gents,' Scarlett cooed to the assembled men. Time to remind these perverted old goats what they're really here for. She did a slow, deliberate pirouette, throwing her head back wantonly, pushing out her chest, giving them a flash of the tops of her tits. Her dress rode up suggestively, providing a quickie glimpse of what they were paying for. The way their eyes followed every reveal of flesh told her she'd got their attention back where it belonged — on the merchandise, not the interruption.

Then she steered the unfortunate girl towards the kitchen, her glued-on smile never faltering.

Danny chuckled, admiring Scarlett's efficiency. She might look like arm candy, but she ruled his girls harder than the bleeding governor of Holloway. Her hostesses were a carefully curated collection of beauties, each dressed in identical sheer white negligees that contrasted with Scarlett's gold. She ensured that the girls looked fresh and presentable. A girl who appeared like she'd been ridden more times than the Northern Line was out.

The buzzer at the front entrance rang, and soon Lord Alexander 'Xander' Blacklock, ninth Viscount, stood on the doorstep, his tall aristocratic figure unmistakable even in the dim porch light.

Even in his seventies, Xander still cut an impressive figure. White-haired, perfectly tailored, with that slick charm that had opened doors his dwindling bank account couldn't – that was until he'd married Lady Prudence.

Danny Steele was his biological son. The product of a housemaid and a moment's weakness, now transformed into Xander's most useful asset. The old bastard felt no paternal love, only heartless scheming about how to exploit his son's criminal empire. To

Xander, Danny was muscle with daddy issues, desperate for recognition that would never come.

Lord Xander embodied everything rotten about the establishment. Aristocracy without honour, breeding without decency. A parasite in silk, trading on a title while his wrong-side-of-the-blanket son danced for scraps from the master's table.

Beside him, a shorter man with the pompous bearing of someone who considered himself extremely important shifted impatiently from foot to foot.

By the time Danny reached the entrance hall, Scarlett had already welcomed the new arrivals, taking their coats with practiced efficiency.

'Daniel, my boy,' Lord Xander called out, his cultured voice carrying the lazy drawl of privilege. 'Allow me to introduce a dear friend of mine. Oliver.'

Oliver Harrington.

Member of Parliament.

And… chairman of the Clean Up Britain campaign.

Of course, Lord Xander relayed none of that. And, of course, Danny pretended ignorance of who the man was.

Inwardly, though, he lapped it up. The moral crusader himself, panting like a dog in heat inside one of London's most high-end brothels. Oliver Harrington was a round-faced man with thinning hair carefully arranged to hide his encroaching baldness. His expensive suit strained slightly over his paunch, and a heavy gold ring adorned his right hand. His watery blue-eyed gaze darted around the entrance hall, cruel eyes burning with sick excitement.

'Mr Harrington.' Danny smiled, shaking the politician's damp hand. 'An honour to welcome you to our humble home.'

If Dorothea Chesterton could see her hero now! The hypocritical wanker spent his days railing against moral decay while preparing to wallow in it by night. This was why Danny's new empire trumped his old dock rackets. The real power wasn't in muscle or territory but in the double lives of men like Harrington.

Harrington's mouth twitched into what might have been a smile on a more attractive man. 'Yes, well, Xander assures me your… club offers the utmost discretion.' Each plummy word was carefully pronounced with the know-how of someone accustomed to public speaking. And getting his way.

'Absolute discretion is our specialty,' Danny assured him. He gestured towards the main salon. 'We cater only to gentlemen of the highest calibre. Your privacy is guaranteed.'

The politician eagerly followed Danny through the corridors.

'I've taken the liberty of preparing our finest champagne.' Danny led them into a private sitting room where a bottle of Dom Pérignon waited in an ice bucket. 'Perhaps you'd like a tour of our facilities before deciding how to spend your evening?'

Harrington nodded stiffly, his attention lingering on a painting of a nude woman that hung on the silk-papered wall. 'Xander speaks very highly of your… accommodations.'

'We cater to all tastes,' Danny explained, pouring champagne into crystal flutes. 'Some gentlemen prefer the communal entertainment in our main salon. Others desire more… personalised attention.'

Lord Xander laughed, the sound brittle in the room. 'What my friend means, Oliver, is that whatever proclivities you might have, they can be satisfied here without judgment or consequences.'

Danny watched Harrington's expression carefully. Despite all his proper gentleman airs, the old pervert couldn't hide that flash of interest in his beady little eyes. This was the delicate dance, giving these hypocrites permission to indulge the very vices they condemned in public.

'Perhaps Mr Harrington would like to see some of our private rooms,' Danny suggested. He led them through a corridor lined with numbered doors.

Behind each door, a different scenario unfolded. In the Green Room, a mock classroom had been set up, complete with desks and a stern 'teacher' disciplining her 'pupils'. The Red Room contained equipment that would make a medieval torturer proud, while the Lilac Room offered the illusion of an opium den from another century.

'Do any of these particular settings appeal to you, Mr Harrington?' Danny watched the politician's pupils dilate with each new tableau.

Harrington cleared his throat, tugging at his collar. 'I…I have somewhat specific tastes. Something perhaps more… exotic?'

Danny exchanged a knowing glance with Lord Xander. 'Of course. I believe I have exactly what you're looking for.'

At the end of the corridor, separated from the other rooms, Danny unlocked a door with a key he kept on his person. Inside, the Gold Room sparkled with gilded mirrors and ornate furnishings meant to evoke mock colonial splendour. Reclining on the four-poster bed, wrists secured to the headboard with golden chains, lay Araminta.

Her eyes, filled with fear and fury, locked on to Danny's with naked hatred.

'Fresh from the Tropics.' Danny gestured towards her with a showman's flourish.

Harrington's breathing quickened, his tongue flicking out for a quick lick of his thin lips, his stare fixed on Araminta with undisguised hunger. 'She's… resistant?'

'Fighting spirit,' Danny confirmed, his tone businesslike. 'Adds to the experience for some of our clientele. The chains are merely precautionary – we find it enhances the colonial fantasy.'

Araminta struggled against her restraints, her voice raw with desperation. 'Please, I have family here. My mother—'

'Silence,' Danny snapped, his smile never faltering. Turning to Harrington, he added smoothly, 'No one will hear, of course. You're free to be... enthusiastic.'

Harrington stepped closer to the bed, his pudgy hand reaching out to stroke Araminta's cheek. She jerked away violently, spitting curses that made the politician's eyes light up with perverse excitement.

'I'll leave you to get acquainted.' Danny backed towards the door. 'The room is yours for the night. Ring the bell if you require anything... additional.'

The night progressed, the clockwork of depravity ticking along just the way it had been designed. Cocaine flowed freely, white lines arranged on silver trays by hostesses trained to avert their eyes while ministers and judges indulged their chemical appetites.

A preening and gloating Danny eventually made his way to check on things in the Gold Room. He wanted to make sure everything was going smoothly with Harrington and the new girl. First-time clients could be unpredictable, and MPs were particularly sensitive about their reputations. As he approached the door, he could hear muffled sounds from within, nothing unusual for this kind of establishment.

He paused outside the Gold Room, hand reaching for the door handle to peek inside and ensure his VIP guest was being properly entertained.

Without warning, the lights flickered once, twice, and then the entire house was plunged into darkness.

***

No one was surprised. Power cuts were all part of the current economic turmoil. But Danny had everything prepared. The generator kicked in with a mechanical groan, while hostesses scrambled to light dozens of candles placed strategically throughout the building. Scarlett directed girls to illuminate the ornate candelabras and antique oil lamps that transformed the brothel into something far more sinister.

The flickering flames cast grotesque shadows on the walls, turning elegant wallpaper into macabre galleries of dancing demons. The men's faces were ghoulish in the uneven light, their features distorted into monstrous masks.

This was the other London, Danny thought with savage pride. Beneath the veneer of civilisation, the city ran on primal instincts – sex, power, violence. The Three-Day Week had simply stripped away the pretence, forcing people to acknowledge the darkness. And nobody understood darkness better than Danny Steele.

The perfect setting for secrets.

Or violence.

He'd barely taken three steps when a bloodcurdling scream echoed through the corridor.

The men who heard it looked shocked, so Danny calmed them with, 'Obviously some play that's getting maybe a bit too enthusiastic.'

Satisfied with his explanation and smile, Danny hurried off, knowing full well something bad had happened. He froze, cursing under his breath. Scarlett stood in the doorway of the Gold Room, her face ghost-white beneath her makeup, one trembling hand covering her mouth.

'Oh my God,' she choked out, staring at him with wide, shocked eyes. 'Danny, look what that fucking animal has done.'

Danny's blood ran cold. He moved quickly to the bed, reaching for the brass candelabra on the nightstand, raising it high. The additional light revealed what the shadows had concealed.

Araminta lay motionless, her eyes staring sightlessly at the ceiling. The white silk sheets around her had turned crimson, spreading outwards from her throat where a vicious wound gaped like a second mouth.

And the Right Honourable Oliver Harrington was nowhere to be seen.

# Chapter Eleven

The Duchess waltzed into the room and stared down at the dead body.

'Well, well, Danny boy. Bit of trouble with the merchandise?'

Behind her loomed Tiny, her ever-present bodyguard who had to duck to fit through the doorframe. Despite his name, he stood well over six feet tall with shoulders that strained the seams of his clothing. He'd been her bouncer back at Sugar Cane Wharf's former floating brothel, *The Sing Song Lady,* and his loyalty had followed her into her new life. His massive presence filled the room with unspoken threat.

Her tone carried the polish of finishing school, but a hint of the East End still lurked beneath the cultivated accent, a reminder of her origins that surfaced whenever business turned ugly. Expressionless, she checked the scene, taking in the bloodied sheets, the cooling corpse of the young woman, and the tang of death hanging in the still air.

Five years ago, she'd been Rita Lawless, East London brothel madam with a reputation for being harder than the flick knife she permanently carried. Now she stood reinvented, a statuesque vision in a cream Yves Saint Laurent trouser suit. Her once-flowing hair had been cropped into a sharp, sophisticated bob that framed her strong-jawed features, a style that would become her signature for decades to come. Three-inch pointed stilettos and a single strand of South Sea pearls completed the look of understated wealth.

But it wasn't just the fancy gear that was different. The brash, loudmouth Rita had become more considered, more deadly, a woman who no longer needed to shout to command attention. The Duchess wasn't just a nickname anymore, but a proper title earned by marrying an actual English Duke who'd fallen for her particular charms and had no idea his elegant wife was systematically building a criminal empire right under his aristocratic nose.

Danny shifted uncomfortably, uncharacteristically nervous in her presence. 'Can you handle it or not?'

The Duchess pulled off her leather gloves with deliberate slowness, one finger at a time. She held his gaze while doing it, establishing dominance through unhurried movement. Then she crossed to the bed, the subtle scent of Chanel No. 5 momentarily cutting through the copper smell of blood.

'Look at her wrists,' she noted, pointing. 'She fought hard. Proper little fighter.' She glanced at him with undisguised contempt. 'Always did like them with spirit, didn't you? More fun to break that way.'

Bristling, he chewed her out. 'You've got the wrong end of the stick. You going to help or stand there with your gob flapping like a bloody Morecambe and Wise routine all night?'

'Twenty grand.'

'What?'

The Duchess straightened up, brushing an invisible speck from her immaculate sleeve. 'Twenty thousand. Cash. My fee for making your little problem disappear.'

His face flushed a nasty purple. 'You're having a giggle!'

'I never laugh about money, Danny.' She pinned him with a scornful glare. 'That's the going rate for body disposal in 1974. Inflation's a killer, haven't you heard? Heath's economic mess has prices rising faster than damp in a Whitechapel basement.'

'Ten.'

Scoffing, she continued. 'Take it or deal with this yourself. Body disposal on my turf comes with a premium, especially when it's this messy.'

She watched him struggle with the figure, knowing he had little choice. The Duchess had connections he could only dream of. People who could make corpses disappear without questions, bent coppers who looked the other way for the right price, crematorium workers who didn't check death certificates too carefully.

'Got a good thing going with the Sixes and Sevens, haven't you?' he said, trying to regain some control. 'Heard you're entertaining cabinet ministers these days.'

The Duchess raised one perfectly shaped eyebrow. 'The Gentlemen's Club has been in my husband's family for centuries. I simply… modernised the entertainment.' Her cold smile never reached her eyes. 'But don't make the mistake of thinking I've gone soft. The West End's my territory now, and I'm running more than just a posh drinking hole.'

She left unsaid what they both knew, that she was well on her way to becoming West London's undisputed Queen of Crime. Her aristocratic title provided the perfect cover for operations that would make East End crims green with envy.

'Still…' She examined the body with professional detachment. 'I never approved of this sort of business. Girls disappearing, families left wondering.' She levelled him with a long stare. 'Reminds me of Joanie.'

His expression hardened. 'Who?'

Her posture shifting subtly, hard bitch Rita Lawless momentarily visible beneath the polish. 'Don't play the fuck-nuts with me, you slag. Joanie.

My girl from the *Sing Song Lady*. Remember her now? The one you beat and made miscarry her kid.'

'Ancient bloody history.' He waved a dismissive hand.

Her words turned dangerously soft. 'Heard she tried to top herself, poor girl.'

Danny slammed his hand against the wall. 'You going to stand there dredging up some sob story, or are you going to do the bloody job?'

The Duchess's gaze darted, blade-quick to Scarlett. 'Take a walk, Goldilocks. The grown-ups need to talk.'

Scarlett's expression contorted, nostrils flaring, lips pursed into a 'how fucking dare you' pout. Her eyes darted to Danny for support, but finding none, she stomped out of the room.

The moment she was gone, The Duchess sent Tiny a small, almost imperceptible nod. The massive bodyguard moved with shocking speed for a man his size. Before he could react, Tiny's fist connected with Danny's stomach, doubling him over. A second blow to the jaw sent him sprawling onto the floor.

The Duchess stepped forward calmly, spiked heel directly against his throat. The polished aristocratic façade dropped completely, and when she spoke, it was pure East End Rita that came out.

'Listen here, you worthless wank-job,' she snarled, pressing just hard enough to make him gurgle. 'You think you're the mutt's nuts now with your fancy gaff and your posho punters gagging for a knee trembler. But you're still the same Danny boy who couldn't find his arse with both hands and a map without my help.'

She increased the pressure . 'You're up to your neck in the brown stuff with this one, mate. A dead girl? On my patch?'

He tried to speak, but the heel against his windpipe made it impossible.

'This is my manor, and when you're on my turf, I give the orders, not you.' She bared her teeth. 'You keep those fancy-pants toffs of yours in line, or I'll have Tiny do stuff to you that will make what happened to this poor girl look like a bloody tea party. Your eyes will be watching your own heart stop beating. Got it?'

She stepped back but still loomed over him. 'This is the last time,' she repeated, her words carrying the finality of a judge passing sentence. 'I bloody mean it. The next body will be yours.'

***

After The Duchess was gone, Danny and Scarlett slipped through what most who came to the high-end brothel in Belgravia had no idea existed — a hidden door concealed behind wood panelling. Servants' corridors they'd once been, now repurposed for a different kind of service. They travelled down the worn stone steps and descended into the bowels of the building. The secret passageway opened into his private monitoring room, a converted wine cellar now housing the most advanced surveillance technology money could buy in 1974.

Bulky reel-to-reel tape recorders whirred steadily, capturing sound from microphones hidden throughout the building. A bank of closed-circuit television cameras fed grainy black-and-white images to little monitors. The equipment had cost him a small fortune, imported from America and installed by an ex-MI5 technician who'd needed certain gambling debts erased. The system was temperamental, requiring constant adjustment, but worth every penny for what it captured – evidence that could destroy the most powerful men in Britain.

Simply told, Danny was running a blackmailing racket. The real power came from knowing the depraved acts influential men indulged in behind closed doors.

And capturing it on camera.

The more powerful the man, the more valuable the blackmail material.

He slammed the hidden panel shut behind them, his expression flushed with fury. The monitoring room felt claustrophobic suddenly, the whirring of tape reels an irritating reminder of the night's disaster.

'High-and-mighty jumped-up slag!' Livid with outrage, he poured himself a large dark rum from the crystal decanter. 'Twenty fucking grand for getting rid of one body. She's forgotten where she came from.'

Scarlett's eyes widened at the sight of the angry purple bruise blooming along his jaw. She tippy-toed over, reaching up to touch his damaged skin with featherlight fingers.

'Oh, Danny! Did that beast of a woman slog you one?' Her tone dripped with indignant sympathy. 'Poor baby.'

He brushed her off, his pride stinging worse than his jaw. The thought of a woman – any woman – getting the better of him was unbearable. That uppity bitch thinking she could manhandle Danny Steele and get away with it. Her and her pet gorilla.

He knocked back his drink in one burning gulp, relishing the heat that spread through his chest.

Scarlett retreated slightly, perching on the edge of the desk, legs crossed primly despite her provocative dress. 'Who was Joanie?' she asked.

His head snapped up, eyes narrowing dangerously. 'Just some worthless scrubber who couldn't handle the rough stuff.'

'The Duchess made it sound like you hurt her pretty badly.'

He slammed down his glass. 'What's it to you?' His fingers ran roughly through his hair. 'Fucking hell, Scarlett, we've got bigger problems than some poxy, brain-dead bobtail from years ago.'

Scarlett reached for the decanter, refilling his glass with steady hands. 'I just wondered, that's all. Losing a baby must be terrible.'

'Christ,' he snorted then threw back the fresh drink in one gulp. 'You getting sentimental on me? She was just damaged goods. Probably not the first time she'd been knocked up.'

Knowing when to leave it alone, Scarlett turned her attention to the business at hand. 'What about the tapes? Did you get everything?'

A triumphant smile replaced his scowl. Danny moved to the bank of equipment, rewinding one of the reels with practiced movements. 'Every sickening second. From the moment our moral crusader walked in until the moment he cut that girl's throat.'

The grainy black-and-white footage flickered to life on one of the monitors. There was Harrington, his respectable face stripped away to reveal a monster, hands around Araminta's throat before he slit it.

'Jesus,' Scarlett gasped, a shudder running through her. 'He's a right brute.'

'He's perfect,' Danny corrected, eyes gleaming with malicious victory. His finger traced the outline of Harrington's features on the screen almost lovingly. 'The chairman of Clean Up Britain himself, murdering a prostitute on camera. This is better than winning the pools.'

Scarlett stared at the footage, her expression unreadable. 'How will you approach him?'

He lunged for Scarlett, making her howl and swung her high. Then Danny pushed her into the wall and flipped her hem up, ready for action. 'You leave the thinking to me, doll.'

With a grunt, he thrust hard into her. 'This is better than the fucking docks ever were. Why break legs when you can break souls instead? Men like Harrington will do anything to keep their dirty little secrets buried.'

# Chapter Twelve

Brother Bertie stood frozen outside the Job Centre, shame eating him alive. The building squatted on the high street like a tombstone, its brick walls screaming failure at every poor bollocks who walked through those doors. They'd tarted it up with some fancy new name – Job Centre – but it was still the same humiliating cattle market it had always been, in his opinion.

A steady stream of broken men shuffled inside, shoulders hunched under the burden of defeat. Young lads who should've been grafting, middle-aged geezers thrown on the scrapheap, older blokes whose lined mugs told stories of work that didn't exist anymore.

Through the smudged glass, he could see the fluorescent hell inside, rows of plastic chairs filled with defeat, pen-pushing nobodies processing human misery like another day at the office. His feet had turned to concrete. His hand might have been severed for all the good it was doing reaching for that door handle.

*Bloodfire!*

He couldn't do it. Couldn't grovel for government scraps. Every instinct in his body was screaming against it, his pride battered but not dead. And pride was a funny thing. Once it got its claws in, it didn't let go easy.

Twenty minutes earlier, Sin had been playing the perfect little wife, humming while she packed his lunch. Her dark eyes had sparkled with the kind of trust that twisted his guts into knots.

'Here you go,' she'd said and snapped the lid onto the blue Tupperware container she'd won at Gertie's party. 'Ham sandwiches, that packet of Golden Wonder cheese and onion crisps you like, and I've put in a thermos of tea. Should keep you going till dinnertime.'

While she'd been up early making his packed lunch, he'd been lying there planning another day of spectacular deception.

'You're too good to me, darling,' he'd choked out, the words scraping his throat raw with guilt.

She'd reached up to fix his collar, her fingers warm against his neck. 'Got to keep my working man properly fed, haven't I? Can't have you wasting away on some building site.'

Her touch had twisted his guts with guilt. If only she knew her 'working man' was worthless.

'Daddy!' Isaac had called from the doorway, the four-year-old dragging his favourite toy car, looking proper poorly. Dark circles under those bright eyes and that wheeze in his chest that made Brother Bertie want to punch walls.

'There's my big man.' Brother Bertie had scooped up the boy who felt fragile and breakable. 'How's that chest feeling today then, soldier?'

Isaac had coughed – a sound that cut right through him. 'It's scratchy, Daddy.'

That wheeze was getting worse. The boy needed his specialist medicine – the expensive private stuff that cost more than most geezers earned in a month. And here he was, more broken than a busted flush and too proud to beg.

'I'm taking him round to Mum's today,' Sin had said, reading his expression with uncanny accuracy.

That kiss she'd given him still burned on his lips. The way she'd whispered 'Love you, Bertram Watson' on his mouth, cushioning her whole body lovingly to him. She'd tasted of tea and trust, believing every lie that came out of his mouth.

Now here he stood, too proud to grovel and too broke to breathe. A real bloody catch, he was.

'Well, well, well. If it ain't Brother fucking Bertie.'

The voice cut through his misery. Brother Bertie spun round to find himself face to face with a ghost from his past – and not one he wanted to see.

Keith Wright stood there grinning. The man had aged badly. His once-sharp features had gone to fat, and his thinning hair was slicked back with enough Brylcreem to grease a motor.

'Wrighty,' Brother Bertie said, his voice flat. 'What rock did you crawl out from under?'

'Cheeky bastard, you are, right?' Wright's laugh had all the warmth of a gravedigger's shovel. 'Could say the same about you, standing outside the dole office looking proper miserable. Having a bit of trouble with the straight and narrow, are we, right?'

Everyone called him Wrighty because the tosser couldn't finish most sentences without ending with a 'right'.

Brother Bertie drew himself up to his full height, letting Wrighty see exactly what five years of hard graft had done to his already dangerous frame. 'I'm doing just fine, mate. Just passing through.'

'Course you are, right? Looking sharp, though, I'll give you that. Always did know how to dress the part, even when you were skint.' Wrighty sized him up from all angles. 'Heard you went legit after that dust-up with Jimmy Southpaw. Proper domestic now, innit? Wife, kid, the whole suburban dream, right?'

Brother Bertie's whole body went rigid, murder flashing in his eyes. 'My family's none of your fucking business.'

'Touchy, touchy. No offence meant. Just catching up with an old mate, right?' Wrighty's grin showed more gaps than teeth. 'Speaking of which, I never could work out why a clever bastard, like yourself, would chuck away easy money for honest graft. Especially when honest graft's getting harder to find these days, right?'

There it was – the hook, dangled with all the subtlety of a hammer to the skull. Brother Bertie kept his feeling to himself, but his pulse was racing. 'Times are hard all over.'

'Too bleeding right they are. Lot of decent, hard-working men finding themselves in uncomfortable situations.' Wrighty's eyes never left Brother Bertie's face, reading every twitch. 'Lucky for them, there's still work available for those with the right skills and flexible consciences, right?'

*Flexible conscience?*

'That so?'

'Oh, very much so. See, I've been doing a bit of independent work lately. Helping connect talented individuals with opportunities that suit their particular gifts, right?' He glanced around. 'Funny thing is, I spend a lot of time around places talking to the right sort of candidates.'

Brother Bertie finally got what the guy was doing here. A vulture preying on desperation, offering criminal work to men who'd lost everything else. The bastard was a parasite who made his living off other people's misery.

'It's delivery work, mainly,' the fucker continued. 'Moving packages from point A to point B. No questions asked. Night shifts, mostly. Cash in hand, no paperwork.' His eyes sharpened. 'The sort of work that pays enough to cover expensive bills.'

The words hit Brother Bertie hard. Medical bills. Izzy's wheezing.

Suddenly, Sin's trusting face came to him.

He'd promised her. Sworn on everything sacred that he'd keep his nose clean.

But how could he watch his boy struggle to breathe when dirty money could fix everything?

His promise to Sin went to war with Isaac's desperate need.

Honor against necessity.

Love against love.

With cold fury, he made his decision. 'You know what, Wrighty? You can take your "delivery work" and ram it up your two-faced arse. I went straight for reasons that matter, and no amount of blood money's going to change that.'

Not deterred in the least, the other man reached into his jacket, pulling out a crumpled piece of cardboard with a phone number scrawled on it. 'Fair enough. But just in case you change your mind and decide my arse has only got one face, you give me a bell. Right?'

He shoved it into Brother Bertie's jacket pocket and slithered off into the crowd. Brother Bertie yanked the card out, crushing it in his fist, ready to heave it in the gutter with the ciggy butts and dog muck.

But he didn't.

He'd made a sacred promise to his wife.

He was done with the gangland life for good. So why couldn't he chuck it away?

# Chapter Thirteen

'The permissive society has become the destructive society,' Oliver Harrington MP roared, his words striking the conference hall with righteous fury. 'From the cesspits of Soho to the drug dens masquerading as nightclubs, we are witnessing the systematic corruption of everything our forefathers fought to preserve.'

Roof-raising applause swept over him in waves of pure validation. Standing behind the mahogany podium at Westminster's grandest conference hall, he surveyed the sea of upturned faces with the arrogant satisfaction of a man who'd just delivered another commanding speech.

The standing ovation confirmed what he already knew; he was the man of the hour, the fighting voice against corruption that Britain desperately needed.

Twenty minutes later, Harrington slipped out through the service exit, avoiding the crush of reporters in the main foyer. The evening air bit sharp and cold, carrying the acrid smell of coal smoke from the chimneys. His Bentley waited in the narrow alley behind the building.

'Wonderful speech, Mr Harrington. Truly inspiring.'

The voice came from the shadows between two industrial bins. A figure stepped forward – a man in his late forties with the lean build of someone who'd grown up fighting for everything he had. The stranger's face bore a jagged scar down one cheek.

Harrington's spine stiffened, the hairs on his neck rising in primitive warning. But years of being a politician ensured that he hid his astonishment well. 'Do I know you?'

'Danny Steele. Local councillor for Sugar Cane Wharf. We met… briefly… Recently.'

Harrington neither confirmed nor denied, another trait honed from years of being a politician. 'What can I do for you, Mr Steele? Though I must say this is hardly the appropriate venue for constituency matters.'

Danny wasn't surprised the MP was playing the 'I ain't got an effing clue what's going on here' card. It was time to stop pissing about and give this posh prick a sharp dose of reality. 'This is about how you're cleaning the country up with one hand while the other one's getting filthy dirty. Blood-red dirty.'

'I beg your pardon?' Harrington's affronted tone flared with indignation.

'Belgravia townhouse. Private membership. Last week.' Danny's gaze never left Harrington's face, studying every twitch and flicker. 'Ring any bells?'

For the first time, fear crawled up the MP's neck, his cheeks turning a blotchy red. 'I haven't the faintest idea what you're talking about,' he sputtered and pulled his cashmere coat tighter around his tall frame. 'Now if you'll excuse me—'

'Funny thing about memories.' Danny stepped directly into Harrington's path, invading his personal space with East End aggression. 'They can get a bit foggy after a few champagnes and lines of Bolivia's finest. But I've got something that might jog yours.'

Harrington drew himself up to his full height, nostrils flaring with disdain. 'Stand aside,' he ordered, his tone that of a man accustomed to immediate obedience. 'I have another engagement this evening.'

'With all due respect, Mr Harrington,' Danny pulled a small envelope from his jacket pocket and held it between two fingers, 'you'll want to see what's in here before you go anywhere.'

Harrington's jittery gaze darted to the envelope, a slither of sweat forming on his upper lip. 'I don't have time for games.'

'No game.' Danny flipped open the envelope and tilted it so only Harrington could glimpse its contents. 'Just a little snapshot. Got plenty more where this came from.'

The colour drained from Harrington's face as he stared at the photograph – himself, unmistakable despite the grainy quality, with a dark-skinned young woman. The image was carefully cropped, revealing nothing explicit but suggesting everything.

'This is preposterous,' he hissed, spittle flying from his thin lips. 'That's clearly a forgery.'

'Is it, though?' Danny grabbed his arm, fingers digging into expensive cloth. 'Want to risk the papers deciding that for themselves? Or would you rather have a little chat? My car's just round the corner.'

For a split second, Harrington's carefully constructed composure slipped, revealing raw panic beneath. 'Ten minutes,' he finally agreed, every syllable dripping with loathing. 'Then I'm leaving.'

As he tucked the incriminating evidence away, Danny felt a rush of vicious, gloating satisfaction. He'd soon show this jumped-up toff-cunt who was calling the shots.

He gestured towards a side street with mock gallantry.

***

Danny's Roller purred through Soho's neon-lit streets. He sprawled in the back seat beside Harrington, who sat rigid with growing dread.

'Where exactly are we going?' the Member of Parliament demanded. He kneaded his liver-spotted hands together, the veins prominent beneath papery skin.

Danny grinned, watching with satisfaction when the older man flinched away. 'You'll see soon enough.'

The car eventually rolled up outside a narrow building squeezed between a book shop and a chippie. The frontage was painted black, with discreet signs advertising 'Private Cinema' and 'Members Only'. Posters in the windows promised exotic entertainment for discerning gentlemen.

'After you.' Danny opened the car door, the courtesy exaggerated.

Harrington remained seated, his body rigid while his fingers locked around the leather seat. 'I'm not going in there.'

'Yeah, you are.' He grabbed Harrington's lapel and yanked him forward. 'Because if you don't, tomorrow's papers get some very juicy snaps of Clean Up Britain that aren't so clean.'

Danny contemptuously flung him into the seat. 'Your choice.'

Shoulders sagged in defeat, the MP stepped out onto the pavement.

***

The screening room stank of stale cigarettes and bodily fluids, its torn red velvet seats facing a large screen. Danny directed Harrington to the front row, while he took the seat directly behind him.

'Best seat in the house,' he announced, signalling to someone in the projection booth.

Harrington stared straight ahead at the blank screen. 'Whatever game you're playing, Steele, it won't work. I have powerful friends.'

'Not powerful enough to save you from this,' Danny snapped back. 'Star of your very own blue movie, you are. Well, more red than blue.'

The screen flickered to life, and Harrington's body went rigid with horror.

There he was, clear and unmistakable in the grainy footage. The exclusive party, the cocaine, the young woman's terrified face. Her struggle against the golden chains. His own face twisted with excitement as he approached her. And then... the violence. His hands around her throat. The knife...

'Turn it off,' Harrington choked, his fingers clawing at the armrests, nails scraping against the worn velvet.

'Not enjoying the show?' Danny leaned forward, his lips almost touching Harrington's ear. 'But you're the main attraction.'

Despite his horror, beneath the initial nausea, beneath the shock of seeing his crime played back in vivid detail, another sensation stirred in Harrington. The familiar heat stirred in his cock. The girl's screams echoed from the speakers, and his pulse quickened with remembered pleasure. Just like that first time he'd indulged his perversion during the war, that young East End girl with the defiant eyes who'd fought so beautifully before he'd broken her.

His breathing deepened, reliving the moment of absolute power. The savage thrill of her futile thrashing beneath him, the exquisite terror in her voice. His body responded eagerly to the memory, blood rushing to his cock, watching himself take what he wanted.

Behind him, Danny observed the telling signs, including the unmistakable bulge forming in expensive trousers.

*The revolting bastard.*

'Getting excited all over again, are we?' Danny taunted, contempt thickening his voice. 'You sick fuck.'

The film ended abruptly, plunging the room into darkness.

'What do you want?' Harrington finally asked, his cultured voice reduced to a rasp.

'Straight to business. I like that.' Danny relaxed back. 'I want advance warning of any police raids targeted at my establishments. Information about what the Old Bill are planning.'

'And if I refuse?' the older man dared.

Usually, Danny would have clumped him one. But there was no need for that in this instance because he had this murdering pervert by the balls and all he had to do was squeeze. 'The film goes to the coppers. You ever been to The Scrubs? I hear it's a shithole.'

Defeated, Harrington nodded. 'How do I contact you?'

Danny patted him on the shoulder like they were best mates. 'I'll be in touch. I have a feeling this is the beginning of a beautiful friendship.'

The fight went out of Harrington completely, the full horror of his new reality settling on him. 'What happened to the girl?'

'Concerned about her welfare now?' Danny barked a harsh laugh that echoed off the grimy walls. 'Bit fucking late for that, mate.'

They emerged into the neon-lit street, where life continued its grubby pace. Danny's Roller disappeared into traffic, leaving Harrington standing alone among the vice dens he'd sworn to destroy.

***

Three streets away, a respectably dressed woman in a worn coat stopped another passerby near the entrance to a strip club. Her hands gripped an old black-and-white photograph – a young woman with bright eyes and an innocent smile.

'Excuse me,' she said, her voice carrying a slight Caribbean lilt. 'Have you seen this girl? She's my daughter. Her name is Araminta.'

The man barely glanced at the photo before hurrying away, just like all the others.

Hyacinth clutched the picture tighter and approached the next person walking past. She'd been searching these streets for hours, showing the same photograph to anyone who would spare her a moment.

She was heartbroken because she didn't know if she would see her adored daughter ever again.

# Chapter Fourteen

'Blimey, Ruddy, you planning on entering a fashion show or working the land?'

After his snide comment, Brother Bertie surveyed the patch of earth before him, leaning on his spade. The allotment stretched out before them, a quarter-acre of neglected London soil that reminded him of Jamaica's earth. Most Londoners couldn't fathom why anyone would want to cultivate a tiny strip of inner-city earth when perfectly good vegetables sat waiting on supermarket shelves. But Bertie understood something they didn't. That working the soil connected him to something deeper than the chaos of London's streets. Here, he could breathe again.

The allotment was his pride and joy.

Ruddy stood beside a pile of old timber, slender hands planted firmly on her jutting hips. Ruddy had evolved into his closest confidante, the one person who could read his shifting moods better than he could himself. Where once Jimmy had been his soul mate, his other half…

He pushed that thought aside. Sometimes the ache of missing his former blood brother hit him so hard it took his breath away. All those years of brotherhood, of having someone who understood him completely. But Jimmy had slammed the door in his face. All because he'd fallen in love with his sister.

Today Ruddy was sporting a psychedelic paisley minidress that barely skimmed her knobbly knees, paired with pristine black go-go boots with red love hearts dotted over them that had clearly never touched honest dirt.

'What's wrong with my clobber?' Her incensed question sliced through the afternoon air. 'Just because we're playing farmers doesn't mean a girl can't appear the business, does it? Besides, these boots are proper leather. Cost me a week's wages, they did.'

Bertie shook his head, unable to suppress a wicked grin. 'Woman, you're dressed for Tom Jones at the Palladium, not digging up cabbages.'

'Don't get your knickers in a twist.' She rolled up her sleeves with characteristic determination and examined his modest patch of vegetables with mock seriousness. 'Besides, someone needs to keep an eye on your gardening efforts. Last week I caught you having a proper heart-to-heart with that beetroot plant. 'Come on then, grow nice and big for Uncle Bertie,' you were saying. I thought you'd completely lost your marbles.'

Brother Bertie rolled his gaze skywards. 'They respond to encouragement!'

'Encouragement?' Ruddy's tone rose with delighted incredulity. 'You were stroking the bleedin' leaves like they were Raquel Welch! Next thing I know you'll be holding christening ceremonies for the carrots and reading bedtime stories to the brussels sprouts.'

She followed up by clasping her hands in an over-the-top motion to her chest and put on a ridiculous accent: 'Once upon a time, there was a lovely little lettuce who dreamed of being in a proper sandwich…'

They both creased up laughing. That's what he loved about his friend, she reminded him that life wasn't to be all serious. It felt good to laugh like this, proper belly laughs that drove away all the worry and stress, if only for a few minutes.

'Right then,' he announced, 'let's christen the shed properly before we do anything else.'

The wooden shed stood crooked at the far end of their plot, its battered door hanging slightly askew. He'd spent the previous weekend reinforcing the rusty locks and adding additional shelving. Not for garden tools, but for something far more precious to his current circumstances.

Inside, Bertie carefully arranged bottles of his special rum blend on the makeshift shelves. Each bottle contained Wray and Nephew Overproof Rum infused with marijuana leaves from plants he'd been cultivating inside the warmth of the allotment shed. The concoction was so potent that those brave enough to try it often found themselves shuddering, before shouting, "Lord have mercy!" after the first sip, which is how it earned its nickname: Lord Have Mercy Rum Punch.

'How many bottles you got stashed away now?' She peered over his shoulder, her perfume mixing with the earthy scent of wacky baccy.

'About two dozen.' His tone carried an undertone of worry. 'Need to shift more of them, though. Word's spreading that the operation has moved here, but not fast enough.'

Brother Bertie took two glasses of his special Lord Have Mercy Rum Punch, the amber liquid glowing like liquid gold in the afternoon light. His transistor radio came next. He handed her the drinks.

'Right then, let's get these beauties set up.' He gestured towards two folded deckchairs.

His friend examined the chairs with growing delight. 'Bloody hell, Bertie! These are proper works of art, they are.'

The first chair bore the bold red, white, and blue stripes of the Union Jack, while the second displayed Jamaica's vibrant green, gold, and black flag.

'Remember that mad artist who squatted upstairs?' Bertie unfolded the Jamaican flag chair with careful reverence. 'Barmy as they come, but talented hands when he wasn't off his face on whatever he was smoking. He made these for us.'

'Disappeared one night, didn't he?' She settled into her Union Jack throne.

He positioned his chair beside hers, the two flags creating a perfect picture of unity.

'To surviving another bleedin' day in paradise.' Ruddy raised her chipped glass.

The rum burned sweet and fierce down Brother Bertie's throat, loosening the brutal knots of tension that had been strangling his shoulders for weeks. He fiddled with the radio dial until Stevie Wonder's, 'You Are the Sunshine of My Life' floated across the allotment.

'Perfect.' She closed her painted lids, her beehive catching the afternoon breeze. 'This is the life, innit? Just you, me, and enough rum to sink a battleship.' Suddenly, one sharp lid of hers opened. 'What's eating you, Bertie? You've had a face on you all afternoon.'

The words tumbled out before he could stop them. 'I lost my job. Three weeks ago now.'

She sat bolt upright, her glass nearly slipping from her grip. 'Why didn't you tell me sooner?'

'Couldn't.' He stared into his rum, unable to meet her penetrating stare. 'Felt such a failure. I can't bring myself to tell Sin.'

'Oh, you daft brush.' Her tone softened with genuine, but exasperated affection. 'Your missus isn't going to think any less of you. Half the blokes in London are losing their jobs with all this economic bollocks going on.'

Brother Bertie shook his head, frustration tightening his jaw. 'Izzy needs his medicine, Ruddy. That chest of his gets worse every winter, and the doctor says he might need special treatment if it doesn't improve. How am I supposed to provide for them selling rum punch from an allotment shed?'

'Don't even think about it.' Her words carried a warning edge.

'Think about what?'

Her body became rigid. 'You know bloody well what. I can see it in your gaze. That dangerous gleam you get when you're remembering the old days. All that easy money, the respect, the power. But that's not you anymore, Bertie. You're a family man now.'

His jaw tightened. 'I know what I am. But knowing and being able to afford Isaac's medicine are two different things, aren't they?'

'Listen to me.' She shuffled forward. 'You think Sin fell in love with you because you were some big-shot criminal? You think little Izzy lights up when he sees you because his daddy's a dangerous man? They love you because you're you. Because you chose them over that Badlands life.'

'Easy for you to say. You don't have a four-year-old who can't breathe properly.'

Her expression darkened, temper on the rise. 'And speaking of family, what about that brother of hers? Jimmy's sitting pretty in his flash Bentley while his sister counts pennies for her son's medicine. Shameful, that is.' She ground her back teeth in disgust. 'He's chosen to cut Sin off because his feelings got wounded. Well, boo-hoo! Your little boy's his nephew, for crying out loud. His own flesh and blood.'

He knew she was right, but it didn't solve his immediate problem. 'Maybe I could just do one job. Something small, something safe. Just enough to get us back on our feet.'

'Bertie Watson, you open up those lugholes of yours and listen good.' Ruddy's tone carried the steel that had earned her legendary status from East to West London. 'There's no such thing as "just one job" and you know it. The moment you step back into that world, it's got you by the nuts and ain't letting go.'

She tapped a finger on the back of his hand. 'You want to know what I think? I think you're scared. Scared of being ordinary, scared of struggling with everyone else, scared that maybe you're not the man you thought you were.'

Her words hit hard. Like he was back in the boxing ring sparring with Jimmy.

She continued, voice softer. 'But being a good father and husband – that's the hardest job in the world, love. Harder than any con or heist you ever pulled.'

Before he could respond, rapid footsteps approached across the allotment. They turned to see Sabina Patel, Bertie's next-door neighbour, her face grave with worry, still wearing her cleaning apron and clutching a crumpled piece of paper.

'Brother Bertie!' she called out, slightly breathless from running. 'Thank God I found you. Your Sin called. She couldn't reach you at home, so she tried me.'

Ice formed in his stomach. 'What's wrong?'

Her words carried urgent concern. 'You need to get to London Hospital. Now.'

# Chapter Fifteen

Brother Bertie bulldozed through The Royal London's corridors, pure panic propelling him on. The antiseptic stench burned his nostrils. The fluorescent lights buzzing overhead cast a sickly pallor over everything, intensifying the dread coiling in his belly.

He spotted Sin before she saw him, hunched against the wall outside the children's ward. Her face was chalk-white, ravaged by tears, her usually perfect hair hanging messy around her shoulders. The sight of his strong wife crumpled in despair sent icy fear shooting straight into his bones.

'Sin!'

She whirled at his voice and flung herself into his arms, clutching him with the desperation of a drowning woman. Her entire body convulsed with sobs she couldn't control, her tears soaking hot patches through his work shirt.

'Thank Christ you're here,' she whispered, her voice splintering into jagged fragments. 'I thought... I thought we were going to lose him, Bertie. He couldn't breathe. He just... couldn't breathe.'

Gently, he eased back, gripping her shoulders. The naked horror in her eyes stabbed him deeper than any blade.

'Where is he? Where's our boy?'

'In there.' Sniffing, she nodded towards a nearby room. 'The doctors are with—'

'Brother... Bertie?'

The hesitant, slurred voice floated from the shadows near the ward entrance. He turned to find a woman he barely recognised shuffling painfully towards them.

Iris Steele moved with agonising slowness, each step a deliberate negotiation. The right side of her face hung slack and immobile, the once-plain skin puckered with angry scars. Her skull was misshapen where surgeons had pieced the shattered bone back together, leaving a grotesque valley of indentations across her forehead and temple. A cloudy film covered her left eye, the pupil fixed and unresponsive. Her fingers shook continuously, gnarled into permanent claws.

That accident had really fucked her up.

The sight of Sin's hardworking mother reduced to this broken creature never failed to shock him. Five years after the accident that had crushed her skull, she remained a ghastly monument to suffering.

'Iris.' Brother Bertie kept his voice gentle. Despite her condition, this woman had always adored her grandson. 'What happened with Izzy?'

Her ruined mouth worked soundlessly for a moment before words emerged, each one pushed through damaged nerves with painful effort. 'He was…watching *Magic…R-Roundabout*. Then he…he just…fell down. Couldn't…get air.'

Her mangled hand fluttered to her misshapen temple, distress contorting her features further. 'I couldn't…remember…Then I did, and called the ambulance.'

He reassured her with gentle care. 'You saved his life, Iris.'

A doctor emerged from Izzy's room, fatigue etched into the lines around his eyes.

'Mr Watson? I'm Dr Fleming. I understand Isaac has also been receiving private treatment for his condition?'

Brother Bertie nodded, his gut twisting.

'How's my son?' The words scraped from his dry throat.

'Stabilised for now. His asthma is progressing more rapidly than we'd anticipated. The standard NHS treatments aren't sufficient anymore.'

Sin's fingers dug painfully into Brother Bertie's arm. 'What does that mean?'

'It means Isaac will need to continue the specialised medication and follow-up care he already receives at the private clinic. Without it...' He didn't need to finish because Bertie didn't need words to understand the graveness of the situation.

Sin's face brightened with desperate hope. 'Thank God your construction job's been going so well, Bertram. At least we don't have to worry about money.'

'We'll sort it,' he heard himself saying, the lie bitter on his tongue. 'Whatever Izzy needs.'

'Good.' Dr Fleming nodded. 'You can see him now. He's had his first treatment, but he's still struggling.'

Brother Bertie steeled himself and followed Sin into the small hospital room. The sight that greeted him nearly drove him to his knees.

His adored little prince lay propped up in the narrow bed, his small body swallowed by the crisp white sheets. A clear plastic mask covered half his tiny face, connected to an oxygen tank beside the bed. His chest heaved with each laboured breath, the effort visibly exhausting him.

Brother Bertie approached on unsteady legs. His son's eyes, glassy with fever, widened at the sight of him.

'Daddy,' Izzy wheezed, the word barely audible through the mask. His fingers scrabbled weakly at the sheets.

Brother Bertie took his son's hand, shocked by how bird-like those tiny bones felt beneath his rough fingers. Izzy's skin burned hot, his pulse fluttering too fast.

'Don't try to talk,' he murmured, smoothing back his son's sweat-damp hair. 'Just focus on breathing, nice and slow.'

Izzy nodded, his eyes never leaving his father's face. Brother Bertie forced himself to smile, to project a calm he was nowhere near feeling.

'The medicine will start working soon,' Dr Fleming said quietly. 'The first dose is already helping, but he needs continuous treatment.'

As if on cue, Izzy's eyelids drooped. His breathing remained laboured but less desperate, each inhale less of a battle.

Brother Bertie bent down and pressed his lips to his son's burning forehead. 'Sleep now, little man. Daddy's watching over you.'

Izzy's eyes fluttered closed, his hand still clutching his father's finger.

In the corridor, Sin gripped his arm, her face shining with relief. 'He's going to be all right, isn't he? We'll increase the private treatment?'

'Of course we will. We'll do whatever it takes.'

*Whatever it takes.*

He used the pads of his fingers to wipe the tears from her cheeks. 'I need to step outside for some air. You stay with our brave lad.'

He kissed her forehead. 'I love you, Sin Watson. More than my own life.'

He walked away before she could witness the devastation in his expression, before she could read the truth written across his features. Each step down that endless Victorian corridor felt heavier than the last.

Inside the phone box outside the hospital, Brother Bertie dialled the number on the piece of cardboard.

The phone rang twice before a familiar voice answered: 'Wrighty here, right?'

Brother Bertie closed his burning eyes, feeling five years of legitimate living crumble around him. 'About that job…'

# Chapter Sixteen

'She tried to hack my cock off.'

A pissed Danny stood frozen in the doorway of the once-tidy front room, his nostrils filling with the metallic tang of fresh blood. The terraced house in Bethnal Green would've been decent enough with its proper furniture, framed pictures on the walls, and small bookcase, but now it resembled a slaughterhouse. A bloke he'd never clapped eyes on before sat perched on a good-quality sofa, a blood-soaked towel pressed to his groin. His face had drained whiter than a fresh bedsheet, sweat clinging to him like a second skin.

Disgust curling his upper lip, Danny surveyed the chaos that had overtaken the otherwise respectable room. 'What the bloody hell went on here?'

The man, Malcolm, according to the post on the sideboard, winced with every slight movement. 'I only touched her! Just a little peck! Next thing I know she's coming at me with that!' He jerked his chin towards the corner.

'HE HAD NO RIGHT TO TOUCH!'

The scream ripped through the room. Danny whipped around. His sister, Chrissie, huddled in the shadowy corner, knees yanked up to her chest, clutching a jagged shard of glass in her trembling fist. Blood trickled between her fingers where the glass bit into her palm. Her gaze darted around the room, never settling, like a trapped rat searching for escape.

Her cat was pressed protectively to her leg, back arched, spitting fury at both men.

Danny's lungs seized up, all the air punched right out of him at the sight of his baby sister. One year it had been since he'd clapped eyes on her, and God knows what had gone on with her during that time, but the truth was if he'd seen her in the street he'd have passed her as a stranger. She was a state and literarily half the woman she was.

A memory flashed through his mind: just twenty minutes earlier, buried in council paperwork when his secretary knocked on his office door.

'Mr Steele? There's a call for you.' Margaret had hovered in the doorway, fidgeting with her pencil. 'A woman. She sounds… not quite right, if you get my drift.'

Danny had assumed it was Scarlett throwing another wobbly. That bird could flip from purring kitten to spitting wildcat in the blink of an eye.

'I'll take it,' he'd said, reaching for the heavy black receiver.

But it wasn't Scarlett. The voice on the other end came small, hoarse.

'I didn't mean to do it.' His sister, Chrissie.

Danny's heart had plummeted to his shoes. The familiar dread had settled in his gut. The same feeling he got every time Chrissie went off the rails.

'Tell me where you are. Don't move. Don't talk to anyone. I'm coming now.'

He'd scribbled the address, already grabbing his jacket.

Now, he stood in this blood-spattered room, the bleeding man on the settee glaring at him.

'Your sister's one stop short of East Ham!' he raved, finding his courage. 'I want compensation! Should ring the plod and get her banged up!'

The air seemed to chill as Danny turned to him, real slow, his gaze narrowing to dangerous slits. 'Who am I?'

Malcolm swallowed hard, remembering exactly whose gangland toes he was treading on. *Fuck me! I could be a dead man!*

So he quickly shot back, 'Umm...Danny Steele.'

Danny gave the knife a twist. 'So you know exactly what happens to gobby little toerags who think they've got the brass to threaten my family?'

He enunciated each word, crystal clear so this knobhead got it into his thicko skull where he was going to end up if he continued down this dead-end street – in the Regents Canal wearing concrete boots.

Terror gripped Malcolm's features. Danny might play the community councillor these days, but the East End remembered. The King of the Docks wasn't a brutal title easily forgotten.

Danny took out his wallet, peeled off several notes. 'You had an accident. Fell on a knife while you were buttering your toast. That's your story.'

Malcolm eyed the money, his scheming mind doing overtime. Mouth curling into a sneer, he spat back, 'Two hundred quid ain't enough for what she did!'

Danny loomed over the seated man, his shadow swallowing him whole. 'It's enough to keep your knackers attached to the rest of you. Because if you breathe a word about my sister, the next bit of glass goes through your ear, into that twat brain.'

Money changed hands. Wincing, Malcolm retreated to another room, leaving the Steele brother and sister to it.

Danny turned to Chrissie and took a handkerchief from his pocket and approached slowly, palms open. 'Let me see that hand, Chris.'

She flinched back, the glass shard raised, her entire body trembling with fear. 'Don't touch me!'

'I won't touch. Just want to stop the bleeding.' He crouched a few feet away, holding out the handkerchief, keeping his movements slow and measured. 'You're hurting yourself.'

Her eyes darted to the blood dripping onto the clean carpet, then back to Danny's face. Something flickered behind the wildness – recognition, perhaps. The shard lowered slightly.

'That's it, love. Let me help.' Danny inched closer.

With a suddenness that startled him, Chrissie dropped the glass. It clattered to the floor, bloodstained and accusing. Her shoulders sagged, the fight draining out of her.

Danny gently wrapped the handkerchief around her cut palm, his thick fingers surprisingly delicate. The wound wasn't deep, but his stomach knotted at how little she seemed to feel it. Her skin felt cold, despite the warmth of the house.

His throat tight with emotions he couldn't name, Danny managed, 'Get your gear. You're coming with me.'

For a moment, her vacant eyes cleared, a flash of the old Chrissie surfacing. Her cracked lips parted, her voice barely above a whisper. 'Tel too.'

''Course.' Danny nodded. 'The cat comes, too.'

He watched her stuff clothes into plastic bags. Plastic bloody bags. His sister always travelled with swanky suitcases, some with her initials on the side. He missed her picking up the bloodied shard of glass and stuffing it into her pocket. She scooped up Tequila, burying her face in his matted fur for a moment. The cat sank into her affection, but his watchful eyes never left Danny.

The knot in Danny's chest tightened at the state of his sister. Never in his lifetime did he think he'd see the day Chrissie moved as a ghost through her own life, appearing shattered beyond repair.

Outside, he ushered her into his roller. Chrissie curled into the passenger seat, knees drawn up, making herself smaller. The cat settled on her lap.

He drove away, throat tight with the words stuck there. The silence stretched between them, years of unspoken truths piling up like corpses.

Finally, rage, and concern battling in his voice, Danny growled, 'What the fuck were you playing at back there, Chrissie?'

She stared out of the window, the orange glow of streetlamps sliding across her hollow features. The handkerchief around her hand bloomed red in places.

Danny slammed his palm against the steering wheel, making her jump. 'You could've killed him! One slip and you'd be banged up for murder!'

Chrissie flinched at the volume, her shoulders hunching further, making herself even smaller in the passenger seat.

'He touched me.' Each word emerged from her lips with visible effort, her voice distant and empty. 'Like before.'

The blood in Danny's veins froze, his grip tightening on the wheel until his fingers ached.

'Before?' The question hung between them, heavy with dread. 'What d'you mean, before?'

Chrissie faced him, something terrible and knowing in her suddenly alive eyes. The vacant fog lifted, replaced by such piercing clarity that Danny nearly drove off the road.

Her gaze burning into him with accusation and pain, she whispered, 'That time you should have saved me.'

# Chapter Seventeen

The front door of the Steele family home banged open, rattling the family photos on the wall. Eric 'Batters' Rogers stomped in holding the hand of his five-year-old grandson, Harry.

'Iris! You about, girl?' His call thundered through the house, loud enough to wake the stiffs over in Tower Hamlets cemetery.

At fifty-six, Batters remained a fearsome sight. His life-beaten face, barrel chest, and thick forearms still put the wind up those who remembered his all-out war with Danny Steele for supremacy as the Number One Face on Sugar Cane's Dock. But grief and guilt changes a man. Losing Mini, first to his own stupidity when he turned his back on her for marrying Jimmy Steele, then to the illness that snatched her far too young, had him hanging up his shooter for good. His grandkids, Mini's young ones, became his salvation.

The sight of Batters Rogers sitting peacefully in the Steele family kitchen still caused most to do a double-take. The Steele-Rogers blood feud was East End legend, yet there he sat, breaking bread with his once-deadly foe, all for those three little ones with Mini's eyes. Don't take the piss, though, because he still carried that don't-fuck-with-me swagger.

'Granddad, did you bring my Thunderbird 2?' Harry tugged at his trouser leg, bouncing with excitement.

Digging into his coat pocket, Batters, gold tooth glinting with his grin, produced a die-cast model of the iconic green aircraft. 'What d'you reckon I am, some mug who forgets promises to his best grandson?'

Harry snatched the toy with a squeal of delight. The boy's face beamed brighter than Piccadilly Circus at night, a miniature version of Mini with Jimmy's stubborn chin. The sight twisted something painful in Batters's gut. His darling daughter, dead and buried before he'd found the nuts to reconcile with her. That shame would follow him to his grave and beyond.

'Go on, then.' He nudged Harry towards the kitchen. 'Let me find your nan.'

The lad scampered off, leaving Batters alone in the hallway.

'Eric? Is…that…you?'

Iris shuffled into the hallway, moving with the uncertain steps of someone three decades older. Those clear eyes that once flashed with intelligence now gazed vaguely in his direction, never quite focusing properly.

His tough features softened, a tenderness reserved only for her breaking through his hardman exterior. No matter what happened between them, seeing her reduced to this shell tore him up inside. 'Brought Harry round for a visit.'

'Oh…that's…nice.' Her words emerged slowly, each one requiring concentrated effort. She raised a trembling hand to smooth her cardigan, a flash of the fastidious Iris still fighting through the fog.

Protective instinct kicking in, Batters guided her into the sitting room, his giant hand supporting her elbow with surprising gentleness. He settled her into her armchair, plumping the cushion behind her back. 'There you go. Want a cuppa?'

'Tea would be…lovely.' She struggled to breathe right.

Each of his visits hammered home what that terrible fall had done to her. The dignified, gentle woman who'd kept the street cleaner than the bloody Queen's drawing room, reduced to this confused shadow.

The sound of the front door interrupted his troubled thoughts. Danny strode in, flash in his tailored suit, the picture of East End success. Behind him trailed a scrawny, dishevelled figure clutching a mangy cat to her chest.

Shock registering on his face, Batters pulled himself upright. 'What the heck! Is that you, Chrissie, girl?'

He couldn't believe his eyes. The vibrant, mouthy firecracker who'd been the talk of every boozer from Mile End to Whitechapel stood before him looking like death warmed up.

The ragged creature in her arms hissed at him.

'Wotcha, Batters.' Her voice kept a ghost of its former tartness. 'Tel,' her chin dipped to indicate her pet, 'remembers you. Never did like you much.'

Barely glancing at his wife, Danny informed her, 'Chrissie's stopping with us for a bit.'

Batters sourly noted that his former enemy didn't greet his wife with a kiss. In fact, the geezer tried to eyeball any and everything other than her. Batters's back molars ground together.

*Treating her like she's already in the fucking ground…*

Iris struggled to her feet. 'I'll…prepare the…spare room.'

Concern marking his heavy brow, Batters moved to her side. 'Let me help you.'

'She can manage,' Danny cut in sharply. 'The doctors up at the hospital say she won't get better if she doesn't help herself.'

The silence hung thick in the room with them all thinking the same thing: Iris was never going to get better.

His tone softening fractionally, Danny nodded to his sister. 'Go settle in, Chris. Get yourself situated.'

When the women disappeared upstairs, a solid quiet fell between the two men. The loaded pause of once mortal enemies maintaining a dodgy truce.

Danny broke it first, with, 'Drink?'

After Batters nod, Danny poured two shots of whisky, passing one to Batters. The ritual of hospitality observed between men who knew each other's capabilities all too well. On the surface, they maintained the appearance of two family men united by grandchildren. Underneath, the old wounds festered.

Keeping his tone neutral, though concern flickered in his eyes, Batters took a small sip. 'Your sister don't look too clever.'

Danny's face shut down faster than a dodgy boozer during a raid. 'Bad patch. She'll pull through. You know Chrissie, she's the comeback kid.'

Batters nodded, respecting the boundary. Family business stayed family business in their world. Although, Iris was another story, and Danny knew full bloody well why that was.

'And Iris? Doctors say anything new?'

'Same old story.' Danny knocked back his drink in one gulp. 'Good days and bad.'

Cocking his brow, Batters fixed him with a pointed stare. 'I hope you're looking after her proper.'

Danny slammed his glass down, jaw tensing. 'She's my bleedin' wife, ain't she? Not yours.' His eyes narrowed to slits, a dangerous glint replacing the public front. 'I don't remember needing no marriage advice from you, Batters. You worry about your own nest, and I'll worry about mine, yeah?'

The words tumbled out before Batters could stop them, raw emotion overriding his usual caution. 'She was my girl first.'

'Ancient history, that.' Danny's calm voice contradicted the tension coiling through his shoulders.

Indignation bubbling up, Batters puffed up his chest, his massive frame dwarfing the armchair. 'Not to me, it ain't. I still remember when we were tight, me and you. Running wild on the docks, watching each other's backs. Brothers in all but blood.'

Danny's jaw tightened, the only sign of emotion on his controlled mug. 'We were kids.'

'Until you went behind my back with Iris.' Batters swirled the remaining whisky in his glass, bitter memories swirling just like the amber liquid. '*My* Iris.'

'She made her choice.' Danny cut him short.

Batters reined in the red mist threatening to descend. 'Looks to me like you set your sights on Iris because she was the daughter of Alfred the greengrocer who had a few bob.'

A muscle jumped in Danny's cheek, his composure cracking for a split second. 'That what you think? That I went after her for her old man's money?'

Heaving his massive shoulders, Batters let out a humourless chuckle. 'Convenient, wasn't it? My girl suddenly carrying your baby.'

'She wanted more than what you were offering.' Danny's voice hardened, his words sharper than a cut-throat razor. 'A future, stability. Someone with ambition.'

'And you had ambition in spades, didn't ya?' Disgust simmering just below the surface, Batters maintained an even tone while his eyes turned to flint. 'Always looking for the next rung up.'

Danny straightened his already immaculate cuffs with self-importance. 'I gave her a good life. Built something decent. Most women would give their right arm to have a councillor for a husband.'

*That isn't the only thing you're up to these days,* Batters thought. Oh yeah, he'd ears had burned with all the rumours about who this so-called King of Porn was. Sanctimonious prick preaching about public decency while running half the filth in London.

Harry's laugh pulled Batters to his feet, grateful for the interruption before he did something stupid. 'Better get this one back to his dad.'

When he strolled away from the Steele house with Harry, Batters couldn't shake a nagging feeling of disquiet. It was the way Danny's lips rippled when he glanced under hooded eyes at his wife, like he was getting ready to spit on her. That wasn't the look of a devoted husband. That was pure contempt.

He'd known Danny Steele since they were scabby-kneed kids nicking apples from the market. The man had ambition carved into his bones. Always had, always would.

And ambitious men didn't stop climbing just because they'd reached what they wanted. They kept going, kept taking, kept hunting for more.

Whatever was going on in that house, Batters would keep his eyes open.

For Iris's sake.

Some dark instinct, honed through decades on the unforgiving streets of the East End, told him all was not as it seemed with his first love. Danny was up to something nasty, he'd bet his last quid on it. And Batters Rogers had survived this long by trusting his gut.

# Chapter Eighteen

Relief swept through Danny when that fuckwit, Batters, and the boy were gone. He bloody hated having that oversized bellend in his house, acting like he still had some claim on Iris after all these years.

'Chrissie's settled, Danny.' Iris came back into the sitting room, her slippered feet dragging across the carpet. 'She…She's…Sleee…Sleeping.'

Danny turned, his lip curling involuntarily at the sight of her. His stomach cramped with revulsion. This pathetic creature, his wife, resembled a monster. He could barely physically look at her. What disgusted him most were her eyes, the way the same silver colour their son, Jimmy, had inherited, darted around the room without truly seeing anything. Sometimes they'd fix on him with momentary confusion, like she was trying to place who he was. Other times, they'd fill with childish tears over nothing at all.

The doctors called it traumatic brain injury. Said the fall down those slippery steps by the Thames had damaged her beyond repair. Talked about neurons and synapses and other fancy medical terms he pretended to listen to while nodding with fake concern.

What they didn't know, or anyone else for that matter was that she hadn't fallen. He'd pushed her. Smashed her head against those ancient stones before leaving her for dead.

That's what fucked him off the most. She should be dead.

'Sit down, you dopey mare.' His voice carried false concern, practiced over countless doctor visits.

She obeyed without question, lowering herself carefully into the armchair, hands folded in her lap. Danny towered over her.

He spoke to her like she was an idiot. 'Do you remember that night, Iris?' He kept his voice conversational, knowing full well she couldn't. 'Down by the Executioner's Steps?'

Iris blinked up at him, confusion clouding her damaged brain. 'St…St…Steps?'

His mouth drooped with utter disgust at her stuttering speech.

'The night you took a tumble.' His lips stretched into a cruel smile. 'Or rather, the night I helped you take a tumble.'

She frowned, struggling to process his words. 'I don't…'

''Course you bloody don't, you piss-poor excuse for a wife.' Danny leaned closer, his breath hot on her face. 'That's the beauty of it. You can't remember dick about that night. Can't remember how I found out about your secret trust fund. Can't remember how I dragged you down those steps and bashed your head in.'

Her eyes widened slightly, a flash of something, fear, perhaps, before clouding over again.

'I should have finished the job properly.' Like he was making some grand speech in the council chamber. 'You surprised me that night, dragging yourself back to the boozer. 'Course, no one was surprised. Poor gin-soaked Iris, on the piss again.'

He crossed to the drinks cabinet, his footsteps heavy. The gleaming array of bottles stood in perfect formation. He selected a bottle of distilled dry gin, Iris's old favourite. Just a quarter left sloshing in the bottom. More than enough for what he had in mind.

'Thirsty, love?' He unscrewed the cap, the distinctive juniper scent blooming in the air between them.

Iris shook her head, a small gesture of defiance. 'Doctor said… no…no…booze.'

'Did he now?' Danny emptied what was left of the gin into a crystal tumbler. 'Well, I say different.'

He returned to her chair, shoving the glass towards her face. 'Drink up.'

Her voice came out small, childlike. 'Don't.... want to.'

His face contorted with sudden, murderous rage. 'You useless fucking moron.'

Viciously, he grabbed her jaw in a bruising grip, fingers digging into the soft flesh of her cheeks. He wrenched her head back, forcing her mouth open. With his other hand, he brought the glass to her lips and poured.

Gin splashed down her throat, making her gag and choke. Some spilled from the corners of her mouth, soaking her cardigan. Her hands fluttered weakly, trying to push him away, but she was no match for his strength.

'That's it, get it down you.' He released her jaw once half the glass was empty, careful not to give her too much.

He needed to play this carefully. Had to be slow.

Untraceable.

Iris gasped for breath, tears streaming down her face, mingling with the spilled gin. Her body shuddered with fear and confusion.

The glass half-empty, Danny returned to the drinks cabinet, placing the tumbler down with a satisfied clink. He glanced over his shoulder to check Iris remained in her chair, huddled and sagging forward.

He discarded the empty bottle and replaced it with a fresh one from the cabinet. Now for the special preparations he gave every new bottle. From his inside pocket, he withdrew a small brown bottle.

No label, nothing to identify its contents. The heavy liquid inside caught the light, silver-white and deadly.

Mercury.

He'd nicked it from the docks years ago, back when they still used it in thermometers and barometers shipped through London. He'd kept it squirreled away, never knowing when such a thing might come in handy in his line of work.

Now it served a different purpose.

Danny uncorked the bottle and tipped a few drops into the bottle of gin. Just enough to continue her deterioration without arousing suspicion. The mercury dispersed through the clear liquid, invisible to the naked eye.

Mercury poisoning attacked the brain, causing tremors, memory loss, confusion, symptoms that were perfectly masked by Iris's existing brain damage. When she finally died, everyone would blame complications from her 'accident'.

Poor, selfless, devoted Danny, losing his damaged wife after years of caring for her.

The perfect crime.

He returned the doctored gin bottle to its place, arranging it precisely alongside the others. The bottle of mercury disappeared back into his pocket, his insurance policy against a wife who'd refused to die the first time.

Danny turned to observe Iris again. She sat with her head lolling slightly, the forced gin already affecting her. A droplet still clung to her bottom lip, poisoned without her knowledge.

'You know what, Iris?' He informed her, 'A man in my position needs a proper wife. Someone with class. Youth. Someone who doesn't make my guests think I'm running a freak show.'

Not Scarlett, though. No, he was eyeing up the debutantes whose rich daddies slipped through his Belgravia brothel. Plenty of toffs with pretty daughters gagging for a husband. The perfect ornament for the glittering empire he was building.

Iris mumbled something unintelligible, her eyelids drooping.

'Don't worry, sweetheart.' An evil smile distorted Danny's mouth, his eyes gleaming with sick satisfaction. 'Won't be long now before I'm a grieving widower. Tragic accident, followed by years of decline.' He adopted the sorrowful expression he'd been practicing in the mirror ready for the day of her funeral.

He moved towards the door, pausing to cast one final glance at the woman he'd tried to murder twice now. Once in rage, now with cunning patience.

'Sleep tight, you pathetic, senseless, useless, worthless crone.' He took perverse delight in every insult with pure loathing. 'Every drop brings you closer to the grave.'

Danny Steele closed the door behind him, already picturing the future.

All he needed was for Iris to finally, mercifully, die.

# Chapter Nineteen

'Fight! Fight!'

The playground erupted into chaos.

Shrill voices cut through the morning, thirty-odd uniformed kids surging forward with hungry bloodlust. At the circle's heart, two boys squared off consumed by pure hatred. The older one, thirteen, had cruel, dead eyes and a sneering mouth. He towered over his target. Below him, a dark-haired eleven-year-old wiped blood from his split lip using his school jumper.

'Your sister's a right brain-dead divvy,' the older boy sneered, his voice dripping venom. 'Like that grandmother of hers. Everyone knows she's mental. Can't even string two words together without dribbling all over herself.'

Savage rage contorted the younger lad's face. 'You're gonna be brain dead when I knock your fucking block off,' he growled, his young voice carrying lethal promise.

The circle pressed tighter. Voices rose in bloodthirsty chants.

The younger boy launched forward, small fists flying in vicious accuracy. His right hook smashed into the bully's jaw, snapping the bigger lad's head sideways. Blood sprayed across grey tarmac. They crashed down in a tangle of flailing limbs and ripped fabric. The younger lad rolled on top, raining blow after blow, brutally determined. His fists split against teeth and bone, but he felt nothing except white-hot fury burning through his veins.

'Take it back, you bastard!' the younger boy snarled. He grabbed his rival's collar and shook him violently. 'Take it back!'

Through his busted mouth, his opponent yelled, 'Won't take back the feckin' truth, will I? She'll probably go the same way as your mum—'

The younger boy's roar of anguish shook the playground. His small fist connected, the force devastating.

'Mr Grimley,' someone squealed.

The kids scattered in all directions. But the younger boy remained straddling the kid who had the nerve to mention his beloved mother.

Mr Grimley, their headteacher, loomed over them. In his right hand, a thick wooden ruler tapped against his thigh in the rhythm of a nail being hammered into a coffin.

'Collins.' His voice carried the authority of the Grim Reaper himself. 'Steele.'

Without another word, Mr Grimley grabbed them both by the scruff of the neck and marched them towards the imposing Victorian school building.

***

Jimmy Steele strode down the school corridor. His urgency had his heart pumping. Anything to do with his kids set off alarm bells that drowned out everything else.

His eleven-year-old son sat hunched on the wooden bench outside the headmaster's office, blood-crusted tissues pressed to his busted lip. The lad's school uniform hung in tatters, white shirt stained crimson, his left eye already on its way to being a black shiner.

Despair mingling with exasperation, Jimmy ran his hand roughly through his dark hair. 'For crying out loud! Not again, Robbie.'

The boy glanced up, defiance flashing through the bruises on his young face. 'He said stuff about Vi, Dad. Proper nasty stuff.'

Before Jimmy could respond, the headmaster's door swung open. Mr Grimley filled the doorframe, tall, his posture ramrod straight in his funeral-black suit.

'Mr Steele.' Grimley's voice carried the weary tone of a man who'd seen generations of stubborn East End boys pass through his office. 'Please step into my office.'

The room was a throwback with its heavy oak desk dominating the space, walls lined with leather-bound books, certificates of academic excellence framed in dark wood. Jimmy lowered himself into the hard-backed chair opposite, feeling every bit the naughty schoolboy despite his expensive clothing.

Grimley settled behind his desk, steepling his bony fingers. 'Third time this term, Mr Steele.'

Struggling to maintain his composure while worry for his son churned in his gut, Jimmy kept his voice level. 'What happened?'

'Robbie broke Timothy Collins's nose. Split his lip. Knocked out a tooth.' Grimley's tone carried no judgment, just cold facts. His pale eyes studied Jimmy with professional detachment. 'The other boy, I understand, said very unkind things about your daughter, Violet.'

*The little fucker.*

Jimmy's stomach twisted into a tight knot. Family. The one thing that could break through his hardman exterior. 'Robbie was defending his sister.'

'I understand that.' Grimley's shoulders dropped slightly, unexpected compassion softening his severe features. 'However, we cannot have pupils resolving differences with their fists.'

Jimmy bit back a caustic retort, the muscle in his jaw twitching with the effort. In his world, fists solved plenty of problems, but Grimley commanded respect even from hardened East End parents. The headmaster ran the best school in the borough. He was strict but scrupulously fair. For working-class families, getting your kids through his doors meant giving them a fighting chance at making something of themselves.

Folding his hands carefully on the desk, Grimley continued. 'The Collins boy will be punished, have no doubt about that.' His voice gentled, the harsh edges smoothing away. 'But there's another matter we need to discuss.' His pale eyes held Jimmy's with unexpected warmth. 'About Violet.'

Jimmy tensed up, a cold dread spreading through him. 'What about her?'

Grimley chose his next words with obvious care. His expression softened further. 'Since your wife passed, Violet has… struggled. Her reading age has fallen behind. Her mathematics even more so.' He paused, his gaze steady and compassionate. 'She's becoming increasingly frustrated. The other children notice her difficulties.'

'She ain't a thicko! One of them not rights.' Jimmy exploded, parental protection and anger rearing up in a combustible mix, his fists clenching involuntarily at his sides.

*Don't you dare write my girl off.* The thought seared through his mind like a branding iron marking his very soul with fatherly defiance.

'That's not what I'm suggesting, Mr Steele.' Grimley skilfully carried on, measured and firm. He believed in always being straight with parents, no matter how hard the truth might be. 'But Violet needs specialised attention that we simply cannot provide. There are excellent schools—'

'For the educational subnormal, that's what they call them,' Jimmy interrupted, his voice hard-edged while his heart broke for his daughter. 'For backwards kids.'

'For children with different learning needs,' Grimley corrected, though his eyes remained kind. 'Children usually thrive when given proper support.'

Jimmy stared at the wooden desk, mind racing. Mini would have known what to do. She'd have read books about it, talked to doctors, found the best solution for their daughter. But Mini was gone, leaving Jimmy fumbling through fatherhood like a man in the pitch dark trying to disarm a bomb. One wrong move, and everything precious could shatter.

Grief rising unexpectedly to choke him, Jimmy swallowed hard, throat tightening with emotions he refused to show. Not here. Not to this man, however decent he might be.

'Try to see it from Violet's perspective,' Grimley carried on, his voice gentle but firm. 'She's bright enough to know she's falling behind. That must be terribly frustrating for her.'

Jimmy scrubbed a calloused hand across his face, the responsibility of single fatherhood pressing down on him, a ton of bricks. Most nights, he sat with Vi at the kitchen table, trying to help with homework. His beautiful twelve-year-old daughter, who couldn't quite grasp the letters on the page or make numbers behave properly. The memory of her tears, her crumpled papers, her small fists banging against the table in frustration, tore at his heart.

His girl growing up without a mother, that's what ripped his heart to shreds.

'I'm doing my bloody best,' Jimmy defended himself.

'That goes without saying.' Grimley nodded, genuine respect evident in his expression. 'You're raising three children alone. That's no small feat.' He fixed Jimmy with a penetrating stare. 'Think about what I've said. For Violet's sake.'

Then his sympathy disappeared, replaced by professional authority. 'As for Robbie, one more fight, and he'll face suspension. I cannot make exceptions, even for understandable brotherly protection.'

Jimmy nodded stiffly, rising from the chair, his legs oddly unsteady beneath him. 'Understood.'

Outside, he found Robbie still slumped on the bench, small shoulders tight with defiance and lingering anger.

'Come on, son.' Jimmy placed a heavy hand on the boy's shoulder, giving it a gentle squeeze that conveyed more than words could.

They walked together down the empty corridor, their footsteps moving in unison.

'Am I in trouble?' Robbie finally asked, his voice small and vulnerable in a way that twisted Jimmy's heart.

Jimmy stopped, turning to face his son. Beneath the hardman exterior, his heart ached at the sight of his boy's battered face. 'You can't spend your life fighting the world, Robbie.' He ruffled his boy's hair with unexpected tenderness.

'But that Collins said Vi was mental. Called her a brain-dead divvy.' His hands balled into fists at the memory, knuckles still raw and bloody.

Jimmy crouched, meeting his son at eye level. He gently took Robbie's injured hands in his own larger ones. 'Words from poxy little tossers don't matter. Family matters.' He squeezed the boy's hands carefully, mindful of the bruises. 'Which is why I need to tell you that you played it all wrong.'

Robbie's head snapped up, confusion clear in those steel-grey eyes so like Jimmy's own.

'Fighting in the playground?' Jimmy shook his head, his voice dropping to a conspiratorial whisper. 'That's amateur hour. Gets you nothing but grief from Grimley and a black eye to show for it.'

'But Collins—' Robbie protested, indignation flashing across his bruised face.

'Let me finish.' Jimmy's voice hardened with the authority that made grown men piss themselves in the East End. 'You've got to think using your loaf, not just your bunch of fives.'

Robbie straightened, suddenly attentive, his stare fixed on his father's face.

'Next time that little prick or anyone else tries dragging Vi through the gutter, you don't do it where the headmaster can catch you.' Jimmy's eyes narrowed, his voice dropping to a whisper filled with deadly purpose. 'Wait for him after school, somewhere quiet. Then make him understand that if he continues poncing about, you'll put his balls through a grinder.'

Robbie's young face scrunched in concentration. 'You mean put the frighteners on him?'

'Make him understand there's consequences.' Jimmy demonstrated with his fist, not quite touching his son's shoulder. 'One warning. Calm, controlled. Tell him exactly what happens if your sister's name ends up in his mouth. No shouting, no losing your rag. Cold and clear, like business.'

Robbie nodded, his bruised face lighting with understanding.

Settling his large hand on his son's slight shoulder, Jimmy guided him towards the exit. 'It's about respect. In this family, we protect our own, but with brains as well as bollocks.'

Suddenly, Robbie looked down at his scuffed shoes, his shoulders drooping. 'I miss Mum.'

The unexpected revelation caught Jimmy hard. A wave of grief, never far from the surface, threatened to drown him. He drew his son into a tight hug, his own eyes burning with unshed tears. Against his chest, he felt Robbie's body trembling with suppressed emotion.

'Me, too, son,' Jimmy admitted, his throat tight with unspoken pain. 'Me, too.'

# Chapter Twenty

Sin adored working with the children. So much had changed about her life since she had traded in the name Steele for Watson. Including her best mate, Kath moving with her husband and sister, Dilly to live in New York. She missed Kath so much.

The classroom hummed with gentle activity, sunlight streaming through the windows of St Philomena's convent school in Poplar, just a stone's throw from Chrisp Street Market.

The special needs school attached to the church had become her sanctuary. A place where she could escape the shadows of her Steele family name and the criminal empire her father had built brick by bloody brick.

'That's it, Sharmima. Now try counting with your fingers,' Sin encouraged, her voice soft but firm.

The little girl with pigtails and brown eyes concentrated fiercely, her tongue poking out between her lips as she touched each finger deliberately.

People called these children slow, but Sin knew better. They weren't, they simply moved at their own rhythm, like this little girl with her exquisite handwriting that would put a calligrapher to shame.

Slow.

Sin hated that word.

A nasty, diminishing word that missed the beauty of these children entirely.

Sin guided the child's fingers. 'One…two… three…'

The love she felt for these children had blindsided her. Years back, all she'd dreamt about was escaping the East End, running from her criminal father and transforming herself into some glamorous model draped in chic clothes. Then she'd held Isaac in her arms for the first time… There was no feeling like it in the world. That rush of everlasting, protective love that had consumed her body. The overwhelming certainty that she would die for this tiny human being without a second thought. Her heart had expanded in ways she'd never thought possible, making room for a love so pure it hurt.

The thought of Jimmy flickered through her mind unbidden. The anger, the hurt, the words that were said that couldn't be unsaid.

She missed him. Despite everything, despite the way he'd turned his back.

Sin missed her big brother.

Did Jimmy ever think of her? Wonder about the nephew he'd never met?

The classroom door opened with a gentle creak. Sister Bernadette entered, her habit perfectly pressed, her spine straight as a ruler despite her seventy-odd years. The nun's eyes held kindness, but her mouth remained set in that no-nonsense line that had terrified and comforted Sin in equal measure all those years ago.

'You're doing wonderful work with Sharmima,' Sister Bernadette praised.

This woman had been her salvation when her mother had sent her away at fifteen, after Sin had attacked her father with a knife, leaving him with that scar he'd wear until his dying day. Her mother, desperate to save her daughter from Danny Steele's notorious shadow, had known Sister Bernadette through her church cleaning work. The nun had arranged for Sin to attend a convent boarding school far from the reach of her father's dangerous retribution.

'Thank you, Sister,' Sin replied and stood straighter instinctively. Old habits die hard around Sister Bernadette.

Since her marriage to Bertie, Sin had found herself turning back to the church, finding comfort in its rituals and certainties. She wished Bertie would consent to having Isaac christened. She sighed inwardly. In time, perhaps. She'd wear him down eventually.

The corner of Sister Bernadette's mouth twitched upwards, the closest the woman ever came to an actual smile. 'That parent I mentioned is here with his children, specifically his daughter. I thought you might show them around. You speak so beautifully about our school.'

Sin nodded, smoothing down her plain dress. 'Of course.'

'They're waiting in the reception area,' Sister Bernadette said, turning to leave. 'The father seems… overwhelmed.'

Sin's heart squeezed. How many parents had she seen with that same lost look? That mixture of love and fear and desperation to do right by their child?

The reception area came into view. A man stood with his back to her, broad-shouldered in an expensive suit. A boy of about eleven or twelve stood beside him, protective arm around a slightly older girl who kept her gaze fixed on the ground.

'Hello there, I'm Mrs Watson. I understand you're interested in our school?'

The man turned.

Sin's heart stopped, nosedived to the floor.

'Jimmy?' Her brother's name escaped her lips before she could stop it.

***

Jimmy stared at his estranged sister, blood buzzing in his ears.

Sin.

His little sister.

Standing right there like it hadn't been five years since they'd clapped eyes on each other.

'Jimmy?' she uttered in shock again, eyes widening.

Memories crashed over him. Defending her against their dad. Teaching her to throw a proper punch. Holding her while she cried.

Bringing that belt down on her back while she screamed.

Slamming a hospital door in her face.

The look in her eyes when he'd told her their mother had no daughter. Christ. He'd seen men shot who looked less destroyed.

His children broke the frozen moment.

'Auntie Sin!' Robbie called out, his young face lighting up with recognition.

Violet hung back, clutching her brother's arm, uncertain. They knew who Auntie Sin was but sensed something wasn't right, some invisible barrier keeping them from running to her like they wanted to. The children had never understood why their beloved aunt had simply vanished from their lives.

He should leave right now. March his kids straight back to the Bentley parked outside. What kind of sick joke was this? Coming to a special school and finding his sister working there?

Yet he couldn't move, couldn't tear his gaze from her face. She looked good. Healthy. Happy even. Her cheekbones still high and proud, but her features had softened somehow. Motherhood had changed her.

Motherhood. Her betrayal with Bertie. The pregnancy that had torn their friendship apart.

'I should go.' Grabbing Violet's hand, he turned to the exit.

'Wait.'

Sin's command stopped him cold.

'You shouldn't waste the visit. Violet deserves to see the school.'

Jimmy glanced down at his daughter, her vulnerable face tilted up towards his, trusting him to make the right decision. This visit was for her. Not for him. Not for the hurricane of feelings tearing through his body.

'Fine,' he responded curtly. 'Show us around then.'

Sin nodded, all business. 'This way, please.'

Showing him through the bright corridors, she explained, 'We focus on each child's individual needs. Most schools label these children "subnormal" and warehouse them. Sister Bernadette and I developed a different approach.'

Jimmy's eyebrows shot up. 'You developed it?'

A hint of pride flickered across Sin's face. 'I researched educational methods while pregnant with Izzy. The ESN schools were barbaric. Children locked away, no proper teaching. I convinced Sister Bernadette we could do better.' She gestured around them. 'Not having too many children in a class, teaching practical skills, dignity. The Church provides the building, but we're creating the approach.'

Jimmy watched his sister kneel beside a young boy struggling with wooden blocks. Her hands guided his, patient, kind. A grudging respect warmed within him.

'Can I try?' Violet asked, pointing to where children painted at easels.

Sin smiled. 'Of course.'

While Violet joined the art session and Robbie explored a bookshelf, Sin stood beside Jimmy, a careful distance between them.

'She's beautiful,' Sin said quietly.

'Yeah. Got her mother's heart. You've done well here,' he admitted, gesturing around the classroom.

'I love it,' Sin gushed, her face glowing. 'Children are honest. No games, no pretending.'

Unlike the Steele family, with all its secrets and lies. The unspoken truth hung between them.

Jimmy studied her from the corner of his eye. The last time he'd seen Sin, she'd been a mess of tears and smudged makeup, begging to see their mother in hospital. Now she stood tall, composed, with a wedding ring on her finger and confidence in her stance.

'Do you ever wonder…' Sin began, then stopped herself.

'What?'

'Nothing.' She shook her head. 'Let me show you our learning area where we've set up stations for different skills. Reading corner, counting table, craft space.'

They ended up in a garden where children played under supervision. Violet had joined them, laughing as she pushed a younger girl on a swing.

'She's already happy here,' Sin observed, her gaze shining with pleasure.

'Looks that way.'

Sin turned to face him, her gaze direct. 'I'd like you to meet your nephew. My boy.'

He didn't see that coming and almost staggered back.

Isaac. Brother Bertie's son. The child who'd cemented the betrayal.

'Being Mister Southpaw, I'm sure you know where I live.' Her voice was even. 'You could bring the children. It would be good for them to know their cousin.'

Jimmy's swallowed back a scoff. Five years of silence, and she thought they could just play happy families? After everything?

'We're leaving,' he announced, then called for Robbie and Violet.

Sin touched his arm, the first physical contact in years. He went rigid, a spark jolting through him. Her touch brought back too many memories of the days when they'd been inseparable, when he'd been her protector instead of her punisher.

'Just think about it.' That was the sister he remembered, never one to give up. 'They're innocent in all this, Jimmy.'

He gathered his children and turned his back on his sister again.

# Chapter Twenty-One

Dash, Jimmy's new property business partner, strolled into the magnificent dining room of the Grosvenor Square mansion like the coolest hip cat in all of London, a city that had given up swinging since the end of the sixties.

His dark hair flopped carelessly across his forehead in that effortless playboy style that drove women wild and made sensible men question their life choices. The morning light caught the silk of his burnt-orange shirt, unbuttoned just enough to reveal that familiar gold chain and dusting of chest hair, while his chocolate-brown flares hugged his thighs with casual perfection. A paisley scarf in shades of amber and cream hung loose around his neck, the kind of groovy touch that screamed expensive rebellion.

'Good morning, beautiful people!' His voice carried like Jamaican sunshine spreading through the stuffiness of the Grosvenor Square dining room.

At opposite ends of the very long polished table sat Lord Xander and his much younger wife, Lady Prudence. Dash's uncle occupied his throne at the head, silver hair immaculate, morning coat pressed to perfection. Lady Pru perched at the far end like a nervous bird, her pale hands wrapped around a delicate teacup.

Dash paused dramatically, tilting his head back and drawing a deep breath through flared nostrils. 'Smell that! That's pure possibility dancing in the air, man. Life calling out to be seized and shaken until it screams for mercy.'

Lord Xander's aristocratic eyebrow arched with disdain. His pale-eyed gaze travelled the length of Dash's ensemble with the enthusiasm of a mortician examining a particularly distasteful corpse.

'Good heavens, nephew. Did you perhaps mistake my dining room for a…theatrical production?'

Dash's grin widened, revealing perfect white teeth that could have advertised toothpaste. With fluid grace, he draped himself into the chair between his uncle and aunt by marriage, sweeping that rebellious hair back with long fingers.

'Far out observation, Uncle.' His eyes sparkled with mischief. 'Life's nothing but theatre when you really think about it.'

He turned towards Lady Pru, that devastating smile softening into genuinely warm. One eyelid dropped in a conspiratorial wink that brought the faintest flush to her pale cheeks.

'Prudence, you're radiant this morning. That shade of blue brings out the glow in your eyes.'

Before she could respond, a uniformed maid appeared with practiced silence, setting a full English breakfast before Dash. The bacon glistened, egg yolks perfect golden orbs waiting to be broken, grilled tomatoes bright as rubies against the elegant Limoges plate.

'Cheers, darling,' Dash murmured to the maid, who coloured prettily before retreating.

Xander's fork paused halfway to his mouth. 'Really, Dash, must you charm every female within breathing distance?'

'Can't help it if women enjoy genuine appreciation, Uncle.' Dash attacked his breakfast with the gusto of a man who lived life at full throttle. 'Speaking of which, I've been meaning to ask about family history... Why did you rarely visit your brother, my father, in Jamaica?'

'Jamaica.' Xander pronounced the word like a terminal diagnosis. 'That dreadful place corrupted his judgment completely. All that oppressive heat and those infernal insects, not to mention the... primitive influences. Really, I can't fathom why any civilised person would choose to remain in such a savage wilderness.'

Dash set down his fork very slowly. His easy charm drained from his features, replaced by something fierce and protective. 'Savage? Uncle, you're talking about paradise itself. Jamaica doesn't corrupt, it liberates. Strips away all the suffocating propriety and lets your soul breathe free.'

Lady Pru appeared captivated by every word. Although the reality was deep down inside she suspected that her husband's nephew was more dangerous and devious than he was.

Dash's eyes took on an almost reverent quality. 'Picture trade winds carrying the scent of Blue Mountain Coffee and aged rum. Hibiscus blooms bright as spilled blood against emerald hills that roll towards turquoise water so clear you can count the fish swimming twenty feet down.'

His voice grew richer, warmer. 'The music, man, steel pans, drums and rhythms that grab your heartbeat and teach it new patterns. Women moving like liquid poetry, their laughter bright as temple bells. Every sunset paints the sky in colours that would make Michelangelo weep with envy.'

Xander's lip curled. 'Romantic tosh. Give me civilisation over that steaming jungle any day.'

'You've never been, have you?' Dash's smile held sharp edges. 'The island gets into your blood like fever, teaches you what it means to truly live instead of just existing.'

'Existing?' Xander snorted. 'I'll have you know this family has maintained proper standards for centuries—'

'Standards.' Dash's chuckle held no warmth. 'Is that what we're calling it?'

The silence stretched taut between them. Lady Pru's teacup rattled against its saucer.

Xander recovered his composure with visible effort. 'Yes, well, Rufus certainly embraced the local… customs. I heard he developed quite an attachment to a native woman. Had her as his mistress, didn't he?'

The change in Dash was instantaneous. His animated features went completely blank, eyes turning to chips of winter ice. The charming playboy vanished, revealing something far more dangerous underneath.

'Wouldn't know about that,' he replied, his voice flat.

Sensing weakness, Xander did what he did so well – he went in for the kill. 'Curious thing, though. Back in '63, your parents rather abruptly shipped you off to New York. Extended visit with your mother, wasn't it? Quite sudden, as I recall.'

Dash's jaw muscle flexed once. 'Business opportunities. Nothing more fascinating than that.'

'Of course.' Xander's smile turned predatory. 'Though the timing seemed rather—'

'What timing?' Dash went perfectly still, his question dangerously quiet.

'Oh, nothing specific. Just seemed coincidental, given certain… events at one of the hotels there.'

Dash's smile returned, but now it promised violence. 'Life's full of coincidences, Uncle.'

'Indeed.' Xander turned his sour attention to his wife with casual cruelty. 'Rather like Prudence here coincidentally developing another headache whenever I require her…companionship. Remarkable how conveniently her ailments align with my needs.'

Lady Pru's skin turned an alarming shade of red. 'Xander, please—'

'Please what?' he snapped venomously. 'Please stop expecting you to fulfil the basic duties of a wife? Please accept that I married a frigid, useless ornament who can't even produce an heir?'

'That's enough!' Dash insisted.

Xander blinked, startled by the interruption. 'I beg your pardon?'

'You heard me.' Dash rose from his chair with fluid grace, every movement controlled and purposeful. 'The lady doesn't deserve your poison.'

He moved around the table and stopped beside his aunt-in-law's chair. With courtly gallantry, he lifted her trembling hand and pressed it to his lips.

'Lady Prudence,' he murmured, his voice gentle as silk. 'You honour this room with your presence.'

She should have stared back with wonder and gratitude, instead her expression was strained. The last thing she wanted was to be caught in the crossfire between these two ruthless men.

In Dash's twisted mind, there was no contradiction in trafficking vulnerable women and defending Lady Pru. She was family. Family was sacred territory, marked by invisible lines that real men never crossed. Whilst business was business, professional, and necessary for survival in a world that ate the weak.

The women he kept locked up and then handed over to sick, perverted brutes were nothing.

His Uncle's wife, on the other hand was untouchable. A woman of pure breeding.

Xander's lips rippled with disgust at his nephew's action. 'Really, Dash, such distasteful gestures—'

'You know what I learned in America, Uncle?'

If Xander had been paying attention he would have noticed his nephew pick up a silver steak knife, testing its weight with professional interest.

Dash finished with, 'All sorts of useful skills during my extended visit.'

With a casual flick of his wrist, the knife spun through the air, landing point first in the table directly in front of Xander's place setting. The blade quivered in the expensive wood like a steel exclamation point.

Xander's mouth flapped open, a strangled noise escaping him. His breath came in short, sharp bursts, chest rising and falling rapidly beneath his morning coat. His pale complexion drained to ashen grey, beads of perspiration forming along his receding hairline.

Dash swept his dark hair back. 'Amazing what a fellow picks up when he's motivated to learn, you dig?'

He offered Lady Pru the crook of his arm, which she gracefully took and stood up so he could lead her out of the room.

'Prudence,' Xander warned. 'Sit down. We haven't finished breakfast.'

She paused at the threshold, her spine straightening with newfound resolve. 'Actually, husband dearest, I believe we have.'

Just before closing the door, Dash popped his head back in and informed his uncle with malicious delight, 'You should see what I can do with a machete.'

Outside, Dash took the stone steps two at a time and swung into his flash Jaguar E-Type. All the charm drained from his face because he was focused on business. He had a new shipment coming in tonight.

# Chapter Twenty-Two

'Bertie, my son!' Wrighty's delighted mug grinned from ear to ear in the doorway of the house in Bloomsbury. 'Glad you decided to take me up on that job opportunity, mate. Not many reliable faces these days.'

He pressed the door shut with a quiet click, plunging them into the low light of a single oil lamp. His voice dropped. 'Fucking power cuts. Got emergency lights downstairs, though.'

Glancing around the hallway, Brother Bertie noted the expensive wallpaper, thick shagpile carpet underfoot. This gaff had serious money behind it, more flash than a Soho strip club.

His pork pie hat was pulled low to hide the hot shame burning his face. He knew full well that he was doing this to get money to help his son, but that still didn't make him feel good about being back in the criminal world. His stomach churned with disgust at the cruel twist of fate that forced a father to choose between his morals and the life of his child.

'Let's not waste time.' He wanted out of here as quickly as possible. 'Got what you need me to move?'

Wrighty's brows shot up, his ferret-style features crinkling with amusement. 'Straight to business? Where's the Bertie Watson who liked to wet his tongue with a little rum before getting into proceedings?'

'Let's just get the raas on with it.' His voice was tight.

Wrighty nodded. 'Simple job. Five packages need moving across town tonight. Just pickup, drop-off, collect your dosh, right?'

'Where's the pickup?' Brother Bertie asked.

'Follow me,' came the reply.

Which Brother Bertie did, to a door which led to a narrow staircase. He frowned because he noticed odd details.

Scratch marks on the walls.

Multiple locks on a side door.

The heavy stench of bleach.

Alarm bells screamed in his head. He didn't like this one bit. Not one bit, at all.

They arrived in a storage room at the bottom of the house. The stink of bleach here was strong, enough for his eyes to water.

*Get out. Now.*

That's what the warning in his head told him.

*But what about Izzy?*

*I'm here now, so I'll go through with it. But,* he vowed, *this is a one-time ting.*

There were rows of cardboard boxes stacked against a wall, and on a shelf a number of packages. Wrighty moved with practiced efficiency, selecting five small packages wrapped in brown paper.

'Here you go, careful with 'em.' He handed them to Brother Bertie one by one. 'Boss is particular about his merchandise, right?'

Brother Bertie's criminal radar buzzed, his neck prickling like a cat in a dog pound. A sound froze him. A muffled cry from somewhere beyond the storage room walls.

Wrighty's expression darkened. 'Ignore that.'

Brother Bertie's gaze drifted to a heavy metal door on the far wall. Triple-locked. 'What's through there?'

'Nothing you need worry about.' Wrighty thrust the remaining packages into Brother Bertie's arms. 'Just get these moved, right?'

Another sound, a sob this time. Brother Bertie's skin went cold all over. 'What the bloodclaat is going on here?'

Wrighty shrugged in a 'not my problem' gesture. 'These jobs have changed since our day. More complicated. More lucrative. Just move the packages.'

The fifth package slipped from Brother Bertie's fingers, tumbling towards the concrete floor. The package hit with a soft puff, brown paper splitting along one edge. A small cloud of white powder escaped, settling on the grey concrete like fresh snow.

Brother Bertie stared, mind refusing to process what he witnessed. He backed away, heart and pulse going into overdrive. 'That's…'

'Fucking hell, Bertie!' The other man dropped to his knees, cursing. He frantically tried gathering the spilled contents. 'You got any idea how much that's worth?'

'This is fucking coke.' The word tasted toxic in Brother Bertie's mouth.

He didn't deal in this junk. Full fucking stop. Never had, never would. The stuff was pure evil, turning decent people into walking corpses who'd sell their own mothers for another hit. He'd seen it destroy, rip families apart, children left starving while their parents chased the white devil.

''Course it bloody is.' Wrighty attempted to frantically scoop powder back into the torn wrapping, white dust flying everywhere.

Brother Bertie's mind raced through the possible fallout. Banged up behind bars for years. Sin left alone. Izzy without a father while his dad rotted in Pentonville. Everything he'd built destroyed in one bloody night.

'I can't do this.' He placed the remaining packages on a shelf, wiping his hands on his trousers. 'Find someone else.'

Wrighty stood, anger flashing across his visage. 'You already touched the merchandise. You're in the shit now, no getting out, right?'

'Fuck that.' Brother Bertie backed towards the stairs. 'I don't care what you tell the head honcho who's running this. I'm gone.'

The sound of a footstep higher up the stairs stopped Brother Bertie cold. Then he turned slowly, and for some reason he couldn't figure out, a paralysing sensation seized every muscle.

A figure descended the stairs, emerging from the darkness.

Brother Bertie stumbled back in stunned disbelief.

'Dash?'

Dash's expression transformed from surprise to cold fury in an instant.

'What the fuckery are YOU doing here?'

# Chapter Twenty-Three

Jamaica, 1954

The rum cellar air hung thick with molasses and oak, cool against the Kingston heat beating down outside. Fourteen-year-old Bertie Watson, wearing his trademark pork pie hat, paused at the bottom of the stone steps, letting his eyes adjust to the dim light. He was doing some work up at the big house, and Cook had sent him to fetch a bottle of dark rum for tonight's pudding, but someone had beaten him here.

A white boy stood with his back to the door, running his fingers over dusty bottles, pulling one out, examining the label, then returning it to try another. His pressed linen shirt gleamed even in the weak light, expensive, like everything else about him.

Bertie leaned against the doorframe, arms folded. 'You're taking the wrong ones. Those are logged in the inventory.'

The boy spun around, nearly dropping the bottle clutched in his pale hands. Posh schoolboy written all over him, from his polished shoes to his carefully combed hair, though there was something not quite right about him, a wildness in his eyes that didn't match the proper clothes.

'Who the hell are you?' the boy demanded, trying to sound authoritative, but his voice split mid-sentence.

'Someone who works here,' Bertie replied calmly. 'Unlike you, who's stealing from your daddy's rum collection.'

This had to be Jack Blacklock, son of the house's owner. The boy who'd been sent away to some fancy English school years ago.

The other boy drew himself up to his full height, the same as Bertie's, though he seemed to think he was taller. 'Do you know who my father is?'

Bertie snorted. 'Do you know how little I care? Fuckery off back upstairs, soft-handed boy.'

For a heartbeat, rage flashed across the boy's face; he was clearly unused to being put in his place this way. Then, unexpectedly, he laughed. A genuine laugh that shook his shoulders and crinkled the corners of his eyes.

'You've got nerve,' he said and set the bottle down carefully. 'No one talks to me like that.'

'Then no one's being honest with you,' Bertie replied, but the edge had gone from his voice.

'Jack Blacklock.' The other boy extended his hand.

Bertie hesitated, then stepped forward and took it. 'Bertram Watson.'

'Everyone calls me Dash,' the boy added, his grip firm despite his soft palms.

'Because you're always running from something?' Bertie asked, shrewder than his years.

Dash grinned, a flash of teeth. 'Because I'm dashing, like Cary Grant.' He struck an exaggerated pose that made him look ridiculous.

'More like because you can't stay still for five fuckery seconds,' Bertie countered, having seen the boy's restless fidgeting even in their brief encounter.

Dash dropped the pose, seemingly pleased to be read so easily. 'What do they call you then?'

'Brother Bertie.' He pushed his chest up with pride at his nickname.

'Brother? You religious or something?'

'Nah.' Bertie moved past Dash to scan the shelves. 'Just someone people know will put an arm around their shoulder when they need it.'

'Sounds boring.' Dash's tone suggested curiosity rather than dismissal.

Bertie found the bottle Cook had requested but didn't leave. Instead, he nodded towards the one

Dash had been examining. 'That one's no good. Too young.'

'How would you know?'

'I listen. I watch. Your father talks about his rum when he's had too much of it.' Bertie stepped deeper into the cellar, to a dusty corner. 'These ones here, he doesn't count these because they're his special reserve. Takes one maybe twice a year.'

Dash followed, interest lighting his face. 'You know a lot about what goes on upstairs for someone who works downstairs.'

'People forget I'm in the room,' Bertie explained simply. 'My sister, Gertie, taught me that. Being invisible has advantages.'

'Gertie? The pretty maid who went to England last year?' Dash asked.

Bertie's expression darkened. 'She's not just a maid. She's the smartest person I know.'

'Sorry,' Dash punched in quickly, surprising both of them with his apology. 'I heard my mother say good things about her. Said the house hasn't been the same since she left.'

The tension eased from Bertie's shoulders. 'Hasn't been the same for me either.'

Something passed between them, a type of recognition.

Dash propped himself against a shelf, suddenly less poised. 'England's miserable. Cold and grey, and everyone talks like they've got marbles in their mouth.'

'Thought you'd know all about that, Harrow boy.'

Dash's eyes narrowed. 'You do listen, don't you? They sent me back. Said I was "unsuitable for continued enrolment."'

'What'd you do? Punch a teacher?'

'Broke into the headmaster's office. Tried to change my marks.' Dash shrugged, but his casualness seemed forced. 'They all made fun of how I talked anyway. Not English enough for England.'

Bertie nodded slowly. He understood not belonging. 'My grandmother says I've been running wild since Gertie left.'

Dash studied the bottle in his hands. 'You didn't answer my question. How'd you know so much about rum?'

'My grandfather worked the cane fields, then the distillery.' Bertie took the bottle from Dash's hands and examined it with expert eyes. 'He taught me how to taste the difference between two-year and seven-year. Said knowing quality matters, even if you can't always afford it.'

Dash gestured towards the special reserve bottles. 'And these would be…?'

'Fifteen years minimum. Smoother than anything you've tasted.' Bertie slid one out carefully. 'Your father saves these for when the important people visit and those folks he needs to impress.'

'How much would one fetch? If someone were to sell it?'

Bertie shot him a sharp look. 'More than I make in six months.'

Dash's gaze wickedly gleamed. 'And if one disappeared, my father wouldn't notice?'

'Not from this particular shelf. Not until Christmas at least.' Bertie found himself caught between caution and curiosity. 'Why? You need money? Thought your kind just asked Daddy for more.'

'My kind,' Dash repeated, not offended but thoughtful. 'My father cut my allowance after Harrow. Says I need to learn the value of things.' His smile turned sardonic. 'I'd rather learn the value of this rum.'

Both boys caught each other's eyes and sniggered, something rebellious and conspiratorial passing between them. That shared laugh, the understanding of breaking rules together, cemented their new friendship.

Bertie should have walked away. Should have taken Cook's bottle and gone back upstairs. Instead, he found himself scheming. 'I might know people who'd pay good money for a taste of this private stock.'

'Split it fifty-fifty?' Dash suggested, no longer the awkward schoolboy but something sharper, more cunning.

'Sixty-forty,' Bertie countered. 'I'm taking all the risk.'

Dash considered this, then nodded. 'Deal.'

'Just like that?'

'Just like that.' Dash carefully extracted the bottle Bertie had indicated. 'I'm bored out of my mind here.

Everybody tiptoes around me because of my father. At least you tell me to fuckery off.'

Despite himself, Bertie laughed. 'That part's free of charge.'

While Dash wrapped the stolen bottle in his jacket, he asked casually, 'Same time tomorrow? I've got ideas for other… opportunities.'

Bertie knew he should refuse. Yet something about this strange boy with his proper English clothes and wild Jamaican eyes intrigued him. 'I finish at six. Meet me by the old flamboyant tree past the south gate.'

'I'll be there,' Dash promised. He tucked the concealed bottle under his arm. At the cellar steps, he paused. 'This could be the start of something big, Brother Bertie.'

'Just don't get caught, rich boy. I'm not going down for you.'

'You won't have to. We'll be the kings of Kingston before we're sixteen.'

'Kings?' Bertie scoffed. 'I'd settle for enough money to get my grandmother proper medicine.'

Dash extended his hand again; this time they were more equals. 'We'll get that and more. Spars look out for each other, right?'

'Spars,' Bertie agreed, testing the Jamaican slang term for a close friend, a fighting partner who had your back. 'For now.'

***

## Jamaica, 1963

The midnight sky over Kingston Harbor held no stars, just perfect darkness for what they planned to do. Two men, no longer boys but not quite men at twenty-one, crouched behind the loading docks, their faces hidden beneath dark caps.

'Tonight we become legends, Brother Bertie.' Dash's whisper carried the excitement of a man about to change his life forever. His watch gleamed dully under the distant dock lights.

Bertie nodded, adjusting the small pack slung across his shoulders. The last seven years had transformed them both from mischievous teens into Kingston's most notorious pair of criminals, the well-connected white boy and his street-smart partner, pulling jobs that required both privilege and local knowledge.

The Oceanview Grand Hotel loomed ahead, its gleaming façade representing the new Jamaica. Just one year after independence, the island buzzed with international attention. Businessmen from around the world had flocked to this conference, investors eager to establish themselves in a nation newly freed from British rule.

'You memorised the guard schedule?' Dash adjusted the leather gloves on his hands.

Bertie nodded and studied the building. His mind was clear tonight, focused on details in a way it hadn't been before.

'Perfect timing with all those rich foreign businessmen storing their valuables in the hotel safe.' Dash grinned. 'Independence opened doors for everyone, even us.'

They slipped from shadow to shadow. The service door opened with the key Dash had acquired from a hotel worker. The corridor beyond stood empty, just as their intelligence had promised.

'Like taking candy from a baby,' Dash murmured and led the way towards the hotel's back offices. His cocky swagger hadn't changed since the day they'd stolen that first bottle of rum.

The office door required Bertie's lockpicking skills, talents honed through dozens of jobs across Kingston. His fingers worked automatically, precise and confident. The heavy door swung open without a sound.

'There she is,' Dash breathed. He pointed to the wall safe behind the manager's desk. 'Fifty thousand pounds from all those rich businessmen who checked in their valuables for the conference. Fifteen minutes and we'll be ghosts.'

Bertie watched Dash kneel before the safe, spinning the dial with criminal know-how.

'When we finish this,' Dash continued, his voice low with excitement, 'we should think bigger. Maybe London. Your sister could help us get established.'

'Leave Gertie out of this,' Bertie snarled.

Dash paused, glancing up with surprise. 'What's eating you? Thought you'd be happy. This is what we've worked towards for years.'

The last number clicked into place. Dash gripped the handle, pulling the safe door open to reveal stacks of cash and velvet pouches that surely contained jewellery. His smile gleamed white in the darkness.

'We did it, Brother Bertie. We bloody did it!' He reached for the money, stuffing bundles into the canvas bag slung across his shoulder.

'I've got to check the corridor.' Bertie backed towards the door. 'Make sure we're still clear.'

Dash barely nodded, too busy with the contents of the safe. 'Hurry back. Can't carry all this myself.'

Bertie hesitated at the doorway for just a moment. Seven years of friendship. Countless secrets shared. Brotherhood forged through risk and reward.

'Goodbye, Jack,' he whispered, using Dash's real name for the first time in years.

Bertie slipped out, closing the door silently behind him. Instead of checking the corridor, he moved quickly towards the service exit, each step carrying him further from the life they'd built together. Outside in the warm Jamaican night, he broke into a run, not stopping until he reached the waterfront three blocks away.

There, with steady hands, he stepped into a phone booth and dialled a number he'd memorised that morning.

'Kingston Police. How may I direct your call?'

'The Oceanview Grand Hotel is being robbed. Back office safe. One man, armed and dangerous.' He hung up before they could ask questions.

Less than an hour later, Bertie watched from the shadows as police dragged Dash from the hotel in handcuffs, his face contorted with rage and disbelief. Even from a distance, Bertie could see his friend scanning the crowd desperately, looking for the partner who had vanished.

Their eyes met across the crowd for one electric moment. Dash's expression transformed from confusion to understanding to pure hatred. He screamed something that was lost in the commotion, but Bertie understood the message perfectly:

*This isn't over.*

Three days later, two ships left Kingston Harbour, carrying the former spars in opposite directions.

Aboard the luxury liner bound for New York, Jack "Dash" Blacklock stood on deck, his father's influence having secured his freedom. Across the harbour on a ship bound for England, Bertie Watson leaned against the railings, watching Jamaica disappear into the horizon.

Neither man knew what the future would bring. But both carried the same certainty in their hearts.

If they ever met again, only one would walk away.

# Chapter Twenty-Four

'Well, look what the tide washed in. The backstabbing Judas who left me to rot. Been waiting years to return the favour.'

Dash's features contorted with savage recognition, his lips peeling back from his teeth like a snarling animal. His gaze burned with years of festering hatred and rage.

The basement air turned to concrete in Brother Bertie's lungs. His legs went weaker than water, but pride kept him standing. The spilled cocaine lay between them, a dusty reminder of choices that couldn't be unmade.

Wrighty, a born survivor, knew when to do a vanishing act.

'Nothing to say, traitor?' Dash descended the final step, his face scolded red with rage. 'Bumboclaat silent now?' He fell into his natural Jamaican.

*Traitor.*

That's what Jimmy had branded him at Mini's funeral. Two best friends, both lost.

'Why did you do it?' Raw pain replaced Dash's rage for a heartbeat. 'We were blood brothers, man. Kings of Kingston.'

'Had my reasons.' Brother Bertie didn't owe him an explanation. Not after what he'd discovered all those years ago.

'Reasons?' Dash spat. He looked about ready to tear the place apart. 'I spent two, fuckery days locked down in a Kingston cell and you're chatting out of your batty-hole about 'reasons!''

He kissed his teeth, long and hard, the contemptuous Caribbean gesture cutting deeper than any insult. His mocking eyes travelled slowly from Brother Bertie's scuffed boots to his worn pork pie hat.

'How the mighty have fallen,' he sneered, bitterness dripping from each word. 'Thought you'd be the King of London Town by now. Instead, I find you crawling with the rats in the gutter, scraping around for a living.'

Brother Bertie squared his shoulders, swallowing the humiliation burning his throat. 'It's an honest living. Something you might want to try one of these days.'

Dash's laughter bounced off the concrete walls, hollow and cold.

'I'm a family man now,' Brother Bertie added, unable to hide the pride thickening his voice.

Dash's head tilted, curiosity momentarily displacing rage. 'A family man?' His gaze drifted to the cocaine scattered across the floor. 'So what's a family man doing in a room filled with coke?'

Brother Bertie's jaw clenched tight. No way was he telling this snake about Izzy's illness. Not his business. Not his right.

Dash's face contorted, the polished façade cracking to reveal something wounded underneath. 'You want to know what happened after you raasclaat called the police?' His voice trembled like he was a boy again. 'Father shipped me to New York like damaged goods. Made me live with my mother. You know how that bitch-woman always hated the sight of me.'

The pain flashing across Dash's face sparked an unwanted memory in Brother Bertie's mind – Dash as a teenager, waiting each day for letters from his mother that never came. How she'd spend months in London or New York, and then barely acknowledged her son's existence when she bothered to visit Jamaica. Brother Bertie had witnessed that neglect firsthand, had seen the crippling hurt it caused, even as Dash pretended not to care.

*Nevertheless*… 'Not my bloody problem,' Brother Bertie said, hardening his heart. He edged towards the stairs, every instinct screaming to escape. 'I'm out. Whatever you're into, leave me out of it.'

'Leaving again?' Dash's voice turned silky. 'Running seems to be what you do best. Wonder if your sister runs, too?'

Brother Bertie froze, one foot hovering above the bottom step. The word 'sister' echoed in his ears, rattling against his skull. His foot lowered slowly back to the concrete floor. The basement seemed to contract around him, air growing thicker, sounds muffling except for the thundering of his own heartbeat.

'Gertie.' Dash took perverse pleasure in saying her name, rolling it around his tongue. 'She's still in London, isn't she? Maybe I should pay her a visit. For old times' sake.'

Brother Bertie's control snapped. With a guttural roar, he lunged forward, hands outstretched for Dash's throat.

Dash sidestepped, his public-school boxing training evident in his stance. Brother Bertie's momentum carried him forward, stumbling past his target. Before he could recover, Dash's fist connected with his kidney, sending white-hot pain exploding through his back.

Brother Bertie spun, swinging wildly, connecting with Dash's jaw. The impact sent shock waves up his arm, the satisfying crack of bone against bone momentarily dulling the pain in his side.

Dash staggered, eyes widening in shock before narrowing with murderous intent. Blood trickled from the corner of his mouth, staining his perfect white teeth crimson.

They circled each other, predatory, muscles coiled. The basement fell silent except for their ragged breathing. Two former partners in crime, now mortal enemies, measuring each other with hate-filled eyes.

Brother Bertie attacked first, charging forward. Dash met him halfway. They collided with bone-jarring force, grappling and twisting. Brother Bertie's superior size against Dash's technical skill.

A brutal exchange of blows followed. Fists against flesh. Elbows finding ribs. Blood spattering across pristine concrete. Each punch carried years of resentment, each block a denial of the other's pain.

They crashed into shelving, cocaine packets raining down around them. Brother Bertie slammed Dash against the wall, feeling savage satisfaction at the shriek of pain that escaped his former friend's lips.

Dash retaliated with a headbutt that sent stars exploding across Brother Bertie's vision. He reeled backwards, blood gushing over his teeth, warm and foul.

Before he could recover, Dash's knee drove upwards, connecting with his groin. Paralysing agony radiated through Brother Bertie's body, dropping him to his knees. Through watering eyes, he watched Dash step back, reaching inside his jacket.

A switchblade appeared, flicking open with a soft, deadly click. Light danced along its polished edge, hypnotic and terrible.

Brother Bertie shifted sideways, to avoid the blade.

Too slow.

The knife sank deep between his ribs. Fire erupted in his side.

Gasping, he staggered backwards, hands clutching the wound. Warm blood seeped between his fingers, soaking his shirt.

Dash stood watching, chest heaving, knife dripping red onto the concrete floor. For an instant, shock registered in his eyes, as though he hadn't truly meant to go this far.

With monumental effort, Brother Bertie stumbled towards the stairs, leaving a dark smear across the floor. Each movement sent lightning bolts of pain through his body.

'Maybe I'll pay Gertie a visit,' Dash shouted nastily after him.

Gasping, Brother Bertie fixed Dash with a death glare. 'If I see you anywhere near my sister, I'll fucking kill you.'

# Chapter Twenty-Five

Sin settled deeper into the worn armchair, the children's *Bible Stories* open across her lap. The candlelight painted uneven shadows across the colourful illustrations, the only illumination in Izzy's small bedroom during yet another power cut.

Her son's breathing slowed, deepened. His thick eyelashes fluttered against rounded cheeks, then stilled. Sin watched him for long minutes, drinking in the miracle of him. After a soft kiss to his head, she tiptoed out of the room and closed the door.

Then two things happened at the same time: the electricity came back on, bathing the hallway in light, and there was a sharp knock at the front door. Frowning, she froze. Bertie had his keys. He never knocked.

Who would come calling at this time?

Only bad news came knocking at this hour.

She moved down the narrow hallway, her teeth worrying her bottom lip. Sin opened the door a crack, to reveal a familiar figure grinning back at her.

Her brother.

Her Jimmy.

Something broke inside her then. Years of lonely exile crashed down, and Sin practically leaped forward and flung herself around him, face buried in his shoulder. The familiar, comforting scent of him sent her reeling back to childhood, to safety.

Jimmy stood rigid beneath her desperate embrace, every muscle tensed. One heartbeat. Two. Three. Then he fiercely hugged her back.

And, oh God, to Sin, in that moment, it felt like her brother had never been away.

***

Jimmy sat on the edge of Sin's sofa, his bulk making the furniture creak in protest. The council flat closed in around him, very snug compared to his house overlooking the river at Sugar Cane Wharf. The place sparkled with a proud cleanliness – not a speck of dust anywhere, the worn carpet hoovered to within an inch of its life.

The silence stretched between them, thick with five years of unspoken words. Jimmy's leg bounced nervously, a habit their mum used to bollock him for. His gaze roved over the room, taking in the evidence of a child – a plastic dinosaur peeking from under an armchair, a finger-painted masterpiece stuck to the fridge.

'Five years is a bloody long time, Sin,' he finally uttered, voice gruff in the quiet room.

Her chin jutted up, the old defiance flaring. 'It wasn't me who slammed a door in your face.'

The dig hit its mark. Jimmy winced, rubbing his fingertips over his stubbled jaw. Christ, looking back, he'd been a total arsehole.

Then Sin's shoulders sagged, her hurt vanishing in a heartbeat. 'I don't want to argue. Not tonight, eh?'

'I shouldn't have thrown you out,' Jimmy admitted. 'At Mini's funeral. It was bang out of order.'

Sin blinked rapidly, surprise flitting across her features. Her mouth opened, closed, opened again. 'You were grieving.'

'So were you.' Jimmy leaned forward, elbows on his knees. 'But she was my wife. And there you were with Bertie, his hand all protective on your belly. Didn't take a genius to know you had a bun in the oven. My best mate and my sister. Breaking every bloody rule—'

'Rules?' Sin butted in, contempt curling her lip. 'There aren't any rules for love. You of all people should know that.'

He glared. 'Now, hold on one bloody minute, that was different.'

'How so?' Sin challenged with rapid-fire. 'It's totally the same. Mini, forever in our hearts, gave up everything for her love for you.' She inhaled deeply, memories flooding back. 'Her father, her family, the only life she'd ever known… For you. She gave it all up because she loved you, you big lummox.' She jabbed a finger at his chest. 'And you're going to sit there and tell me I couldn't do the same?'

'It's not the same.' Jimmy held tight to his convictions, though doubt flickered in his eyes. 'Batters wasn't my blood brother.'

'No, just your mortal enemy,' Sin shot back. 'Which was worse, according to the East End gospel. You crossed battle lines for love, Jimmy.'

'Bertie should've told me. Face to face. Man to man.' He shook with emotion, thinking of the man he'd once hailed as brother not coming to him. It still hurt. 'Not skulked around behind my back.'

'He's a black man in Britain, for crying out loud.' She threw her hands in the air with despair. 'It was 1969. It wasn't that easy. Still isn't.'

Jimmy recoiled, the accusation searing him. His stomach clenched tight with indignation. 'You know it had fuck all to do with that. I never saw Bertie's skin colour—'

'Well, maybe you should've,' Sin cut in, breathing hard. 'Known what it was like for him living here.'

'Don't twist my words,' Jimmy growled, frustration boiling in his veins. He jumped to his feet, towering over her, hands spread wide. 'You know what I bloody well mean. His blood runs as red as mine. I'd put a fist through the face of anyone who called him out because of his colour.'

Sin's voice softened, the sting going out of her. 'Like my Isaac's.'

The name hung between them. Jimmy's nephew. His flesh and blood he'd never met. Frigging hell, how had it come to this?

'Can I see him?' Jimmy tentatively asked. 'The boy?'

Sin got up, padded across the worn carpet, beckoning Jimmy to follow. Suddenly, he was nervous, heart pounding like a teenager on his first date. Family. Blood. The thing that mattered most in the world.

The boy's bedroom was tiny, barely room for the single bed and small chest of drawers. Sin stayed in the doorway while Jimmy approached the sleeping child with reverent steps. The floorboards creaked beneath his weight.

Isaac, Izzy, that's what Sin said they called him, lay sprawled across dinosaur-patterned sheets, one arm flung above his head. His skin gleamed copper in the candlelight, his tight curls a halo around his face. Jimmy crouched beside the bed, breath caught in his throat.

His hand hovered over the boy's head; he wanted to touch but was afraid to wake him. 'He's beautiful, Sin.'

A commotion in the hallway outside shattered the moment of peace. A thud, the sound of something jangling and dropping on the hall floor. Sin bolted into the hallway. Following her, Jimmy automatically reached for his shooter.

Brother Bertie stood swaying in the doorway, one hand pressed to his side, crimson seeping between his fingers. His pork pie hat tottered on his head, his face ashen beneath its usual bronze. Life flowing out of him with each passing second.

'Bertie!' Sin's scream tore through the flat.

But Bertie's glazed eyes fixed on Jimmy, disbelief warring with pain in his expression.

'Jimmy,' he rasped, blood bubbling at the corner of his mouth. Then his knees buckled, body crumpling to the floor with a sickening thud.

# Chapter Twenty-Six

'Get Ruddy on the blower. Now!' Jimmy barked, his arms already sliding under Brother Bertie's limp body.

Sin stood frozen, eyes round as saucers, unable to comprehend the desperate turn of events.

'For fuck's sake, Sin! Shift yourself!' He hoisted Brother Bertie into a fireman's lift, staggering slightly under the dead weight. Blood smeared across his crisp white shirt, warm and sticky against his skin.

Sin jerked as if slapped and darted for the phone.

Jimmy hauled Brother Bertie up the narrow staircase, careful not to bang his head against the wall. Sin had pointed out their bedroom earlier when showing him around the maisonette.

'Don't you dare die on my sister's bed, you selfish prick,' Jimmy muttered, fingers already working on Brother Bertie's blood-soaked shirt buttons.

The shirt peeled away, revealing the ugly wound between Brother Bertie's ribs. A vicious slash that bubbled with each shallow breath. Jimmy hissed through clenched teeth, his stomach plummeting to his boots.

'For crying out loud, Bertie,' he whispered, reaching for a nearby towel. 'What mess have you got yourself into?'

He pressed the towel against the wound, wincing when fresh blood immediately soaked through. The bedroom light cast Brother Bertie's ashen face in harsh relief, every line etched deeper by pain.

'Not as bad…' a raspy voice startled Jimmy, 'as that mess in Wapping… when you lost that fight 'cause you spotted a pair of tits in the crowd.'

Jimmy's head snapped up. Brother Bertie's eyes were open, clouded with pain but unmistakably alert, a ghost of his old mischievous smile playing across his bloodless lips.

'Jesus Christ,' Jimmy breathed. 'You're supposed to be out cold, you daft twat.'

'Take more than a little jab to keep me down.' Brother Bertie's attempt at bravado ended in a wet cough that brought fresh blood to his lips.

Jimmy shook his head, increasing pressure on the wound. 'Little jab? Someone's stuck you like a bloody Christmas pig.'

'You should see the other fella.' Brother Bertie's voice was barely audible, each word clearly costing him.

'I bet he's halfway to bleedin' Timbuktu while you're leaking all over your missus's bedspread.' Jimmy's light tone contradicted the desperate pressure he maintained on the wound. 'Proper selfish, that is.'

A weak laugh escaped Bertie's lips. 'Some things never change, eh? Still a cheeky little gobshite.'

'And you're still uglier than a docker's armpit,' Jimmy shot back, falling into their old rhythm with natural ease. 'Hold this tight against it.'

He guided Brother Bertie's rough, calloused hand to the towel, noting how badly the fingers trembled.

His one-time best friend shifted, face contorting with pain. 'How's about you…stop fussing and get me a glass of Lord Have Mercy? Dying man's request.'

'You're not dying on my watch.' Jimmy's voice roughened; it betrayed the casual banter. 'Sin would never let me hear the end of it.'

'Wouldn't be the first time you've disappointed a woman.' Brother Bertie's attempted wink turned into a grimace.

'Who did this to you, Bertie? Must've been someone who knew what they were doing with a blade.'

Brother Bertie's bloodshot eyes suddenly focused sharply on Jimmy's face. 'Dash,' he gasped, the name expelled with venom. 'Fucking Dash.'

Jimmy froze, his beefy hand hovering above the drawer. The name sent a jolt through his system, too much of a coincidence. His expression must have changed because Brother Bertie's bloodshot eyes narrowed.

'Tell me you're not doing business with him?' Brother Bertie demanded, voice suddenly stronger.

Jimmy's silence answered for him.

'Bloodfire, Jimmy!' Despite is weakness, Bertie managed to clutch Jimmy's wrist with surprising strength. 'Stay away from him. Far away.'

'What's he to you?' Jimmy demanded. He leaned closer.

Brother Bertie's eyes drifted towards the ceiling, focusing on something distant. 'We were brothers once,' he whispered. 'Blood brothers. Back in Kingston.' A sad smile touched his lips. 'Nobody like me and you, Jimmy boy.' His grip on Jimmy's wrist loosened. 'Just… trust me. Stay clear of him.'

'You're not making sense,' Jimmy pressed, frustration mounting. 'What's he doing?'

Brother Bertie shook his head weakly, refusing to elaborate. 'Bad business, Jimmy. Worse than you can imagine.'

Rage exploded in Jimmy's gut, hot and familiar. His large fists clenched involuntarily.

'I'll fucking find out myself then,' he growled, the promise deadly in its simplicity.

Brother Bertie's eyes rolled back, and he dropped into unconsciousness. His hand lay limp on the bed, fingers splayed, mere centimetres from Jimmy's own.

Jimmy stared at their nearly touching hands, a lump the size of the East End lodged in his throat. Their fingers lay side by side on the blue cotton bedspread, so close yet miles apart. Two men bound by something that went deeper than words, neither one able to bridge that final gap.

'Don't you bloody leave us now,' Jimmy whispered fiercely, his voice rough with emotion. 'We've got unfinished business, you and me.'

'Ruddy's bringing her doctor friend!' Sin yelled, her feet bounding up the stairs.

She exploded into the room, bolted across, and sank to her knees by her husband's side.

'Hang on, brother.' The words slipped out unbidden from Jimmy. 'Just hang on.'

***

Brother Bertie floated through darkness, voices ebbing and flowing around him. Pain hauled him back to consciousness. Burning, searing pain that twisted through his side with every shallow breath. His eyelids were so heavy but he forced them open. Sunlight sliced through the gap in the curtains, stabbing into his skull.

Ruddy sat beside the bed. Dark circles shadowed her eyes, her usually spot-on slap was smudged from a night's vigil.

'Well, well, well.' She sat straight but didn't reach for him. 'Sleeping Beauty decides to join the land of the living.'

Brother Bertie tried to speak, but his throat felt lined with sandpaper. He winced, fingers probing his side. Thick bandages wrapped his torso, the skin beneath them pulled tight with stitches.

'Doc says you're lucky,' Ruddy informed him. She reached for a glass of water. 'Knife missed anything vital. Though if you'd been any slower getting here, you'd be measuring for a wooden overcoat right now.'

She helped him drink, Brother Bertie gulping greedily, water spilling down his chin.

'Jimmy?' he croaked when she pulled the glass away.

Ruddy's eyes narrowed, sharp with disapproval. 'Gone. Left once the doc patched you up.'

Memory flooded back. Jimmy's face hovering above him, their conversation, the warning about Dash. Brother Bertie shifted, pain shooting through his side like a hot poker.

Ruddy jabbed a bony finger into his shoulder. 'You've made a proper cake of things now, ain't ya?' Her voice rose, words tumbling out in a furious torrent. 'I bloody warned you, didn't I? "Stay away from that shady game," I said. But, oh no, Bertram Watson knows best! And now look at ya!'

Brother Bertie didn't turn his face away in shame. He'd done what he'd had to. Faced with such a stark choice, any father would have. 'Had no choice, did I?'

'There's always a choice!' Ruddy snapped. Her hand gestures sliced through the air. 'Could've swallowed your sodding pride and told Sin your job went down the karzie. Could've come to me for help.'

'Izzy needed his medicine,' Brother Bertie mumbled, the words sounding pathetic even to his own ears.

Ruddy's mouth twisted. 'And now what does Izzy need? A father in a box?'

The bedroom door creaked open. Sin stood in the doorway, her slim frame silhouetted against the hallway light. Her eyes, puffy and red-rimmed, fixed on Brother Bertie with an expression that tore at his guts.

'I'll leave you two to it.' After a stiff nod, Ruddy gathered her handbag. She squeezed Sin's arm as she passed. 'I'll be back with more supplies.'

The door clicked shut behind her. Sin remained motionless, arms wound tight around her torso, fingers digging into her own flesh.

'Sin—' Brother Bertie began, his voice barely audible.

'Don't!' The single word wrung out of her. She moved then, steps deliberate, stopping at the foot of the bed. She gripped the iron bedframe. 'The doctor said you'll live.'

The coldness in her voice frightened him more than the lightning flash of anger in her eyes ever could.

Sin drew a deep breath, her chest rising and falling rapidly. 'You're back in it, aren't you?' she asked, voice wrenching with heartbreaking disbelief. 'That East End underworld. After everything you promised.'

Brother Bertie tried to sit up, desperate to explain, but pain forced him back down. 'It wasn't like that,' he protested, voice straining. ''I lost my job,' Brother Bertie confessed, the words bursting from him. 'Weeks ago.'

Sin's breath caught. 'You've been lying to my face?'

'I was going to tell you—'

'When?' Sin chucked at him, her pain erupting to new heights. She slapped her palm against the bedframe with a metallic clang. 'After you got yourself killed?'

Brother Bertie flinched, each word striking true. 'I was protecting you!'

'Protecting me?' She stalked around the bed, movements eating up the floor. 'From what? The truth? That my husband's a boldface liar?'

'From worry!' Brother Bertie shot back, frustration overwhelming pain. 'From knowing we couldn't afford Izzy's medicine! From seeing how bloody useless I am!'

Admitting the last nearly crippled him. What father, what husband, wants the world to know that about them?

But Sin was oblivious to his wretched inner turmoil. 'So instead you dive back into that villainous racket?'

Tears glistening in her eyes. She trembled visibly, fists clenched at her sides.

Brother Bertie desperately reached for her hand like he was worried she would slip away from him forever. 'It was just temporary. Till I found proper work.'

Sin snatched her hand away, jerking backwards, putting distance between them. 'Once you're in, you're in for life, that's the only flipping rule that matters in gangland. You can't dabble with that crowd, Bertie. It's not like having a flutter down the bookies or nipping out for a quick pint. It owns you, body and soul. The moment you shake hands with the devil, he's got you marked. And those bastards, whoever they are, don't give two tosses about your promises to me or your son. All they see is another mug to use and throw away when they're done.'

Bertie shook his head at the harsh reality of her words. He would never go back, would he? This was a one-time thing, wasn't it?

He couldn't stand to see the expression in her eyes. Like he'd ripped her heart out.

'I can't do this again.' Sin wrapped her arms around herself, her expression brimming with pain and hurt. 'I won't put Izzy through it.'

Brother Bertie's heart stuttered, all the colour draining from his skin leaving him chilled and scared like he'd never felt fear in his life. 'What are you saying?'

'You made your choice when you went back to that life.' Her voice hardened, resolution replacing hurt. 'When you chose that gangland business over honest struggle.'

'It wasn't a choice!'

'It's always a choice!' Sin's control shattered. Tears streamed down her face unchecked. 'You chose your pride over your family! You chose to lie instead of letting me help you carry the burden!'

Brother Bertie's vision blurred, panic rising in his chest. 'I love you. I love Izzy. More than the air I breathe, more than my own beating heart. You two are my whole life. My reason for getting up every morning. My reason for trying to be a better man. You're asking me to choose between right and wrong, but you ARE my right. Our boy...Christ, our beautiful boy...he's the best of both of us. You and Izzy are everything good I've ever done. Without you both, I'm just another broken-down former villain with nothing left to live for. Please, love, please give me another chance.'

'Then prove it.' Sin stood in the doorway now, her slight frame rigid with determination. Her tear-streaked face held no compromise. 'Because I swear on everything holy, Bertram Watson, if you go back into the East End Badlands, me and Izzy will vanish from your life forever.'

# Chapter Twenty-Seven

Danny settled into the grimy back-row seat at the seedy blue movie cinema and gestured for Oliver Harrington, MP – murderer – to join him. The politician's pale face had already lost its colour at the sight of naked flesh writhing across the massive screen.

The sleazy moans and grunts echoed through the cramped screening room, the soundtrack of degradation that had Harrington's refined sensibilities in proper knots. Danny savoured every moment of the knobhead's discomfort with the same relish he'd shown during their first meeting when he'd made the other man understand who was boss of this arrangement.

'Lovely cosy establishment, this, very cosy indeed,' Danny drawled, his scarred face twisted into a cruel grin. 'Perfect place for gentlemen of discerning tastes to conduct private business.'

On screen, a blonde actress was giving enthusiastic vocal appreciation to her male co-star's efforts.

'Get on with it,' Harrington hissed, his cultured voice barely audible over the moaning soundtrack. 'What do you want now?'

Danny smile widened. 'Well now, seeing as your moral crusade's going so well, I thought we might expand our arrangement.' He settled in closer, his breath hot against Harrington's ear. 'I want introductions. Social events where I can meet your cabinet mates, your parliamentary friends. Time I started moving in more elevated circles.'

Harrington's spine unexpectedly straightened like he knew something Danny didn't. 'Absolutely not. That's completely out of the question.'

Danny blinked, certain he'd misheard. In his world, nobody refused Danny Steele. Ever.

'Come again?'

'I said no.' Harrington's voice carried surprising steel. 'I won't introduce a common criminal to government ministers. Find another way to expand your sordid empire.'

Rage exploded through Danny, hot and vicious. 'Seems you've forgotten who's got the film of you murdering that bird.'

'I haven't forgotten a damn thing.'

The calm certainty in Harrington's voice sent ice down Danny's spine. This wasn't the terrified politician he'd broken weeks ago. This was different. Wrong.

Danny's brutal hands shot out, seizing Harrington viciously by the throat. His firm fingers found the vulnerable windpipe, applying just enough pressure to cut off air without leaving visible marks. Harrington gagged, face beginning to turn purple.

'Listen very carefully, you poncy, posh knob,' Danny snarled, on the verge of giving this inbred piece of British aristocracy the kicking of his life. 'One little squeeze and I can crush your windpipe flat. Won't kill you straight away, mind. You'll spend the next few minutes drowning in your own blood, choking on pieces of your throat.'

Harrington's eyes bulged, his hands clawing uselessly at Danny's iron grip. He was terrified.

'But I'm feeling generous today.' Danny loosened his hold just enough to let precious air flow back. 'So you're gonna tell me why you've suddenly grown a pair.'

Harrington gasped desperately, his cultured voice reduced to a panicked whisper. 'Lord Xander…he told me not to cooperate. Said he'd handle everything.'

The revelation shook Danny up. His brutal grip loosened completely, releasing Harrington's bruised throat. The MP slumped to the side, one searching hand pressed to his neck.

'He said what?'

'Lord Xander knows about our arrangement,' Harrington wheezed. 'He said you'd gone too far this time. That I should refuse any new demands.'

Danny's features went white, then flushed crimson. Apoplectic rage roared through him. The old bastard. His own father, interfering in his business, protecting his toff mates from Danny's perfectly legitimate blackmail operation.

'Get out.' Danny's voice had dropped to a lethal whisper. 'Before I change my mind about letting you walk out of here breathing.'

Harrington didn't need telling twice. He scrambled from his seat, stumbling towards the exit in the blind terror of a man fleeing death.

Rigid disbelief held Danny frozen in the seat. Frothing at the mouth, volcanic anger coursed through his veins, black and murderous. The old man had protected his parliamentary friends, pulled rank on his own son.

'The geriatric cunt thinks he can still yank my strings,' Danny growled to the empty room. 'We'll see about that.'

***

Outside the cinema, Harrington burst onto the Soho street in a panicked frenzy. His aristocratic face was flushed, his suit dishevelled, his quivering hands still pressed to his bruised throat. He needed to get away from this cesspit, back to the civilised world where men like Danny Steele couldn't touch him.

Across the narrow street, he didn't notice the thin figure who froze completely.

Chrissie Steele's haunted eyes widened in absolute terror, her face draining of all colour.

*That's him,* her traumatised mind screamed. *That's the evil monster who destroyed me.*

The man from her nightmares. The so-called distinguished gentleman who'd torn her fifteen-year-old world apart in that squalid flat, leaving her broken and bleeding.

Chrissie's piercing stare followed his every movement, memorising his face all over again. The predator who'd stolen her innocence, walking free while she lived every day mentally still imprisoned by his cruelty.

Her thin fingers tightened around the razor-sharp glass in her pocket, and for the first time in months, Chrissie Steele smiled.

# Chapter Twenty-Eight

Danny's brutal fist hammered the ornate brass knocker with vicious force, each blow banging through the refined silence of Grosvenor Square. The heavy door swung open to reveal a silver-haired butler in a pristine uniform. His keen blue eyes widened in alarm at the sight of Danny's barely contained violence.

'You know me. I've been here before,' Danny bit out. 'So move yourself out of the effing way.'

The butler didn't bat an eyelid. Or shift himself. 'I'm afraid Lord Xander is not receiving visitors this evening—'

'His poxy Lordship will see me. Trust me on that.'

Shoving the butler aside, Danny barrelled into the opulent entrance hall.

'XANDER!' he roared through the mansion, decades of suppressed resentment finally breaking free. 'Get down here!'

***

Upstairs in his private study, Lord Xander barely glanced up from his leather-bound ledger at the sound of that familiar voice downstairs. His patrician features remained impassive, though his fingers tightened almost imperceptibly around his fountain pen.

*That boy.*

Setting down his pen, deliberately calm, Xander straightened his silk cravat and smoothed his silver hair. Decades of public-school discipline had taught him never to show weakness, never to let emotion rule behaviour. Whatever tantrum his illegitimate son was throwing, he would handle it nobly, composure intact.

The study door burst inwards, splintering under brutal force. Instead of waiting downstairs, Danny's rage had propelled him to find his father.

'What do you think you're playing at, coming here?' Xander's refined voice carried icy disapproval. 'You know our business is conducted at the club.'

With a casual flick of his wrist, he waved away the two hulking thugs he kept on staff for moments such as this. He'd been controlling Danny since the fool drew his first breath and had never needed back up. In fact, he could handle his bastard-born son blindfolded and pissed to high heaven.

Danny stepped inside, his features twisted into a bitter smile. 'What's the matter? Ashamed your posh friends might find out about your East End bastard?'

Xander sighed. Not this. Again. He was tired of it. 'Daniel. State your business.'

'You interfered with my arrangement with Harrington.' Danny's voice dropped to a lethal whisper. 'Told him not to cooperate with my perfectly legitimate requests.'

Xander stood and moved to his drinks cabinet, his steps unhurried, his movements betraying nothing of his thoughts. Crystal clinked against crystal in a soft, practiced ease.

'Oliver is a friend. I merely advised him against entangling himself with…unsavoury characters.' His icy stare fixed on Danny with cool calculation. 'Surely even you can understand the wisdom in that.'

The casual dismissal ignited something volcanic in Danny's chest. His tailored suit couldn't contain the raw fury building inside him.

'Unsavoury?' Danny's laugh held no warmth whatsoever. 'Do you have any idea what your *friend* did in my establishment the night you brought him there?'

Xander's features revealed nothing, though his grip on the whisky tumbler tightened fractionally.

'I have no idea what you're implying.'

'Mister Clean Britain Up,' Danny informed him savagely. 'Seems he's got quite the appetite for violence. Particularly enjoys hurting young women.'

Irritation flickered in the depths of Xander's eyes. 'Oliver has his…enthusiasms. That's what your establishment caters to.'

The casual admission froze Danny's blood.

'Enthusiasms?' Danny's voice came out strangled. 'That what you call what he did to that girl? What he did to my sister when she was fifteen?'

Chrissie was his half-sister and, thank God, they did not share the same father. Chrissie's father, Ezra, had been a good, upstanding man who had rescued Danny's mum at the worst time in her life.

'Such dramatics, Daniel.' Xander took another measured sip of whisky, his cultured voice oozing bored aristocracy. 'The Steele girl was hardly innocent. How can any woman be who grew up in the squalor and immorality of the East End of London.'

The words hit Danny, the force devastating. His controlled façade shattered completely, revealing the horrified realisation. 'You knew. You knew all these years what that fucker did to Chrissie.'

Too late, Xander recognised his slip up. His pale eyes hardened with harsh calculation, but the damage was done.

'Ezra's girl,' Danny continued, his voice thick, horror dawning. 'My mum's daughter. You stood by and let him destroy a fifteen-year-old kid.'

Xander took a measured sip of whisky, his aristocratic bearing unchanged. But Danny caught the slight pause, the momentary stillness that betrayed hidden knowledge.

'I'm afraid you've lost me, Daniel.'

'Have I?' Danny's voice turned raw, desperate. The councillor's dignity crumbled completely, revealing the wounded boy underneath. 'All these years, all this bollocks between us, and you can't even admit what you are. What you've done.'

Something shifted in Xander's pale eyes, not panic, but a cold assessment of the situation before him.

'And what exactly am I, in your estimation?'

'My father!' The words tore from Danny's throat, his vulnerability agonising. 'Why couldn't you just call me son? Just here, between us? Just once in my whole fucking life?'

The admission hung there between them, raw and bleeding.

Xander studied his bastard son, detached, the way he might examine an interesting specimen. When he spoke, his cultured voice carried the casual cruelty of absolute blue-blooded privilege.

'Because you're not my son, Daniel. Rather, you're the consequence of a moment's weakness with a housemaid.' His penetrating gaze never wavered. 'Sons inherit titles, build dynasties, carry on family names. You're simply…useful.'

The words landed, surgically precise, destroying decades of desperate hope in a single breath. Danny's face went completely white, then flushed scarlet, homicidal rage zipping through him.

'Useful,' Danny repeated, in a daze. This wasn't news to him, and he'd always known this was the truth. But to hear it from his lips. It was like being punched in the lungs and having a plastic bag shoved over his head at the same time.

Then Danny Steele, former King of the Docks, now reigning King of Porn admitted something he could never breathe to another living soul.

He was hurt.

Gutted.

The pain sat in his chest with an unbearable pressure, pressing down on his ribs until he could barely draw air. All those years of building his empire, of becoming someone who mattered, someone who commanded respect and fear, and still, to this man, he was nothing. Less than nothing. A mistake. An embarrassment.

His throat burned with words he'd never be able to say. All the times he'd imagined this moment, fantasised about finally being acknowledged, recognised for what he'd achieved.

The worst part? He hadn't even been wanting love from this man. Love was for fools and weaklings. All he'd ever wanted was acceptance. A nod. A moment where Xander looked at him and saw something worth claiming.

But he'd been a fool to think blood meant anything to someone like Lord Xander Blacklock.

His father carried on twisting the knife, oblivious to his turmoil; he clearly had no idea of the wound he'd created.

'Precisely. A tool to be employed when necessary, discarded when convenient.'

Danny's powerful hands shot out, seizing his father by his upper-crust throat, using crushing force. For the first time, genuine surprise flickered in the older man's bulging stare.

'Fifty-odd years.' Even though his instincts were to squeeze, he still couldn't. 'Of wanting your approval, your recognition. Thinking maybe one day you'd be proud of what I built.'

Suddenly, Xander's body convulsed violently. His features distorted in agony, a hand clutching desperately at his chest.

'My…heart…'

Danny released his grip, and Xander gasped and dropped forward. The great Viscount Alexander Blacklock, reduced to a grunting wreck on his own antique carpet.

'Help…me…' Xander wheezed, his aristocratic dignity completely shattered.

Danny stood motionless. Detached. His scarred face showed no trace of mercy or regret.

He watched and said nothing.

Xander's contorted features abruptly went slack, his terrified eyes staring sightlessly at the ornate ceiling. The refined study fell silent except for Danny's controlled breathing and the distant tick of a clock.

A soft intake of breath from the doorway made Danny turn. Lady Prudence stood frozen in the entrance, her plain features taking in the scene. Her husband's lifeless body, Danny's calm satisfaction.

For a long moment, they regarded each other across the corpse of the man who had caused so much suffering. Then Lady Pru's gaze shifted to Xander's still form, and something almost like relief flickered across her features.

She said nothing. Danny said nothing. The silence stretched between them, heavy with mutual understanding.

Without a word, Danny straightened his silk tie and walked past her, his expensive shoes echoing through the marble hallway. Lady Pru watched him go, then quietly closed the study door.

She returned forty-minutes later, put on the performance of her life finding his body and crying out that he'd had a heart attack long after Councillor Steele had departed.

Viscount Alexander Blacklock was dead.

And the world was a cleaner place for it.

# Chapter Twenty-Nine

Gertie held Hyacinth's shaking arm, her protectiveness tender, guiding her through the desolate wasteland that Sugar Cane Wharf had become. The skeletal remains of cranes stood frozen in the grey London sky, their rusted limbs reaching nowhere. Warehouses gaped open, their broken windows staring blind over the murky Thames. Where once docker's shouts and cargo ships' horns had buzzed in the air, now only the wind whistled through empty buildings, carrying the stench of decay and abandonment.

'This used to be the beating heart of the East End.' Gertie's gaze roamed around, her red, gold, and green head wrap bright in the gloom. 'Now it's deader than Lazarus before the Lord called him forth.'

The high street stretched before them, a graveyard of boarded-up shops and peeling paint. But there, standing defiant among the ruins, was a converted warehouse that somehow radiated warmth.

'Mini's Place'

That's what the sign above read in cheerful yellow letters that refused to be dimmed by the surrounding bleakness.

'Why they call it that?' Hyacinth asked.

Gertie's face softened. 'Mini Rogers was Jimmy Steele's wife. Beautiful girl, taken too young by a brain tumour. She had the biggest heart in the East End, always helping anyone who needed it. When she died, her brother, Lucas, decided to keep her spirit alive by creating a sanctuary for young women, especially those in trouble and with nowhere to go.'

They pushed through the heavy wooden doors into a space that blazed with human warmth despite the institutional trappings. Harsh strip lighting couldn't dim the genuine welcome that touched every corner. Donated furniture, a battered velvet armchair with springs poking through, wooden chairs salvaged from church halls, a Formica table with chipped edges, had been arranged to create intimate spaces where people could talk without the whole world listening. The smell of instant coffee and Players cigarettes mixed with the lingering sweetness of digestive biscuits. A coal fire glowed in one corner, radiators clanked cheerfully, and somewhere a kettle whistled with promise.

Lucas Rogers emerged from behind a makeshift reception desk, and Hyacinth's eyes widened. At thirty-two, he stood six feet plus with huge hands that once cracked skulls for his old fella, Batters. Now those same hands fixed broken girls at Mini's Place.

This bruiser had channelled the pain of his sister's death into purpose. Lucas might have hung up his knuckle-dusters, but the steel was still there underneath. Any predator thinking the kids were easy pickings would learn the hard way that this gentle giant still had teeth.

'Gertie!' His voice rumbled with recognition and a welcoming smile, but there was a troubled glint in his gaze. 'What brings you here?'

'This is Hyacinth,' Gertie introduced. 'Her daughter's gone missing. Police won't listen because she's a young Caribbean girl who came over from Trinidad.'

Lucas looked upset. Not that he hadn't heard this before, but it still left him shaking at how unfair the world could be, especially when it came to girls and women. 'How long's she been gone?'

'Three weeks,' Hyacinth whispered. Desperation clawed at her throat. 'She came here because she had a job. Then nothing. No word, no call.'

'What's her name?' a quiet voice asked from the doorway.

Dr Edmund Fairchild stepped forward. He gave the impression that he wouldn't say boo to a goose.

At fifty-four, medium height with wire-rimmed spectacles and thinning hair, he was the sort of bloke you'd walk past without a second glance. Unremarkable in every way. But there was an alertness to his calm presence that caused Hyacinth to straighten slightly.

'Araminta,' she managed, the name torn from her chest. 'Araminta Marshall. She's only nineteen. My sweet girl never hurt nobody.'

Edmund nodded gravely, his hands clasped behind his back. 'We'll do everything we can to find her. I promise you that.'

Lucas pulled out a large, black notebook where they recorded interviews. 'Tell us everything. What this job was, where she was planning to stay, who she knew, any contacts she had.'

For the next hour, they listened in complete silence while Hyacinth poured out every detail about her missing daughter. When her tears came, Gertie's maternal instincts took over, producing a clean handkerchief. When her voice failed, Edmund waited patiently, his steady presence anchoring her until she found strength again.

'We've got good contacts,' Lucas assured her, leaning forward in his chair, corded forearms resting on his knees. Authority rang through every word. 'People who know the streets, know what goes on in the shadows. If Araminta's out there, we'll find her.'

'And if someone's hurt her?' Hyacinth could barely ask.

'Then they'll answer for it,' Lucas replied, deadly certainty in every word. 'That's a promise.'

Hyacinth carefully unwrapped a small framed photograph and placed it on the table. The image showed a stunning young woman with luminous dark skin and bright, hopeful eyes that seemed to sparkle with dreams of her London adventure.

Hyacinth didn't need to say who it was. Araminta wore a beautiful coral-coloured shift dress with three-quarter sleeves. The dress fell just below her knees, modest yet stylish, and a delicate white collar framed her graceful neck. Her straightened hair was curled around her ears. But it was her smile that held the attention, innocent sparkle brimming with excitement.

'That's my Araminta,' Hyacinth whispered, pride and pain thickening her voice. 'I sent money back home for her so she could get that dress made.'

After Gertie had walked Hyacinth back to the bus stop, the two men stood in the empty reception area. The cheerful atmosphere had evaporated, replaced by cold dread that settled in their bones.

'Are you thinking what I'm thinking?' Lucas asked, his large frame rigid.

Edmund's unremarkable face had hardened into granite. 'The whispers about that exclusive place in Belgravia. High-end clientele, young women who disappear into thin air.'

'And someone new in town with a new trafficking network,' Lucas growled. Rage boiled up, driving every step. 'Promising them legitimate work, then…'

He didn't need to finish. They both knew how these stories ended. Had seen too many broken girls stumble through their doors, if they were lucky enough to escape at all.

'I'll call my contact at Scotland Yard,' Lucas got the ball rolling.

Edmund added, 'And I'll reach out to my friends in social services. Newspapers.'

They stood in grim silence, two men who'd seen enough evil to recognise its stench when it came calling. Somewhere out there, Araminta Marshall was either fighting for her life or already beyond their help. But they'd move heaven and earth to find out which.

In the East End, family protected family. And every girl who walked through Mini's doors became family.

***

Edmund stepped outside into the grey afternoon, fishing a packet of Player's No.6 from his jacket pocket. The familiar ritual of lighting up gave his hands something to do while his mind processed the horror of another missing girl. He drew the smoke deep into his lungs, letting the nicotine calm his racing thoughts.

The narrow alley behind Mini's Place was supposed to be empty, but something prickled at the back of his neck. Years of working with damaged souls had given him a sixth sense for when he was being watched. He stood perfectly still, cigarette halfway to his lips.

'Whoever you are, do come out,' he said quietly, his voice carrying through the stillness. 'No point skulking in the shadows.'

A figure emerged from behind the rusted bins, clutching a mangy cat to her chest like a shield. Edmund's breath caught. The woman was painfully thin, her blonde hair a bit of a tangle, dark circles carved deep under haunted eyes. But it was the way she held herself that told the real story, wound tight, ready to bolt at the first wrong move.

And she was beautiful. He'd never seen a woman like her before in his life.

Of course, being a professional to the core he would never mention this. Above all, a vulnerable woman needed to feel safe.

Underneath that unremarkable exterior beat the heart of a warrior for justice. Not the sort who settled scores with fists and blades, but the kind who fought battles in courtrooms and council chambers. He'd turned his back on a cushy academic career to work in London's grittiest corners. His quiet voice carried more authority than most men achieved with shouting and threats. He had a gift for seeing straight through to the broken bits that needed mending.

And all his years of experience told him that this tall woman before him was shattered in ways that ran bone-deep.

Keeping his movements deliberately slow, he took another drag from his cigarette before speaking. 'Would you like to come in?'

No sudden movements, no pressure. Just an invitation hanging in the cold air.

The woman stared at him; her eyes had seen too much. Her arms tightened around the cat, which regarded Edmund with suspicious yellow eyes but didn't hiss. That was something, at least. In his experience, animals knew who to trust.

Hugging the cat tighter to her chest, fighting the tremor threatening her voice, she asked, 'Do they help older women here, too?'

The words came out raspy, damaged, but held an edge that could cut glass. She hated how small she sounded.

Edmund considered her carefully, noting the defensive posture, the way she kept her distance, the cat held like armour between them. Gently, without judgment, he replied, 'If you need help, I can—'

'I never said it was me, now did I?' Panic flaring in her eyes, the words burst out, full throttle, in a torrent of fire, a flash of the fierce woman she used to be.

'Of course not,' he replied calmly, his voice steady with absolute certainty. He'd heard this dance a thousand times before. The need for help warring with pride, fear, shame. 'My apologies.'

Emboldened by his acceptance, she stepped closer, her worn boots scraping against the grimy pavement. The cat's purr vibrated between them, oddly soothing in the tense air. Voice strengthening with desperate need, she continued, 'She needs answers to questions from someone close to her.'

Then she startled him by producing a wicked piece of glass. 'She was going to do her usual thing and sort it out. Then she remembered this place and told me to see what I could find out – for her, of course.'

As quick as she had taken the makeshift weapon out, she swiftly hid it back away.

Instinctively, he wanted to take it from her but knew he couldn't.

Edmund nodded slowly, stubbing out his cigarette against the brick wall. 'If it's going to help her feel better, she should ask this person close to her.'

'But I'm scared.' She shook before him, finally admitting she was the person in trouble.

When he spoke, his voice carried the power of absolute truth. 'Fear means you're still fighting. That takes more courage than most people have in their whole bodies.'

For a heartbeat, her guard dropped completely. He saw the terrified girl beneath the hard shell, the one who'd been broken so badly she'd built walls out of barbed wire just to survive another day. Hope flickered in her damaged eyes, fragile but real.

Then alarm seized her again, the shutters brutally slamming back down.

Clutching the cat, she whirled away from him and fled down the alley, her footsteps echoing off the damp brick walls in frantic rhythm.

Edmund watched her disappear. Because he was worried.

Worried about the plans she had for that glass.

# Chapter Thirty

The crystal ashtray exploded against the wallpaper, missing Danny's head by inches.

'You lying pillock!' Scarlett Fox shrieked, her flame-red hair wild with fury. She resembled a beautiful demon from Hell. Those doe eyes blazed with the kind of rage that could strip paint from walls.

Scarlett in a temper was magnificent. All fire and venom wrapped in alabaster skin. But Christ, she could be a proper handful when she got her dander up.

'Now steady on, love,' he began, raising his hands in mock surrender. 'What's got your knickers in a knot this time?'

Spinning to face him, her negligee swirling around her thighs, she planted her fists on her hips.

'Don't you dare "love" me, you two-faced snake! You promised me you'd divorce that pathetic vegetable you call a wife months ago!'

Her high and shrill voice was no doubt giving the neighbours an earful, but Danny couldn't bring himself to care. Not when she appeared this fuckable in her fury.

'Scarlett, sweetheart,' he tried again, then took a cautious step forward. The plush carpet cushioned his approach. 'These things take time. Legal complications and all that bollocks.'

'Time?' The word came out strangled, her disbelief obvious. She grabbed an expensive perfume bottle from the dressing table, hefting it threateningly. 'How much bloody time does it take to get rid of one brain-addled woman?'

Danny's jaw clenched. If only she knew how right she was. The stubborn old bitch just wouldn't have the decency to turn up her toes, no matter how much mercury he slipped into her gin. Iris clung to life; she had the tenacity of a dock rat, and it was driving him mental.

'She's sicker than we thought,' he lied smoothly, his silver tongue working overtime. 'The doctors say it won't be long now.'

Scarlett's laugh was bitter, viciously cutting through the air. 'Quacks! What do they know? Meanwhile, I'm stuck here playing the perfect dolly bird while you gallivant home to that drooling wreck every night!'

Tears of rage sparkled in her eyes, but Danny knew better than to mistake them for weakness. Scarlett didn't do vulnerable – she did dangerous.

'You know what I think?' she continued, her voice dropping to a venomous whisper. Stepping closer, her bare feet silent on the carpet, she thrust her face up close to his. 'I think you enjoy having us both. The respectable wife and the slice of side muff.'

'That's not true and you know it,' Danny growled, his own temper fraying. His fingers itched to grab her, shake some sense into that beautiful, stubborn head.

'Prove it!' she screamed, hurling the perfume bottle at the mirror. It shattered in an explosion of glass and expensive scent. 'Get rid of her or I'm gone! Tonight!'

Cursing a blue streak, she stalked over to the wardrobe and flung its doors open and reached for her Hermès leather suitcase.

*Enough with this load of old cockle!*

In three quick strides, Danny caught her wrist, spinning her back to face him. 'You're not going anywhere.'

Something primitive burned in her eyes, fear mixed with excitement. They stared at each other, predator and prey, though which was which remained unclear.

'Watch me,' she whispered, but her voice lacked conviction. Her pulse fluttered under his thumb in a frantic rhythm.

'No,' he said simply and crushed his mouth to hers.

The kiss was brutal, desperate, all teeth and tongue and barely contained violence. She fought him for a heartbeat before melting into his arms, her nails raking down his back through his expensive shirt. They crashed into the wall, sending a framed photograph tumbling to the floor.

What followed was animalistic, two wounded creatures tearing at each other, equal parts love and hatred. The silk negligee didn't survive. Neither did Danny's shirt. Their movements were savage, intense, all pretence stripped away, leaving only animalistic need and the taste of blood from bitten lips.

Afterwards, they lay tangled in the wreckage of silk sheets, breathing hard. Danny's back stung from her scratches, and Scarlett's throat bore the marks of his desperate kisses. The expensive flat looked like a battlefield.

'I meant what I said,' she whispered against his chest, her voice hoarse from screaming. 'Get rid of her, Danny. Soon.'

'I will,' he promised, already planning his next move. Iris had dodged death too many times. 'Just give me a few more weeks.'

After Danny left, Scarlett waited ten minutes before reaching for the telephone beside the bed. Her hands were steady now, all traces of hysteria gone.

'It's me,' she said when the familiar voice answered. Her tone was completely different now –

controlled, businesslike, deadly calm. 'Everything's proceeding according to plan. He's getting desperate.'

She listened to the response, a cold smile playing at her swollen lips.

'Don't worry,' she purred, examining her reflection in what remained of the shattered mirror. 'It's all in hand.'

***

'Iris!' Danny's voice boomed through the hallway, echoing off the polished tiles. After his encounter with his bit of skirt on the side, he was on the warpath, not in the mood for any more defiance. 'Slip your coat on, we're going out!'

He'd had enough of waiting for the poison to do its work. Time for a more direct approach.

'Iris, come on!' he called again and loosened his tie with impatient fingers. The confrontation with Scarlett had left him wound tight, ready for action.

But it wasn't Iris who appeared at the top of the stairs. Chrissie descended slowly, a thin dressing gown wrapped around her body.

*For fucks sake!*

Annoyance twisted Danny's features. 'Chrissie, not now, all right.'

Standing at the bottom of the stairs, blocking his path to the kitchen, Chrissie lifted her chin, defiantly determined. 'Me and you need to have a chat.'

'Well, I don't need to speak to you,' he snapped, moving to push past her. 'I've got business to attend to.'

Her thin arm shot out, barring his way with surprising strength. 'I won't have it, Danny. Not anymore.'

His snorted in exasperation. 'Won't have what, exactly?'

'Living in fear.' She pressed on. 'Someone told me that fear means I'm still fighting. That I've got more courage than most people have in their whole bodies.'

Danny rolled his eyes, his patience hanging by a thread. Between Scarlett's tantrum and now this bollocks from his half-sister, he was ready to throttle someone. 'Spare me the fucking philosophy lesson, Chrissie. What do you want?'

She took a shuddering breath, her haunted eyes fixed on his face. 'I want to know about that day. When I was fifteen. During the war.'

His jaw tightened. 'Forget about it.'

'I can't forget!' The words tore from her throat, raw from decades of pain. 'You asked me to deliver a packet to an address in Whitechapel. Said it was important.'

Danny's face went carefully blank. 'So?'

'I thought it was black market stuff,' she continued, gaining strength with each word. 'You were always involved in dodgy dealings during the war. Food, cigarettes, stockings for the ladies.'

He shrugged, feigning indifference. 'Everybody was at it back then. Had to survive somehow.'

Tears tracked down her hollow cheeks, but her voice remained steady. 'When I got there, I knocked on the door. This kind-looking lady answered. Invited me in for tea.'

'Chrissie—'

'No!' She slammed her palm against the wall, the sound echoing through the hallway. 'You're going to listen for once in your miserable life!'

Danny's eyes narrowed, but he stayed silent.

'She gave me tea,' Chrissie whispered, her voice almost breaking with the nightmarish memory. 'Sweet tea with something in it that made the room spin. Made me feel sick and dizzy. Then these men came out of the back room.'

Her whole body trembled, but she forced herself to continue. 'There were three of them. Posh voices, expensive suits. But their eyes…their eyes were like animals.'

'That's enough,' Danny said sharply. 'You don't need to—'

'It was only one of them in the end.' The words came out in a broken whisper. 'The others just watched. He wouldn't stop, Danny. No matter how much I screamed, how much I begged. He just kept… he kept…'

She doubled over, wrapping her arms around her stomach. The memory still had claws that tore at her insides.

'But I got away,' she continued, straightening with visible effort. 'Climbed down the coal chute while they were arguing about what to do with me. Ran through the streets bleeding and crying until I found you.'

Danny's face had gone stone-cold. 'And I took you home. Cleaned you up. Sorted you out.'

'Yes.' She stepped closer, dropping to a dangerous whisper. 'My big brother. My protector. You sent me there.'

'With a simple job to do. So what's the problem?'

'The problem,' she frowned at him, 'is what you were doing on that street in the first place? If you were there, why didn't you deliver the packet yourself?'

Danny's control finally snapped. 'Because I didn't get there in fucking time, did I!'

The words hung in the air between them, loaded with meaning. Chrissie went very still, her face draining of what little colour it had.

'What do you mean,' she asked quietly, 'you didn't get there in time?'

Danny blanched, realising what he'd revealed. 'Nothing. I meant nothing. You're twisting my words.'

But Chrissie was reaching into her coat pocket, her fingers closing around the familiar jagged glass from the broken mirror. The shard emerged, wicked and sharp, reflecting the hallway light in dangerous angles.

She pressed it to his throat, just hard enough to draw a thin line of blood. 'You better start talking, Danny, because you know what I'm capable of. I will chop you into tiny little pieces.'

Danny looked down at the glass, then back at her face, and laughed. Actually laughed, the sound cold and cruel in the confined space.

'All right then, since you're so desperate to know.' He sounded smug, completely unafraid. 'I set the whole thing up, didn't I? Those three toffs, they had money and reputations to protect. I was going to catch them in the act, get some lovely photographs, and blackmail the bastards for years.'

Chrissie's hand shook, the glass trembling against his skin.

'But on the way there, I got jumped by the Murphy brothers,' he said. 'Beat the stuffing out of me, they did. Took me two hours to crawl out of that alley. By the time I got to Whitechapel, you were already running down the street like your arse was on fire.'

The glass slipped from Chrissie's nerveless fingers. She reeled backwards, her palm opening in a red line where the shard had cut deep. But she couldn't feel the physical pain. Nothing could compete with the agony exploding in her chest.

Oh my God, NO! She must have heard wrong. Her big brother never…

'You…' Chrissie fought not to crumble, clinging to what little sanity she had left. 'You set it up. You sent me there knowing…'

'It wasn't meant to get that far!' Danny protested, but his statement lacked conviction. 'It was supposed to be foolproof!'

Chrissie pressed her bleeding hand to her mouth, tasting copper and betrayal. All these years, she'd carried the guilt, the shame, the terror. All these years, she'd been grateful to the brother who'd saved her.

'You used me as bait?' Chrissie didn't even know where she was anymore.

'Like I said, water under the bridge.' Danny brushed Chrissie off and went in search of his wife. 'Iris? We need to go out, darling.'

Chrissie wasn't sure if she was sitting or standing. Living or dying. Nevertheless, a truth was settling in her bones, cold and final.

She'd spent years hating the men who'd hurt her, never knowing the real monster had been holding her hand on the way home.

# Chapter Thirty-One

Danny's harsh fingers gripped Iris's thin arm, practically dragging her bewildered frame through the grimy backstreets of Whitechapel. Iris appeared bewildered, her winter coat hanging loosely on her gaunt body, the fabric flapping with each hesitant step. Those vacant eyes stared ahead, clouded and confused, while her auburn hair hung limp beneath a tatty headscarf.

*Finally,* Danny thought, satisfaction coursing through his veins. *Finally going to be shot of this fucking vegetable.*

'Come on then,' Danny muttered, his voice dripping false tenderness while his grip tightened broilingly on her arm. 'The doctor's going to sort you right out.'

The building reeked of carbolic soap and piss. Dr Marcus Brightman – struck off the medical register three years back for his fondness of young nurses and dodgy prescriptions – greeted them with a smile framed by crusty lips. His surgery occupied the basement of a crumbling Victorian terrace, the kind of place where screams got swallowed by thick brick walls.

'Ah, Mr Steele!' Brightman's watery eyes gleamed with avarice, and he rubbed his filthy palms together. 'And this must be the lovely Mrs Steele.'

Danny's lip curled with disgust. *Lovely? She's a fucking embarrassment. Brain-fried slag who can barely string two words together.* The greengrocer's daughter had served her purpose, elevating him from dock scum to respectable businessman. Now she was an albatross around his neck dragging him down.

'She's been playing up something chronic,' Danny lied smoothly. 'Violent episodes, throwing things about. The specialists reckon a good shock might reset her thinking box.'

*Or scramble what's left of it completely. Either way, I win.*

Brightman nodded sagely, though his shifty gaze suggested he'd swallow any bollocks for the right price. His tongue darted out nervously, before he explained, 'Electroconvulsive therapy can work miracles, absolutely. Though I must warn you, Mr Steele, the treatment can appear rather… intense to the untrained observer.'

'Intense how?' Danny's curiosity sparked, anticipation building in his chest.

The doctor's grin turned wolfish. 'Perhaps you'd benefit from witnessing the procedure first? I have another patient scheduled which will help clarify expectations, you understand.'

Power over life and death always fascinated him. Perverse excitement quickened his pulse. 'Go on then.'

Still holding on tight to his wife, Danny descended with the doctor deeper into the building's bowels, past peeling wallpaper and damp stains that resembled dried blood. The treatment room contained medical equipment that belonged in a bloody museum. A battered electroshock machine from the 1940s, its metal casing scarred and dented, crude copper electrodes dangling from frayed wires. Sparks occasionally leaped from loose connections, crackling, the energy malevolent.

A middle-aged woman lay strapped to a rusty gurney, her terrified eyes darting between the two men.

'Please,' the woman whimpered, tears streaming down her sunken cheeks. 'I changed my mind. I don't want this anymore.'

Brightman was deaf to her pleas, adjusting dials with practiced indifference, whistling tunelessly under his breath. 'No anaesthetic, you understand. Can't afford the proper setup. But the convulsions clear the mind wonderfully. Burns out all the troublesome thoughts.'

Danny leaned forward eagerly, his breathing shallow, anticipation building.

'Voltage set to maximum effectiveness,' Brightman announced cheerfully, his finger hovering over the activation switch. 'Brace yourself, Mr Steele. Here we go.'

The machine emitted a mechanical whine before unleashing its electrical fury. The woman's scream pierced the fetid air, a sound of pure, primal agony that seemed to scrape paint from the walls and burrow into Danny's skull. Her spine arched violently, tendons straining beneath her skin, limbs thrashing, their force inhuman. The leather restraints creaked ominously under the brutal assault.

Danny watched, transfixed. This wasn't the clinical procedure he'd envisioned. This was savage butchery.

Her convulsions intensified, her battered body slamming repeatedly into the metal gurney, each impact a sickening thud. A wet crack echoed through the room, ribs snapping under the violent muscle contractions. Foam bubbled from her lips, tinged pink with blood where she'd bitten clean through her tongue. Her eyes rolled back, showing only bloodshot whites.

The stench of burnt flesh filled the air. Urine and shit stained her dress where her body had betrayed her completely.

'Fuck me,' Danny breathed, his face draining of colour, bile rising in his throat.

The seizure seemed to last an eternity before her broken form finally went limp. Her breathing came in ragged, rattling gasps. Blood trickled from her nose and ears.

Danny swallowed hard, his stomach churning. *Christ, that's brutal. But necessary. A few more sessions and I can have Iris committed permanently. Natural deterioration, the doctors will say. Tragic accident.*

'Textbook perfect!' Brightman declared cheerfully, wiping blood spatter from his spectacles. 'She'll be right as ninepence once the confusion clears. Though I must admit, some patients never quite… recover their full faculties. Occupational hazard, I'm afraid.'

Danny's pulse quickened. *Even better.*

'Now then,' Brightman continued, turning towards Iris, enthusiasm renewed. 'Shall we prepare Mrs Steele?'

Danny glanced at his wife, still standing docile and bewildered by the door, drool glistening on her chin. He felt nothing, not pity, not guilt, certainly not love. If anything, her presence made this easier. Iris was completely defenceless, and here he was — the one person in the world who should be protecting her — deliberately putting her in harm's way. Whatever remnants of the woman he'd once married had died the night he'd tried to murder her. What stood there now was just an inconvenient shell and he was about to finish what he'd started. The sight of her pathetic, trusting vulnerability made his resolve harden, feeding his wicked justification.

*She's already gone. This just finishes the job properly.*

Before he could respond, the basement door exploded inwards, a thunderous crash that shook dust from the ceiling. Batters Rogers towered in the doorway. Fury twisted his granite features into pure murder.

'What the bloody hell is this?' he roared, his voice shaking the foundations. His piercing gaze swept the scene, the primitive torture device still sparking, the woman's broken form twitching on the gurney, Iris waiting innocently for her turn.

Danny straightened, trying to regain his composure, teeth grinding with irritation. 'Private medical consultation, Batters. None of your bleedin' concern.'

'Private medical consultation?' Batters rushed closer, his huge frame radiating menace, veins bulging in his wide neck. 'I heard that poor cow screaming from the friggin' street. You call this medicine? This is torture, you sick bastard!'

Brightman cowered behind his machine, all his earlier confidence evaporating, hands shaking violently. 'I'm a qualified physician! This is established treatment! Perfectly legal!'

'Qualified my arse!' Batters snarled, spittle flying from his lips. 'You're a struck-off quack working out of a basement. I've seen more medical expertise in a knacker's yard.'

Danny positioned himself between Batters and Iris, his territorial instincts flaring, false bravado puffing out his chest. 'She's my wife. I'll decide what's best for her treatment.'

'Treatment?' Batters advanced another step, his voice dropping to a dangerous whisper that promised violence. 'You were about to strap her to that contraption and fry what's left of her brains. That's not treatment, that's pure fucking barbaric.'

Danny scoffed, 'Medical science, Batters. You wouldn't understand.'

'Fuck! You!' Batters reached for Iris's free arm, his touch infinitely gentle despite his fury, voice softening. 'Come on, love. Let's get you somewhere safe.'

*No! Not when I'm this close!*

But Iris pulled back towards Danny, her damaged mind seeking familiar territory, clinging to the devil she knew. Her voice emerged slow and halting, each word requiring tremendous effort.

'Danny's…my husband. He'll…take care… of me.'

Danny's triumphant smile spread across his face, victory tasting sweeter than aged whisky, vindication flooding his veins. Even brain damaged, the stupid cow chose him.

*That's right. Stick with Daddy.*

Wrapping a possessive arm around his wife's frail shoulders, he pulled her closer, relishing Batters's devastation. ''Course I will, love. Always have, haven't I?'

Batters stared at Iris in disbelief, his protective instincts warring with heartbreak, massive shoulders sagging. The woman he'd loved first, the woman who'd chosen another man's ambition over his devotion, now choosing her destroyer over her potential saviour.

'Iris, sweetheart, you don't understand what he is planning—' His voice cracked from desperate emotion.

'She understands perfectly,' Danny interrupted, savage satisfaction widening his grin. 'Don't you, darling? I'm the one who'll always take care of you.'

Iris nodded slowly, those vacant eyes gazing up at him. Damaged trust. A small smile played on her lips. 'But… I want… Batters… Take me… Home.'

He didn't need asking twice and secured her to his side.

Danny let them go. Batters wouldn't be around all of the time, and when he wasn't, he'd bring Iris back here for her much-needed treatment.

# Chapter Thirty-Two

Chrissie placed the shard of glass beside her on the old steps behind Mini's Place. She was still carrying the glass from the broken mirror from the lavs in Spitalfields, the one Malcolm said she'd tried to hack his cock off with.

The night pressed down, thick and impenetrable around her. The murky Thames sloshed against the embankment below, barely visible in the darkness. The darkness suited her mood just fine.

Fifteen. She'd been fifteen years old. Just a kid. And Danny had sent her there knowing what would happen.

Her own brother.

Chrissie lit up a fag, the brief flare illuminating her bony face, shadows pooling in the hollows of her cheeks.

'A big brother protects his little sister,' she whispered into the darkness. 'That's what they're for.'

That's what she'd believed all these years. That Danny had accidentally come upon her in the street.

Lies. All of it.

Tequila rubbed himself along her ankles, mewing softly. The only living creature that gave a toss about her.

'What kind of brother does that, Tel?' Her voice broke, raw with pain. 'Sets up his baby sister for a pack of crawling maggots?'

The cat let out a violent hiss when a rat scurried past her feet, disappearing into the shadows. Even vermin had somewhere to go. Not her. Not anymore.

All these years she'd been carrying this wound, this gaping hole inside her. Filling it with booze and blokes and loud laughter. Playing the hard-faced tart who feared nothing and no one. And underneath it all, the terrified fifteen-year-old girl, calling for her big brother to save her.

But he'd never been coming to save her. He'd been the one who'd fed her to the wolves.

'Your own blood's supposed to be the one thing you can count on,' she told the cat, who stared up at her with knowing amber eyes. 'Family's supposed to mean something.'

Not to Danny Steele. Not even his little sister was sacred. Just another body to be used in his climb to the top.

She picked up the glass shard, turned it over in her palm. In its jagged edge, she saw fragments of her reflection – distorted, broken.

'Who'll feed you, eh?' She stroked Tel's matted fur with her free hand. 'Who'll take care of you when I'm gone?'

The cat meowed, rubbing her leg.

Chrissie raised the shard, its edge catching moonlight.

'Time to clock out,' she whispered.

***

Edmund Fairchild locked the doors of Mini's Place, tugging them twice to ensure they were secure. The battered leather satchel under his arm bulged with case files he'd review before bed. Sleep was a luxury in his line of work.

The night air bit at his face as he turned up his collar. No streetlights illuminated this stretch of Sugar Cane Wharf. The council had bigger priorities than lighting up this forgotten corner of the East End.

A plaintive mewing stopped him mid-stride.

Edmund paused, head tilted. The sound came again, insistent, distressed. He followed it towards the river steps, fumbling for the small torch he kept in his pocket.

The weak beam caught a scrawny cat pacing frantically at the top of the stone steps. Edmund recognised it immediately, the puss that belonged to the tall blonde woman he'd spotted lurking outside Mini's Place several times this week. Lucas had identified her as Chrissie Steele, sister to notorious former gangland boss, Danny Steele.

Edmund crouched, extending his hand towards the agitated animal. 'Hello there. What's got you so upset, then?'

The animal darted down the steps, crying louder, then back up to Edmund, its behaviour unmistakable. *Follow me.*

Edmund directed his torch beam down the steps. The light caught a slumped figure halfway down.

'No! Not on my watch!' he vowed.

He rushed down the worn steps, nearly slipping on the damp stone. His first-aid training kicked in before conscious thought. Pulse, breathing, injuries. The woman lay curled on her side, one arm outstretched, fingers loosely curled around what appeared to be a shard of glass. Blood pooled beneath her wrist.

Edmund knelt beside her, his voice gentle but firm. 'Ms Steele? Chrissie? Can you hear me?'

Her skin felt cold under his fingers as he pressed them to her neck. A pulse, faint but present. Edmund set his bag down, shrugging off his coat to drape over her.

The cat circled anxiously, butting its head against Chrissie's limp hand.

Professional concern softened Edmund's features as he glanced at the loyal animal. 'Good cat. You did well.'

His experienced hands pulled off his scarf to wrap around her bleeding wrist. He'd seen this before. Too many times. Young women with nowhere to turn, pain too great to bear. His efficient fingers applied pressure to stem the bleeding.

Leaning closer, his breath visible in the cold night air, Edmund spoke, quietly authoritative. 'I need to get you to hospital, Ms Steele.'

Her eyes fluttered open at that, unfocused at first, then sharpening in her sudden panic. She jerked upright, her strength shocking, bony fingers digging into his forearm.

'No,' she rasped, terror flashing across her gaunt face. 'No hospitals. No ambulances.'

Edmund attempted to reason with her, his tone steady despite her grip. 'You've lost blood. You need—'

'I said no.' Her voice held surprising authority for someone so weakened, chin jutting forward in stubborn defiance. 'They'll lock me up. Put me in the nuthouse.'

Edmund assessed her quickly. The cut wasn't as deep as he'd feared. With proper care, she might not need stitches.

Running a hand through his hair, he offered an alternative. 'At least let me call someone for you. Family?'

A bitter laugh escaped her lips, her eyes darkening in a pain that went far beyond physical. 'Family's the reason I don't want to be here no more.'

Despite her dire situation, a flash of her famous sharp wit surfaced through her pallor. The corners of her mouth twitched upwards in a ghost of her former dazzling smile.

'If you take me to The London, might as well get Angela Rippon to broadcast it on the evening news.' Her voice grew theatrically dramatic, though undermined by its weakness. '"Chrissie Steele tried to do herself in." That'd give the East End something to gossip about over their Kellogg's cornflakes.'

Then her eyes rolled back, the momentary spark extinguished as she slumped against him, consciousness fleeing.

Edmund's decision was made in that moment. He gently gathered her into his arms, surprise registering on his face at how little she weighed. For a woman nearly six feet tall, she felt no heavier than a child. Her bones pressed against him through her thin coat, all angles where there should have been curves.

The cat watched him, tail twitching suspiciously, amber eyes narrowed in feline judgment.

Adjusting Chrissie's weight in his arms, Edmund addressed the animal with surprising seriousness,. 'She's coming with me. You, too, if you want.'

As if understanding, the animal followed Edmund up the steps. The night wrapped around them as he carried Chrissie towards his car, her breathing shallow against his chest. His warehouse flat had medical supplies, privacy, safety. Everything she needed.

'Hold on, Chrissie,' he murmured against her platinum hair, determination hardening his gentle features. 'This isn't where your story ends.'

# Chapter Thirty-Three

*Where the bleedin' 'ell is this?* Chrissie thought, her bleary eyes darting about a room she'd never clapped eyes on before. Mind you, it wasn't the first and wouldn't be the last time that had happened. Usually occurred when she got off her face and couldn't recall which mug she'd gone off with. Whose bed, well, once again she didn't know, once again, not the first sodding time.

The room stretched before her, vast and industrial. Exposed brick walls climbed to a high ceiling crossed with thick wooden beams. Massive iron columns rose from the concrete floor, now softened by rich Turkish rugs in deep burgundies and midnight blues. Dusty sunlight filtered through tall, arched windows that framed a view of abandoned wharves and the restless Thames beyond.

This wasn't some bloke's grotty bedsit. This was… different.

Bookshelves lined one entire wall, packed tight with leather-bound volumes and paperbacks stacked in wobbly towers. A worn leather sofa faced a small fireplace where embers still glowed. Near the kitchen area, all copper pots hanging from a rack and mismatched crockery visible through glass-fronted cabinets, stood a record player with vinyl albums neatly arranged beside it.

The space breathed calm intelligence, carefully arranged yet lived-in. Potted plants thrived on windowsills. A wooden desk cluttered with papers and academic journals stood in one corner.

Only when Chrissie attempted to sit up did she moan in pain and notice the bandages wrapped around her wrists.

The memories flooded back.

The river steps, the glass shard, the darkness she'd tried to embrace.

'So you're awake.'

A voice from across the room startled her. A man emerged from the kitchen, carrying a steaming mug. She recognised him immediately. Captain Four Eyes from Mini's Place. Smaller than her and losing his hair. Definitely not her type.

More shocking than his appearance was the sight of Tel, purring and rubbing himself against the man's legs like they were old mates. The cat who normally spat and clawed at anyone who came within spitting distance of him, acting like a lovesick kitten.

*Traitor!* she mentally screamed at the animal. Tel merely blinked lazily and wandered off to explore some distant corner.

But Chrissie knew what she had to do. 'I suppose you'll be wanting payment.' Men always wanted a slice of action. That's how the world turned, wasn't it?

She awkwardly started to try taking her top off, no easy thing with slit wrists. Her fingers fumbled with the buttons, clumsy with bandages.

The man froze. Then calmly placed the mug on a side table and approached, keeping a careful distance.

'Please don't do that,' he said quietly, eyes averted. 'That's not why I brought you here.'

Suspicion darkened her gaze. 'Then why did you? Nobody does nothing for free in this poxy world.'

'Edmund Fairchild,' he offered, making no move to shake her hand. 'We've seen each other at Mini's Place. I work with Lucas Rogers.'

Chrissie let her hands drop to her lap, wincing at the sting in her wrists. 'I know who you are. Don't mean I understand why I'm in your gaff. Or not pushing up bloody daisies.'

Edmund's lips pressed into a thin line. 'You were quite adamant about not going to hospital. Given your state, I thought it best to respect your wishes.'

'How bleedin' noble.' Chrissie glanced around again, more deliberately this time. 'Nice little setup you've got here. Bit odd for a brainbox, ain't it?'

'I prefer unconventional spaces,' Edmund replied.

*Unconventional spaces? The poor bollocks would probably have a coronary if he knew some of the ones I'd seen the inside of.*

'Tea?' He offered.

Chrissie snorted. 'Got anything stronger?'

'Not for someone who's lost blood.'

Her eyes narrowed. 'You patched me up pretty good for someone who ain't a proper doctor.'

'I've been around long enough. Picked up a few things.' Edmund's tone remained even. 'Knew how to keep you from bleeding out, at least.'

'And what else do you do, Professor?' Her voice dripped with insinuation.

Edmund brought her a cup of tea, placing it on the coffee table within her reach rather than handing it to her directly.

'As you probably know, I run a programme at Mini's Place for women in crisis.' He settled into an armchair opposite her. 'Before that, I worked at Cambridge in psychological research. I've seen too many young women dismissed as hopeless cases. I prefer a different approach.'

Chrissie eyed him warily. 'And what approach is that?'

'One that recognises trauma doesn't define a person.' His gaze met hers, direct but not invasive. 'You can stay here until you're well enough to leave.

The loft upstairs is yours. It has its own door and lock. I'll sleep down here.'

Disbelief contorted her features. 'Just like that? No questions asked?'

'I imagine you've had enough of people demanding answers from you.'

Chrissie's fingers twitched towards her bandaged wrists. 'How long was I out?'

'About eighteen hours. I gave you a mild sedative after treating your wounds.'

'And you just sat here watching me sleep? Bit dodgy, that.'

A hint of amusement flickered across Edmund's face. 'I checked your vital signs periodically. Otherwise, I allowed you to rest.'

Chrissie pushed herself up straighter, grimacing at the pain. 'I need to see this upstairs room of yours. Make sure it ain't some kinky professor dungeon where you demand I bend over because I didn't finish my homework.'

After her saucy remark, beneath hooded eyes, she waited for a reaction. Nothing. The guy didn't even blush.

Instead he got up and gestured towards the spiral staircase. 'Can you manage the stairs?'

Pride pushed her to her feet despite the wooziness. 'I can manage just fine, thank you very much.'

The climb was slow, each step shooting pulses of pain through her wrists. Edmund followed several steps behind, close enough to catch her if she fell but maintaining a deliberate distance.

The loft space took her breath away. Unlike the cluttered warmth below, this room was spare, almost monastic. A double bed with crisp white sheets stood beneath a skylight. A simple wooden wardrobe occupied one corner. The entire outer wall consisted of French doors opening onto a small balcony.

'Bathroom's through there.' Edmund indicated to a door to the side. 'It locks.'

'Fancy pants,' Chrissie muttered, turning slowly to take it all in. She moved to the French doors, pushing them open and stepping onto the narrow balcony. The cooling air stung her skin.

The Thames stretched before her, dark and powerful. Only then did she recognise her surroundings – she was still in Sugar Cane Wharf.

'You live here alone?' she asked, stepping back inside.

'Yes.' Edmund folded his arms. 'But I was married once. Got three grown kids and two grandchildren up in Manchester.'

'Then what do you want from me?' Chrissie demanded, her patience exhausted.

Edmund considered her for a long moment. 'Have you ever watched someone drown, Ms Steele?'

The question caught her off guard. 'What?'

'I have. When I was twelve. A boy in my neighbourhood fell through ice on a pond. I stood there, frozen, watching him slip away.' Edmund's expression remained neutral, but his eyes held old pain. 'I've spent my life making sure I never stand by and watch again. That's my angle.'

He moved towards the stairs. 'There are clean clothes in the wardrobe. Nothing fancy, but they should fit. Food in the kitchen when you're hungry. Stay as long as you need to heal.'

Chrissie stared at him, decades of street wisdom failing to detect the lie. 'What if I rob you blind?'

'There's nothing here worth stealing,' Edmund replied simply. 'The front door isn't locked. You're free to leave whenever you choose.'

With that, he descended the stairs, leaving Chrissie alone in a room filled with more kindness than she'd encountered in years.

She moved back to the French doors, watching the dark-water below. The same river she'd sat beside last night, ready to leave this world for good.

# Chapter Thirty-Four

'Mr Harrington!'

The insistent call of his name stopped Oliver Harrington, MP, dead in his tracks in the corridors of Westminster. When he saw who it was, he groaned inwardly.

*God give me strength!*

Ben Gausky, a persistent hack who'd been sniffing around his Clean Up Britain campaign for weeks. If there was one species Harrington truly despised, it was journalists. In his considered opinion, they should bring back the death penalty for the lot of them.

The scruffy reporter seized his chance, rushing forward while yanking a battered notebook and chewed pen from his grubby mackintosh. Other MPs strolled past in the background, their conversations creating a low hum of political gossip that could turn deadly if the wrong words were overheard.

'Ben Gausky, *Evening Tribune*,' the journalist panted, scribbling notes before Harrington could escape. 'Any comment about the film, sir?'

Harrington's patrician features arranged themselves into their practiced mask of moral authority. Thirty years navigating Westminster's treacherous waters had taught him to deflect awkward questions with consummate skill. He glanced nervously at the passing MPs, noting how Lord Pemberton slowed his stride, ears practically flapping with curiosity.

'I'm afraid you'll have to be more specific, Gausky.'

'The film showing you with a young woman who appears to have been badly hurt.' Gausky's pen hovered over his notebook, ready to capture every damning word. 'We have the footage in our possession. Any comment before we print the story and send the evidence to Scotland Yard?'

The colour fled from Harrington's face, leaving his skin waxy and pale. His stomach dropped through the floor, a sickening plunge that left him gasping. The marble corridor spun around him, walls closing in until he could barely draw breath.

'I… I have no idea what you're referring to,' he managed, his tones dissolving into a strangled rasp.

The journalist remained dead serious. 'Really, sir? Because the footage is quite clear. Shows you with a very young black woman. A woman who, in my opinion, appears dead, after you have finished attacking her, to be more precise. The public have a right to know.'

Harrington's world tilted on its axis. His carefully constructed life – the ministerial position, the respect, the moral crusade – crumbled to dust in that single moment. Danny Steele had betrayed him. Who else could it be? No one else knew about the film.

'No comment,' he croaked, knocking past the journalist.

The drive to his Buckinghamshire estate passed in a blur of country lanes and mounting terror. His Jaguar's engine purred, but Harrington heard only the thundering of his pulse in his ears. Thirty-five years of marriage, three children, a dozen grandchildren, all of it would be destroyed by dawn.

The Georgian manor house rose before him in all its grand splendour, pale stone facade catching the late afternoon sun.

'Darling, is that you?' His good and unsuspecting wife, Constance, called from the drawing room, her cultured tone warm with affection earned over decades of devotion.

His beloved Connie, who still looked at him with the same adoring eyes she'd worn as a debutante. She'd trusted him completely, never questioning his late nights or mysterious business trips. The perfect political wife, now about to be dragged through the gutter press alongside him.

'Yes, my dear,' he answered, his voice barely steady. 'Just need to… handle some correspondence in the study.'

His heavy footsteps echoed through the panelled hallway, past portraits of distinguished ancestors who'd served Crown and country with honour. The study door closed behind him, a soft click that sounded like a prison cell.

The Purdey shotgun hung in its glass case, a thing of beauty crafted by English artisans. Harrington's trembling fingers fumbled with the lock. He'd used it for grouse shoots on Scottish moors, pleasant autumn days filled with laughter and good fellowship. Now it would serve a different purpose entirely.

He thought of the young girl's terrified eyes, her desperate pleas for mercy that had only inflamed his twisted desires. The memory would follow him to Hell, where he surely belonged.

The gunshot shattered the evening stillness, sending birds screaming from the roof.

***

Scarlett Fox flopped back on the bed in her flat next to Danny after their marathon, sex session. He was properly done in, but she sprang to her feet the way only young people know how.

After wrapping a Chinese-style dressing gown around her, she asked, 'Coffee, darling?'

Nodding, he then swung his legs from the silk sheets, admiring his reflection in the gilt-framed mirrors that adorned every wall. Still had it at, even in his fifties, he told himself. The body of a man twenty years younger, kept sharp by violence and vanity in equal measure.

Scarlett returned with a strong coffee and the morning papers, playing the perfect mistress to the hilt.

Danny grunted approval, reaching for the paper. His coffee turned bitter in his mouth the moment he spotted the headline that blazed across the front page.

**MORAL MP'S MURDEROUS SHAME & DEATH**

The newspaper trembled in Danny's grip. Below the screaming headline, grainy photographs showed scenes from the investigation and promises of full police inquiry into Harrington's suicide.

'Fucking hell,' Danny breathed, his face draining of colour.

Scarlett pressed closer, apparently alarmed by his reaction. 'My goodness, what is it, baby?'

'Harrington's dead.' The words scraped his throat raw. 'Topped himself last night. Says here the police have got the film.'

'What film?' Scarlett's eyes widened.

God, the girl could be as thick as shit sometimes.

Through gritted teeth he explained, like he was chatting to an idiot, 'The film of him killing the girl. The one we – me and you – made at the party.' Danny's hands shook as he scanned the article. 'Our bloody insurance policy.'

She shot upright, her stricken gaze going wild with terror, pupils dilated with raw panic.

'They've got our film? How is that possible?'

'I don't know, do I?' Danny's voice rose to a snarl. His mind churned with possibilities, each more dangerous than the last. Someone had betrayed him. Someone with access to his most secret sanctuary had sold him out to the highest bidder.

'But that means…' Scarlett's chest heaved, her breathing coming in short, desperate gasps. She pressed trembling fingers to the base of her throat. 'Danny, that means they know about the house, about everything we do there!'

Scarlett flew to the wardrobe, flinging its doors with such force they banged against the walls.

'We need to pack! Get out of here!' Her voice pitched into hysteria, hands clawing through items of clothing.

'Calm down—'

'Calm fucking down?' She whirled to face him, her red hair wild around her shoulders. 'We're finished! They'll trace it back to us, they'll arrest us both!'

She paced the bedroom like a caged animal, her movements becoming more frantic with each step.

'We need to run! Pack everything and scarper out of London before—'

Danny grabbed her bare arms and shook her. 'Get a grip, woman! Falling apart won't help anyone.'

'You're right, as always. I'm sorry.' She sagged against him, suddenly fragile. 'It's just… the thought of prison…'

Danny's gut twisted with protectiveness and suspicion. 'No one's getting banged up. We need to get to the house. Find out how those bastards got hold of our film.'

Danny had a very bad feeling about this.

# Chapter Thirty-Five

'Faster, Danny!' Scarlett's breathless voice squealed, her russet hair whipping around her pale face. She twisted in the passenger seat to peer through the rear window. 'What if they're already there?'

'Shut your gob and let me drive.' His fingers gripped the steering wheel of his Roller. Bile rose in his throat despite his outward bravado. Someone had betrayed him. Someone with access to his most guarded secrets had sold him out.

'There!' Scarlett's finger jabbed towards the windscreen, emerald eyes widening in shock.

The coppers were already at the house. Uniformed filth swarmed around his Georgian townhouse. Danny's gut churned, sickening dread mounting.

'Fucking bastards!' The words exploded from Danny's throat. He slammed on the brakes, the Roller lurching to a halt. He was in the mood to rip someone's head clean off.

A massive figure emerged from the front door of his townhouse. Danny's blood turned to ice water in his veins. That unmistakable bulk, those beady eyes, that smug grin spreading across brutal features.

Detective Abbot.

His stomach twisted into knots of pure dread. Of all the bent coppers in London, why did it have to be this tosser? If that bastard was here, it meant his moron partner would be lurking nearby, too. Danny's gaze swept the scene, alarm growing.

There. Detective Long emerged from behind a police van. Danny's windpipe seized up with alarm. These two tossers together meant serious trouble.

'Danny, we need to go!' Scarlett clawed at his arm, her nails digging into his flesh. 'Turn around, drive away!'

'Like fuck am I running.' Danny Steele had never run from a fight in his life.

His shoes hit the pavement with deliberate authority and he strode towards his violated sanctuary with the swagger of a man who owned half of London's underworld.

Abbot's gravelly voice boomed across the square dripping with obvious relish. 'Well, well, well. What have we got here then?'

Long quickly added, 'Fancy meeting Councillor Steele among all this muck.'

Four decades of criminal enterprise had taught Danny the value of a good performance.

'Abbot. Long.' His tone was the height of innocence despite the circumstances. 'What's all this about then? Bit of a commotion for a quiet morning.'

Abbot's stare gleamed, predatory satisfaction evident. 'Just happened to be in the neighbourhood, were you, Danny boy?'

'Routine patrol,' Danny replied, his practiced smoothness not letting him down. 'Heard there might be some dodgy activities in the area. Thought I'd check it out personally.'

Long's grin widened into something genuinely unpleasant. 'How very public-spirited of you. Always checking out for community standards, aren't you?'

'Someone reported suspicious comings and goings.' Confidence growing, Danny continued peddling his lies. 'Young women, foreign accents, men in flash motors. Thought it might need investigating.'

Abbot's bulk shifted closer. 'Investigating, were you? Very thorough investigation, I'm sure.'

'That's what they voted me in for,' Danny insisted, stubbornly defiant. 'Clean Up Britain starts right here in Belgravia.'

They were interrupted when a young constable approached at a run, his face flushed and excited. 'Sirs! You need to see this! Inside the house!'

Abbot and Long exchanged glances like they'd hit the jackpot.

'Shall we, Councillor?' Abbot nodded in exaggerated courtesy. 'Since you're here on official business and all.'

Danny's stomach plummeted, but every instinct told him to maintain the charade. His feet moved with forced confidence, following the coppers into the house.

The interior revealed systematic destruction. Artwork hung askew on cream-coloured walls while uniformed officers catalogued evidence, their efficiency methodical. Overturned furniture and scattered papers testified to thorough searching.

They climbed the grand staircase to the second floor, then stopped before what appeared to be a solid bookshelf lined with leather-bound volumes. The young constable pressed something behind a false spine, and the entire section swung inwards.

Danny's secret monitoring room lay exposed. Banks of television screens showed multiple camera angles of bedrooms below. Recording equipment lined the walls. Shelves held hundreds of film canisters, each labelled with dates and initials that would destroy the lives of the powerful.

'Well, get a load of this,' Long breathed, his features lighting up, savage joy in his expression. 'It's like Pinewood Studios in here! Lights, camera, blackmail!' Nasty delight twisted his grin. 'Hope you're ready for your close-up!'

Abbot's gaze swept over the equipment; he was obviously relishing this. 'Very professional setup, Danny boy. Must have cost a bob or two.'

'I've never seen this room before in my life,' Danny croaked, but his denial sounded fake even to his own ears.

Abbot's whole face burned bright from triumphant hatred. 'Daniel Steele, you're nicked!'

Two uniformed coppers seized Danny's arms, their satisfaction vicious. The cold metal handcuffs bit into his wrists. His suit wrinkled under their rough handling.

'Get your filthy hands off me!' Danny snarled, struggling against the restraints. 'I know my rights!'

Abbot's meaty fist grabbed a handful of Danny's silver hair, yanking his head back. 'You've got the right to shut your gob before I shut it for you.'

A scratchy brown blanket dropped over Danny's head. The coarse wool stank of previous arrests. Danny Steele, the King of Porn, reduced to shuffling blindly, police protection hiding his shame.

'Move!' Abbot commanded, shoving Danny forward, the force enough to send him stumbling.

Danny seethed.

Someone close to him had orchestrated this betrayal.

But who the fuck was clever enough to outsmart Danny Steele?

***

Two hours later, Danny sat in Interrogation Room Three, his expensive suit wrinkled from rough handling. The two coppers circled him.

Lowering his bulk into the chair opposite, Abbot got stuck in. 'Been a naughty lad, haven't you? Filming people you've got no business spying on.'

'Blackmailing them,' Long piled on with venomous pleasure and clucked his tongue. 'Powerful folk who don't appreciate having their private moments turned into *Candid Camera*.'

Abbot chuckled at that. '*Candid Camera*. That's a good un.'

'What the fuck did you think you were playing at, Danny?' the copper continued, face creased with something resembling concern. 'Me and you, we grew up in homes where we hardly saw our dad because he was working all hours trying to keep the family together.'

Danny's defiant expression faltered. Abbot's voice had lost its copper's authority, becoming something more personal, more dangerous.

Abbot rubbed his forehead with thick fingers, suddenly looking every one of his fifty-odd years. 'That's how it is for people like us. Always has been, always will be.'

Long shifted on the table's edge, his weasel features arranging themselves into uncharacteristic seriousness. He nodded towards Abbot, then fixed his cool, laser intense gaze on Danny. 'Now, the other half, they've always lived like kings, held the power.' He shook his head like they were down the pub having a chat over a pint. 'Don't know what it is to have their bellies empty and growling because it hasn't seen food for days.'

Danny's throat went dry. These two bent coppers weren't gloating anymore, they were giving him an education he'd never asked for.

'What we're telling you, Danny,' Abbot offered, 'is that if you don't cooperate and decide to talk, these powerful people will see that you never make it to court.'

Long threw in, 'Probably ensure you never leave this here station alive.'

Abbot's voice dropped to barely above a whisper. 'Think you'll be safe behind bars? Think again.'

Danny suddenly grasped the terrible and deadly situation he was in.

Long told him straight: 'You've been swimming with sharks, Danny boy. Time to realise you're just another fish.'

Danny's shoulders sagged, the crushing realisation heavy. 'So what's the deal?'

Abbot took over. 'Certain people would appreciate it if we took away and destroyed your film collection. In exchange, your name never gets mentioned, this arrest never happened, and you walk out of here breathing.'

Danny knew when he was cornered.

'Deal.'

He might be licking his wounds, but he was beaten. It would take more than a couple of dodgy plods to bring down Danny Steele.

He would rebuild.

Bigger and stronger.

With twice the bite and half the mercy.

# Chapter Thirty-Six

Brother Bertie stood frozen in the marble entrance hall of Lord Xander's Grosvenor Square mansion, the black funeral wreath on the massive oak door banging shut behind him like the gates of Hell itself.

Black crepe draped every mirror, death announcements fanned across a silver tray, and the staff glided past with black armbands tight around their sleeves. The butler, a proper stuffed shirt with a face like he'd been sucking lemons since birth, eyed Bertie's cheap suit, not disguising his disdain.

'I'll inform Mr Jack of your… arrival.' The butler's nostrils flared. 'Your name?'

'Watson. Bertram Watson.'

The sharp click of heels on marble saved him from further scrutiny. His stab wound pulsed with a dull throb, his body's own alarm bell reminding him he was in the home of the man whose blade had put it there.

Just then, Ruddy appeared from a side door, her gaze widening in stunned disbelief when she clocked him.

'Bertie? What in God's green earth are you doing here?' She drew him through double doors into an elegant morning room. 'Have you lost your marbles?' Up close, her face was pale with worry beneath her heavy makeup. 'You should be at home with that wound, and you do know that Dash lives here.'

Bertie touched his side, the stabbing pain a constant reminder. 'I need to see him, Ruddy.'

'You need your head examined, more like.' She circled him, incensed. 'That maniac tried to gut you like a Sunday roast, or have you forgotten?'

'How's Lady Pru holding up?'

'Don't change the subject, you cheeky sod.' Ruddy jabbed a scarlet-tipped finger into his chest. 'I know why you're here.'

'Do you, now?'

''Course I bloody do.' Her voice dropped to a furious whisper. 'After everything, you're risking it all for what?' She shook her head in disbelief. 'You can't do this, Bertie. What about your promise to Sin?'

His stomach twisted. The memory of Sin's tearful face flashed through his mind.

'I know what I'm doing,' he muttered, avoiding Ruddy's accusatory stare.

'Do you? Because from where I'm standing, it looks like you're about to flush five years of honest living down the bog faster than last night's curry.'

Before he could respond, the door banged open. Dash filled the frame, dressed head to toe in black mourning clothes that emphasised his height.

'Bertie Watson in my house.' He smiled, slow and deadly. His eyes flicked to Ruddy. 'Fuck off.'

Ruddy planted her hands on her hips. 'This is Lady Prudence's house, not yours, Mr High-and-Mighty Blacklock.'

'Fuck. Off.' Dash delivered each word in brutal clarity.

Ruddy hesitated, giving Bertie one last desperate look. 'Don't do nothing stupid, you hear me?'

The door banged behind her, leaving Bertie alone with the devil in a groovy linen suit.

Dash stalked forward, every movement controlled. 'You've got some fucking nerve.'

Bertie stood his ground, ignoring the throb in his side. He forced himself to breathe slowly, evenly, refusing to show weakness. Sweat prickled his back despite the chill.

'I need a job.' He inhaled deeply. 'My boy needs medicine.'

Dash's face froze. Then his face split into a smile of pure triumph. White teeth gleamed in his handsome face, victory dancing in his eyes.

'Say that again.' Dash leaned forward, elbows on knees. 'I want to hear those sweet, sweet words one more time.'

Bertie's throat tightened. Humiliation burned. 'You heard me.'

'The righteous man.' Dash waved his hands. 'The family man. Mister Straight-and-Narrow.' He took a sip, eyes closed in appreciation. 'Begging me for work.'

'I ain't begging,' Bertie growled, his jaw muscles bunching.

Dash's eyes snapped open. 'Aren't you?' He moved closer, invading Bertie's personal space. 'Looks like belly crawling from where I'm standing.'

Bertie's fists clenched, then unclenched. The urge to smash that smug face burned in his veins, but he pushed it down. Too much at stake.

'You offering work or not?'

Dash circled him again, close enough that Bertie could smell his expensive cologne, feel the heat radiating from his body. 'What happened?' Dash's voice dropped to a mock-whisper. 'The straight life not paying the bills?'

Bertie kissed his teeth. 'Fuckery! I've had enough of this crap.'

Twisting on his heels, he headed for the door.

'Wha' happen now? Running away again?' Dash jeered, his posh tones slipping easily to the Jamaican of his youth. 'Same old Bertie, always ready to turn him tail when tings get serious.'

Bertie kept walking.

'Wait!' Dash called out, his voice suddenly dead serious. 'I've got work for you.'

Bertie paused, hand on the doorknob. 'What's the job?'

'I'll contact you.' Dash's voice had returned to its polished English. 'Tomorrow night. Be ready at nine.'

Bertie pulled open the door. He'd taken one step into the hallway when a knife whistled through the air and embedded itself in the doorframe, inches from his face. The blade quivered with the force of the throw.

Bertie froze but didn't turn back.

'If you betray me again,' Dash's voice was soft, deadly, 'I'm going to stick that right through your heart. And then cut it out.'

# Chapter Thirty-Seven

The power was back on, at least for tonight. Shadows danced across Violet's bedroom walls as Jimmy tucked the blanket around her thin shoulders. His girl looked up at him with that soft gaze and the loss of his Mini twisted in him from head to toe.

'I like my new school, Dad,' Violet said, fingers worrying at the edge of her blanket. 'Nobody makes fun of how I talk there. Sister Bernadette says I'm clever.'

Jimmy lovingly smoothed her hair back from her forehead. ''Course you are, princess. You're a Steele, ain't you?'

Robbie, already in his jim-jams, leaned against the doorframe with arms crossed, trying to look tough even with his cowlick sticking up. 'Anyone gives you any trouble, Vi, you knock their block off with that right hook I showed you.' He punched the air with a small fist. 'Pow! Right in the hooter!'

'Nobody's knocking anyone's head off,' Jimmy said but couldn't help the small smile that tugged at the corners of his lips. He pressed a kiss to Violet's forehead. 'Night, princess.'

'Night, Daddy.'

He ushered Robbie to his own room, decorated with football posters, pride of joy going to a photo of this year's England World Cup Team. The boy scrambled into bed, pulling the covers up to his chin.

'Not too hot for all them blankets?' Jimmy asked, tucking him in anyway.

'S'fine,' Robbie mumbled, already settling in.

Jimmy clicked off the bedside lamp. The room fell into darkness, save for the thin strip of hallway light bleeding under the door. He was halfway out when Robbie's small voice stopped him.

'Dad?'

'Yeah, son?'

'Sometimes…sometimes I don't remember what Mum looked like.' The words tumbled out in a rush, like he'd been holding them in for ages. 'Her face gets all foggy in my head.'

Jimmy froze. The familiar pain knifed through him – quick and vicious. For a moment, he couldn't speak past the lump in his throat.

'Dad?' Robbie's voice sounded smaller; was he worried he'd said something wrong?

Jimmy moved back to the bed, lowering himself onto the edge. 'Listen to me, son. It ain't what a person looks like that sticks with you. It's what they were.' He rested his hand on Robbie's shoulder. 'Your mum, she was sunshine on your face after weeks of rain. She was the warm bit in the middle of a fresh loaf. She was the one who'd fight the whole bloody world for you lot and still have enough left to make everyone feel special.'

The silence stretched between them, comfortable now.

'You've got her in you,' Jimmy added softly. 'In how you look after your sister. How you notice things others don't. That's my Mini, that is. And you'll never forget that part of her, no matter what.'

'Okay,' Robbie whispered, sounding relieved.

'Night, son.'

'Night, Dad.'

Jimmy stepped into the hallway and pulled the door nearly closed, leaving just a crack the way Robbie liked it. He stood there for a moment, listening to the ordinary sounds of his household settling down for the night – Harry's soft snoring from the next room, pipes creaking, the distant hum of a late-night bus.

Family. The one thing no one could take from him. The one thing worth any price.

He tugged on his leather jacket, his mind shifting gears to the business waiting for him outside. The clock on the wall read half nine. Perfect timing.

Downstairs, he checked his reflection in the hall mirror. Jimmy Southpaw, feared Face of the East End, stared back at him. Gone was the tender father from upstairs, replaced by the hard-eyed gangland boss with a job to do.

He slipped out onto the terrace of his house on Molasses Quay, glancing both ways before heading down the steps towards the riverfront of Sugar Cane Wharf. The blackout had hit this part of the docks tonight, plunging everything into shadows except for the occasional emergency lamp that cast eerie pools of yellow light on the wet cobblestones.

Jimmy moved with purpose, staying in the shadows. The Thames lapped hungrily at the wharf's edge, its inky surface reflecting what little moonlight broke through the cloud cover.

He reached their meeting spot, a forgotten loading bay beneath a crumbling warehouse. A figure stood waiting in the darkness.

'Did he fall for it?' Jimmy called out softly.

The figure stepped forward into a faint splash of moonlight. Brother Bertie's unmistakable pork pie hat sat at its usual jaunty angle, his broad shoulders filling out his jacket despite the wound still healing in his side.

'Hook, line, and bloodfire sinker, mate.' Brother Bertie grinned, teeth flashing white in the darkness. 'Dash reckons I've come crawling back with my tail between my legs, the mug. Actually thinks I'd pick him over my own flesh and blood.'

Jimmy felt the tension in his shoulders ease for the first time in days. It had worked. Their plan was in motion.

Brother Bertie placed a canvas bag on a stack of pallets and rummaged inside, producing a bottle with a flourish. 'Thought the occasion called for something special.'

'Lord Have Mercy,' Jimmy breathed, recognising the infamous rum punch that had fuelled so many of their youthful adventures. 'Ain't touched that stuff in five years.'

'Then you're well overdue.'

Brother Bertie uncorked the bottle, took a deep swig, and passed it over. Jimmy accepted it with something close to reverence, then tilted it back. The fierce liquid scorched down his throat, punching him in the chest and leaving him spluttering.

'Bloody hell!' He coughed and spluttered and then wiped his mouth with the back of his hand. 'You still brew this poison in a fucking radiator or what?'

Brother Bertie's rich laugh echoed off the stone walls. 'Secret recipe, my friend.'

Jimmy recovered enough to take another, more cautious sip, then let out a satisfied grunt. 'Now we're talking,' he said, offering the bottle.

They settled onto crates facing the river, passing the bottle between them. For a while, they sat in companionable silence, two kings surveying their domain, the dark water, the sleeping cranes, the hulking warehouses that had shaped their lives.

'Remember?' Brother Bertie nodded towards a patch of muddy foreshore visible in the moonlight. 'We used to spar right there. Remember your fight with Terry "The Tank" Thompson?'

'Jesus.' Jimmy shuddered at the memory. 'Everyone thought he'd flatten me. Six straight knockouts, he'd had.'

'Terrifying bruiser,' Brother Bertie agreed. 'Built like a bloody brick shithouse.'

'I still see his ugly mug in my nightmares.' Jimmy chuckled. 'But we showed him, didn't we?'

'Fifth round. Beautiful left hook. His legs went all jelly-like before he hit the canvas.' Brother Bertie mimed wobbling knees with his hands. 'The punters nearly tore the roof off with their cheers.'

Brother Bertie stood suddenly, bouncing on the balls of his feet. 'Come on then.' He raised his fists in a classic boxing stance. 'Let's see if you've still got it, Southpaw.'

Jimmy cocked his head to the side and arched a brow. 'You having a laugh?'

'Dead serious, man.'

Jimmy's face split into a 'you're fucking on' grin. He shrugged off his jacket, squared up, and they circled each other, just like old times. Brother Bertie threw a slow jab that Jimmy easily slipped, countering with a light tap to the ribs.

'You telegraph that left,' Brother Bertie chided, dancing back. 'Always did.'

They moved together in the ancient rhythm, muscle memory taking over. Brother Bertie feinted, Jimmy bobbed, their shadows merging and separating on the wet stones.

Back to being brothers forged by fire and fists.

'Remember what I taught you?' Brother Bertie called.

'Float like a butterfly, sting like a—' Jimmy started.

'Bollocks to Ali's catchphrase,' Brother Bertie interrupted. 'What did I teach you?'

Jimmy grinned, throwing a combination that ended with his signature left hook. 'Bosh 'em so they'll be picking up their teeth in Dagenham.'

'That's my lad.'

They sparred for a few more minutes before exhaustion and the rum caught up with them and Brother Bertie groaned from the ache in his side where the stab wound was healing. Breathing heavily, they collapsed back onto their crates, sweat cooling on their brows despite the chilly night air.

As the quiet stretched between them, sitting shoulder to shoulder with the man he'd once trusted with his very life, Jimmy felt the bitterness of the past start to dissolve. Hadn't he punished Bertie and Sin enough? Five years of turning his back on them, of denying himself the only real friend he'd ever had.

And for what?

Because they'd fallen in love?

Brother Bertie's thoughts were racing down a similar path. He'd never meant to hurt Jimmy, never imagined that falling for Sin would destroy the bond that had defined his life. The weight of Jimmy's anger, of his cold silence over the years, had been a constant hurt Bertie lived with every day. He'd missed his best friend, missed the easy camaraderie, the fun and unshakable loyalty that had seen them through the ups and downs of life.

Jimmy's voice cut through the heavy silence, rough with emotion. 'I was a right twat, wasn't I? Acting like you'd stabbed me in the back when all you did was love my sister.'

Bertie swallowed hard, his eyes stinging. 'I never set out to hurt you, Jimmy. You have to know that. But Sin... she's my world. Her and Isaac.'

'I know.' Jimmy inhaled deeply. 'I was just so fucked off, so bloody proud. Thought I could punish you by pretending you didn't exist. But all I did was punish myself, didn't I? Missed out on years with my brother, with my sister and nephew.' He shook his head. 'Missed out on family.'

Bertie reached out, gripping Jimmy's shoulder with a force that spoke of their shared history, of a bond that had been battered but never truly broken. 'We're here now, aren't we? Brothers again, like we always should've been.'

The hurt and betrayal of the past seemed to melt away, replaced by a fierce determination to rebuild what had been lost, to be the family they were always meant to be.

Brother Bertie took another swig from the bottle. 'How you managing, for real? With the kids and all?'

Grief squeezed Jimmy like it always did. 'One day at a time. Violet's better now she's at Sin's school. Robbie's... well, he's ready to take on the world. And Harry's just Harry – more bloody energy than sense.'

'Must be tough without Mini.'

The words hung between them, honest and painful. Jimmy stared out at the river, his throat tight.

'Some days I wake up, and for a second, I forget she's gone,' he admitted quietly. 'Reach across the bed for her. Then it hits me all over again.' He rubbed his chest where the ache lived permanently now. 'Other days, I can't even remember the sound of her voice. Scares the shit out of me, that does.'

Brother Bertie nodded, understanding in his eyes. 'When my mum passed, Gertie told me something I never forgot. Said grief ain't about forgetting – it's about learning to carry what you lost inside you without breaking apart.'

Jimmy took the bottle, grateful for the burn that hid the tremor in his voice. 'Wise woman, your sister.'

'Wise pain in the arse, more like.'

They shared a small chuckle before Brother Bertie's face turned serious again.

'I nearly lost my head when I thought of losing Izzy the same way. Can't imagine how you do it, mate.'

'You just do, don't you? For them.' Jimmy nodded towards the direction of his house. 'Anyway, enough of this soppy bollocks. Tell me about Dash.'

Brother Bertie's expression hardened. 'The stupid wanker's given me bouncer duty at a house. Starting tomorrow night.'

'Where?'

After he gave him the address in Bloomsbury, Jimmy's face darkened with fury, the veins in his neck pumping harsh with blood. 'That bloody bastard! That's one of my properties! I gave him fifty grand to develop that place into luxury flats.'

'Well, I doubt that's what he's using it for,' Brother Bertie said grimly. 'When I was there, I saw chains bolted to a wall in the basement. Didn't like the look of that at all.'

'You think he's holding people there?' Jimmy's stomach twisted.

Brother Bertie shrugged, careful not to claim certainty. 'Might be. Might be just kinky bedroom shit for all I know. But with all the coke that was there, and the women's voices…' He let the implication hang.

'That could be where Hyacinth's girl disappeared to,' Jimmy added meaningfully. Brother Bertie had passed on to him what Gertie had told him about her friend's missing daughter.

'That's what we need to find out.' Brother Bertie's jaw tightened. 'I need to get inside, see what's really going on. He also wants me to tend door on a house in Bermondsey. If he's really doing what we suspect…' He trailed off, expression grim.

'Then we shut the fucker down.' Jimmy's voice was steel. 'No one uses my business for that filth. No one.'

Brother Bertie nodded. 'Just like old times, eh?'

'Better.' Jimmy's mouth curved into a wolfish grin. 'We're smarter now.'

They stood side by side, gazing out at the river that had witnessed so much of their lives. Their triumphs, their failures, their bond that neither time nor betrayal could fully break.

'Be careful, Brother B,' Jimmy said, surprising himself with the old nickname. 'Under all that groovy-man-dig-it shit, Dash is a very dangerous man.'

'So are we.'

They bumped fists like they used to back in the day. They were back to being brothers.

Bound by loyalty, not just blood.

# Chapter Thirty-Eight

The Bermondsey terraced house appeared ordinary enough, but Gertie Watson had learned that evil often wore respectable faces. Hyacinth stood beside her, maternal desperation etched in every line of her tired face.

Heart pounding with determination, Gertie declared, 'We knock on that door and we ask our questions direct.' Her voice carried the steel of conviction, though her palms had grown damp with nervous sweat. 'No point dancing around the truth when we need to find your girl.'

Clutching her worn handbag like a shield, Hyacinth nodded, her heart brimming with the hope she was too scared to show. 'You think they might know where my Araminta is?'

'The Lord works in mysterious ways, sister.' Gertie's sturdy frame moved purposely towards the peeling blue door. 'Perhaps He's led us here for good reason.'

The heavy wooden door swung open before they reached the front step.

A man emerged into the grey London afternoon.

Gertie Watson recognised him in stunned shock.

*Sweet Jesus, no. Not him. Not here.*

The last face she thought she'd encounter in London, or anywhere else on God's green earth.

Her body betrayed her instantly; violent tremors seized her limbs while ice-cold terror erupted across her skin. Every muscle turned to water. Her red, gold, and green head wrap loosened, threatening to slip from her suddenly unsteady head. The pavement seemed to shift beneath her feet.

Gasping for air, she felt her vision blur at the edges.

Salvation only came when Hyacinth's startled grip caught her elbow, preventing her complete collapse.

'Gertie!' Hyacinth gasped, alarm sharpening her Trinidadian accent. She pulled back, supporting her church sister's swaying form. 'What's wrong with you? You look like you've seen the Devil himself.'

*Because I have,* Gertie's mind screamed. *I have.*

They retreated quickly, Gertie's legs moving on pure instinct while her thoughts fractured into a thousand painful shards.

Dash stepped further into daylight, his flowing dark hair catching the weak sunlight like a fallen angel's halo. He remained completely oblivious to the two women frozen some distance away. His arrogant gaze swept the street; he possessed the confidence of a man who owned everything he surveyed. And crushed everything he didn't.

Dread clawed at Gertie's throat, making each breath a struggle. Her survival instincts screamed louder than her shock.

Her desperate strength gripping Hyacinth's wrist, she dragged her church sister into the narrow alley between two houses. Rough brick scraped her shoulder, the pain grounding her in the present moment.

*Hide. Must hide. Can't let him see me. Can't let him know I'm here.*

'Gertie, you're scaring me.' Hyacinth's whispered voice carried genuine fear as she pressed against the cold brick wall. 'Who is that man? Why are we hiding like criminals?'

Gertie struggled to control her panicked breathing, her mouth turning bone dry. Each word scraped her throat raw as shameful memories crashed over her like poison waves.

'That man is Jack Blacklock.' Old pain filled her voice. 'Dash, they called him in Jamaica. Evil walks upright in a tailored suit when it wears his face.' She pressed her palm against the rough brick, needing something solid to anchor her to reality. 'He's one of

Satan's own disciples. A serpent walking on two legs.'

Hyacinth felt ice sweeping through her. The way Gertie spoke his name, the horror in her friend's face, this man was dangerous beyond measure.

Backing further into the shadows, she clutched her handbag tighter than a lifeline. 'Dear Lord in Heaven.' The prayer escaped her lips in a strangled whisper. 'Is he… does he have something to do with missing girls? With my Araminta?'

Pain lanced through Gertie's chest as she fought back the images trying to surface. 'Pray to the Almighty that he doesn't,' she whispered, her voice breaking. 'Pray harder than you've ever prayed in your life.'

*Please God, not another girl. Not another innocent.*

Dash walked back inside, leaving Gertie's skin crawling with disgust and her stomach churning with a sickness she fought hard against.

The blue door remained open, a mouth waiting to swallow more victims.

Another figure emerged from the house's shadowed interior.

'No.' The word escaped Gertie's throat, a wounded animal's cry. Her legs nearly gave way completely as recognition struck, sending shockwaves through her disbelieving body.

'No! No! No!'

Her brother stepped into daylight, his trademark pork pie hat slightly askew. He glanced both ways down the street before following Dash's path, unaware that his sister's world was crumbling to dust in a nearby alley.

Choking on anguish, Gertie slumped deeper into the alley's shadows. 'Lord Jesus, no. Not my Bertram.' Tears streamed down her face, carving tracks through years of carefully constructed strength. 'Satan has claimed my precious brother. He's walking in the Devil's very shadow.'

Her world shattered into a thousand jagged pieces.

***

'I saw you last night.'

Gertie Watson sat rigid at her kitchen table, her black leather-bound Bible positioned beside her flat palm. The rich aroma of rice and peas simmered on the stove, mingling with the golden scent of macaroni pie browning in the oven. Domestic warmth filled every corner of the cramped boarding house kitchen, but her voice carried the chill of a funeral parlour.

*How do I tell him? How do I say the words?*

Brother Bertie paused in the doorway, confusion creasing his handsome features. His trademark pork pie hat cast shadows across his eyes. He stepped inside with careful movements, genuine bewilderment radiating from his posture.

'What you talking about, sister?'

She watched her beloved brother settle into the wooden chair opposite her, each movement twisting her stomach tighter. Removing his hat, he placed it on the rough table surface next to her sacred book. Two symbols of their divergent paths – his criminal world beside her spiritual salvation.

Gripping the Bible's worn leather cover until her fingers ached, she forced the words past her constricted throat. 'I saw you with Dash Blacklock.' The words wrenched out, broken, the edges sharp. 'What were you doing with that boy? You know he's no good, Bertram.'

Brother Bertie's skin took on an ashen-brown pallor. 'How could you have seen me? Where—'

Raw fury erupted from years of suppressed pain. Gertie's fist crashed onto the table, the force explosive. The Bible jumped. Brother Bertie's hat trembled. The sound bounced through her beloved kitchen with the finality of a judge's gavel.

Brother Bertie jerked backwards in his chair, genuine alarm flickering across his features. He'd never seen his sister display such volcanic rage. His hands instinctively gripped the chair arms, bracing against her unexpected violence.

She continued, in desperate urgency. 'I saw you last night. In that house in Bermondsey. Someone told us that girls are kept there. Bad things happen in that place.'

Brother Bertie rallied, his voice gaining strength as he leaned forward. 'You've got it all wrong. You don't understand—'

'One of my church sister's daughters has gone missing.' Gertie cut through his protests, her voice rising to a near shout. Her chest heaved with the effort of speaking these terrible truths. 'Was she in that house? Tell me the truth.'

Shaking his head, grave and solemn, Brother Bertie met her desperate gaze. 'There were no black girls there, Gertie. I swear on Isaac's life.'

Gertie's composure shattered completely. Hot tears spilled down her dark cheeks as decades of suppressed anguish finally broke free. Her sturdy shoulders shook, violent tremors, each sob tearing from her chest as physical pain.

'I have to help find that girl. The wickedness of men...' Her voice broke into jagged pieces, each word cutting her throat raw. 'You don't know what happened to me—'

'Gertie, listen—'

'Have you never thought how I got the money to buy this house?' The confession poured from her broken soul. 'Where a single woman like me found that kind of cash?'

Brother Bertie fell silent, his body going completely still. Something in her tone warned him that sacred ground was being crossed. His beloved sister needed to speak her truth after all these years of suffocating silence.

Gertie's fingertip caressed the worn leather of her Bible; she sought comfort from its familiar texture.

Her breathing came in shallow gasps as she fought to form the words.

Voice barely above a whisper, she began, 'I was Rufus Blacklock's secret girlfriend. Some would call it being his mistress, but that sounds too fancy for the arrangement it was.' Her gaze flicked fearfully up to check Brother Bertie's reaction, then dropped because she couldn't bear to see disgust replace love in his eyes. 'I was young, desperate. He was an older man with money. All I could think about was how that money would help our life, help my beautiful brother.'

Brother Bertie's jaw ticked. Jesus Christ, he had no idea how he was managing to hold it down. His hands slowly knotted into fists on the table.

Her face crumpled with remembered pain as she continued, 'I liked him at first. He was fun, taught me how to gamble and play cards.' Each word felt dragged from a festering wound. 'Then it wasn't fun no more.'

She swallowed hard, the bitter disgust of shame coating her throat. What she was about to reveal had haunted her for decades, poisoning every quiet moment.

Gertie forced herself to say: 'Rufus came to me one day and said his son was coming home from school in England. Said the boy was getting to be a man and needed to learn how to be one.' Her hands shook violently, the tremors spreading up her arms. 'Said it was about time Jack lost his virginity, and he couldn't think of a better person to do it.'

Suddenly, Brother Bertie's harsh breathing was audible in the room, red-blazing rage building behind his controlled façade. A vein pulsed in his temple.

*Sweet Lord, give me strength to say this.*

Straightening her spine in remembered defiance, her voice gained strength. 'I was outraged. Refused point blank to do it.' Pride and pain warred in her expression. 'That's when Rufus told me I would have to leave. How could I leave? Where would our money come from? We had nothing, Bertram. Absolutely nothing.'

The kitchen fell silent except for the gentle bubbling of rice and peas. Brother Bertie's breathing had turned shallow and dangerous, his chest rising and falling, barely contained fury held in check.

Voice breaking with self-loathing, she whispered, 'So when that boy came home from England, I did it.' The confession tore from her throat, each word a piece of her soul being ripped away. 'He was a nasty, entitled boy. Pinching and biting like I was his personal plaything.'

Brother Bertie's chair scraped backwards violently. He shot to his feet, pure volcanic fury erupting from every muscle. His powerful frame trembled, the effort of containing his rage becoming too much.

'Raasclat!' The ripe Jamaican curse exploded from him, carrying years of suppressed vengeance.

She gathered courage from his protective fury. Her eyes hardened, remembered fire blazing within them. 'A few days later, he tried to touch me again. Thought I was his personal dessert whenever he fancied a taste.' Her voice turned lethal. 'I gave that boy a mighty box around the ears. Told him that was a one-time occurrence. If he ever touched me again, I'd come for him in the night. Not him – his man thing. Chop it off and stuff it in his entitled mouth.'

Voice rising to a cry of despair that seemed to tear from her very soul, she continued, 'That's when I knew I never meant anything to Rufus. That I was less than human to him. Just a thing to be used.' Tears streamed down her face unchecked. 'I am so ashamed, Bertram. So bloody ashamed.'

She braced herself for his revulsion, his disappointment, his inevitable withdrawal from her contaminated presence.

Instead, her brother's voice came soft and certain, cutting through her self-hatred, gently precise.

'I knew.'

Gertie's world shifted. 'What?'

He moved around the table, nearer to his sister. 'I found out what happened. I heard Dash bragging about it years later, before we planned a job together in Kingston.' His hands trembled; suppressed violence. 'I wanted to kill him, right there, on the ground he stood on, with my bare hands. Instead, I set him up for the police.'

*He knew. All this time, he knew, and he never looked at me with disgust.*

He gathered his beloved sister in his powerful arms, her smaller frame folding into his protective embrace. For once, she wasn't the pillar of strength, she was the one receiving the love she'd given so freely to him over the years.

'I love you, my brave sister. What happened wasn't your fault. You did what you had to do because we were poor and desperate. A man with money took advantage of your situation.'

He held her tighter, his powerful arms forming a fortress around her broken heart. 'You don't worry about Dash Blacklock anymore. That bastard is going to get exactly what's coming to him.'

# Chapter Thirty-Nine

The manila folder slipped from Chrissie's fingers, scattering papers across the threadbare carpet of Mini's Place reception area.

'Bugger it,' she muttered, dropping to her knees to gather them up. Her wrists, still pink with healing scars, protested at the movement.

She was still lodging in Edmund's warehouse flat. It had given Chrissie something she'd never expected. Peace. She'd grown fond of their evenings together, on the balcony, Edmund reading some book written in German, while she devoured Jackie Collins's *The Bitch*, pretending not to notice how his eyes occasionally drifted her way. At night, she'd lie awake listening to his gentle snoring from downstairs, finding unexpected comfort in the sound. It made her feel safe. What a soppy mare she was turning into.

The heavy front door banged open, bringing with it a gust of icy wind and a soaking-wet bloke in a mackintosh.

'Morning, Chrissie,' he called, shaking water from his coat. 'Lucas and Edmund about?'

She recognised Ben Gausky, the *Tribune* reporter who'd broken the Harrington story that was still sending shockwaves through London.

Chrissie jutted her chin towards the back offices. 'Through there, if they'll let you in.'

Lucas emerged, Edmund appearing moments later, wire-rimmed glasses perched on his nose, cardigan buttoned wrong. Chrissie's fingers twitched with the urge to walk over and straighten it. That man needed looking after.

Warmth flooded Edmund's tired eyes when he spotted the journalist. 'Ben, good to see you. Come through to the office.'

Chrissie hesitated, uncertain if she was included.

Edmund paused, turning back to her. 'Coming?'

She blinked, genuine surprise registering on her face. A girl who'd left school at fourteen being invited into important conversations? Four weeks ago, she'd been ready to bleed herself dry on riverside steps. Now she was being treated like she had something worth contributing.

The office smelled of tobacco and cheap aftershave. Lucas settled behind his desk, his massive frame making the chair beneath him groan in protest. Edmund perched on a wooden stool, while Chrissie leaned against the filing cabinet.

Ben pulled a manila envelope from his satchel, his eyes grave beneath his shaggy fringe. 'These are stills from the film that led to Harrington's downfall.'

He spread black-and-white photographs across the desk. Chrissie moved closer, peering over Lucas's broad shoulder.

The images ripped the air from her lungs.

A young black woman, barely out of her teens, lying motionless on expensive sheets. And looming over her, a distinguished, silver-haired older man.

Oliver Harrington, MP.

The same sadistic monster who had brutalised her.

That face…

Her features twisted violently, acid bile burning her throat. Blood roared in her ears.

*Oh my God, He's got me again.*

*Trapped.*

*Helpless.*

*No, he ain't. You're here, amongst friends.*

*Inhale. Breathe. Calm your beating heart.*

*That's right, girl. You ain't that scared little bird anymore. You're a woman now.*

Chrissie straightened up, chin lifting with renewed purpose. Time this evil monster got his comeuppance.

Lucas's broad shoulders tensed, a muscle twitching in his jaw. 'Christ.'

Edmund pulled a different photograph from his desk drawer. A young woman, smiling, dressed to the nines in her Sunday best. 'The woman is Hyacinth Marshall's daughter.'

He placed it next to the stills. The same face, transformed from joyful innocence to vacant stillness.

'Araminta,' Lucas confirmed grimly.

'I know Gertie. Hyacinth's friend,' Chrissie told them. 'Her brother is married to my niece.'

Ben's gaze flashed with heat. 'There've been rumours about nasty parties in a house in Belgravia. Important men, young women brought in for entertainment. Some of them forced. This must have been one of them.'

A heavy silence fell over the cramped office. Lucas shuffled the photos back into their envelope, his massive hands surprisingly gentle.

'We have to tell Hyacinth,' Edmund said, removing his glasses to pinch the bridge of his nose.

Lucas nodded, his large frame tense with controlled fury. 'I'll call Gertie. Ask her to bring Hyacinth in.'

'Wait,' Edmund interjected, placing his glasses back on with care. 'This needs to be handled delicately. It's not just what we tell her, but how,' he insisted, his normally gentle voice firm and full of conviction. 'This news will destroy her world. We need someone who can…'

His voice trailed off, but his eyes drifted towards Chrissie.

Lucas followed his gaze, massive arms folded across his chest. 'Need a woman there. Someone who understands…'

Chrissie suddenly realised what was not being said. 'Me? You want me to be there?'

Edmund's eyes softened behind his wire-rimmed glasses. 'Sometimes it takes someone who's walked through darkness to guide others through it.'

Chrissie's first instinct was to run. What did she know about comforting mothers?

But the image of that poor dead girl. What that evil man had done to her, too.

'I'll do it,' she heard herself say.

Edmund leaned forward, concern etched across his gentle features. 'Are you sure? This could trigger your own trauma.'

Chrissie squared her shoulders, lifting her chin, stubborn determination coming to the fore. 'That's exactly why I need to do this. I understand. I know what it's like to be hurt by men who think they're untouchable.'

And she wasn't only thinking of that bastard Harrington. She was thinking about her brother too.

***

Hyacinth and Gertie sat in the small counselling room at Mini's Place. The hope in Hyacinth's eyes skewered a knife in Chrissie's gut. That hope was about to be extinguished forever.

Hyacinth's fingers knotted together anxiously in her lap. 'You've found my Araminta?'

Edmund glanced at Chrissie, giving her the smallest nod. She reached out, taking Hyacinth's warm hands in her cold ones. 'Hyacinth, I'm so sorry. We have news about Araminta, but it's not what you've been hoping for.'

Gertie stiffened. 'What you saying, girl?'

'We have evidence that Araminta was at a private party about three weeks ago,' Chrissie continued, her voice gentle but direct. 'A party where very powerful men were present.'

Hyacinth's fingers tightened around Chrissie's, her eyes widening, mounting dread in their depths. 'My girl wouldn't go to such things. She's a good Christian girl.'

'She was probably forced there,' Chrissie explained, maintaining steady eye contact despite the pain reflected back at her. 'These men, they lie. They promise jobs, opportunities. They don't tell you what they really want until it's too late.'

Understanding dawned in Gertie's eyes. She placed a protective arm around Hyacinth's shoulders.

Chrissie took a deep breath, the heaviness of what she had to say pressing on her chest. 'At this party, something terrible happened…'

Without faltering, she told this grieving mother what had happened to her daughter.

The scream that tore from Hyacinth's throat would haunt Chrissie for years to come. Primal, maternal agony that no words could soothe. Hyacinth pitched forward, her body convulsing with grief so violent it seemed it might tear her apart.

Gertie tried to hold her, but Hyacinth was beyond comfort. She slid from her chair to the floor, keening, rocking, her arms wrapped around her middle as if physically holding herself together.

Chrissie knelt beside her on the floor, saying nothing. No empty platitudes. No useless reassurances. She simply placed a hand on Hyacinth's back, offering the only thing that mattered – presence in the unbearable moment.

Minutes passed. Hyacinth's raw screams eventually softened to whimpering sobs. Chrissie remained beside her, hand steadily moving in circles on her back.

When Hyacinth finally looked up, her eyes were vacant with shock, her voice hoarse from screaming. 'Where is she? I need to bury my child.'

Hyacinth's eyes darted wildly between them, her breath coming in short, desperate gasps. 'My baby girl. Where is she? I need to see her. Take her home.'

'Hyacinth,' Chrissie said gently, her hand never leaving the woman's trembling shoulder, 'I need to tell you something else. Something hard to hear.'

Hyacinth stared at her, already shattered but somehow bracing for more.

'They… they might never find Araminta's body.' Chrissie forced herself to maintain eye contact.

'These people, they know how to make bodies disappear.'

A fresh wail tore from Hyacinth's throat, her hands clawing at her own chest. 'No proper burial? No resting place? She needs to be with the Lord!'

'I know,' Chrissie said softly, her own voice threatening to break. 'For a Christian woman, I know what that means.'

Gertie murmured prayers, rocking with Hyacinth.

'When I was fifteen, a man hurt me, too.' Her disclosure was steady despite the thunder of her pulse. 'He was with men who thought they were above the law. Men who thought they could break me and walk away.'

Edmund's eyes widened slightly. He'd never heard Chrissie speak so openly about her past.

'For years, I let them win.' Chrissie's hands curled into fists. 'I let the hurt eat me from inside until there was almost nothing left. Then I grew strong. The men who hurt us think we'll stay broken. But we don't have to. Your Araminta can't come back. That pain won't ever leave you. But you can make sure she matters. You can make sure she's not forgotten.'

'How?' Hyacinth whispered, the single word heavy with grief.

'By not letting them bury what happened,' Chrissie replied, fierce determination burning in her eyes. 'By telling her story. By making sure other girls don't fall into the same trap.'

Eventually, Gertie helped Hyacinth to her feet. 'I'll take her home with me tonight. She shouldn't be alone.'

As Gertie guided Hyacinth towards the door, the older woman paused, turning back to Chrissie, her eyes red-rimmed.

'Thank you,' she said simply. 'You understood.'

After they left, silence filled the counselling room. Edmund handed Chrissie a cup of tea, his fingers briefly brushing hers.

'That was remarkable,' he said quietly, eyes studying her, seeing past the survivor to the extraordinary woman beneath.

Lucas nodded in agreement. 'Never seen anyone handle a situation like that better. Not even the professional grief counsellors we've brought in.'

Chrissie stared into her teacup, suddenly drained. 'I just did what I wished someone had done for me.'

Lucas cleared his throat, straightening in his chair. 'We could use someone like you here, Chrissie.' Abruptly, he stopped and restarted. 'No, that's all wrong because there is no one like you. Chrissie you are unique. We'd like you to work here on a permanent basis. I mean. If you wanted.'

She looked up, stunned disbelief widening her eyes. 'What, like a proper job?'

'We can't pay much,' Lucas admitted, rubbing his broad hand across the back of his neck. 'But there's a small stipend for counsellors. And you've got a gift, whether you realise it or not.'

A job. Purpose. A reason to get up in the morning that didn't involve running from her own demons.

'I'd like that,' Chrissie agreed with conviction. 'I want to help other women.'

Edmund's smile carried a warmth that sent an unfamiliar flutter through Chrissie's chest.

Maybe she wasn't just Chrissie Steele, Danny's broken sister, after all.

# Chapter Forty

Danny's key slid into his mistress's flat's lock, feverish anticipation coursing through him as he thought about claiming Scarlett's sexy-as-shit body. Thinking about groping those plump titties of hers stirred his blood.

'Scarlett?' His voice bounced off cream walls. 'You hiding from me, sweet puff?'

Nothing.

The silence felt wrong.

Probably having a bath. The bird loved her long soaks in that ridiculous marble tub, surrounded by enough French bubbles to drown a small army.

But the bathroom stood empty. Danny's gut churned. Where the fuck was she?

The bedroom told a different story. Wardrobe doors hung open, revealing bare hangers swaying in accusatory motion. Her dressing table – usually cluttered with diamond earrings and designer makeup – showed only faint outlines in the dust where her treasures once sat.

Danny's mind struggled to process the evidence. She'd cleared out completely. Every silk dress, every lace nightie, every designer shoe worth more than most people's monthly wage – gone.

*She's done a runner.*

The thought hit him with dull surprise rather than panic. Made sense, really. The police raid had spooked her, poor little thing. Probably panicked when she saw those coppers swarming the place, decided to lay low until the heat died down.

Smart girl. He'd always said she had more brains than most people gave her credit for.

His foot kicked against something as he turned towards the door. Papers scattered and fanned out across the bedspread.

His private business calendar.

Danny's blood turned sluggish in his veins. That calendar lived in his office safe, locked away from prying eyes behind six inches of reinforced steel. How the bloody hell had it ended up here?

He picked up the leather-bound book, his fingers nerveless. Red ink circled specific dates in handwriting he recognised – Scarlett's distinctive loops and curves.

*Tuesday 14: Harrington meeting, 8 p.m.*

*Friday 17: Film collection review, midnight.*

*Monday 2: Bank transfer authorisation, 3 p.m.*

Every secret appointment. Every clandestine deal. Every blackmail exchange.

Danny's mouth went dry. The meetings with Harrington weren't common knowledge – only three people knew those details. Himself, Harrington, and…

*How did she get this?*

His hands trembled. She couldn't have…could she? The bird barely understood half the words that came out of his mouth during business discussions. Always asking him to explain things twice, those big innocent eyes wide, showing her confusion.

But there it was, spread across the bed in her own handwriting. Not just the meetings – the locations, the times, even notes about which films to bring for the blackmail sessions.

*No. She's not clever enough for this.*

Danny shook his head violently. He was seeing conspiracies where none existed. The calendar must have fallen out of his briefcase, and she'd picked it up, maybe tried to help by organising his schedule. Scarlett was many things, but criminal mastermind wasn't one of them.

The bank transfer date circled in red ink made his stomach lurch. But that was just coincidence. She'd been grateful when he'd made her a silent partner, confused by all the legal jargon. He remembered explaining everything twice while she'd nodded, trusting, bewildered.

*Check the accounts. Make sure everything's normal. Prove yourself wrong.*

Danny shoved the calendar into his inside pocket and rushed from the flat, tearing towards his car, wild panic fuelling every step.

***

'Mr Gleeson will see you now, Councillor Steele,' the receptionist's cut-glass accent informed Danny inside the Anglo-Merchant Bank.

Gleeson's office occupied the top floor, windows offering a commanding view of St Paul's.

'Councillor Steele!' Gleeson rose from behind his antique desk, thin face arranged in professional welcome. 'How may we assist you?'

Danny settled into the leather chair, his bulk dwarfing the furniture. 'Need to check my accounts, Gleeson. All of them. Immediately.'

The bank manager pulled a thick ledger from his desk drawer, which he opened. His pale fingers traced columns of figures while Danny watched, his anxiety growing.

'I'm afraid there's been some significant activity, Councillor.' The words carried careful neutrality. 'Your business partner, Miss Fox, has been quite active recently.'

*Business partner?*

His powerful hands gripped the chair's arms while his mind reeled.

'What's she been up to?' His voice sounded strange in his own ears.

'Substantial withdrawals, sir. Legal transfers, properly authorised and documented.' Gleeson reached into a filing cabinet, nervous. 'Miss Fox has been exercising her partnership rights rather extensively.'

He placed a manila folder on the desk between them. Danny stared at it like it might explode.

'How much?' The words scraped his throat raw.

'I'm afraid she's withdrawn virtually everything. The accounts have been systematically emptied over the past month.'

Danny's world tilted. His criminal empire, built through decades of violence and intimidation, drained dry by a woman he'd trusted with his bed and his business.

'Show me.' Danny's voice dropped to a dangerous whisper.

Gleeson shared the opened the folder with him. Document after document spread across the polished desk surface. Bank transfer forms, withdrawal authorisations, partnership agreements – all bearing Danny's own signature.

Danny leaned forward, studying the papers, his horror growing. His handwriting on every page, witnessed and legally notarised. But seeing them laid out together, the pattern became undeniable.

'This one here,' Gleeson pointed to a withdrawal form dated three weeks earlier, 'authorised the transfer of fifty thousand pounds.' His finger moved to another document. 'Then this one, dated five days later, another thirty thousand.'

Danny's hands shook as he picked up the papers. Each signature perfectly legal, each authorisation properly executed. He remembered signing every single one – Scarlett bringing them to him, her breathless explanations about protecting their assets, her confused questions about legal terminology while she positioned the pen in his fingers.

'And this final authorisation,' Gleeson's voice carried professional sympathy, 'executed just two days ago. The remaining balance of approximately two hundred thousand pounds.'

The documents told their own story. Months of patient manipulation, pillow talk designed to position papers in front of him while his attention focused on her silk-clad, lithe body. Every signature obtained through careful seduction, every authorisation secured through trust he'd given freely.

Danny's fury erupted without warning. His fist slammed onto the antique desk, sending papers cascading to the floor and an ornate inkwell exploding into crystal fragments.

'That scheming whore!' His roar echoed off mahogany panelling while Gleeson scrambled backwards with terror-filled eyes.

The thieving bitch had played him from the very beginning. The devoted mistress, the grateful partner, the confused innocent asking helpful questions about his business – all performance designed to systematically drain his accounts.

While he'd been congratulating himself on his sexual conquests, she'd been stealing his entire fortune using the patient skill of a master thief.

Every disaster that had befallen him in the past week suddenly made perfect sense. The blackmail film that destroyed Harrington. The police raid that exposed his monitoring room. All orchestrated by the woman who'd shared his bed and whispered sweet lies in his ear.

Danny straightened his tie, portraying deliberate control, smoothed his silver hair, and fixed the cowering bank manager with a smile that promised bloody retribution.

But beneath his forced calm, one thought burned, a brutal rage was building, dangerous as dynamite with a lit fuse.

That backstabbing, light-fingered, two-faced cunty-floozy had no idea who she'd started a war with.

The first thing he needed to do was hunt her down. She was going to pay for every penny She'd stolen, and the interest would be measured in blood.

# Chapter Forty-One

Rage, thick and venomous, pumped through Danny's veins the moment he spotted her flame-red hair through the gleaming glass of the Starlight Lounge located in a hotel in Mayfair. He'd been hunting her for a couple of days, and finally word had reached him where she was holed up.

The thieving slag was holding court at the Art Deco bar, playing the perfect rich bitch while his world collapsed around him.

*With my fucking cash!*

The hotel lobby was all polished mahogany, crystal chandeliers, and toffee-nosed punters who'd never set foot east of Aldgate. Danny pushed past a gaggle of foreign businessmen, his fists bunched tight. She'd picked her stage well, the crafty cow. Public, respectable, crawling with witnesses who'd remember the distinguished silver-haired gentleman losing his bollocks at the sparkling cocktail bar.

Scarlett Fox sat perched on a velvet barstool, legs crossed, cigarette holder balanced between fingers. The vision of her stopped Danny dead in his tracks. Gone was his chirping dollybird. This woman wore power the way other birds wore perfume, thick, intoxicating, dangerous. Her emerald-green silk dress clung to every curve, the fabric catching the light from the geometric mirrors that lined the back wall of the bar. Gems glittered at her throat, wrists, ears. Real rocks, not the fake shit he'd bought her for show.

Two mountains of muscle flanked her. Professional bruisers, the kind of hard-faced cunts who'd snap necks without spilling their drinks.

'Danny Steele. The great King of Sleaze, reduced to hunting down birds in hotel bars,' Scarlett purred, not bothering to turn round.

How the fuck had she clocked him? The mirrors – of course. Must've been watching him stalking towards her in the polished glass behind the bar.

'Keep your bloody voice down,' Danny hissed, glancing round at the other punters. 'Maybe we can have a private word?'

'Private?' She gestured to her silent guardians. 'I don't think so. These days I prefer witnesses when dealing with dangerous men.'

'Cut the poxy drama,' he snarled and stepped closer. 'You've robbed me blind, you manky slag.

Cleaned out my accounts, nicked my properties. I want it back. All of it.'

Both bodyguards moved closer instantly, hands reaching inside their jackets. Scarlett raised one manicured hand without even glancing at them. They froze mid-motion, disciplined as trained attack dogs.

Her green eyes glittered, malicious amusement in them. 'Rob you? Oh, Danny, you always were prone to over-the-top exaggerations. I simply collected what was rightfully mine.' Then she added insult to injury by saying, 'I left you twenty quid. Very generous of me because I could've left your mouth writing cheques that your arse couldn't cash.'

Danny nearly went for her. 'I gave you everything! Set you up proper, treated you better than Princess Margaret!'

'Treated me?' Her lips rippled with disgust. 'You used me, Danny. The way you use everyone.'

'I don't know what garbage you've been fed, but I treated you better than any bird I've ever known.'

Scarlett raised her champagne glass in a mocking toast. 'Most of the money goes to Mini's Place. Seems fitting, don't you think? Your ill-gotten gains helping the kind of women you've spent your life using.'

'You can't do this,' Danny gritted out in desperation, tottering on the edge of defeat.

'I already have.' She stubbed out her cigarette with a twist of her fingers. 'And there's nothing you can do to stop me. Nothing at all.'

One of her brutes took a menacing step forward. Time to go. Danny's legs felt unsteady as he pushed back from the bar. The great Danny Steele, reduced to begging scraps from a bird who'd played him for the biggest fool in London.

'Word to the wise, *dead girl,* this isn't over.' Cursing a blue streak beneath his breath, he stomped off towards the revolving doors and out on to the street.

Scarlett's laugh followed him towards the lobby. Rich, triumphant, utterly without mercy.

'Oh yes it is, Danny. It's been over for longer than you know.'

A few moments later, a figure rose from an elegant leather chair on the other side of the room and walked over to Scarlett. This person had been observing the nasty encounter.

'You did good,' they praised her.

Scarlett knocked back another glass of fizz. 'How much longer?'

The newcomer smiled. 'Not much longer now.'

# Chapter Forty-Two

The sounds of high-pitched moans and pounding flesh echoed through the thin walls of the Bermondsey knocking shop. The Sweet's 'Ballroom Blitz' blared from speakers, barely masking the mock groans of female pleasure.

Brother Bertie stood by the reception desk, face carved from stone. Five days he'd been working security in this dump, playing the heavy for Dash's operation. Five bloody days watching punters come in with hungry eyes and leave with that satisfied swagger. Every minute here twisted his guts into knots, but he had a job to do. Get evidence. Find proof of what Dash was really running.

'What you after tonight, handsome?' Pammy preened and leaned towards the businessman, her bosoms threatening to spill from her low-cut leopard-print top. Her face was a proper work of art. Three layers of foundation caked into the deep lines around her mouth, false eyelashes thick as spider legs, and lips painted blood-red. Sixty if she was a day but dressed like a twenty-year-old on the pull.

The man remembered his wedding ring and yanked it off into his pocket. He nervously coughed, before asking, 'Heard you got specialities.'

Pammy's crimson lips split into a grin that didn't reach her cold eyes. ''Course we do, love. Whatever tickles your fancy.' She lowered her voice, though not enough that Brother Bertie couldn't hear. 'Got girls who'll let you play rough, if that's your game. Chains, whips, the whole bloody circus. Got some foreign birds, too – proper exotic.'

The businessman licked his lips. 'Rough?'

Brother Bertie's jaw tightened; he resisted the urge to smash the fucker's face in. But he couldn't blow his cover. Not when they were so close.

'No permanent marks.' Pammy winked. 'But they'll take whatever you dish out.'

She slid a dog-eared menu across the desk. 'Price list. Premium services on the second page.'

Brother Bertie maintained his thousand-yard stare, bile rising in his throat. The thought of Dash running this meat market boiled his blood. After what that animal did to Gertie in Jamaica and now trafficking women through properties that Jimmy had invested in… The bastard would pay.

'I'll take the domination package.' The businessman slid over a wad of notes. 'And the East Asian girl.'

'Third floor, end of the hall.' Pammy pocketed the cash without counting. 'Suki's waiting, all leather and chains. Don't mark her face, mind. That's her fortune.'

The businessman scurried upstairs, stinking of anticipation and Brut aftershave.

'Need a piss,' Brother Bertie announced, seizing his chance.

Pammy waved a dismissive hand. 'Don't be long. Rush hour starts in twenty minutes. City boys will be piling in soon.'

Brother Bertie nodded and moved down the hallway. The toilet was in the basement, past rooms where grunts and theatrical cries leaked through paper-thin walls. The narrow stairwell stank of cheap perfume and disinfectant.

Halfway down, Brother Bertie paused. There – in the wall. A seam that shouldn't exist. He ran thick fingers over the surface, felt it give slightly. He glanced back up the stairs. Empty.

Brother Bertie pushed. A hidden door swung inwards, revealing darkness beyond. Jimmy's suspicions had been right. There was more to this operation than just a knocking shop.

He slipped through, easing the door shut behind him. He found himself on another staircase, this one leading to the basement of the neighbouring house.

The sounds here raised the hairs on his neck. No fake moans, no tacky music. Just whimpers and muffled pleas.

Brother Bertie descended, keeping to the shadows. The basement opened into a stark, brightly lit room with concrete floors and drains. Four men in surgical masks moved between metal-framed beds. On each bed lay a woman. Young. Terrified. One thrashed against restraints while a masked man held a syringe. Others lay motionless, eyes vacant, doped to the eyeballs.

Brother Bertie ducked behind a stack of wooden crates, pulse thundering in his ears. His mouth filled with sour saliva, stomach churning like a cement mixer. Cold sweat broke out across his forehead, dripping down his temple. His muscles coiled tight, every fibre screaming at him to charge in, to rip these bastards limb from bloody limb.

'Fresh batch. Need them ready for distribution by Friday. The brass house in Belgravia has been shut down, so the West Indian one goes to a house of correction in Chelsea.'

Brother Bertie's gaze locked on a dark-skinned girl, no more than eighteen. His breath caught. Could it be Araminta, Hyacinth's missing daughter? Then she turned her head, and he saw it wasn't her. But someone's daughter all the same.

One of the masked men bent over a naked woman, jabbing a needle into her arm. 'This one's fighting the dose. Wants to be difficult.'

'Give her more. But don't turn her into a zombie. Dash wants them broken, not vegetables.'

Brother Bertie bit down on his tongue until he tasted blood. His fingernails dug crescents into his palms. These scum. These fucking cockroaches. The savage urge to wade in, fists flying, knife slashing, filled his chest with burning fury. He could take all four of them. Snap their necks like twigs.

But the rational part of his brain, the part that had planned this with Jimmy, held him back. Charging in now would save no one. These girls would still be captives, and Dash would remain free, trafficking more victims through his evil human pipeline.

The door at the far end opened. Brother Bertie pressed deeper into the shadows, swallowing the acid that rose in his throat. Wrighty entered, clipboard in hand.

'Inventory,' Wrighty announced, moving between the beds. 'Got clients waiting in Mayfair, South Ken, and Chelsea. Need four processed tonight.'

'Quality control takes time. These cunts need to learn who's boss before they go to the clients.'

One of the girls sobbed. 'Please… I want to go home.'

She was viciously backhanded. 'Shut it or I'll give you to the boys for practice.'

Bastard!

Brother Bertie's vision washed red. An avenging savagery uncaged itself in him, turning his breathing ragged and dangerous. His hand moved to the knife at his belt before he stopped himself. Every muscle tensed as he fought for control and, with superhuman effort, he pulled back from storming in there.

*Just walk away, Bertie. For Jimmy. For the plan.*

But his soul was screaming. These were somebody's daughters, somebody's sisters. Any other day, he'd have booted that door down without a second thought, and shown those evil fuckers some street justice. Now he was trapped between his protective instincts and cold strategy, and it was killing him inside.

He slipped back up the stairs and through the hidden door. In the brothel stairwell, he paused, dragging air into his lungs, the stench of disinfectant now a relief compared to the horror he'd witnessed.

He wiped sweat from his face with hands still itching to batter every last one of those men until they didn't exist. His shirt clung to him, soaked through.

He straightened his jacket and climbed back to reception. Pammy glanced up from her magazine, fixing him with a long stare.

'Long piss,' she remarked.

'Tummy trouble,' Brother Bertie grunted, resuming his position by the door.

Careful to not let it show, he was still shaking inside, consumed by both horror and rage. This wasn't just about bringing down a criminal anymore. This was about stopping a monster.

Dash would pay. For Gertie. For every girl on those beds. Brother Bertie would see to that personally. And when he got his hands on that flash bastard, God help him, because Bertram Watson wouldn't.

# Chapter Forty-Three

Brother Bertie slammed his fist down on Jimmy's desk, rattling the whisky glasses. 'You don't understand what I saw in that place. It's not just a knocking shop. It's a bloody abattoir.'

Jimmy Steele sat behind his massive oak desk in the back office of 'Odds On', his betting shop headquarters on Commercial Road.

'Tell me again.' His request was dangerously quiet. 'Every detail.'

'They're processing women like fucking cattle. Drug them up, break them down, then distribute them to brothels across London. Dash has got a production line going. Industrial scale. I counted twelve girls in that basement, but God knows how many more come through.' Brother Bertie paced the office, unable to stay still, the fury burning through his veins. 'These girls… they're scared out of their minds. Drugged to the eyeballs.'

Jimmy's silver-grey eyes hardened to steel. 'And you're sure Dash is running this?'

'Heard his name clear as day. Christ, Jimmy, it's sickening.' Brother Bertie swallowed hard, the memory of those women's vacant eyes twisting his guts. 'And all through properties you invested in.'

Jimmy hurled his whisky glass across the room, shattering it against the wall. 'That lying, scheming cunt! He told me luxury flats. Cash-in-hand tenants who needed discretion. I'd never have touched it if I'd known.'

'I know that.' Brother Bertie dropped into the chair opposite Jimmy. He hesitated, steeling himself for Jimmy's reaction. 'We need to go to the Bill.'

Jimmy's head snapped up, eyes blazing. 'You gone soft in the head?'

'It's trafficking, Jimmy. These girls need help.'

'And when did going to the filth ever solve anything in the East End?' Jimmy growled. 'Besides, half the bent coppers in Soho are probably on Dash's payroll. They're more crooked than a dog's hind leg.'

'Then what do we do?'

Jimmy pulled open his desk drawer, withdrew a document, and pushed it towards Brother Bertie. 'Take a gander at this. Property deeds for the Bermondsey house.'

Brother Bertie flipped to the last page, scanning the signatures. His blood froze. 'Your signature. On every fucking page.'

'That crafty cunt got me to sign my name all over the properties we invested in together,' Jimmy snarled. 'His name? Nowhere. He signed for some company abroad somewhere. If this goes tits up, I'm the one they'll nail to the cross.'

'Fuck the paperwork!' Brother Bertie exploded, surging to his feet. 'There are women being drugged and raped in that basement right now. I don't give a monkey's if you end up in chokey. We have to do something.'

The words hung between them, a line crossed. Brother Bertie had never spoken to Jimmy like that, not even in their worst rows.

Jimmy's eyes narrowed. 'Careful, Bertie.'

'No, you be careful.' Brother Bertie leaned over the desk, palms flat on the wood. 'I saw what they're doing. It's playing on repeat in my head. Girls chained to beds, screaming while they're jabbed with needles in their arms. And one of them…' His voice caught. 'One of them could've been Gertie all those years ago. Could've been Sin.'

Jimmy's expression flickered at the mention of his sister.

'You wanted evidence,' Brother Bertie continued. 'I've given it to you. Now what are you going to do about it?'

The muscles in Jimmy's jaw worked overtime. 'Let me think on it.'

Brother Bertie straightened up, disgust written across his face. 'While you're thinking, more girls are being tortured.'

He turned and stalked out, slamming the door behind him.

Jimmy sat alone in the flickering candlelight, the impact of Brother Bertie's words pressing down on him. The thought of his properties being used for trafficking made his skin crawl. But there was more at stake than Bertie knew. Much more.

The question now wasn't if he'd act, but how bloody the reckoning would be.

***

The bitter Thames wind sliced through Jimmy's jacket, carrying the stink of the river and rotting wood. He leaned against the crumbling brick wall behind the River Rat boozer, eyes fixed on the Executioner's Steps. In centuries past, condemned men had been marched down these worn stone steps at low tide, chained to the wall, and left for the river to claim them. The place had always given Jimmy the willies, but tonight it suited his purpose.

The click of high heels on stone announced her arrival before he spotted her. The Duchess stepped into the pool of yellow lamplight, six feet of pure elegance in a white mink coat that gleamed in the darkness.

She glanced around at the grimy waterfront, nose wrinkling. 'If this place is your idea of wooing a girl, you need to go back to dating school, darling. Most women prefer dinner, not a place of execution.'

'Haha!' Jimmy responded without an ounce of humour. 'Rita—'

'It's The Duchess now, and don't you forget it.' She cut him dead. 'Rita's long dead, bless her dodgy, twisted-hearted soul. I'm one of the toffs these days.'

She moved closer, her massive bodyguard, Tiny, coming into view at the top of the steps. She levelled Jimmy with one of her playful smiles. 'Though I've always had a soft spot for you, Jimmy, handsome. Even when you were just a cocky tearaway with those gorgeous eyes.'

'Knock it off.' Though he didn't say it with anger. This was the little game she loved to play, reminding him that they had stepped out a time or two before Mini had come into his life.

The Duchess studied his face, her expression softening. 'You know, those kids of yours need a mother, Jimmy.'

The words hit him like a punch to the gut. His heartache bubbled up, fresh and raw. 'I know.'

'It's been what now? Five years since Mini?' She touched his arm, her voice gentle. 'You can't keep sleeping on one side of the bed forever, love.'

'The thought of another woman there…' Jimmy shook his head. 'Nah. Ain't going to happen.'

'What have you found out?' He changed the subject, voice hardening.

He'd gone to her to do some snooping for him.

The Duchess glanced around, then leaned in. 'Your Jamaican friend? He's bad news. Trafficking girls from all four corners of the world, especially the West Indies. Word is, another batch is arriving tomorrow night at that warehouse you both own by the river, right here in Sugar Cane Wharf.'

'Jesus.' Jimmy scrubbed a hand over his face.

'He's got powerful friends, this Dash. Politicians. Foreign diplomats. Rich bastards with special tastes.' The Duchess tapped her red nails against her fur coat. 'Be careful, Jimmy. This isn't some street row. This is organised.'

'I don't have a choice,' Jimmy said. 'I can't let this continue in my properties.'

Jimmy's mind turned to Brother Bertie. Back in the day, Bertie would've been by his side in a heartbeat. They'd have torn through Dash's operation like a hurricane. But now…Bertie was married to Sin, had Izzy to think about. A family man. Jimmy couldn't drag him into this bloodbath.

The Duchess must have read his expression because she scowled hard at him in disbelief. 'Going it alone? That's suicide, Jimmy.'

'Then I'll die doing the right thing.'

The Duchess studied him, then nodded slowly. 'Your father would call you a fool.' He kept schtum. He never discussed his old man with anyone. That was family business and should stay behind closed doors.

He pushed off from the wall, breathing in the cold night air. 'Tomorrow night. The warehouse.'

'And what exactly do you plan to do?' The Duchess called after him.

Jimmy paused at the top of the steps, his silhouette black against the streetlights. 'Whatever it takes.'

# Chapter Forty-Four

Jimmy Steele scaled the warehouse wall, fingers bloody from gripping the rough brickwork in the pitch-black of the power cut. His black clothes clung to him in the damp river air, sweat trickling down his spine. The Three-Day Week blackouts might be hell for most of London, but tonight they were his ally.

He hauled himself onto the flat roof, breathing hard. Below him, the muffled growls of Alsatians patrolling the perimeter cut through the night. Vicious bastards. He'd watched the guards earlier, two blokes with torches circling the building every fifteen minutes. Amateur hour.

A skylight offered a view into darkness. Jimmy pried it open with his knife and lowered himself into the warehouse, dropping silently onto a stack of crates. The candle he lit cast a tiny bubble of light in the vast blackness.

The air hit him first, stale and rancid, and an underlying sweetness that turned his stomach. The stench of unwashed bodies and fear. And underneath that, something worse.

Death.

This was bad. Really bad.

Jimmy moved deeper into the warehouse, keeping the candle shielded. Rows of shipping containers lined the main floor, modified with crude airholes punched through the metal. From inside came soft whimpers, hushed voices in languages he didn't recognise.

'Hello?' he whispered, approaching the nearest container. 'I'm here to help.'

A terrified face appeared at one of the holes, a woman no older than twenty.

'Please,' she breathed, her accent Eastern European. 'Men come soon.'

Jimmy pulled out his lock picks. 'How many of you in there?'

'Six. Please hurry.'

The padlock gave way under his skilled fingers. Inside, six women huddled together on filthy mattresses, dressed in little more than rags. The stink of human waste and unwashed bodies billowed out.

'Christ,' Jimmy muttered. 'Can you walk?'

They nodded, wide-eyed with terror and disbelief.

'Stay quiet,' he instructed. 'Wait here while I check the rest.'

Three more containers yielded similar scenes, more women all petrified, many bearing bruises and injection marks on their arms. A production line of misery.

But it was what he found at the back of the warehouse that seared itself into his brain forever.

A small, enclosed area. A metal door. Jimmy's candle illuminated a sign: DISPOSAL.

The padlock on this door was serious business. Took him twice the time to crack. The door swung open, and the stench smothered him, and he almost gagged. The sickly-sweet smell of putrefaction.

Three bodies lay on concrete, partially wrapped in plastic. Women who hadn't survived the 'processing'. One with a needle still jutting from her arm. Another with a face beaten beyond recognition. The third, her eyes staring at nothing.

Jimmy staggered back, acid burning up his throat. He bent double, heaving onto the concrete floor.

This wasn't just trafficking. This was systematic murder. And he'd provided the fucking real estate.

He wiped his mouth, his hand shaking. A businessman. That's what he'd told himself. Building his empire, expanding beyond the East End. And he'd been played for a mug by Dash, signed his name to this house of horrors.

Never again. Not while he breathed.

Jimmy forced himself to move, to think. These women needed to get out. He needed evidence. Needed to destroy Dash completely.

At the far end of the warehouse stood a partitioned office. Jimmy picked the lock and slipped inside, raising his candle. Filing cabinets lined one wall. A desk cluttered with paperwork dominated the centre.

He rifled through the papers. Shipping manifests, client lists with coded names, payment records. The scale of it staggered him. This wasn't just London. This was international.

A telephone sat on the desk. Jimmy lifted the receiver, dialled Brother Bertie's number from memory. His pulse hammered in his throat while it rang.

'Yeah?' Brother Bertie's voice, cautious.

'It's me. I'm at the warehouse.'

'Jimmy? What the fuck—?'

'Listen to me. It's worse than we thought. Much worse. There's bodies, Bertie. Women who didn't survive. They're murdering them.'

'Jesus Christ.'

'I've found documents—'

'Get out of there, Jim. We'll go to—'

'No police. We handle this ourselves. I'm getting the women out now—'

The door behind him crashed open. Two goons stood silhouetted, torches blazing in Jimmy's face.

'Oi! What the fuck?'

Jimmy dropped the phone, shouting into it: 'Warehouse on Sugar Cane Wharf! Now!'

The first man charged, torch swinging for Jimmy's head. Jimmy ducked, driving his fist into the man's gut. The second one pulled a knife, lunging forward.

'Run!' Jimmy bellowed towards the women. 'Get out! All of you!'

The blade just missed his forearm. Jimmy hissed, grabbing a paperweight from the desk and smashing it into his attacker's face. Bone crunched beneath the impact.

Women screamed outside the office, fleeing towards the exit. The guard dogs barked frantically. More footsteps pounded through the warehouse. Reinforcements.

Jimmy grappled with the knife-wielder, both men crashing into the desk. The candle toppled, flame catching a stack of papers. Fire bloomed instantly, racing across the cluttered surface.

'Fire!' someone shouted.

Jimmy drove his knee into his opponent's groin, then slammed his head into the wall. The man collapsed in a heap.

The first guard was back on his feet, swinging a truncheon. It connected with Jimmy's shoulder, sending lightning bolts of pain down his arm. Jimmy roared, charging forward, tackling the guard through the office doorway.

They hit the concrete floor hard, rolling. Jimmy straddled the man, raining down blows until the guard stopped moving.

Smoke billowed from the office. Flames licked up the walls, fuelled by decades of dust and grime. The wooden beams overhead smouldered.

Women streamed towards the exits, wild-eyed and screaming. Jimmy staggered to his feet, scanning the chaos for more of Dash's men.

A massive shape loomed from the smoke, a brute with tattooed knuckles and a shaved head. 'You're fucking dead.'

Jimmy spat blood onto the floor. 'Come on then.'

The fire spread, hungry fingers, crawling across the warehouse ceiling. Ancient timber crackled and popped. The temperature soared, sweat pouring down Jimmy's face.

The animal charged. Jimmy sidestepped, hooking a foot behind the man's ankle. As the giant stumbled, Jimmy drove an elbow into his temple, sending him sprawling.

Through the spreading flames, Jimmy glimpsed more of Dash's men arriving. Four, maybe five of them. Too many.

A burning beam crashed down twenty feet away, sending up a fountain of sparks. The shipping containers had become metal ovens in the growing inferno. A violent shudder ran through Jimmy at the thought of what would've happened to those terrified women if he hadn't reached them in time. They would have been roasted alive.

Jimmy backed towards the exit, the heat searing his lungs with every breath. Women continued to flee past him, their wails mixing with the roar of the fire.

The tattooed giant was back on his feet, blood streaming from his temple. Behind him, the other men advanced through the smoke, faces twisted, murderous intent in their eyes.

The warehouse was becoming a blazing tomb. And Jimmy stood alone between Dash's men and the escaping women.

The fire spread before his eyes, hungry tongues of flame devouring everything in their path. There was no going back now.

# Chapter Forty-Five

'Jimmy! Jimmy!' Brother Bertie shouted into the dead phone. The line had gone to static after the sounds of a struggle and Jimmy yelling about Sugar Cane Wharf.

Brother Bertie slammed the receiver down, his heart pounding.

Jimmy in trouble.

Warehouse on fire.

Bodies of murdered women.

This was a life-or-death situation.

Jimmy's life or death.

He paced the maisonette's sitting room, mind racing. Sin had gone to help Sister Bernadette at the church evening service. She wouldn't be back for hours. It was just him and Izzy home tonight.

Brother Bertie stopped, staring at his son's bedroom door. Inside, his four-year-old boy slept peacefully, chest rising and falling with the innocent rhythm of childhood. His boy. His pride and joy.

But Jimmy was in danger. Jimmy who'd been more than a friend – a brother in all but blood. The man who'd saved his life countless times back in the day. Who'd had his back through thick and thin.

'Fuck,' Brother Bertie muttered, running calloused fingers over his face. 'Fuck, fuck, FUUUCK.'

Years ago, there would have been no choice. He'd have been out the door before the phone hit the cradle. But now? Now he had Izzy. He had promised Sin he'd never leave their boy alone. Promised on his mother's grave.

Brother Bertie opened his son's door, the hall light casting a soft glow over Izzy's sleeping form. The boy's chest wheezed slightly with each breath. His dark curls spread across the pillow, tiny fists clutched around his favourite teddy bear.

The clock on the wall ticked, each second dragging out his indecision.

Jimmy might be dying right now.

Brother Bertie closed his eyes, his promise to Sin warring with his loyalty to Jimmy.

He moved to the phone and dialled Gertie's number, his fingers trembling. 'Come on, pick up,' he chanted.

'Hello?' Gertie's familiar voice, warm and strong.

'It's me. Need you to come over. Now. Emergency.'

A pause. 'Bertram? What's happened?'

'Jimmy's in trouble. Warehouse fire at Sugar Cane Wharf. I need to go, but Izzy's asleep. Can you come stay with him? Sin's at church.'

'On my way. Fifteen minutes, tops.'

'Thanks, sis.' Brother Bertie hung up and scribbled a note for Sin in case she came home before Gertie arrived.

*Had to help Jimmy. Emergency. Gertie coming to sit with Izzy. Love you. B.*

He grabbed his knife from the drawer, checked the blade, and tucked it into his boot. From the wardrobe, he pulled out his old leather jacket, the one with the reinforced pockets where a man could hide things the law wouldn't approve of.

Brother Bertie returned to Izzy's room, guilt and fear churning in his gut. He bent down and placed a gentle kiss on his son's forehead, breathing in the sweet innocent smell of him.

'Sleep tight, little lion,' he whispered. 'Daddy will see you in the morning.'

***

The naked blonde writhed on the velvet chaise longue, her pupils blown wide with coke and champagne. Dash buried his face between her breasts, then dragged his tongue down her flat stomach to the line of white powder waiting there.

The private room in the brothel in Chelesea pulsed with pounding music and expensive debauchery. Dash inhaled sharply, the cocaine hitting his bloodstream in a blissful rush. He threw his head back, teeth bared in a wolfish grin.

This was power. This was living. The man who'd conquered London's filthy soul.

A staff member materialised at his elbow. 'Call for you. Private line. Business.'

Dash waved the girl away, wiping powder from his nose with a manicured finger. 'This better be fucking important.'

The phone sat in an alcove, away from prying ears. Dash picked up the receiver, irritation pulsing through his coke-fuelled high. 'What?'

'Boss.' His man's voice tight with panic. 'The warehouse is burning. Sugar Cane Wharf. Southpaw was there.'

Dash's euphoria evaporated. 'What the fuck did you just say?'

'Southpaw. Jimmy Steele. He broke in, freed the merchandise. Place went up like a tinderbox. We got four men down.'

'Where is he now?'

'Don't know. Might still be inside. Fire brigade's on their way.'

Dash pounded his fist into his thigh. That fucking mug had finally worked it out. All those deeds with Jimmy's signature and none of his own. The perfect setup. If anything went wrong, Jimmy would take the fall.

But there was something else gnawing at him.

Brother Bertie.

Working security at the Bermondsey house, asking questions, poking around. Dash had done his homework — found out that Bertie and Jimmy Steele were once thick as thieves, closer than blood brothers. If those two had patched things up, if Bertie was feeding information back to Jimmy...

That fucking traitor.

The same backstabbing betrayer who'd sold him out in Jamaica all those years ago.

History repeating itself.

Dash's rage crystallised into icy clarity. 'Send men to Brother Bertie's place. That council dump on the Isle of Dogs.'

'What you want done?'

Dash dragged a finger across his throat. 'Send a message. Proper old-school.' He smiled, cold and vicious. 'I want that backstabbing bloodclaat to know what happens when you cross me twice.'

# Chapter Forty-Six

Brother Bertie tore through the blackout-shrouded streets, lungs burning, each breath a gasp in the freezing air. The distant orange glow from Sugar Cane Wharf blazed against the night sky, guiding him like a hellish beacon.

The smell hit him first, burning timber, melting metal, and something worse. Something that churned his guts and quickened his already pounding pulse.

Flesh.

Women stumbled past him, terrified, half-naked. Their faces were streaked with soot and tears. All with haunted expressions that spoke of unspeakable horrors. Brother Bertie gently caught one by the shoulders.

'A man inside. Tall, dark hair. Have you seen him?' His voice softened, recognising the trauma in her petrified eyes.

The woman stared, uncomprehending or too traumatised to speak. She pulled away, vanishing into the smoke-thick night.

Brother Bertie charged forward, the brutal heat slamming into him. Inside the warehouse entrance, proper fucking chaos reigned. Thick black smoke billowed in choking clouds. Burning debris crashed from the ceiling. Screams of trapped women mingled with the inferno's thunderous roar.

'Jimmy!' he bellowed, voice swallowed by the flames.

Through swirling smoke, he spotted a cluster of men in the warehouse centre. Jimmy stood surrounded, bloodied but defiant, wielding a metal pipe against three circling attackers. A fourth lay motionless at his feet.

Brother Bertie didn't hesitate. He snatched up a length of burning timber and charged, bringing it down on the nearest thug's skull. A sickening crack. The man dropped like a sack of spuds, blood spurting from his shattered head.

Jimmy's face split into a wild grin, blood streaming from a deep gash across his forehead. 'Bertie! You mad bastard!'

'What, and let you have all the glory?' Brother Bertie shot back, their old rhythm clicking into place like it had never gone.

They stood back to back, facing the remaining thugs across the burning battleground. One pulled a knife, its blade gleaming orange in the firelight.

'You're both dead men,' the knife-wielder snarled, eyes narrowed to slits. 'Dash is gonna have your fucking heads mounted on his wall.'

Jimmy spat a glob of blood and saliva onto the concrete. 'I'm right here if you want it, you gutless cunt.'

The thugs charged. Brother Bertie blocked a punch and rammed his knee into his attacker's bollocks, bone connecting with soft tissue. The man doubled over, and Brother Bertie delivered an uppercut that sent teeth scattering across the warehouse floor.

Behind him, Jimmy's pipe connected with flesh and bone, the meaty thud followed by an agonised howl.

'We need to get out!' Jimmy shouted over the fire's hungry roar. 'This whole fucking place is coming down!'

A massive section of ceiling collapsed nearby, unleashing a tornado of glowing embers. The heat scorched Brother Bertie's skin, sweat evaporating instantly from his face.

'There's more women trapped in the back!' Jimmy pointed towards a row of shipping containers glowing red in the inferno. 'We've got to get them out!'

They sprinted across the warehouse floor, ducking beneath falling beams. Brother Bertie's lungs screamed with every toxic breath. The locks on the containers had been damaged but not fully opened. Jimmy attacked one with his pipe while Brother Bertie wrestled with another, the scorching metal searing his palms.

His container swung open, revealing five terrified women huddled together, skin marked with bruises and needle tracks, eyes wide in disbelief.

'Move!' Brother Bertie shouted, gesturing towards the exit. 'Run! Now!'

The women bolted past them. Jimmy had the second container open, helping more captives to freedom. The smoke thickened until Brother Bertie could barely see Jimmy ten feet away.

'That's all of them!' Jimmy bellowed, voice hoarse. 'Let's scarper!'

They turned towards the exit, but a terrible groaning sound rose above the inferno's roar. Brother Bertie glanced up to see a massive steel support beam, glowing white-hot, tearing free from its moorings directly above Jimmy's head.

'Jimmy!' He lunged forward without thought, shoving his friend clear with every ounce of strength.

The world exploded into blinding agony. The beam crashed down, pinning Brother Bertie's right leg to the concrete. His scream tore through the warehouse, primal and raw.

Jimmy scrambled to his side, face contorted with horror. 'Bertie! Hold on, bruv. Just fucking hold on.'

Jimmy braced himself against the beam, muscles straining, with all his might and mind, trying to lift the crushing weight. It didn't budge an inch. Brother Bertie's vision swam, darkness creeping at the edges.

'Leave me,' he gasped through gritted teeth. 'Get your arse out while you can.'

'Shut your fucking mouth.' Jimmy's eyes burned with determination. He snatched a length of pipe from the floor and jammed it under the beam, creating a crude lever. 'When I lift, you pull yourself free. Ready?'

Brother Bertie nodded, gathering the tattered remains of his strength. Jimmy threw his full weight onto the lever, neck veins bulging like cables. The beam shifted – mere inches.

Agony exploded through Brother Bertie's body when he dragged himself backwards, feeling tissue tear and bone splinter. The pain whited out his vision, but some animal instinct kept him pulling until his mangled leg slid free.

Jimmy dropped the lever and hauled Brother Bertie upright, draping his arm across his shoulders. 'I've got you, brother. Not letting go.'

Brother Bertie's leg dragged uselessly, and they staggered towards the exit. The warehouse was fully engulfed, the heat unbearable. A wall of flame blocked their path.

'We go through!' Jimmy shouted. 'Deep breath!'

They plunged into the fire, clothes smoking, skin blistering. Three steps. Four. Five. Then suddenly, blessedly, cold night air hit their scorched lungs.

They collapsed onto the cobblestones outside, coughing and retching and urgently tapping the embers from their clothing. Brother Bertie's gaze fell upon his leg, and his stomach violently heaved.

Every Jamaican curse word he knew slammed through his mind at the sight of his leg.

*Jesus fucking Christ!*

The limb was unrecognisable. Crushed bone jutted through torn flesh, blood pooling beneath him on the stone.

'Bit of a mess,' he managed, shock numbing the edges of his agony.

Jimmy tore off his jacket, wrapping it around Brother Bertie's shattered leg as a tourniquet. 'You're gonna be all right. You hear me? You saved my fucking life in there.'

Brother Bertie felt the darkness closing in, blood draining from his body faster than his heart could pump it. 'Sin's… gonna do her nut…' he mumbled, words slurring.

Jimmy's panicked face hovered above him, features blurring into smears of light and shadow. 'Stay with me, Bertie! Don't you fucking dare!'

'Bertie!' Jimmy shook him, desperation rising. 'Bertie!'

No response. Blood continued to pump from beneath the makeshift tourniquet, staining the cobblestones black in the night.

'No, no, no.' Jimmy pressed trembling fingers to Brother Bertie's neck, searching for a pulse. Nothing. 'Don't you fucking do this to me!'

Jimmy's gaze frantically searched the growing crowd of onlookers. 'Help me! Somebody help! He's dying!'

Brother Bertie tried to respond, but the darkness claimed him. The last face he saw, before his body went limp in Jimmy's arms, was the face of his son, Isaac.

# Chapter Forty-Seven

One kick splintered the cheap lock. The flat lay silent and dark.

'Nobody home,' one of the thugs Dash had sent to pay a surprise call on Brother Bertie said.

He and the two others tore through the flat like rabid dogs. Records shattered against walls. Cushions gutted. Photos stomped underfoot.

A tiny sound halted them mid-destruction. A faint wheeze from down the hall.

'What's that?' he growled, drawing his knife.

He pushed open the bedroom door. No one inside.

The wheeze came again, from the wardrobe.

Mills yanked the door open. A boy crouched inside, eyes wide with fright, a teddy clutched to his chest. His breathing came in painful gasps.

'Fuck's sake!' Mills scoffed with disdain. 'There's a kid.'

Dex appeared in the doorway. 'Must've hidden when he heard us break in.'

His thin chest heaved desperately.

'We didn't come for the kid,' one protested. 'He's having trouble breathing. Shouldn't we help him?'

'Not our business,' the more vicious of the three declared. 'Let's go.'

***

Sin rounded the corner to her landing and froze. The front door of her home hung from one hinge, splintered around the lock.

Sister Bernadette's evening prayers that had filled her with peaceful certainty mere minutes ago vanished. A sickening fear washed over her.

'Bertie?' Sin called, pushing the broken door fully open. 'Bertie, you home?'

The sight punched the breath from her lungs. The main room lay devastated.

'Bertie!' she cried out, panic rising in her throat.

Only silence answered. Her gaze fell on a scrap of paper on the floor. Bertie's handwriting.

*Had to help Jimmy. Emergency. Gertie coming to sit with Izzy. Love you. B.*

Sin's blood turned to ice water in her veins. Gertie wasn't here. The flat stood empty except for the destruction. And Izzy—

'Izzy!' The name tore from her lips. 'Izzy, baby! Mummy's home!'

She ran towards his bedroom, pulse thundering in her ears. Flung open his door. The room appeared empty, his *Thunderbirds* bedspread rumpled but vacant.

'Izzy?' Her voice cracked with the first tendrils of terror. 'Where are you hiding?'

The wardrobe door stood partially open.

Sin dropped to her knees, peering inside. First, she saw just the little brown hand clutching his teddy bear. Then her eyes adjusted to the shadows.

Her son lay curled in the corner. Motionless.

'Izzy?' The word escaped as barely a whisper.

She snatched him towards her. Touched his cheek. Cool. Too cool.

'No.' The word slipped out, soft with disbelief.

Her trembling fingers slid beneath his body, one hand supporting his lolling head. The terrible limpness of him sent a physical jolt through her chest. With painstaking gentleness, she drew him into her arms, cradling him against her thundering heart.

'Izzy?' She jostled him with desperate gentleness. 'Izzy, wake up for Mummy.'

Minutes passed in desperate futility. Her arms ached. Her lungs burned. Still she continued, wild-eyed, refusing to accept what her hands told her – that his body grew colder with each passing minute.

Sin gathered Izzy into her arms with heartbreaking care, his body curled against her breast. She cradled him like she had when he was a newborn, one hand supporting his head, the other wrapped protectively around his little body. His dark curls tickled her chin, just as they had countless times when she'd carried him sleeping to his bed.

She staggered to her feet and outside, her vision blurred with tears.

'HELP ME!' she screamed, her voice tearing from her throat. 'SOMEBODY HELP MY BOY!'

Doors opened. Neighbours appeared in nightclothes, faces shifting from irritation to horror when they saw what Sin carried.

'What happened?' Sabina from next door gasped.

'He's not breathing.' Sin sobbed, clutched Izzy tighter, backed away when people reached towards him. 'Don't touch him! He needs air!'

Sin's mind fractured. One part knew. One part refused to know.

'Someone call an ambulance!' she shrieked, rocking Izzy in her arms. 'He needs his medicine!'

The neighbours exchanged glances, their pitying expressions only feeding Sin's frantic denial.

'Don't stare at me like that!' she spat and spun in a circle, her boy's head lolling against her shoulder. 'He's going to be fine! Izzy! Izzy, wake up for Mummy!'

Heavy footsteps pounded up the communal balcony. Gertie appeared, breathless, her dark eyes widening in horror at the scene before her.

'Sin! What—' She stopped and took in the broken door, the neighbours gathered in hushed silence, the child in Sin's arms.

'He won't wake up, Gertie,' Sin whimpered, her voice childlike with confusion.

Gertie moved forward slowly, tears already streaming down her face. 'Let me see him, darling,' she said softly, reaching out trembling hands.

'No!' Sin jerked away. 'No one touches him!'

'Please, Sin,' Gertie coaxed, tears in her eyes but a firmness in her tone. 'Let me help my nephew.'

The thick emotion in her sister-in-law's voice penetrated Sin's haze of denial. She stood frozen, allowing Gertie to press gentle fingers against Izzy's neck.

Gertie's face crumpled, her shoulders sagging. 'Oh, Sin,' she sobbed, her voice breaking. 'He's gone. Our beautiful boy is gone.'

'No.' Sin shook her head violently, eyes wide with devastating horror. Colour fled her face. 'No, no, no!'

Izzy wasn't going to wake up. Not ever again.

The realisation ripped through Sin's body. Her knees buckled. She clutched Izzy tighter, pressing her face into his curls, inhaling the lingering scent of his baby shampoo.

Then came the scream.

It started deep in her belly, tearing upwards through her chest, erupting from her throat in a sound none present would ever forget. Not human.

Not animal. The gut-wrenching sound of a mother's soul shattering into irrecoverable pieces.

# Chapter Forty-Eight

Pain ripped through Brother Bertie's consciousness, dragging him from merciful darkness into brutal reality.

White ceiling tiles swam into focus above his pounding head. Antiseptic stench filled his nostrils, sharp and clinical. His mouth tasted of blood and charcoal. Every breath sent fire through his ribs.

Hospital. He was in a hospital.

Brother Bertie tried to shift, and agony exploded up his right leg. The pain was so savage, so all-consuming, that bile surged up his throat. He bit down hard, swallowing the bitter taste, cold sweat beading across his forehead.

'Easy, Bertram.' Gertie's familiar voice cut through the fog of confusion. 'Don't try to move, love.'

Brother Bertie turned his aching head towards her soothing voice. Gertie sat beside his bed. She looked tired. Wiped out. Behind her, Ruddy perched on the windowsill. In the corner, Jimmy stood motionless, his face grey and haunted.

Ruddy had been crying. Proper crying. And Ruddy thought tears were for angels with nothing better to do with their time.

Paralysing terror pooled in Brother Bertie's guts.

'What happened?' His voice came out as a rasp, throat raw from smoke inhalation. 'Why am I…'

Then it all crashed back. The warehouse. The flames. Jimmy surrounded by thugs. The burning beam falling…

Brother Bertie's gaze shot to his leg. It lay elevated, wrapped in pristine white bandages that couldn't hide the unnatural angle of the limb beneath. The pain wasn't just from the injury, it was the deep, bone-grinding ache of permanent damage.

'How bad?' The words scraped from his damaged throat.

Gertie reached for his hand, her calloused fingers gentle around his. 'Bad enough, Bertram. Doctor says you'll need surgery. You'll walk again, but…'

'But?'

Gertie's dark eyes glistened with unshed tears. 'You'll need a stick for the rest of your days. I'm sorry, love. So bloody sorry.'

A walking stick. For life. Brother Bertie absorbed this information, strangely detached. He'd saved

Jimmy's life, pulled him clear of that beam, and now he'd carry the consequences until his dying day.

Oddly, he felt no regret. Jimmy was alive. That mattered more than any stick.

'The women? Did they get out?'

'All of them,' Gertie confirmed, squeezing his hand. 'You and Jimmy saved every last soul in that warehouse.'

Relief flooded through Brother Bertie's battered body. At least those poor girls were free.

But a nagging worry tugged at his foggy brain. An important detail he was forgetting…

'Where's Sin?' The question tumbled out before he could stop it. 'And Izzy? Have they been to see me?'

The silence that followed was deafening. Gertie's hand tightened around his. Ruddy turned away, shoulders shaking. Jimmy's face drained of what little colour remained.

Cold, suffocating fear slithered up Brother Bertie's spine. The kind of dread that whispered of unspeakable horrors, of lives destroyed beyond repair.

'Gertie?' His voice barely rose above a whisper. 'Where's my boy?'

Gertie's face crumpled, tears spilling down her dark cheeks. She opened her mouth, but no words emerged.

The door exploded inwards, slamming into the wall, a crash that made Brother Bertie's damaged head throb. Sin stood in the doorway, her face a mask of pure devastation. Gone was the woman who'd kissed him goodbye that morning. This creature had hollow, red-rimmed eyes and skin the colour of old bone.

'WHERE WERE YOU?' Her voice tore through the room like shattered glass, each word dripping with venom. 'Where the fuck were you when our son needed you?'

Brother Bertie's blood turned to ice water. The way she said 'needed' – past tense – sent terror shooting through his veins.

'Sin, what—'

'DEAD!' Sin advanced on his bed, her face contorted into a mask of fury mixed with grief. 'Our beautiful, innocent boy is DEAD! Because you couldn't stay away from your filthy criminal world!'

Izzy gone?

*No. That can't be.*

Brother Bertie thought he was being pulled under, into a dark hole he'd never emerge from. The shaking started in his bones, hit his blood, and took over his whole body.

'NO!' The word escaped as a strangled gasp, his throat closing around the sound. 'No, Sin. Not Izzy. Please, not—'

Brother Bertie tried to sit up, trying with all his might to reach her, but agony shot through his leg, and he collapsed back onto the pillows. His hands shook uncontrollably, the tremors spreading through his entire body.

'He was four years old!' Sin's voice reached a pitch that bordered on inhuman. 'Four fucking years old, and he died terrified and alone because his daddy chose HIM over his own child!'

Sin pointed a condemning finger at Jimmy, who stood frozen in the corner.

'I had to help Jimmy,' Brother Bertie whispered, his voice breaking. 'There were women trapped—'

'I DON'T GIVE A SHIT ABOUT JIMMY!' Sin lunged forward, her fingernails raking down his face, leaving bloody furrows.

Brother Bertie barely felt the sting of her nails. All he could feel was the burning, lashing guilt consuming his entire soul, ripping him from the inside out. She was right. Dear God above, she was absolutely right. He'd let Izzy down. His beautiful boy had needed his daddy, and he'd chosen Jimmy instead.

So he didn't defend himself against the punishment she meted out.

'Sin!' Gertie leaped up, trying to pull her back, but Sin fought like a wildcat.

'GET OFF ME!' Sin shook her off, her fists pounding into Brother Bertie's chest, each blow sending fresh agony through his damaged ribs. But the physical pain was nothing compared to the knowledge that his child was gone forever.

How was he going to go on without ever seeing his son again?

Jimmy finally moved, grabbing Sin around the waist and dragging her away from the bed. 'Sin, stop! You'll hurt yourself!'

Sin rounded on him, and Jimmy physically recoiled. His sister's face had collapsed in on itself, eaten away with grief and fury that burned so hot the fire burned right through him.

'Hurt myself? HURT MYSELF?' Sin screamed at him. 'You think I give a fuck about hurting myself when my son is lying... lying…?'

She wrenched free from Jimmy's grip, rounding back to husband, renewed venom in her glare.

'He trusted you!' Spittle flew from her lips. 'My baby boy trusted his daddy to keep him safe, and you threw that away for your precious criminal brotherhood!'

Brother Bertie's whole body was shaking now, violent tremors he couldn't control. Cold sweat poured down his face, mixing with the tears he couldn't stop.

'I left him sleeping,' he whispered, the words feeling foreign in his mouth. 'He was safe. I asked Gertie to check on him…'

'I got there too late,' Gertie shook her head, still in a daze. 'There was a delay on the East London line from Whitechapel to Wapping. By the time I arrived…'

The unfinished sentence hung in the air, damning them all.

Sin's laugh was a sound devoid of any human warmth. 'Well, are you proud now? Are you fucking proud of what your friendship cost? My beautiful boy is cold and dead because you two couldn't resist playing soldiers one more time!'

Brother Bertie felt his chest caving in, lungs refusing to work properly. His perfect, laughing boy.

'I'm sorry,' he choked out, the words pathetic and useless. 'I'm so sorry—'

'Sorry?' Sin's voice dropped to a whisper more terrifying than any scream. 'Sorry doesn't bring back my son, does it? Sorry doesn't change the fact that he died alone and scared while you were off being a fucking hero!'

A keening sound of anguish left her. 'I BEGGED you to let me christen him! Begged you! And you said no! Now he's dead and his soul can't get to Heaven because of your stubborn pride! He's in Limbo forever - FOREVER! - because you wouldn't let me save him.'

Gertie was not standing for that and pushed herself forward. 'Don't you dare speak that foolishness over that precious child! There ain't no Limbo in my Bible! Jesus said 'Suffer the little children to come unto me' - and He meant ALL children! That baby's soul is safe in the arms of the Almighty, baptized or not! God don't condemn innocent babies for what grown folk didn't do!'

Sin ignored her sister-in-law and leaned over her husband's bed, her face inches from his, breath hot with grief and an expression of pain Brother Bertie would never forget. 'Your hands are covered in blood, Bertram Watson. My son's blood. And I will never, EVER forgive you for that.'

Jimmy stepped forward, his face ashen. 'Sin, it wasn't supposed to happen. We thought—'

'WE?' Sin whirled on him, her fury reaching new heights. 'There is no WE anymore! I hate you both. Hate you for dragging my innocent child into your filthy, no-good world.'

Brother Bertie watched her love for him curdle into pure hatred.

She paused at the door, fresh agony torturing her.

'And most of all, I hate myself for ever believing you'd changed.' Her shattered expression took in her husband, took in her brother. 'I never want to see either of you again. Ever.'

Brother Bertie lay there shaking, violent tremors racking his broken body. A freezing sweat covered his skin, making the hospital gown cling to his chest. He couldn't stop the convulsions, couldn't catch his breath, couldn't process the magnitude of what had just happened.

'Everyone out,' Gertie said quietly. 'Now.'

Ruddy slipped from the room without a word. Jimmy lingered, his face a mask of devastation.

'Bertie, I—'

Brother Bertie turned his face away, unable to bear the sight of the man whose life he'd saved at the cost of his child's.

Jimmy's footsteps faded into the corridor. Brother Bertie closed his eyes, but all he could see was Izzy's face. His perfect, trusting boy.

The bed dipped. Gertie's strong arms gathered him close, cradling his head against her shoulder just like when he was a child in Jamaica.

'It's going to be all right, Bertram,' she whispered, her own tears falling into his hair. 'Somehow, precious baby brother, it's going to be all right.'

But Brother Bertie knew better. Nothing would ever be the same again, and the brotherhood with Jimmy that had once meant everything now tasted like ashes in his mouth.

# Chapter Forty-Nine

Sin knelt alone in the empty church, her forehead pressed against the cold wooden pew, her fingernails digging crescents into her palms. Three o'clock in the morning, and God was nowhere to be found.

The funeral director had Izzy now. Preparing him. Dressing him in his Sunday best.

How was she going to watch while her baby was put in the ground?

'Why?' The word escaped her lips, echoing through the cavernous silence. Then louder, her head snapping up towards the altar. 'WHY?'

Her voice bounced back at her from the stone walls. The crucifix hung impassive above the altar, Jesus suspended in eternal agony. Sin staggered to her feet, moving towards it with unsteady steps.

'You took my boy.' Her voice cracked, raw from days of sobbing. 'My innocent child. Was it because I doubted? Because when I first found out I was carrying him, I thought about getting rid of him?'

The admission tore up her insides. The secret sin she'd carried since those terrified early days when she'd sat in the back street abortionist's house in Stepney before changing her mind. And then Bertie had arrived and taken her away.

'Was that it?' Sin's voice rose, hysteria edging in. 'Did you mark Isaac then? Curse him from the beginning because his mother was weak?'

She paced before the altar, her footsteps thunderous in the silent church. Three candles flickered in the darkness, casting monstrous shadows across the stations of the cross.

'I changed my mind! I chose him! I loved him more than my own life!'

Sin snatched up a prayer book from the nearest pew and hurled it at the altar. It struck with a dull thud, pages fluttering.

'You let them into our home! You let them kill my baby while I was here worshipping you!'

She tore at her hair, clumps coming away in her fists. Four nights now without sleep. Four nights of Izzy's empty bed. Of the terrible silence where his laughter should be.

'Where were you?' Sin sobbed, collapsing at the foot of the altar. 'I trusted you to protect him. I prayed every night.'

Her hands pressed flat against the cold stone floor, her tears falling between her splayed fingers.

'Bertie wasn't there. You weren't there. No one protected my boy when he needed them.'

She lifted her head, staring up at the crucifix through tear-blurred vision.

'What kind of God takes a child from his mother?' she whispered. 'What kind of God lets innocent babies suffocate while their fathers are off playing heroes?'

Sin pushed herself onto her knees, meeting the painted eyes of Christ.

'Was it my punishment? For loving Bertie more than you? For lying with him before we were married?'

The silence pressed in around her, heavy and accusing. No answer came. No divine comfort reached down to soothe her shattered heart.

Sin crawled to the altar steps and pulled herself up. Her fingers found the small golden tabernacle where the Eucharist was kept. The body of Christ. The promise of resurrection.

'He was four years old,' she said, her voice dropping to a whisper. 'He'll never grow up now. Never fall in love. Never have children of his own.'

Her hand closed around a candlestick.

'They're going to bury him. Put my baby in the cold ground next to strangers.'

The last fragile thread holding Sin together snapped clean. A terrible decision gripped her as she carefully set down the candlestick down.

'No,' she whispered. 'No, I won't let them.'

She stood straighter, certainty solidifying within her grief.

'You took him from me,' she said to the crucifix. 'But you don't get to decide where he rests.'

Sin wiped the frozen tears from her face using the back of her hand. No one had warned her that grief wasn't only soft, it was angry, it was bloody, it went hunting for revenge.

She turned her back on the altar and walked down the centre aisle.

Before the church doors closed behind her with a final, thunderous boom, she vowed, 'I know what I have to do now.'

***

When emotional pain became unbearable, he always did a runner. That's what Brother Bertie had done after the business with Dash when they were young, run all the way to England on a ship. When he'd lost Sin all those years ago for the first time, he'd run straight into the arms of gambling. And that's what he was doing now to get away from the crippling agony of losing his family.

He was getting out of this hospital. Where he was going, he didn't know. Just away. He gripped the metal rail and hauled himself upright from the bed.

Fire shot through his wounded leg and entire body the moment his feet touched the cold lino floor. He doubled over, shots of short breath punching in and out of him, sweat beading across his forehead. The torment was so intense his vision blurred.

He waited for the worst of it to pass, then set his gaze on his battered grip in the corner. It had accompanied him all those years ago from Jamaica, full of dreams and hope. Now it would carry him away from the worst nightmare any father could face.

He dragged himself across the room, not caring that his leg was threatening to buckle with each step. Getting the case on the bed nearly broke him. It gaped open, waiting to swallow what was left of his life.

He began chucking in his belongings. Then froze when he found the photo of Izzy. His darling child grinning at the camera, clutching his favourite toy car.

Brother Bertie's chest convulsed, a sound erupting from him that a man makes when his soul is being torn apart. His whole body shook as sobs ripped through him, shoulders heaving with the force of his grief.

'My beautiful boy,' he whispered, his voice splintering on every word. 'Daddy's so sorry, baby. So bloody sorry.'

He'd never hear his son laugh again. Never feel those small arms wrap around his neck. Never watch him grow into the good man he was meant to become.

Unlike him because he wasn't a man anymore. He was a monster who'd chosen crime over his child's safety.

Brother Bertie snapped the case shut and automatically reached for his pork pie hat, settling it on his head.

But what right did he have to wear it anymore?

It was his father's hat. Gertie's gift before she left Jamaica, when he was just a scared boy watching his sister board that ship to England. He'd worn it through every triumph, every disaster. Planned to pass it down to Isaac when he was old enough.

This pork pie hat meant everything. Heritage, family, hope. Honour. Everything he'd destroyed the moment he'd chosen Jimmy over Isaac.

He lifted the hat from his head with infinite care, cradling it between his palms. For a moment he just held it, feeling the soft texture beneath his fingers, remembering Gertie's proud smile when she'd placed it on his young head all those years ago.

He placed it on the bed.

'I don't deserve you.' A shuddering breath ran through him. 'Not after what I've done.'

Brother Bertie grabbed his grip case and limped out of the room. His leg screamed blue murder with every movement, but he forced himself forward. The hospital corridor stretched ahead, empty except for the soft hum of fluorescent lights. The exit doors loomed ahead.

Brother Bertie's injured leg buckled without warning.

The grip case hit the ground first, bursting open with a violent thud. His belongings scattered across the polished floor. He collapsed beside them, his damaged leg folding beneath him at an impossible angle.

Agony exploded through his body, red-hot, taking no prisoners.

'Bertram!'

His sister's commanding, sing-song voice sliced down the corridor. Kissing her teeth with extreme annoyance, she bore down on him in quick, decisive strides. Gertie dropped to her knees beside him, strong hands checking for injuries, her dark eyes blazing with worry and fury.

'What the bloody raas are you doing, boy?' He didn't need to see her face to know she was pissed.

'I was leaving.' The words came out strangled, barely human.

'Leaving to go where exactly?' Her question was rough.

'Anywhere.' A sob threatened to tear loose. 'Far away from here. From what I've done.'

Gertie began gathering his scattered belongings without a word. Her face was a mask of fierce concentration, but he caught the tremor in her hands, the way her mouth tightened at the corners.

'And what exactly have you done, Bertram?'

'I killed him.' His voice broke completely, dissolving into a keening wail that echoed off the hospital walls. 'I killed my boy, Gertie. I killed my beautiful, innocent boy as surely as if I'd put my hands around his throat and squeezed the life out of him myself.'

Gertie's hands stilled on his scattered clothes. Then she spoke, gentle, but steadfast and firm. 'Our beloved Isaac left us because animals took him from us. You think running away honours his memory? You think disappearing serves his spirit?'

Bertie bowed his head. 'Sin's right to hate me. I deserve every bite and lash of her rage.'

'You loved him. In this world, with all its ugliness and violence, you loved that child with everything you had.' A fierceness entered her voice. 'When I saw you with him I was proud to call you brother.'

He stared over at his scattered belongings. 'I don't know how to go on without him. How to forgive myself?'

Brother Bertie closed his eyes and tried to find an answer, but all he could hear was Izzy's laughter fading into silence, and the terrible, echoing emptiness of a world without his son in it.

# Chapter Fifty

The title of Viscount Blacklock belonged to him now, Dash thought with arrogant smugness as he poured another generous measure of whisky. His gaze swept the study with its leather and mahogany, ancestral portraits staring down with frozen disapproval. With his uncle finally in the ground, every asset, every property, every penny was his for the taking. The aristocratic life denied him during his Jamaican upbringing was now his reality. All except this Grosvenor Square mansion. That remained Lady Prudence's. His mouth twisted into a cunning grin that never reached his eyes. He'd have the deeds locked in his safe before the year's end. His uncle's mousy widow stood no chance against a man of his ambition.

And he would begin tomorrow after they had buried the cantankerous, old bastard.

The fate of Bertie's kid had been...unfortunate. The fool should've known better than to stab him in the back - again.

'Should've kept your blasted nose clean, you bumbaclot,' Dash muttered, his upper-class tone mixing with his Jamaican curse. 'That kid's death is on you, not me.'

A sharp knock interrupted his scheming thoughts.

'Enter,' he called, straightening his posture to appear more lordly.

Ruddy burst in, dressed in sombre black. She carried a silver tray with a crystal decanter containing dark, ruby-red liquid. She practically slammed it down on the desk.

'Lady Prudence asked me to bring you this,' she ground out. 'It's for your vigil tonight.'

Dash frowned. 'Vigil?'

'Yeah, vigil. Night before a Blacklock funeral, the new lord spends the night with the dead one. Some posh tradition.' Her eyes blazed with barely contained fury. 'Though what I'd really like to do is chuck this right in your bloody face after what your men did to poor little Isaac.'

Dash bared his teeth in a mirthless grin. 'First thing after the funeral, you'll be out on your arse. I don't need mouthy staff who don't know their place.'

'This was Lord Xander's favourite port,' Ruddy continued, ignoring his threat. 'Lady Pru says you have to drink it before going to the funeral home. Part of the title transfer, apparently. Lady Pru says it's essential for a proper Blacklock succession.'

Dash's lip curled. More aristocratic nonsense, but he'd play along. These rituals were part of his birthright, after all. Although the thought of spending the night with his uncle's corpse creeped him out. But appearing weak before this East End boiler wouldn't do.

After his cool nod, Ruddy filled a glass, her hand steady despite her obvious hatred.

He sniffed it appreciatively. 'To Uncle Xander,' he smirked, 'thanks for finally dying and giving me what's rightfully mine.'

Dash drained the glass in one go, savouring the rich, complex flavours. Sweet with an unusual bitter undertone.

'Interesting taste,' he murmured, already feeling an unusual warmth spreading through his limbs. 'Strong stuff.'

'The best quality,' Ruddy replied, a strange smile playing at the corners of her mouth. 'Car's waiting whenever you're ready.'

Dash stood, but his legs felt oddly heavy. The room swam before his eyes.

'What the bloody...' he slurred, grabbing the desk for support.

Ruddy watched him, the hatred in her eyes replaced by cold satisfaction as he struggled to remain upright.

'You... what've you...?' His tongue felt too large for his mouth.

The last thing Dash saw was Ruddy's face, hard as flint.

Then everything went black.

***

St. Bartholomew the Great loomed ancient and imposing against London's morning sky. For centuries, the Blacklock family had been entombed in the church's private vault beneath. Black-clad figures filed solemnly through its massive Norman doors, a who's who of British aristocracy come to pay their final respects to Alexander, the previous Viscount Blacklock.

Lady Prudence sat in the front pew, a vision of elegant grief in black crepe and lace. A small handkerchief dabbed occasionally at her eyes—which were actually dry—beneath her veil. The enormous mahogany casket before the altar gleamed under the church lights, brass handles burnished to a high shine, the Blacklock family crest prominently displayed.

'A fitting tribute,' murmured an elderly countess beside her. 'Xander would have approved of such grandeur.'

Lady Pru nodded, her gloved hands clasped tightly in her lap. 'He always insisted on the best.'

She glanced at Ruddy, standing discreetly at the side of the church. Thunder rumbled in the distance.

How appropriate, she thought. A storm for a stormy man.

Ruddy observed the gathering from her position. The cream of society mingled with politicians and business associates, all here for a man most of them had despised. Hypocrites, the lot of them.

Her gaze narrowed when she spotted The Duchess—Rita Lawless that was—entering on the arm of her elderly Duke. Only those observing closely would have clocked the nod that passed between them.

The enormous coffin sat before the altar, custom-made at Lady Pru's insistence. When the undertaker had enquired about its unusual size, she'd coolly informed him that Lord Alexander had specifically requested a casket large enough to accommodate the family regalia to be entombed with him. The Blacklock name and a generous donation to the undertaker's preferred charity had prevented further questions.

A side door opened, and a well-dressed man slipped in, unnoticed by most. He took a place among the pallbearers, his expensive mourning attire identical to theirs. The funeral director had been generously paid to add him to their numbers at the last minute.

The church bells tolled eleven o'clock. The organist began the solemn processional as the vicar moved to his position.

'We are gathered here today to commemorate the life of Lord Alexander Blacklock, Viscount of Blacklock...'

The service proceeded with all the pomp and circumstance befitting a peer of the realm. Hymns were sung with proper British restraint. Eulogies delivered with clipped, unemotional tones by associates who spoke of duty and family legacy rather than genuine affection.

The vicar invited the congregation to bow their heads in prayer. The church fell silent save for the rising wind outside, rattling the stained-glass windows.

Just then, a noise sounded from somewhere. A scratching, barely audible above the vicar's monotonous drone.

'And we commend his soul to your eternal care, O Lord—'

A distinct thump interrupted the vicar mid-sentence. There was no mistaking it this time. The sound came from the coffin.

'Did you hear that?' a woman whispered too loudly, earning disapproving glares that quickly turned to wide-eyed stares as another thump followed.

The vicar faltered, prayer book trembling in his hands. He glanced desperately at Lady Pru, who sat frozen, attention locked on the coffin.

A muffled groan emanated from within the ornate box. In horror, the vicar dropped his prayer book, the thud echoing in the sudden silence.

'Good God,' exclaimed a red-faced peer, monocle falling from his eye.

The coffin rocked slightly on its stand. A collective gasp of disbelief and stupefied shock rippled through the congregation. Two elderly ladies clutched each other's arms.

Lady Pru stood shakily, one gloved hand pressed to her throat. 'My God,' she cried, voice carrying throughout the hushed church. 'Is he—is Xander alive?'

The mourners erupted in commotion. People rose from their seats, necks craning for a better view. The vicar backed away from the altar, crossing himself repeatedly.

The casket rocked more violently now.

The Duchess rose majestically from beside her confused Duke. 'Open it!' she commanded, every inch the aristocrat despite her East End origins. 'For heaven's sake, someone do something!'

Lightning flashed through the windows, illuminating the scene in stark, theatrical light as the coffin lid burst open with a terrible splintering sound.

Lady Pru fainted dramatically, collapsing into the arms of a startled baron beside her. Her perfectly timed distraction drew half the congregation's attention away from the coffin.

Those still watching saw a nightmarish scene.

Dash, the new Viscount, erupted from the satin-lined interior, gasping and wild-eyed. His elegant funeral garments were rumpled and stained with bodily fluids. His hands were bloody from clawing at the coffin lid. Behind him, partially visible, lay the actual corpse of Lord Xander. Dash had been lying on top of a dead body.

Pandemonium broke loose. Women screamed. Men shouted. The vicar retreated all the way to the vestry door, face contorted in fright.

Dash fell out of the coffin to the stone floor with a thud. He babbled incoherently, trying to speak but could only produce guttural sounds, spittle flying from his lips. His fingers kept brushing frantically at his clothes, as if trying to remove the contamination of the corpse.

One of the pallbearers stepped forward with two others. 'It's the new Viscount!' he exclaimed for all to hear. 'He's having some sort of breakdown!'

The Duchess moved through the chaos with remarkable poise. 'The poor man needs medical attention immediately!' she announced and then, with a subtle gesture toward the pallbearer who had spoken, she continued, 'Please assist us in taking him somewhere quiet.'

The three men half-carried, half-dragged Dash towards a side door, his legs kicking feebly, still weak.

As they passed Lady Pru, now 'recovering' from her faint with Ruddy's assistance, she leaned close to Dash's ear. 'Good riddance to the bastard who murders innocent children.'

The Duchess remained behind to manage the scandalised crowd. 'I suggest we continue the service for dear Xander,' she proclaimed, taking control of the situation. 'Though perhaps with the casket closed.'

As the vicar nodded gratefully and ushers rushed to secure the lid once more, Ruddy caught The Duchess's eye across the nave. The smallest nod passed between them.

Outside, in the pouring rain, the three men bundled Dash into the backseat of the waiting black car. Only now, away from the church, could the driver's identity be seen clearly.

Jimmy.

His silver-grey eyes held no mercy, no humanity. Just the cold certainty of vengeance.

'Church service is over,' Jimmy growled. 'But the funeral's not over yet. Yours is just beginning.'

# Chapter Fifty-One

The car raced eastward, wipers slashing frantically against the torrential rain. Jimmy's fury filled his motor, cold and deadly. They drove past Tower Bridge, through Wapping, deeper into the heart of his territory. The warehouse district loomed ahead, abandoned buildings, broken windows staring over the murky Thames.

Sugar Cane Wharf.

The car pulled to a stop outside a derelict warehouse, rust bleeding down its corrugated sides. Two mountainous men stepped out from the shelter of a doorway, nodding at Jimmy in the driver's seat. He returned the nod, then climbed out into the downpour.

'Get him inside,' Jimmy ordered, his tone flat and emotionless. 'I'll be waiting.'

He strode through a side entrance while his men wrenched open Dash's door and hauled the semi-conscious man onto the cracked concrete.

The icy rain seemed to revive Dash. His drugged stupor began to lift, replaced by dawning terror. His stomach turned to liquid, pure animal panic flooding his system. This wasn't supposed to happen to him. He was the Viscount bloody Blacklock.

'Let me go, you fucking pricks!' Dash thrashed in their grip, his mind in turmoil with desperate plans of how to escape. 'Do you know who I am?'

One of the men, face gnarled and scarred from too many fights, laughed. ''Course we do, sunshine. You're the man who killed Mr Steele's nephew.'

Dash lost what little colour he had left. These weren't men who could be bought or reasoned with. They dragged him through a battered door into the cavernous belly of the warehouse. The rain hammered on the metal roof, a deafening drumbeat. When his eyes adjusted to the gloom, he saw him.

Jimmy Southpaw.

He sat waiting on a wooden chair in a pool of watery light from a hole in the roof. His silver-grey eyes held no emotion whatsoever. Only his hands, folded in his lap, betrayed his tension, the fingers curled into loose fists.

The men released Dash, sending him stumbling forward onto his knees.

'Leave us,' Jimmy said quietly.

The men nodded and retreated, footsteps fading into silence.

'Jimmy,' Dash implored. He attempted to flash that charismatic grin that had charmed so many before. 'This is all a massive misunderstanding—'

Jimmy cut him off, his voice slicing through the damp air. 'Shut your mouth.'

Dash struggled to his feet, hands shaking, betraying the terror he fought to hide.

'Whatever you think happened—'

'Your men broke into Bertie's home.' Jimmy spoke with casual detachment. Behind his calm exterior, memories flashed. Memories he would never forget. How could he ever erase the picture of Sin's uncontrollable grief in the hospital? 'My sister found her son dead in his bedroom wardrobe.'

'I never ordered that shit,' Dash jumped in quickly, words tumbling over each other. 'I told them to find Bertie, that's all.'

'You sent men with guns to a family home.' Jimmy finally unfolded himself from the chair to his feet. He drew himself up, big and strong and menacing. Behind his impassive face, he pictured Isaac's small body gasping for breath, abandoned and terrified. 'And now a little boy is dead.'

'I didn't know the kid would be there!' Dash backed away. He bumped into a rusted pillar, the sharp metal biting into his back. Clammy sweat soaked through his shirt. 'Christ, Jimmy, I'm not a monster!'

Jimmy tilted his head, studying his former business partner with icy detachment. 'The women locked in your basements. The ones you trafficked. I bet they'd disagree.'

A flash of cunny crossed Dash's face. He could still talk his way out of this. He'd talked his way out of worse in Jamaica. 'And I made you richer! We are partners!'

Jimmy advanced on him, each step deliberate, like a big cat stalking prey. 'Partners? You used me as your fucking fall guy. Put my name on everything. The properties where you kept those women, the warehouses for your cocaine.'

'I'll make it right,' Dash coaxed in a seductive tone. 'I can disappear, you'll never see me again —'

'That's right. You'll never see anyone again.'

The first blow came without warning. A short, savage uppercut that snapped Dash's head back against the metal pillar. Stars exploded behind his eyes when he slumped to his knees.

Jimmy stood over him, removing his jacket and carefully folding it. He placed it on the chair, then rolled up his shirtsleeves, exposing muscular forearms marked with old boxing scars.

The beating was brutal. Jimmy's fists reduced Dash's handsome face to a pulpy mess. Each blow fuelled by images flashing through his mind.

Sin's tortured face at the hospital, contorted in unbearable grief.

Bertie, broken physically and spiritually.

Blood spattered the floor, splashed across Jimmy's white shirt. Still he continued, on and on and on, shattering the jaw that had given orders to leave a four-year-old to die.

With each impact, Jimmy felt the savagery of justice. At some point, Dash stopped begging. Stopped moving. His breath came in wet, bubbling gasps through broken teeth and split lips.

Jimmy didn't stop. He was lost to the violence, the vengeance, his vision narrowing to a red tunnel. He didn't hear himself growling like a wounded animal, didn't feel the tears mixing with Dash's blood on his face.

'Boss?'

The voice came from far away, jerking him back to reality. One of his men stood at the door, concern etched on his battered face.

'You want us to finish him?'

Jimmy blinked, suddenly aware of his surroundings again. He stood over Dash, chest heaving, fists torn and bleeding.

'No,' he glanced down at the broken man at his feet. 'This is for Isaac.'

Jimmy knelt beside Dash, whose eyes fluttered, consciousness fading. He leaned close, whispering into what remained of the man's ear:

'You killed my family. Now I'm killing you.'

His hands closed around Dash's throat, thumbs pressing into the windpipe with implacable force. Dash's eyes bulged, terror giving him one last surge of strength. His ruined hands clawed weakly at

Jimmy's wrists. Blood bubbled from his lips while he fought for air that wouldn't come.

Jimmy's face remained expressionless, even when Dash's struggles weakened, then stopped altogether. Even when the body beneath him went limp and the eyes stared sightlessly at the warehouse ceiling.

Finally, he released his grip and stood. Slipped his jacket back on over his ruined shirt.

'You know what to do,' he instructed his men. 'Weighted chains, into the Thames where it's deepest.'

One final time, he dispassionately stared down at the corpse on the warehouse floor. The blood on his hands would never wash clean, not if he lived a thousand years. But for Izzy, he'd gladly burn in Hell.

This was personal. Primal.

This was family.

# Chapter Fifty-Two

'Not on your life!'

Gertie Watson planted her stout form with iron willed resolve across the doorway of her Whitechapel boarding house, arms folded tight across her chest, blocking entry to the man who stood on her doorstep.

Jimmy Steele.

'If you've come here to drop more grief at my brother's door, you can turn your tail around right now.'

He'd expected this reception, maybe even deserved it. 'I'm not here for trouble, Gertie. Just want to see how he's doing.'

'How d'you think he's doing?' Her voice cracked with fury. 'Lost his boy, lost his wife, leg busted to pieces. All because he answered your call for help.'

The accusation hung between them like a curse. Jimmy's mouth tightened, but he kept his tone level.

'I need to see him.'

Gertie studied his face, searching for malice. Found only exhaustion and pain that matched her own. With a grudging step backwards, she jerked her head towards the narrow staircase.

'You know where to find him.' Her voice dropped to a deadly whisper. 'And Jimmy? Don't you dare pile more pain on his shoulders.'

***

Brother Bertie heard the familiar tread on the stairs and sighed deeply. Not another well-wisher. He appreciated people visiting, truly he did, but exhaustion had settled into his bones. So tired of putting on a brave face, of pretending the pain in his leg was worse than the agony in his chest.

'Come in.'

The door opened, and Brother Bertie's entire body went rigid. Every muscle tensed as Jimmy's tall frame filled the doorway. Expensive grey suit, perfectly groomed, but those eyes held depths of pain that fancy clothes couldn't hide.

The sight of his former best friend sent shockwaves through Brother Bertie's damaged system. His chest tightened, making breathing difficult.

'Bertie.' Jimmy's voice carried warmth beneath the careful control.

'Jimmy.' Brother Bertie struggled to sit up straighter, fire shooting through his damaged leg. The doctors had said he'd walk again, but the walking stick they'd promised him hadn't arrived yet. He felt helpless, trapped in this bed while his old friend appeared so tall and strong.

Jimmy seemed to hesitate before entering slowly. Like a magnet, his gaze landed on the medical supplies cluttering the bedside table, stark evidence that Bertie would never be the same again. That he'd never do the boxer's dance they'd shared ever again.

He choked up, guilt squeezing his insides. They'd been back together for such a short time and look what it had cost Bertie. A crushed leg. A son.

He pulled up the single wooden chair.

'Thought I'd check on you. See how you're healing.'

Pain flickered across Brother Bertie's gaunt features. 'Leg's mending. Slow but sure.' His voice came out hoarse, barely above a whisper. 'Doctors say I'll always need a stick, but I'll walk again.'

'Good. That's good.' Jimmy leaned forward, elbows on his thighs, hands clasped. The silence stretched between them, heavy with unspoken words. 'Dash won't be a problem anymore.'

His one-time best friend closed his eyes and inhaled deeply. Bertie's face was a mash up of emotions. Relief warring with grief, satisfaction tangled with emptiness.

'Does it help?' Brother Bertie finally asked, his eyes re-opening. He was exhausted, totally wrung out, physically and in his head. 'Knowing he's gone, does it fill the hole? Because Izzy's still gone, Jimmy. I'm still going to need to place my beloved son in the ground.'

'Bertie, about what happened—'

'Don't.' The word exploded from Brother Bertie's throat, raw and desperate. 'Just don't, Jimmy. I can't hear how it was worth it, how we saved those women. Not when my boy...' His voice broke completely.

Jimmy's face darkened, the careful mask slipping. 'Your boy died because Dash was a twisted, psycho cunt. Not because of what we did.'

'My boy died because I wasn't there!' Brother Bertie's fist slammed into the mattress, sending waves of pain through his injured body. 'I promised Sin I'd stay legitimate. Promised her the criminal world would never touch our family again. Then you called, and I—' The words choked in his throat.

Helpless anguish washed over him.

'You came to help stop a trafficking operation,' Jimmy said. 'To save innocent women.'

'I chose you over my son!' The raw agony in Brother Bertie's voice filled the small room, seeming to crack the very walls. 'I left him sleeping, defenceless, while I went off playing gangsters with you. Helping to fight your battles.'

Jimmy shot to his feet, the chair screeching again. His face flushed crimson with rage. 'My battles?

Dash used my properties for his sick games! He turned me into an unwitting landlord to his brothels and drug operations. I was the one being played!'

'And I was the mug who helped you clean up the mess!' Brother Bertie struggled upright and gripped the iron bedframe for support. 'I should have said no. Should have stayed home with my family.'

Jimmy breathed hard between ragged gasps, his hands clenched into fists at his sides. 'But you didn't. You came running because that's who you are. Because you couldn't stand the thought of those women suffering.'

'And witness what it cost me.' Brother Bertie's laugh held no humour, just bitter emptiness. 'Everything. My son, my wife, my leg. All gone because I thought I could be a hero one more time.'

Jimmy stared at his oldest friend, seeing the broken man beneath the proud exterior.

'You think I don't carry that guilt?' Jimmy's voice rose, echoing off the bare walls. 'You think I don't see Isaac's face every time I close my eyes? But I won't let you wallow in self-pity when you chose to help.'

Face draining of colour, Brother Bertie hauled himself upright. 'Self-pity? My four-year-old son is dead because I chose our friendship over his safety. That's not self-pity, that's cold, hard fact.'

'Your son is dead because evil men exist!' Jimmy stepped closer. He towered over his injured friend. 'Because Dash was a murdering psycho who wanted to hurt you through your family. Don't you dare cheapen Isaac's memory by turning this into some grand tragedy about choices.'

Eyes blazing with fury, Brother Bertie's voice turned deadly quiet. 'Cheapen his memory? You weren't there when Sin found him. You didn't see her trying to wake our dead son, screaming until the neighbours came running.'

God help! For the rest of his days he would have to live with what Gertie had told him had happened.

'You lost me my sister twice!' Jimmy's control suddenly snapped. 'First time, you got her pregnant and I found out at Mini's funeral. Cut her off completely. Then, just when we're talking again, when she's ready to forgive, because of you, she won't have anything to do with me.'

Brother Bertie flinched as if physically slapped. 'Jimmy—'

'No! I finally had my sister back, and now she's gone forever because of YOU!'

Jimmy turned towards the door just as thunderous footsteps pounded up the narrow stairs. Gertie burst through the doorway, her face twisted with protective fury and something glinting in her powerful hands.

'GET OUT!' she roared and raised a wicked-looking cutlass above her head. 'Get out of my house, you soul-destroying devil!'

Jimmy stepped back, hands raised defensively. 'Gertie—'

'Don't you Gertie me!' She advanced, the cutlass weaving deadly patterns in the stale air. 'I heard every word, you cold-hearted bastard! My brother sacrificed everything for you. EVERYTHING! And this is how you repay him? Leave my Bertram alone!'

Jimmy backed towards the door, keeping his eyes fixed on the lethal blade. 'I'm going.'

'And don't come back!' Gertie followed him to the landing, cutlass still raised menacingly. 'Not ever! You hear me, Jimmy Steele? You're dead to this family!'

***

Inside his car, Jimmy buried his head in his hands and wept. Tears for Isaac, the nephew he'd only recently met and fallen in love with – a bright-eyed boy who'd called him Uncle Jimmy with such innocent joy. His sister, his beloved Sin, who had been his anchor in the world. Their broken bond mended with such fragile hope, only to be brutally severed again. And Bertie. His closest friend. His brother in everything but blood. No other soul had understood him the way Bertie did.

All gone.

East London's most feared gangland crime boss sobbed in a way he hadn't since his beautiful wife had passed on, his broad shoulders shaking with the force of grief that threatened to rip him apart.

# Chapter Fifty-Three

'The chamber's packed to the rafters, Councillor Steele,' Danny's secretary gasped. 'Standing room only. I've never seen anything quite this… enthusiastic.'

Danny had literarily just stepped foot inside Sugar Cane Wharf Town Hall before his secretary barrelled into him delivering her eager news. He'd come here seeking the comfort of familiar territory, somewhere he still held sway. The Victorian building represented his last bastion of respectability. Wood-panelled corridors where his voice carried authority, where lesser mortals deferred to his political position.

His secretary scurried alongside, wringing her hands the way women did when catastrophe was brewing. Her nervous energy churned Danny's gut with unspoken dread.

Since when did council meetings draw crowds? Usually these administrative gatherings attracted nothing more exciting than a handful of pension-age busybodies and the odd journalist hunting free refreshments.

The double doors to the council chamber loomed ahead, carved oak reinforced with brass hinges that had survived two world wars. Muffled voices buzzed beyond the wood – hundreds of them, all talking at once in that particular way crowds did when they smelled blood in the water.

After smoothing his fingers down the lapels of his jacket, Danny pushed through the doors with the swagger of a man who'd faced down violent dockers and corrupt politicians.

The sight that greeted him stopped his stride.

Every seat crammed with bodies. People lined the walls three deep, faces turned towards the front, predatory anticipation in their expressions. The press gallery overflowed with local reporters, cameras clicking and notebooks scribbling. Bright lights had been rigged to illuminate the proceedings, casting everything in harsh white glare that made details sharp-edged and unforgiving.

*Christ, what's all this about then?*

But Danny Steele hadn't survived decades in the East End by showing weakness. He flashed his trademark grin and raised a carefree hand in acknowledgment.

'Afternoon, Mrs Patterson!' he called out to a familiar face in the third row. 'Hope young Kevin's doing well at his new job!'

The woman's return smile seemed strained, and she barely managed a weak wave.

'Mr Henderson!' Danny projected his voice towards another constituent. 'How's the wife's hip coming along?'

Henderson nodded reluctantly, avoiding eye contact.

*Funny. Usually they're all over me with their problems and requests.*

Danny maintained his outward confident calm while his mind raced, almost out of control. The crowd's energy felt wrong – fired up with anticipation rather than the usual civic boredom, like punters gathering round a bare-knuckle fight baying for blood.

Complete silence fell the moment Danny took his position. Four hundred pairs of eyes swivelled towards him, laser focused.

At the front of the chamber, Council Leader Geoffrey Kerr sat behind the ornate Speaker's table, his usually florid face pale beneath the bright lights. To his right stood a woman Danny recognised with growing wariness, Mrs Dorothea Chesterton, the moral crusader who'd been banging on about vice and corruption for months.

This wasn't the flustered housewife who'd complained about street walkers and dirty bookshops. This version wore her steel-grey hair pulled back in a severe chignon, her navy suit tailored to military standards. Her pale eyes held the cold fire of righteous vengeance, and her mouth curved in a smile that promised public execution.

*What's the frigid old cow up to?*

Kerr's voice boomed through the chamber's acoustics. 'Councillor Steele. Please take your seat. We have… matters to discuss.'

Danny walked between packed benches, maintaining his easy confidence despite the crowd's strange hostility. Whispers followed his progress:

'That's him.'

'Dirty bastard.'

'About bloody time.'

*About time for what?*

He settled into his usual chair on the front bench, crossing his legs, deliberately nonchalant. Whatever game was being played, Danny Steele could handle some middle-class morality queen who had delusions of importance.

Mrs Chesterton rose from her position beside the Speaker's table, her. She carried a manila folder thick with documents, handling it the way a prosecutor might hold evidence.

Her crisp accent projected clearly to the back of the chamber. 'Ladies and gentlemen of Sugar Cane Wharf, we gather today to address matters of public morality and civic responsibility.'

Danny's muscles tensed slightly. The theatrical old bat was building tension before she delivered whatever accusations she'd prepared.

'Six months ago, I brought to this council's attention the proliferation of vice establishments in our community. Brothels operating brazenly. Young women exploited. Our neighbourhood's reputation dragged through the gutter.'

Murmurs of agreement rippled through the chamber. Danny kept his expression neutral, but sweat gathered under his arms.

*She's banging on about the brothels again. So what? I promised to look into it.*

'I was assured by Councillor Steele that immediate action would be taken. These establishments would be investigated. Closed down. The perpetrators prosecuted to the full extent of the law.'

Her pale eyes fixed on Danny, their intensity uncomfortable. Danny's mouth went dry, though he couldn't pinpoint why.

Opening her folder with theatrical deliberation, Mrs Chesterton smiled, icy satisfaction on display. 'Instead, I discovered rather more disturbing developments.'

She pulled out a series of glossy photographs, holding them high enough for everyone to see. Danny squinted at the images, his blood chilling as recognition dawned.

Himself, entering an establishment on Commercial Road. One of three he owned on that stretch. The chamber stirred, interested. Danny felt hundreds of eyes boring into him but forced his face into an expression of righteous indignation.

Standing, confident and authoritative, he projected his voice to every corner of the room. 'Ladies and gentlemen, what you're seeing is exactly what Mrs Chesterton requested – a thorough investigation.'

He turned towards her, his smile patronising. 'I told you I'd look into these establishments personally. How else does one gather evidence about criminal activity except by going undercover?'

Several council members nodded thoughtfully. Danny felt the crowd's mood shift slightly in his favour.

'Any police officer will tell you that infiltration is the most effective method of exposing corruption.' Danny's tone carried decades of practiced authority. 'I risked my personal reputation to gather the evidence this council needed.'

Mrs Chesterton's smile never wavered. 'Investigation, Councillor? How interesting. And what exactly were you investigating in this particular moment?'

She produced another photograph. Danny's confident expression froze.

The image showed him inside the parlour, clearly visible despite the dim lighting. He sat in the main chair while a young brunette performed services that left no doubt about the nature of his visit. But worse – far worse – another shot showed him accepting a thick brown envelope, his fingers clearly grasping the bulging packet.

*That conniving, backstabbing whore, Scarlett. She set this up.*

The chamber erupted with gasps and angry shouts. Danny's carefully constructed defence crumbled. He felt like he was being hanged, a man dancing and kicking in the air.

His face flushed purple, rage and humiliation heating his cheeks. 'You don't know what you're dealing with, Mrs Chesterton. There are forces at work here beyond your understanding.'

The crowd's laughter hit him. Cruel, contemptuous, utterly without mercy.

Mrs Chesterton's sharp gaze glittered, her triumph gleeful. 'The only force at work here, Mr Steele, is justice. Long overdue justice for a man who's corrupted this community for far too long.'

Around the chamber, faces showed disgust and righteous satisfaction. Danny realised with growing horror that he was witnessing his own public execution.

'I know exactly what you are,' Mrs Chesterton continued, her refined accent cutting through the noise. 'A pathetic old criminal whose time is up.'

Council Leader Kerr rose slowly, he declared in an ominous tone, 'Councillor Steele, in light of this evidence, I have no choice but to call for your immediate resignation from this council and all associated positions.'

Multiple voices shouted from around the chamber. 'Seconded!'

Danny stood on unsteady legs, his silver hair dishevelled, fury and humiliation mottling his face. The legendary Danny Steele, reduced to public disgrace by a housewife with nothing but a camera and unshakeable moral conviction.

Abandoning all pretence of respectability, he snarled, naked fury distorting his features. 'You sanctimonious old dried-up trollop. You don't know who you're fucking with.'

Mrs Chesterton filed away the incriminating photos, taking meticulous care, her expression serene with victory. 'As you would no doubt say in the filthy world you belong to, I have got you well and truly by the short and curlies.'

Danny stumbled towards the chamber doors, the crowd's contemptuous laughter following him into the corridor. Fleeing, he caught fragments of conversation from the older residents – people who remembered when Danny Steele was the undisputed King of Sugar Cane Wharf. The man everyone approached when they needed help, a few bob extra, or business sorted. The man who'd dealt with troublemakers at Executioner's Steps behind his pub, where problems had a way of disappearing permanently.

But times were changing. A new government was coming to power, promising that the lights would stay on and the old ways would be swept aside. The dark days of power cuts and economic chaos were ending, and with them, the reign of gangland figures who'd thrived in the shadows. Danny Steele's era was finished, relegated to whispered stories about how the East End used to operate before civilisation returned.

Mrs Dorothea Chesterton had executed him with nothing more than truth, a handful of photographs, and the unstoppable force of social justice.

# Chapter Fifty-Four

*Jimmy will understand. Blood's thicker than water. Family helps family.*

Danny Steele pushed through the revolving doors of 'Odds On', his son's HQ on Commercial Road. The neon sign buzzed and flickered in the miserable drizzle, casting sickly pink light across the wet pavement where punters huddled under umbrellas, clutching betting slips with desperate hope.

Three days since the council humiliation, and Danny's empire had collapsed faster than dominoes in an earthquake. But sons respected their fathers. Especially sons who owed everything to their old man's guidance and connections.

Two granite-faced bouncers flanked the entrance – proper hard cases with scarred fists and dead eyes that had seen too much violence.

'State your business,' the taller one told him.

Danny's chest puffed with automatic authority. 'Jimmy's father. He'll want to see me.'

The bouncer's expression never changed. Stone-hearted. Remorseless. 'Wait here.'

*Since when do I wait for anyone?*

He disappeared inside while his partner watched Danny with the casual interest of a butcher eyeing livestock. Rain soaked through Danny's once-expensive coat, but he didn't dare move without permission. The great Danny Steele, standing in the gutter while hired muscle decided whether he deserved an audience.

The muscle returned, jerking his thumb towards the entrance. 'Up the stairs. Third door. Wait in the chair outside.'

The waiting area outside Jimmy's office held a single wooden chair positioned deliberately in front of a massive oak door. Danny perched on the hard seat, his bulk overflowing the narrow frame.

*He's probably just finishing up. Important business. Like father, like son.*

Twenty minutes crawled past.

Forty minutes.

Angry tension twisted and knotted his belly. The great Danny Steele, sitting in a corridor waiting for scraps of attention from his own flesh and blood.

*This is taking the piss. I'm his father, for Chrissakes!*

The office door finally opened.

Jimmy emerged from his sanctuary wearing his finest charcoal-grey suit, the one that cost more than most blokes earned in three months. His silver-grey eyes – inherited from Iris but colder than hers had ever been – swept over the man waiting in the corridor.

But the man perched on that uncomfortable chair wasn't the towering figure from Jimmy's childhood memories. This version appeared smaller somehow. Deflated. News of how he'd lost his council seat and been humiliated had reached Jimmy's ears.

News travelled fast in the East End, especially when it involved the spectacular downfall of someone who'd ruled through fear for decades.

Danny struggled to his feet, 'Son, good to see you. You're doing well for yourself here.'

He followed Jimmy inside. Mahogany desk. Leather furniture. Crystal decanters filled with expensive spirits.

*The boy's built a proper empire. Chip off the old block.*

Confident and easy, Jimmy settled behind his desk and gestured towards the drinks cabinet. 'Help yourself, Dad. You know where everything is.'

The casual dismissal stung, but Danny poured three fingers of excellent whisky while Jimmy continued reviewing papers. Just busy with business. Nothing personal. The amber liquid burned his throat but couldn't warm the growing chill in his chest.

'So.' Jimmy finally raised his eyes. 'What brings you to my humble establishment?'

The gentle mockery in 'humble establishment' wasn't lost on Danny, but he forced a paternal smile. 'Can't a father visit his son without an agenda?'

Jimmy's expression remained unreadable. Waiting. His stillness reminded Danny of a predator preparing to strike.

Danny settled into the leather chair opposite the desk, crossing his legs, deliberately casual. 'I've had some temporary setbacks, Jimmy. Nothing serious, you understand. Just the usual political nonsense that comes with success.'

'Temporary cock-ups.' Jimmy leaned back in his chair, fingers steepled. 'That what you call getting your arse handed to you by Mrs Dorothea Chesterton?'

Heat flooded Danny's face, his breathing turning quick and shallow. 'You saw the news then.'

'Hard to miss. Made quite the splash in all the local rags.'

Jimmy watched his father's confident expression begin to crumble. The great Danny Steele, reduced to explaining away public humiliation to his own son. The sight should have given Jimmy satisfaction, but instead he felt only cold emptiness.

For years, Jimmy had feared this man's disapproval. Craved his respect. Accepted constant criticism about never measuring up to the family reputation. All those times Danny had reminded him he'd never be the man his father was.

Now, seeing Danny squirm in that leather chair, Jimmy realised the balance of power had shifted permanently. The revelation tasted bitter rather than sweet.

'The thing is, son,' Danny continued, his voice taking on a wheedling quality Jimmy had never heard before, 'we're family. Blood. We should stick together when times get rough.'

'Family?' Jimmy set down his whisky glass, real slow to show he was in complete control. 'When exactly did you start caring about family, Dad?'

'I built everything for you, son. For the family. Every deal, every scheme, every bloody thing I ever did was to give you opportunities I never had.'

*Why is he being so cold? This is Jimmy. My boy. He understands how the world works.*

'Bollocks.' Jimmy's terse interruption cut through Danny. 'You built it for yourself. You always put yourself first, then convinced everyone else it was for their benefit.'

Danny felt the conversation slipping away from him, his breathing becoming harsh and uneven. This wasn't going according to plan. Jimmy was supposed to welcome his father's experience, recognise that blood was thicker than water.

Instead, his son regarded him, employing the cold assessment of a businessman evaluating a toxic investment.

'Look, I'll be straight up with you.' Danny leaned forward desperately, his voice developing a tremor he couldn't control. 'I need help. Temporary assistance until I get back on my feet. We could work together, combine your legitimate operation with my experience. Build an empire bigger than either of us could manage alone.'

Jimmy's silence stretched until he said, 'Let me understand this correctly. You want me to bail you out of the hole you've dug for yourself. After years of telling me I'm second-rate. After sabotaging every opportunity I ever had to prove myself.'

'That's not—'

'Remember my boxing career, Dad?' Jimmy rose from his chair, his long strides eating up the distance between them. 'I was good. Really bloody good. Had a genuine shot at the heavyweight championship. Real chance to be something beyond the family business.'

Danny's face went pale, his breathing turning shallow and panicked. He remembered. And truth was, he'd do it all again.

'But you couldn't handle it, could you? Couldn't stand the thought of your son achieving something you never could. So you tried to sabotage it.'

'Jimmy, that was—'

'What? What was it?' Jimmy stalked closer, his looming presence filling the space around Danny's chair. 'Business? Family loyalty? Looking out for my best interests?'

Danny's mouth worked soundlessly. The accusations were true, but Jimmy was supposed to understand. Supposed to appreciate the lessons about knowing your place in the world. Danny's chest heaved with desperate, ragged breaths.

'You always said I'd never measure up to the great Danny Steele.' Jimmy stopped directly in front of his father's chair, staring down with pitiless eyes. 'Turns out you were right. I'm fucking better.'

The devastating force of the words hit Danny between the eyes. He lurched to his feet, suddenly aware that his son towered over him by several inches. When had Jimmy grown so bloody tall?

'You sanctimonious little prick. I made YOU. Made you everything you are.'

'You made me nothing.' Jimmy's silver-grey eyes held no warmth, no recognition, no respect. 'Everything I am, I built despite you. Not because of you.'

Danny's face flushed purple with hot rage, his breathing becoming laboured and harsh. For a moment, Jimmy saw a flash of the old intimidation tactics. The physical presence that had terrorised the East End for decades. Terrorised him and squashed him under this man's thumb for too many years.

But Jimmy was done with cowering like some yellow-bellied tosser. He felt nothing. No fear. No yearning need for approval. Nothing but cold assessment of a pathetic old man clinging to dead power.

'You ungrateful cunt.' Danny's massive fists bunched at his sides, his breathing turning into angry pants. 'After everything I've done for this family. After all the sacrifices—'

'Sacrifices?' Jimmy's laugh held no humour, just bitter amusement. 'You sacrificed other people. Anyone who got in the way of what Danny Steele wanted.'

Danny lunged forward, his speed surprising, his meaty hands reaching for Jimmy's throat. But decades of good living had made him slow and clumsy, while Jimmy had stayed sharp. Muscle memory from boxing training kicked in automatically.

Jimmy caught his father's wrists mid-lunge, twisted, and drove Danny backwards until he slammed into the office wall. Framed photographs crashed to the floor in an explosion of glass and splintered wood. Danny's face contorted in shock and pain as Jimmy's superior strength pinned him in place.

The humiliation burned worse than acid. The legendary Danny Steele, pinned to a wall by his own son like a common thug.

Jimmy's grip was iron. Unbreakable.

'You want to talk about family? How about the way you treated my queen, Mini? Don't you think I fucking knew? All those snide remarks questioning My wife's loyalty to the family she chose with heart. You never forgave me for marrying Batters's girl, did you? Well, guess what, Dad? My Mini was worth ten of you.'

Danny scrambled out of his son's grasp the moment Jimmy released him, stumbling backwards, eyes wild, his breathing laboured. His expensive suit was rumpled, his dignity shredded.

'You could never hurt me.' Danny bared his teeth in a feral snarl, stabbing his finger into his own chest. 'I'm the fucking King. The King of EVERYTHING!'

He stormed towards the door, slamming it behind him.

# Chapter Fifty-Five

Brother Bertie got ready to see his son in the House of the Dead. Next week he would be sending Isaac on to his journey to the angels.

Brother Bertie blamed his busted leg for not visiting Isaac at the funeral director's. Reality was different - he was too broken to face his dead son. The mere thought of seeing his beautiful boy's still face was ripping his heart to shreds.

It was Gretie who had forced his hand.

*'You're his father, Bertram,'* his sister had reminded him. *'He needs you to be brave for him one last time.'*

He felt crushed inside. Crucified. How does a father say goodbye to their child?

What words could possibly matter when his boy would never hear them?

He remembered Izzy's first steps, those chubby little legs wobbling, his face lit up with such fierce pride when he'd made it across the room. Brother Bertie had scooped him up, tossed him in the air, caught him safe. Always caught him safe.

Except when it mattered most.

The thought of those tiny hands, cold now. That laugh silenced forever. Those eyes that would never open again, never look up at him full of trust and mischief. His son's small body in that box – it was wrong in every way a thing could be wrong. No parent should have to choose a coffin for their child. Should have to think about the earth swallowing them up.

What would he even say? Sorry I wasn't there? Sorry I chose Jimmy over you? This pain would never leave him. He'd carry it to his own grave, this failure that no amount of time could ever wash clean.

His fingers shook so badly, he fumbled with the black tie, the silk slipping through his grasp like water. A month since Izzy's death, and his hands still shook from morning till night. The simple task of dressing had become a monumental effort that left his head hanging low and him defeated.

'Here, let me.' Gertie reached for the tie, her hands gentle but efficient.

'Stop fussing over me.' Brother Bertie pulled away, wincing from the sharp pain shooting up his damaged leg. 'I can manage.'

'Shut your mouth and let me help you.' Gertie's tone brooked no argument. She knotted the tie, her eyes filled with concern and love that tightened his chest.

Every morning brought the same crushing reality. Izzy was gone. Sin had filed for divorce. His belongings had been dumped in the street outside their flat, his precious records scattered across the pavement in jagged pieces.

The front door rattled under Ruddy's distinctive knock. She entered without waiting for an invitation. New lines around her eyes and mouth showed the strain of the past weeks. Even her usual swagger was subdued.

'Right then,' Ruddy announced, surveying Brother Bertie's appearance, her eyes critical. 'Time to go pay your respects.'

Brother Bertie despised needing their support, despised the way they flanked him like bodyguards protecting an invalid. But his leg couldn't bear his full body mass yet, and the alternative was staying in his former room at Gertie's, staring at walls that closed in tighter each day.

He had to be strong. Izzy wouldn't want to see his father crying.

The funeral parlour loomed silent in the grey morning light, all Victorian stonework and sombre shadows. Gertie had let him know that Sin had purchased a small white coffin.

Mr Thornton, the funeral director, met them at the entrance. His usually composed demeanour showed cracks, and sweat slicked his pale forehead.

'Mr Watson, I'm afraid we have a most irregular situation.' Thornton's voice wavered, his professional calm fractured. 'There's been an incident.'

Icy dread flooded Brother Bertie's veins. 'What kind of incident?'

'Your son's coffin… it has disappeared.'

His damaged leg buckled, and only Gertie's quick reflexes kept him upright.

'What do you mean, disappeared?' Ruddy's voice turned deadly quiet, the tone she used before violence erupted.

Thornton mopped his forehead with a pristine handkerchief, hands visibly shaking. 'We arrived this morning to prepare for the service, and the coffin was simply…gone. Vanished. In forty years of business, I've never encountered anything remotely…'

'Gone where?' Brother Bertie's voice emerged as a strangled whisper, his chest constricting until he could barely breathe.

'We've searched everywhere. The police have been notified, but there's no sign of forced entry, no evidence of theft. It's completely baffling.'

Brother Bertie felt his world tilting sideways. His son's body, missing. The final goodbye he'd been preparing for, stolen from him. The last thread connecting him to his boy, severed.

'I took him.'

The voice from the doorway froze everyone in place. Sin stood silhouetted in the entrance. But this wasn't the Sin he'd loved and lost. This woman radiated cold composure, her eyes empty of warmth or recognition.

Rage flared in Brother Bertie's chest, cutting through the shock and despair. He had never been so angry in his life. 'Where is he, Sin? Where's my boy?'

Her lips curved in a smile devoid of any human warmth. 'Somewhere you'll never find him. I've laid Izzy to rest where neither you nor Jimmy can pollute his innocent soul with your criminal corruption.'

Brother Bertie let out a cry of agonising heartbreak.

'You can't do that!' Ruddy snarled with outrage and stepped forward, fists clenched. 'That's his son, too!'

'*Was* his son,' Sin insisted, her voice steady and merciless. 'Before he chose his criminal brotherhood over his child's life.'

Gertie released Brother Bertie's arm and she advanced on Sin with righteous fury. 'From the beginning I warned my Bertram about you. I said your love would turn to poisonous hate, that you'd bring him low and nothing but pure pain.'

Sin's composure flickered for a moment, uncertainty flashing in her hollow eyes.

'May God have mercy on your soul,' Gertie continued, her voice building to a thunderous crescendo, 'because I damn you to eternal torment for this cruelty!'

Visibly shaken, Sin straightened her shoulders, her voice gaining biblical power. 'He's safe from all of it now. The violence. The gangland. I've saved my son from becoming another casualty of your world.' She took a sharp breath. 'He'll rest in peace, far from the blood and brutality that claimed his life. Where saints watch over him instead of gangsters.'

She twisted and departed, leaving them all in the deepest shock.

'Run after her!' Ruddy shouted. She grabbed Brother Bertie's sleeve, even knowing full well he couldn't with his leg. 'Find out where Izzy is! Don't let her get away!'

But Brother Bertie remained motionless, the fight draining from his broken body. 'Let her go,' he whispered, watching Sin disappear into the grey morning. 'Perhaps it's for the best. He's in the ground now, laid to rest. Best not disturb him.'

His voice broke on the final words.

'Leave him. Let the angels take care of him now.'

# Chapter Fifty-Six

Steam danced from the pot of beef stew on Edmund's ancient stove, filling the warehouse with the rich aroma of home cooking. Six months had passed since Chrissie spent on these river steps with a shard of mirror glass. Six months since Edmund had carried her broken body up those spiral stairs. Six months of healing, working, finding her way back.

Humming, Chrissie stirred the thick broth with a wooden spoon, tasting a small sip from the edge. She added another pinch of salt, then glanced across the open space to where Edmund sat in his armchair, wire-rimmed glasses perched on his nose, case files spread across his lap. Tel, her once-mangy cat, now sleek and contented, curled at his feet.

'You planning to read all bloody night?' she called over, the East End swagger in her voice softened by affection.

Edmund looked up, that gentle smile spreading across his face, crinkling the corners of his eyes. The same smile that greeted her every morning across the breakfast table, the same smile that bid her goodnight from the bottom of those spiral stairs.

'Just finishing this report,' he replied, stretching his arms above his head. 'The council's finally approved additional funding for Mini's Place.'

Chrissie nodded, pleased but unsurprised. The centre had flourished these past months, with three new counsellors hired and a second location opening in Hackney. Her own caseload had grown to fifteen women she worked with regularly, most referred to her by word of mouth.

'Hyacinth came by today.' Chrissie reached for two mismatched bowls from the cupboard. 'Brought me flowers.'

Edmund set down his papers, giving her his full attention. 'How is she?'

'Still grieving, as you'd expect.' Chrissie ladled stew into the bowls. 'But she's starting that support group for mothers. Five women already signed up.'

From devastation to purpose. That had been Hyacinth's journey, mirroring Chrissie's own in many ways. The woman who'd lost her daughter had channelled her grief into helping other mothers whose children had fallen prey to the same predators.

Edmund cleared the small dining table of books and papers, setting out cutlery and napkins with the domestic ease they'd developed. This unspoken choreography of their evenings together had become Chrissie's unexpected sanctuary.

'You've given her that,' Edmund said quietly. 'A way forward.'

Chrissie shrugged off the praise, though a warm flush spread across her cheeks. 'She'd have found it herself eventually.'

They sat across from each other at the table, knees occasionally brushing beneath. The rain tapped gently against the windows, turning the warehouse into a cozy island amid the industrial wasteland of Sugar Cane Wharf.

They discussed work through dinner, the easy back-and-forth of two people whose passions aligned. No pretence, no performances. Just two people who understood each other's purpose.

When had this happened? Chrissie wondered, watching Edmund gesticulate enthusiastically about expanded counselling services. When had she stopped thinking about leaving? When had his warehouse become home?

After dinner, Edmund insisted on washing up while Chrissie took her customary place on the balcony with a ciggy. The night air carried the brackish scent of the Thames, the distant hum of the city beyond. From this height, she could see the lights of dockside pubs, hear faint music carried on the breeze.

Inside, Edmund put on a record, Nina Simone, one of Chrissie's favourites. The familiar notes floated through the open French doors, wrapping around her like an embrace.

Edmund joined her on the balcony, two glasses of red wine in his hands. He passed one to her, their fingers touching in that familiar way that still sent electricity through her veins.

'Penny for your thoughts?' he asked, leaning against the railing beside her.

'I used to think I was just damaged goods,' she confessed, her voice low and raw. 'That no one would ever want me except for what I could do for them. What my body could give them.'

Edmund stepped closer, close enough that she could feel the warmth radiating from him in the cool night air. 'And now?'

'Now I know that's bollocks,' Chrissie replied, a small smile tugging at her lips. 'Now I know I've got more to offer than that. I've got… talents.'

She set her glass down, her heartbeat thundering in her ears. For the first time in her adult life, Chrissie Steele was approaching a man not from fear, not from obligation, not from desperation – but from choice. From strength.

'I think I'm ready,' she said softly, the words barely audible above the music and the river below.

Edmund's brow furrowed slightly. 'Ready?'

'To be loved properly,' Chrissie clarified, her voice steadier now. 'For who I am. Not what I can give or do.'

Understanding dawned in Edmund's eyes, followed quickly by a warmth that melted something final inside her chest.

'I've been ready since the day you started filing those papers at Mini's Place,' he admitted. 'But I needed you to be ready, too.'

Chrissie closed the last distance between them. Her hand reached up to touch his face, fingers tracing the lines around his eyes, the soft curve of his lips.

'I'm damaged,' she whispered, vulnerability naked in her voice.

'I'm bald.'

Ridiculous man!

Her elbow playfully dug into his side.

'I like you,' she said, the simple phrase containing worlds of meaning.

'Like you, too,' he replied, his voice husky with emotion.

Chrissie glanced back at the open French doors, at the warmth and safety beyond. At the life they'd built together without naming it.

'I don't want to go home.'

Edmund's hands came up to cradle her face, his touch so soft. 'This is your home.'

And, just like that, Chrissie and Edmund kissed for the first time.

# Chapter Fifty-Seven

Pork pie hat low, Brother Bertie sat in his Jamaican flag-backed deck chair on the allotment, savouring the rich burn of Lord Have Mercy Rum Punch and listening to Dennis Brown's sweet tones on 'I Am the Conqueror' drifting from his transistor radio. Six months now since Izzy's death, and not a single day passed without him thinking of his boy.

It was getting easier. The sharp edges of grief had worn smooth with time, but there would always be a gaping hole in his heart, widened by never knowing where his son's final resting place lay. True to her word, Sin had vanished completely. He hadn't caught so much as a glimpse of her since that terrible morning at the House of the Dead.

But his gut told him he would see her again. The East End had a way of hanging on to its own, wrapped around them tight as an umbilical cord, always dragging them back home eventually.

'Aye! Aye! Where's my bloody glass, then?'

Ruddy's distinctive bellow cut through the music. Brother Bertie sat up straighter, spotting her bowling along the dirt path between the vegetable patches, her knobbly knees jutting above her minidress as usual. But today she carried something in her right hand. A long, elegant object that caught the afternoon sunlight.

'What you got there, you mad woman?' Brother Bertie called out, setting down his mug.

Ruddy's beehive bobbed with each purposeful step. 'Got you a present, haven't I? About bloody time, too.'

Brother Bertie's pulse quickened as she drew closer. The object in her hand was unmistakably a walking cane, but not the hospital-issued metal monstrosity he'd been using. This was a thing of beauty, crafted from dark, polished wood that gleamed with a rich mahogany sheen.

'Ruddy, you shouldn't have—'

'Shut your gob and take it.' She thrust the cane towards him, her eyes bright with anticipation. 'Had it specially made for you by a mate down the Silver Vaults. Proper craftsman, he is.'

Brother Bertie's hands closed around the smooth wood, and he immediately sensed its perfect balance and craftsmanship. The cane felt substantial without being heavy, elegant without being showy. But when his gaze travelled to the top, his breath caught in his throat.

The handle was a silver lion's head, exquisitely engraved with flowing mane and regal bearing. Every detail was perfection.

'My mate who crafted this,' Ruddy gently explained, 'said every day you place your palm on that lion, it'll remind you that you're still standing when lesser men would've crumbled to dust.'

Brother Bertie traced the intricate engraving, the cool silver warm beneath his touch.

'It's beautiful, Ruddy. I don't know what to say.'

She winked, her trademark mischief returning. 'Oh, it'll protect you in other ways, too.'

Brother Bertie frowned, studying her face for clues. 'What do you mean by that?'

Ruddy tapped her nose with one painted fingernail. 'You'll find out soon enough, won't you?' She winked. 'I would show you, but I've got a little tickle of personal business to take care of myself.'

That night, in his bedroom, Brother Bertie examined his new cane more closely. He'd been leaning it carefully near the wall when the Lion of Judah handle shifted slightly under his palm. Curious, he gripped the silver top and drew it upwards.

The handle separated from the shaft with a soft click, revealing a gleaming steel blade hidden within the wood. Not just any blade, this was a sword, perfectly balanced and honed to a lethal edge that could slice through bone without effort.

Brother Bertie stared at the concealed weapon, understanding flooding through him. Ruddy hadn't just given him a walking stick. She'd armed him with a blade that would fool any copper, any rival, any threat that mistook his limp for weakness.

The Lion of Judah wasn't just symbolic protection, it was real, deadly, and perfectly disguised.

Brother Bertie smiled for the first time in months, sliding the blade back into its wooden sheath with a satisfying click. Broken he might be, but he was still the king of his domain.

And kings, even wounded ones, always kept their claws sharp.

# Chapter Fifty-Eight

Jimmy slid into the Bentley's driver seat, his gut twisting tight. Instantly, the hairs on the back of his neck prickled. Thirty-odd years of survival in the East End screamed danger.

His hand flashed towards the glove compartment where his shooter waited.

Too fucking late.

Quick as lightning, a thick belt whipped around his throat from behind.

'Move a bleeding muscle and I'll choke the life right out of you, you cruel, selfish bastard.'

The leather bit deep into his windpipe. A figure rose from the backseat shadows, beehive hairdo wild with rage, deadly eyes blazing pure murder.

Ruddy.

Jimmy's massive frame bucked instinctively, but the belt pulled tighter. She'd positioned herself perfect - one knee braced behind the seat, both hands twisted in the leather, cutting off his air supply with practiced skill. His vision blurred at the edges.

'What's the matter, Jimmy? Cat got your tongue?' Her voice dripped venom beside his ear. 'Well you can bollocks to that idea if you think I'm finished with you, you worthless piece of shit.'

Jimmy's powerful shoulders strained, every muscle screaming to break free. This scrawny bint had caught the most feared man in the East End like a mug punter. The humiliation burned fiercer than the leather crushing his throat. He was The Southpaw. Men crossed Commercial Road rather than meet his glacial stare. Now this knobbly-knee nobody held his life in her bony hands.

'Easy now, Ruddy.' His voice came out strangled. 'Whatever's got your—'

'Shut your lying gob!' The belt yanked tighter. 'Nothing easy about watching a proper man get destroyed by you Steele cunts.'

Black spots danced in Jimmy's vision. His lungs burned for air. Every instinct roared to grab her wrists, snap them clean, show this manky bitch what happened to people who crossed Jimmy Steele. But she held the angle perfect - one wrong move and she'd snap his neck good.

'You want to know what it's been doing to my Bertie?' Her breath scorched his ear. 'Watching him drag himself round on that walking stick, crying for his dead boy every bleeding night?'

Jimmy's chest heaved, desperate for oxygen.

Isaac.

The name tore through his skull.

'When a man loses his son and don't know where the little angel's laid to rest, that breaks him forever. Breaks him right down to his rotten core.'

'Sin made her own—' Jimmy gasped.

'Her own choices?' The belt bit deeper. 'That vicious bitch took that beautiful boy's coffin and buried him God knows where. Away from Bertie. Forever. For what? Because she couldn't bear to glance at the man who tried to save her own bleeding brother?'

Jimmy's temples pounded. His powerful fists ground in his lap, itching to crush her scrawny throat. But Ruddy's fury burned white-hot, and grief gave people superhuman strength. She knew exactly what she was doing.

'Since '63 I've known Bertie,' she hissed. 'Seen him face down the hardest geezers in London without blinking. Now he sits in that flat, staring out at the river, wondering if his little boy's cold somewhere.'

The leather dug into Jimmy's flesh. Each word hit harder than any fist.

'I curse the bleeding day you Steeles ever clapped eyes on him. He was golden before you lot sunk your claws in.'

'He was as dodgy as the rest of us—'

'Don't you fucking dare!' The belt jerked vicious. 'That man loved his boy more than his own breath. Loved your poisonous sister despite all the shit she dragged with her from that twisted relationship with your wicked father.'

Jimmy's vision swam. His chest burned. This was his patch, his motor, his frigging Commercial Road. Nobody - man, woman, or Devil - put hands on Jimmy Southpaw and lived to brag about it. But the belt stayed rock-steady round his flesh.

'You listen good.' Her lips brushed his ear, deadly soft. 'You stay the fuck away from Bertie. He's swallowed more grief than any man should stomach, and I won't watch you finish destroying him.'

'And if I don't?' Jimmy wheezed.

'Then next time I won't piss about with warnings.' The belt loosened just enough to let him breathe. 'I'll do it proper and smile while you turn blue.'

Jimmy's shoulders bunched, ready to explode. His biceps strained beneath his jacket, every fibre screaming for violence. But Ruddy's words cut deeper than any blade. The fight drained out of him like dirty water.

'I'm sorry.' The admission tasted bitter.

'Your sorry don't mean bollocks. Won't bring back that little angel or heal what's broken in my Bertie.'

The belt suddenly loosened and dropped round his neck.

Then she was gone.

# Chapter Fifty-Nine

The black telephone rang inside Jimmy's office. His forehead furrowed into deep lines when he recognised the voice on the other end of the line.

'Jimmy, it's your mum. I need to see you. Now.'

His fingers tightened around the receiver, an ominous sensation descending over him. Since her accident, five years back, his mum hadn't phoned him, not once and that was because the doctors up at the hospital had explained that remembering phone numbers and the simple act of dialling was beyond what her damaged brain could manage.

So how was she managing it now?

Alarm shot through Jimmy, propelling him upright. 'What's wrong, Mum? You all right?'

He heard her pull in a deep stream of air. 'Get yourself to the house, love. Now.'

With a sharp click, the line went dead.

Jimmy snatched his Bentley keys from the desk and tore through the streets of Whitechapel into Sugar Cane Wharf, foot flattened to the floor, tyres shrieking round corners. Every red light felt like bloody torture. His chest squeezed tight, lungs struggling for air.

He barged through the front door of the terraced house he'd grown up in, his own key still working in the lock.

'Mum? MUM!'

'In here, love.'

Following the voice to the sitting room, Jimmy froze dead in the doorway. His aunt Chrissie perched on the edge of the settee. Gone was the wreck that had bolted from him in the squat. She'd filled out proper, her face plump and glowing, platinum hair buffed and styled. Word on the street said she'd shacked up with that professor geezer who helped Lucas run Mini's Place.

'Where's Mum?' Jimmy demanded, gaze darting around the familiar room.

'I'm here, my love.'

He spun round so fast he nearly toppled over. Iris stood in the doorway, and Jimmy gawped because she looked like… Mum. His mother before that terrible accident had turned her into someone else entirely.

The shuffling, confused woman had vanished. No more halting, muddled speech patterns, no trailing off mid-sentence or repeating herself. This voice belonged to before. Strong, clear, certain.

When their eyes met, Jimmy felt every bit of air rush from his lungs. Those eyes. The vacant, glassy stare had disappeared completely, replaced by intelligence so fierce it forced him back a step.

'Mum?' The word crawled from his throat, barely audible.

Jimmy's legs went wobbly beneath him. He grabbed for the doorframe, vision swimming. A gentle smile warming her lips, she moved towards him purposefully, back straight, head high. No hesitation. No confusion. When she reached up to press the backs of her fingers to his face, tears welled in Jimmy's eyes.

'My lovely boy.'

He crushed her slight frame against his chest. His beloved mum, truly returned from wherever the accident had sent her. Emotion clogged his throat, thick and suffocating. He wasn't one for prayer, didn't buy that Heaven-above and Hell-below rubbish, but right then he thanked whatever power had brought his mum back to him.

'How? I don't understand. The doctors said your brain…' He pulled back, searching her face. 'They said you might never…'

Iris's expression darkened. She glanced at Chrissie, who nodded encouragement, then leaned close to whisper in Jimmy's ear, her breath warm against his skin.

'Your dad tried to murder me.'

The chilling announcement hit Jimmy like a savage uppercut from his boxing days. Every drop of colour drained from his face, leaving him ashen and shaken. He staggered backwards, mouth opening and closing without sound.

'What? No. That's not— Mum, you're going off your trolley again. Dad?'

'Park yourself down, son.' Iris guided him to the armchair, her touch gentle but unyielding. 'You need to hear this properly.' Her fingers dug into his shoulders. 'Remember what I taught you when you was eight. That the truth is sometimes the hardest thing to swallow.'

Jimmy collapsed into the chair, breathing shallow and rapid. The room tilted and spun around him.

'It was no accident,' Iris continued, voice steady and clear. 'The day we buried your Mini, I was by the river, needing air during the wake. Danny appeared from nowhere, dragged me to the Executioner's Steps—'

'Nah.' Jimmy shook his head violently. 'That's bollocks. Dad said you took a tumble down the stairs after too much gin.'

Iris's face hardened with the memory. 'He smashed my head against those stone steps, again and again, until everything went black.'

Jimmy shot to his feet, fury boiling through his veins. 'He did WHAT?'

'When I came round, I was lying at the bottom with my skull split open and my memories scattered to the wind.' Iris sank onto the arm of his chair, suddenly looking ancient and worn. 'But the hospital treatment started working about two years ago. Slowly, bit by bit, everything flooded back.'

Jimmy stalked around the small room like a rabid beast, fists balled tight. 'Why didn't you tell me? Why didn't you—?'

'Because your father was still trying to finish the job.' Iris's words stopped him cold. 'Mercury in my gin bottle, Jimmy. Little drops every day, meant to complete the evil task he started at the river.'

Blood drained so fast from Jimmy's head he had to brace himself against the wall. Words failed him, the horror of what had been happening inside his own family almost too much to stomach.

'But I figured it out,' Iris carried on, grim satisfaction lighting her features. 'Caught him red-handed one night when he thought I was sleeping. So I switched the bottles. Let him think his plan was working while I got stronger every day.'

That was it!

Face twisting with murderous rage, Jimmy bolted for the door, violence blazing in his silver-grey eyes. 'I'm going to tear his fucking head off and stuff it up that murdering arse—'

'Sit down.' The steel in Iris's command could have sliced through bone. 'You need to hear all of it before you do anything stupid.'

Jimmy turned back, chest heaving, sweat beading his forehead.

His mother's gaze shifted to his aunt. 'Tell him, Chrissie.'

His aunt lifted her eyes to meet his, and Jimmy saw decades of buried agony etched in every line of her face. Her words emerged husky and fragile.

'During the war, I was attacked. Danny sent me to deliver a packet to some posh fellas in Whitechapel.' Chrissie paused, eyes fluttering closed for a moment. When they opened, they burned with long-suppressed fury. 'I was just an innocent girl. Fifteen years old and green as grass. He said it was black market gear – food or cigarettes or whatever.'

Jimmy's brow furrowed. 'I know something happened, but Dad told me he saved you. That's what family does, they look out for each other.'

'Looked out for me? Saved me? That total cunt!' The old Chrissie erupted suddenly, drawing power from decades of buried rage. 'It weren't no delivery, now was it? Three posh toffs waiting in that house, eating me up with their animal eyes like I was nothing but meat. Danny set me up as bait. He planned to catch them with their trousers down, take pictures, blackmail the bastards for years, but he never showed because some rival gang jumped him.'

Chrissie's gaze bored into her nephew, unflinching. 'Saved me? My own brother set me up like a lamb for slaughter.'

Jimmy lurched from the room, retching violently into the kitchen sink. Iris's footsteps padded after him, motherly hands gentle on his back as he clutched the sink edge.

'I'm sorry, son. I know it's hard to hear.'

He splashed cold water on his face, trying to rinse away the horror. When he returned to the sitting room, Chrissie had composed herself, though wet tracks glistened on her cheeks.

Her tone turned venomous. 'I only found out the truth recently. When I confronted him, he tells me it's all ancient business, bad timing.'

The front door knocker rattled. Iris rose smoothly from her chair, her movements still startling to Jimmy after years of watching her shuffle and stumble.

'That'll be our other guest.'

A minute later, when the woman entered, Jimmy nearly lost his mind. 'What the bloody hell is *she* doing here?'

His dad's fancy piece. Or former, since she'd given him the boot.

'Everyone knows me as Scarlett now,' she addressed Jimmy directly, like they were alone in the room. 'But that wasn't always my name. Back when I worked on the *Sing-Song Lady,* people called me Joanie.'

She moved beside Iris. 'I was seventeen, a naïve girl selling herself and pregnant with child. When I defended myself against one of Danny's business partners, your father beat the baby right out of me.' Her throat bobbed as she swallowed hard. 'I've never been able to have another. I wasn't even properly grown, and he robbed me of ever becoming a mother.'

Iris picked up the thread. 'Through my contacts, I heard what he'd done and tracked Scarlett down. Then we started planning.' She grabbed the younger woman's hand, squeezing tight. 'Didn't we.'

Scarlett nodded and finally sank into a chair while Iris continued.

'I asked if she could stomach getting close to Danny. Playing the devoted mistress.'

Jimmy's jaw slackened. His own mother had selected his dad's mistress.

'Being with him turned my stomach every single day,' Scarlett admitted. 'But I did what needed doing. Every smile, every kiss, every time he put his filthy hands on me, I endured it all for this moment.'

Jimmy gaped at the two women. 'You've been working together all this time?'

'Danny only ever had a tiny piece of my trust money,' Iris revealed, cold satisfaction gleaming in her eyes. 'After the bank job in '69, I moved most of it to another account. The stupid bastard never suspected a thing.'

'We've spent the last two years systematically destroying his empire.' Scarlett's expression triumphally glowed. 'Every raid on his properties, every blackmail victim who found the courage to fight back, every business deal that went sour.'

'You orchestrated all of it?' Wonder filled Jimmy's voice.

'He's got nothing left now except the clothes on his back,' Iris declared with grim pleasure.

Chrissie barked out appreciative laughter. 'Bloody hell, Iris. You're like that bloke in the telly show, *Kung Fu*. Been planning this for years while everyone thought you was mental.'

Jimmy stared at the three women. His brilliant mother, his wounded aunt, and the girl his father had destroyed and underestimated. The scales fell from his eyes as he finally saw his father clearly. Not the mighty King of London's Gangland, but a pathetic monster who preyed on those who trusted him most.

His own family.

'For years, I thought my father was the strongest man I knew,' Jimmy murmured, emotion thickening his words. 'But it's you three. You're the ones with real backbone.'

Iris captured her boy's trembling hand between both of hers, her grip firm and steady. Her eyes held all the steel Danny had never possessed, all the cunning he'd never suspected, all the justice he'd never shown.

'We have to do something about your father, son. If we don't, he'll destroy us all.'

# Chapter Sixty

Danny considered just strangling Iris. Putting his large hands around her neck and cutting her air off. Watching the light dim and die in her eyes. He'd had enough of waiting for her to kick the bucket. It was time he took action. He continued planning his murderous thoughts while walking down the side street in Sugar Cane Wharf, a few streets up from his boozer, the River Rat. He stopped and leaned his hand on the wall for a breather. The oddest thing was he'd just had a cuppa at home, and since he'd left his head didn't feel right. His eyes blurred, and the world about him wavered, coming and going. He took two deep breaths, pushed off the wall, and started on his journey again. This time, he only managed three steps before the ground fell away from him and he collapsed into blackness…

Icy water splashed across Danny's face, jolting him awake. His eyelids flew open to blackness. No, not total blackness – faint moonlight glinted off the river nearby. He tried to move but found his arms bound tight behind him, his ankles strapped together. Panic surged through him when he realised a filthy rag gagged his mouth, the taste of oil and dirt flooding his tongue.

Where the bloody hell was he?

Danny thrashed about, twisting his head to scan his surroundings. Then he saw it – the ancient stone steps leading down to the Thames. Executioner's Steps. His insides liquefied with terror.

*Christ Almighty. Not here. Not these fucking steps.*

His frenzied eyes darted upwards and spotted the makeshift noose dangling from the sturdy iron davit that jutted from the old stone wall – once used for loading cargo from barges, now prepared for a very different load.

*No! No! No! They couldn't. They wouldn't.*

Danny bucked and writhed on the cold stone, muffled screams trapped behind the gag. Sweat poured from him despite the chill, soaking his expensive shirt.

'He's awake then.'

The soft female voice sliced through the darkness, freezing Danny mid-struggle. Footsteps approached from the shadows, unhurried, deliberate. A figure stepped into the weak moonlight, and Danny's eyes bulged in their sockets.

Iris.

His wife stood tall, straight-backed, her movements fluid and graceful. Nothing like the shuffling, confused wreck he'd been living with for years.

'Enjoying your special cuppa, Danny?' She knelt beside him, yanking the gag from his mouth. 'I put some of your mercury gin in it. Thought you might like a taste of your own medicine.'

'You deceitful bitch!' Danny railed, blood trickling from his torn lip. 'You can't do this to me! Do you know who I am?'

Iris's laughter cut through the night air. 'Oh, I know exactly who you are. A man who tried to murder his wife. A poor judge of character who never bothered to notice I was getting better, not worse.'

More footsteps sounded on the stones. Chrissie and Scarlett materialised from the darkness, both staring down at him, hatred burning in their eyes.

His brain scrambled for a way out. This couldn't be happening. Not to him. Not to Danny fucking Steele.

'Scarlett, baby,' he pleaded, forcing charm into his voice. 'Help me out here. We can sort this mess, yeah? I'll give you anything you want.'

'My name is not Scarlett.' Her eyes glittered with malice and pure hatred. 'It's Joanie. From the *Sing-Song Lady*.'

The revelation shattered Danny's life like a mirror smashed with a hammer. His mouth hung open, still not able to comprehend what was going on. Scarlett was Joanie, the prostitute from the floating brothel? Nah, someone must be pulling his fucking nuts.

'That's not possible,' he gasped, genuine terror flooding his system. 'You can't be her.'

'I changed everything about myself to get close to you.' The truth of her words battered inside Danny's brain. 'And it worked. The great Danny Steele never recognised the girl whose baby he beat out of her.'

She took a step closer to him, her mouth shaped into an ugly sneer. 'A worthless scrubber. A poxy, brain-dead bobtail. Damaged goods. That's what you called me when I asked you about Joanie.'

She gobbed with all-out disgust on the ground near his feet.

Danny could barely catch the air into his lungs. This was all wrong. He was Danny Steele. The King of the Docks. The puppet master, not the puppet.

'You've gone mental, the lot of ya,' he snarled, pure bottle rising where fear had been. 'Jimmy will rip you apart when he finds out what you've done.'

Heavy footsteps sounded on stone. Danny's head whipped around to see his son emerging from the shadows, eyes cold and merciless.

'Jimmy!' Relief flooded through him. 'Thank Christ! Get me out of this, son!'

Jimmy stared at him, expression blank. 'They told me everything, Dad.'

The relief curdled instantly. 'Don't listen to these mad bitches! They're lying! I'm your father!'

'No father would do what you've done.' Jimmy's voice shattered with revulsion. 'To Mum. To Chrissie. To that girl.'

Danny's mind raced frantically. This wasn't real. Couldn't be real. His own son wouldn't do this.

'Jimmy, listen to me.' He adopted the voice that had always worked before – authoritative, commanding. 'I built everything we have. Everything you are. You think you can run things without me? You're nothing without me, boy.'

Jimmy's face hardened. 'I'd rather be nothing than be like you.'

With a nod from Iris, Jimmy hauled Danny to his feet. The older man struggled wildly, twisting and kicking, but his son's strength overwhelmed him. Jimmy dragged him towards the dangling noose.

Utter panic overtook Danny. 'Don't do this! I'm your father! YOUR FATHER!'

His screams echoed off the stone walls as Jimmy forced the noose over his head and tightened it around his neck.

'Jimmy, please,' Danny sobbed, all pretence of strength abandoned. 'I love you, son. You're my boy.'

For one fleeting moment, doubt flickered across Jimmy's face.

'Finish it,' Iris commanded, her voice steel. 'Or I will.'

The doubt vanished. Jimmy stepped back, joining the women who formed a semi-circle facing Danny.

In that moment, with the rope tight around his neck and the Thames flowing black below, Danny's fear transformed into rage. If he was going out, it wouldn't be begging.

'You ungrateful fucking bastards,' he spat, venom dripping from every word. 'I made every one of you. And you'll be nothing when I'm gone. NOTHING!'

Jimmy shoved him backwards off the edge of the stone platform. The rope snapped taut.

Danny's legs kicked frantically, his body twisting in the air. His eyes bulged, desperate gurgling sounds escaping his throat as his neck snapped. The four watched in silence until the thrashing stopped altogether.

Chrissie's quiet voice broke the silence. 'Justice for Araminta.'

Another figure materialised from the darkness. The Duchess, resplendent in fur despite the grim setting, surveyed the scene with seasoned eyes.

'I'll take care of the body,' she announced briskly. 'He won't be the first to disappear from these steps. And, I'll put it about that he did a runner to America because his empire had fallen.'

Iris nodded her thanks, then turned away from her husband's swinging corpse. The others followed suit, leaving The Duchess to her work.

The reign of the docks' most brutal king ended not with a bang, but with the quiet splash of a body being claimed by the hungry river.

# Epilogue

## 2015

The August sun blazed down mercilessly on Brother Bertie's allotment, turning the small patch of earth into his own slice of Caribbean paradise. He was well into his seventies now. His eyes still held that mischievous glint that had charmed half of London in his heyday. His Lion of Judah walking stick leaned against his beloved Jamaican flag deck chair, the silver lion's head catching the brilliant sunlight.

'The Millionaire' crooned from his battered transistor radio as Connie Francis's velvety-smooth voice drifted across the vegetable patches. Brother Bertie sipped his legendary Lord Have Mercy Rum

Punch, the ice cubes clinking against the glass in a rhythm that matched his contentment.

'If you hike that hemline any higher, love, the boys down at Billingsgate will be getting an eyeful of your breakfast,' he drawled, eyeing Ruddy's outfit with theatrical disapproval.

At seventy-five, Nora 'Ruddy' Baxter still possessed the same gobby spirit that had terrorised East End card tables for decades. Her flame-orange minidress barely covered her bony thighs, paired with white patent boots that reached her knees. The beehive wig perched on her head defied both gravity and good taste, lacquered to within an inch of its synthetic life.

'Shut your trap, you ancient goat,' she fired back, planting her fists on her angular hips. 'Just because your old todger hasn't seen action since the Three-Day Week doesn't mean the rest of us have thrown in the towel.'

Brother Bertie nearly choked on his rum punch. 'Ancient goat? This from someone who was already past her sell-by date when the Beatles were still playing the Cavern Club.'

'Past my sell-by date?' Ruddy's voice pitched higher, outraged. 'I'll have you know I could still pull a toyboy if I put my mind to it. What about you, Methuselah? When's the last time you had anything stiffer than that walking stick of yours?'

'Cheeky mare!' Brother Bertie slapped his thigh, delighted. 'There's life in this old lion yet. The stick's for show. Intimidation factor, innit?'

They glared hard at each other before dissolving into their familiar chorus of wheezing laughter. The ritual insults were as much a part of their friendship as the rum punch and reggae music.

Brother Bertie was reaching for the rum bottle when Ruddy's sharp intake of breath made him freeze.

'You've gotta be fucking kidding me.'

Her voice carried a mixture of disbelief and pure, volcanic rage. Brother Bertie followed her stare down the narrow pathway between the allotments, his own glass slipping from nerveless fingers to shatter on the ground.

Ruddy shot to her feet, her features twisted and contorted. She almost lost her footing because the heaviness of the rage nearly dragged her down.

Brother Bertie was dizzy for a moment, yanked back to a past that had been looming larger and larger lately. Forty odd years evaporated in the space of a heartbeat, leaving him staring at the ghost of his greatest love and deepest torment. Using his Lion of Judah cane for support, he hauled himself upright on unsteady legs, his arthritic joints protesting every movement.

Sin.

Once his wife. Always the mother of his child.

Time had carved deep furrows into her once-beautiful face, turning her dark hair silver-white beneath a simple black headscarf. But those eyes – Christ, those eyes were exactly the same. Now glistening with depths of pain that made the old anguish flood through him.

She stopped short of reaching them, her hands clasped before her.

'Bertram,' she greeted, her voice softer than he remembered but unmistakably hers.

Ruddy exploded, zooming off like a firework. 'You've got the bloody nerve of the Devil hisself, coming here!' she spat and shook. 'Showing your face in Bertie's place after all these years! You stick to your side of the borough and we'll stick to ours, you heartless cow!'

'Ruddy.' Brother Bertie's voice cut through her tirade, quiet but firm. 'Give us some time, love.'

Ruddy whipped around, her beehive quivering with indignation. 'Bertie, you can't be serious! After what she—'

'Please.'

The single word carried forty years of exhaustion, and Ruddy's fury deflated slightly. She grabbed her handbag, huffing and puffing like a steam engine.

'Fine. But you mark my words, Sin Steele,' she jabbed a bony finger at the older woman, 'you hurt him again and I'm coming to get ya. And I won't be using my handbag next time.'

She stomped away down the path, muttering curses that would make a docker blush.

The silence that followed felt sacred and terrifying. Brother Bertie's heart hammered against his ribs as he studied the woman who had once been his everything. In his bones, in his very soul, he knew why she'd come.

'You've come to tell me about my boy,' he whispered, his voice breaking on the words. 'My Izzy.'

Sin stepped closer, tears sparkling in her dark eyes like diamonds. She nodded slowly.

'Yes, Bertram. I'm ready to tell you where he's laid to rest.'

Brother Bertie wasn't sure his ancient heart could take this revelation, although it was what he'd needed to know for over forty years. His hands shook on his cane.

Sin's voice was barely audible. 'I buried him here. In the allotment.'

The words hit him harder than any punch he'd ever taken. Brother Bertie collapsed back into his chair, gasping for breath, the cane clattering to the ground. His vision blurred as the earth seemed to shift beneath him.

'Here?' he choked out. 'All this time?'

Sin knelt beside his chair, her own tears flowing freely now. 'I laid our beautiful boy so that his father could watch over him. Guard him. Keep the evil spirits from his soul. Every flower you've planted, every vegetable you've grown – you've been tending his garden, Bertram. You've been with him all along.'

She stood slowly, extending her hand towards the border of the allotment where Brother Bertie had always grown his prize marigolds – bright-orange blooms that caught the morning sun and seemed to glow with their own inner fire.

'There,' she whispered. 'Way deep under the marigolds. I know you've never planted food in this section, only blooms. Our little lion sleeps under the flowers of remembrance.'

Brother Bertie struggled to his feet, his legs shaking. Forty-three years of wondering, of guilt, of endless nights imagining his son alone in some unknown grave – and Isaac had been here all along. Right here, where his father came every day to find peace.

Without thinking, they moved together towards the flower border. Brother Bertie knelt carefully, his old knees protesting, and touched the rich soil with trembling fingers. Sin knelt beside him, and for the first time in four decades, their hands met over the earth that held their child.

'Forgive me,' she whispered. 'Forgive a mother's grief.'

Brother Bertie couldn't speak past the lump in his throat. Instead, he squeezed her hand – still warm, still familiar after all these years – and together they stayed there in the blazing afternoon sun, finally united in love over their sleeping boy.

***

A week later, the River Thames sparkled like scattered diamonds under the late afternoon sun as the luxury riverboat, *Sweet Harmony,* cruised past

Tower Bridge. Music pounded from the deck speakers – a mix of reggae, soul, and classic rock that had everyone from eight to eighty swaying to the rhythm. The party was in full swing, celebrating forty years of marriage between two people who'd proved that love could conquer the darkest of pasts.

Chrissie Fairchild stood at the bow, her silver hair swept up in an elegant chignon, wearing a stunning emerald-green dress that still showed off her legendary curves. In her eighties, she remained a force of nature, tongue-lashing sharp wit, and fierce protectiveness. The scars on her wrists had faded with the good years.

'Ladies and gentlemen!' Her voice carried easily over the music. 'Forty years ago, this old tart married the most patient man in London!'

Raucous cheers erupted from the crowd gathered on deck. Dr Edmund Fairchild, now ninety-two and still besotted with his wife, raised his champagne flute with a trembling but determined hand.

Standing proudly near him was Charlie, one of their twin children. Chrissie had nearly dropped dead from shock when she'd fallen pregnant at the grand age of forty-six. The doctors called it a miracle, Chrissie called it a bloody nightmare, till those twins arrived and turned her world upside down in the best possible way.

Everyone at the celebrations knew to keep it schtum about their other twin, Gina, or why she wasn't present at the celebrations. Their daughter was a dead ringer for Chrissie back in the bad ole days. A knockout with that same wild streak, same mouth on her, same knack for finding trouble or making it when it didn't find her first. Edmund took it on the chin like he did everything, but Chrissie? It ate her up inside something terrible. Some mornings she'd grab the paper, heart in her mouth, half-expecting to see Gina's face splashed across the front page. The apple never fell far from the tree in the East End, and that was a fact.

'And forty years later,' Edmund responded, his Cambridge accent as crisp as ever, 'she's still the most magnificent woman I've ever met!'

More cheers, wolf whistles, and ribald comments flew from the assembled guests. Ruddy, resplendent in a shocking-pink ensemble that defied both age and gravity, hollered, 'Get a room, you dirty old codgers!'

Brother Bertie, leaning heavily on his Lion of Judah cane but grinning from ear to ear, watched the celebration with deep satisfaction. It lifted his heart to see so many of the old faces here.

'Oi, you lot!' Chrissie barked again. 'Anyone who wants to hear embarrassing stories about my husband's courting techniques, gather round!'

The crowd surged forward eagerly. Edmund groaned dramatically, hiding his face in his hands while suppressed laughter shook his shoulders.

'Right then,' Chrissie began with wicked relish, 'picture this. 1974, and this posh Cambridge geezer tries to impress me by…'

***

Brother Bertie slipped away when the crowd started doing the Candy Dance to Cameo's famous song. He needed a moment's peace to process the overwhelming joy of the day. He made his way to the quieter stern of the boat, where the water frothed white behind them and London's skyline stretched out in all its historic glory.

The Thames held so many memories, some dark as midnight, others bright as sunshine. Today felt like redemption flowing past Tower Bridge, washing away decades of secrets and lies with each gentle wave.

Heavy footsteps approached behind him.

Jimmy appeared at the rail, two crystal tumblers in his hands, both filled with amber liquid that caught the golden light.

'Thought you might fancy a proper drink.' He offered one of the glasses.

A certain someone in their life had gone all out to heal their wounds and ensure they made peace. And neither of them, at that moment, realised that this certain someone was spying on them now, a huge grin of accomplishment lighting up their face. They triumphantly punched the air and did a victory shuffle before quietly leaving the men to it.

Instead of taking the glass Jimmy offered, Brother Bertie reached inside his jacket and pulled out a battered silver flask. He held it up with a knowing smile.

Jimmy grinned and tipped the whisky in the glasses over the rail.

Brother Bertie unscrewed the flask and carefully filled both glasses with Lord Have Mercy Rum Punch.

'Cheers, brother,' he toasted.

They clinked their glasses together, savoured the familiar taste that was so much more than simple booze. It was the taste of growing into manhood together, their days sparring on the river's golden sand, of the heartbreak that trips you up when you least expect it, the bittersweet flavour of joy and love and family that endures through everything.

Both men sighed contentedly.

'Remember that time we were smuggling those bloody monkeys down the Thames?' Jimmy mused, swirling his drink. 'Must've been summer of '64. You convinced me it was easy money.'

Brother Bertie chuckled, the memory as clear as yesterday. 'Easy money, my raas! Nearly got eaten alive by those vicious little bastards, didn't we? That one with the wonky eye kept trying to bite my ear off.'

'And you started singing that Jamaican folk song to calm them down,' Jimmy continued, his grey eyes twinkling. 'Claimed music soothed the savage beast.'

'Hill and gully rider!' Brother Bertie sang softly, grinning. 'Hill and gully! Worked a treat – until that big one escaped and started swinging from the boat's rigging.'

'Swinging straight into the police launch patrol,' Jimmy corrected. 'That Sergeant nearly had a heart attack when a monkey landed on his head.'

'Worth every minute in the cells to see that copper's face.' Brother Bertie wheezed with laughter. 'Thought he was having hallucinations!'

'We were young and stupid enough to think smuggling exotic animals was a good career move,' Jimmy protested. 'Never did find out what that dodgy zoo owner really wanted them for.'

'We were never proper gangsters that day, were we?' Brother Bertie reflected, his voice growing softer. 'Just two lads having an adventure on the river.'

Jimmy nodded slowly, understanding the deeper meaning. 'Lads who became brothers.'

They raised their glasses in silent toast.

To friendship that had survived betrayal, to love that had conquered loss, to the river that had witnessed their darkest moments and brightest triumphs. The crystal clinked softly as they drank, the intoxicating rum warming their throats and their hearts.

Behind them, Chrissie's laughter rang out like silver bells across the Thames, joined by Edmund's delighted chuckle and the voices of everyone who'd found their way from darkness into light.

The boat sailed on through the golden evening, carrying its cargo of redeemed souls towards whatever tomorrow might bring.

# Free Novella

Join Our Exclusive Book Club

If you haven't already, plunge into the gangland world where the Steele and Watson Crime Family Drama started.

# Dangerous

## A LOVE & HATE SERIES PREQUEL

**Fate throws them together. The streets try to tear them apart.**

Bertram Watson, aka Brother Bertie, newly arrived from Jamaica, finds himself on the run in London's gritty streets. Jimmy Steele, son of a feared gangster, is bleeding out in a warehouse after a botched heist. Their paths cross in a twist of fate that will change their lives forever.

As Bertie's Jamaican street smarts clash with Jimmy's East End savvy, they form an unlikely alliance. But with rival gangs closing in and dangerous secrets coming to light, their newfound friendship is put to the ultimate test.

In this thrilling novella, loyalties are tested, blood is spilled, and love is pushed to its limits in the unforgiving world of London's underworld.

# Dive into the Love and Hate Series

If you haven't already Books 1 and 2 in the Love and Hate Series are
Available on Amazon and FREE on Kindle Unlimited

## Love And Hate
## Book 1

THERE'S A THIN DEADLY LINE BETWEEN LOVE AND HATE

**London 1967**

The East End docks are ruled by one man - Danny Steele, the infamous and ruthless King of the Docks. Blood brothers, Jimmy 'Southpaw' Steele and Bertram Watson, aka, Brother Bertie are rising stars in Jimmy's father's gangland empire. Needing cash in a hurry, they go behind Danny's back and pull a criminal job that threatens to tear the underworld apart.

If Danny discovers what his son and best friend have done, he won't just kill them - he'll make them suffer first. And Danny Steele always finds out.

While Jimmy's sister, Sin chases her dreams in London's glittering fashion scene, she ignites a dangerous, forbidden affair that could destroy them all.

In this brutal, gangland world, family love is the deadliest weapon of all.

The explosive first book in the gritty and thrilling Love and Hate Series

# Honour And Vengeance
## Book 2

BOUND BY BLOOD.
TORN APART BY LOYALTY AND BETRAYAL

**London 1969**

The East End docks are closing. Danny Steele's once-mighty criminal empire is crumbling. When he plans a dangerous bank heist, his son Jimmy 'Southpaw' Steele and his brother in crime, Brother Bertie are dragged deeper into a criminal underworld.

But Jimmy doesn't know that his best friend harbours a deadly secret -- Brother Bertie can't forget the woman he's forbidden to love, and it could destroy their brotherhood forever. While Sin Steele struggles to escape her father's shadow, her own dangerous feelings threaten to expose truths that could tear the Steele family apart.

When gang warfare erupts, the heist turns into a collision course with betrayal and vengeance. In gangland London, honour is just another word for revenge, and the price of family betrayal is always paid in full.

Brace yourself for this brutal British Crime Thriller.

**Book 2** in the hard-hitting, gritty **Love and Hate Series.**

Available on Amazon and FREE on Kindle Unlimited

# Want More Jimmy Southpaw And Brother Bertie?

**The Big Mo Series**

Enter a world of ruthless ambition and deadly family feuds!
The Steele and the Watson families are back in the epic Big Mo Gangland Series
Available on Amazon and FREE in Kindle Unlimited.

**IN GANGLAND MEN REIGN BUT IT'S THE WOMEN WHO RULE**

## Dirty Tricks
## Book 1

**Mo Watson is caught in the crossfire of a vicious gangland war.**
**She'll need every dirty trick in the book to survive.**

Pint-sized teen tearaway, Maureen 'Big Mo' Watson, creates mayhem running her own street gang. Her dad is long gone and she won't listen to the pleas of her mum and granddad, Brother Bertie When she's talent-spotted by local villain Barker, Mo jumps at the chance to start climbing the criminal underworld ladder.

Then a vicious and violent East End gangland war to the finish breaks out between Mo's boss, Barker and fearsome gangster, Jimmy Southpaw, the head of the notorious Steele family. Mo is soon in the thick of this brutal struggle. But why are Barker and Jimmy really fighting? And will Mo live long enough to find out?

# Fight Dirty
## Book 2

**In Gangland It's The Women Who Fight Dirty**

Notorious East End gangster, Jimmy Southpaw, has made his long-lost granddaughter, Maureen 'Big Mo' Watson, the head of his criminal empire. But not everyone is happy about it. Including Mo's tough as nails new stepmother, Kristal Steele.

When a mysterious new gangster goes to war with her, Mo begins to doubt her ability to fill Jimmy's shoes. Feeling her enemies circling Mo contacts ruthless bad boy, Nico Sinclair to help find out who's trying to take her criminal crown.

Who is this gangster taking Mo on?

Will Jimmy think he's made a mistake choosing Mo as his gangland heir?

# Wicked Women
## Book 3

**There's another deadly Queen of Crime in town.**
**Classy, elegant and beautiful.**
**And the cruellest woman you'll ever meet.**

Maureen 'Big Mo' Watson, the Queen of Gangland, stumbles upon her late father's blueprint for the perfect heist—a crime meant to be Robbie Steele's swan song before his mysterious demise. Suddenly, Mo finds herself pitted against The Duchess, a ruthless aristocrat who strikes fear into the heart of even Mo's grandfather, the legendary East End gangster Jimmy Southpaw.

Jimmy thinks he's finally tracked down the answer to the question that has tormented him for years. Who killed his son and heir, Robbie?

What everyone thinks they know is blown away in a storm of violence that blasts the guilty and innocent alike. Mo is at the centre of it all. At every turn, shadows of the past are haunting her.

Is it one of these shadows that's finally going to put her in the ground?

Will she survive the shocking truth about her father's death.

Available on Amazon and FREE on Kindle Unlimited

# Play Dirty
## Book 4

**The electrifying finale to the Big Mo Gangland Thriller Series**

When an explosive incident shakes Big Mo to the core, she realises that gangland is no place to raise her young son. She wants out – for good. But when a ruthless enemy emerges, threatening to topple her empire and loved ones, Mo is forced to confront the dark crimes and secrets from her family's past.

Ducking and diving through a world of betrayal and vengeance, Mo finds herself drawn back into the arms of old flame, Nico Sinclair, once one of London's most notorious gangsters.

From Mayfair's glitter to the East End's grit, can Mo escape the underworld alive?

In a game where family ties strangle and playing fair was never an option, there's only one rule for survival:

# Check out Amazon for all of our books

Dreda Amazon Books UK
Dreda Amazon Books US

Reviews: We write for you!
We adore hearing what you think about our books. Reviews help other readers find books. So do please leave a review.

For news and staying in touch head over to:
www.dredamitchell.com including signing up to our newsletter for goodies and free stories.
https://www.facebook.com/dredasaymitchell/
https://www.tiktok.com/@dredaryanauthors?lang=en

# All About Dreda & Ryan

Her Majesty Queen Elizabeth awarded Dreda an MBE in her New Year's Honours' List, 2020! She has appeared on Queen Camilla's Reading Room.

Ryan and Dreda are a husband and wife team who write across the crime and mystery genre - psychological thrillers, gritty gangland crime and fast-paced action books.

Dreda scooped the CWA's John Creasey Dagger Award in 2004, the first time a Black British author has received this honour.

Spare Room, their first psychological thriller was a #1 UK and US Amazon Bestseller. Lee Child, named her 2022 novel, Say Her Name his best book of the year so far. She is one of the twelve acclaimed female authors of International Bestselling, Marple, a new reimagined Miss Marple anthology. Dreda is a passionate campaigner and speaker on social issues and the arts. She has appeared on television, including Celebrity Pointless, Celebrity Eggheads, BBC 1 Breakfast, Sunday Morning Live, Newsnight, The Review Show and Front Row Late on BBC 2. She had Fun! Fun! Fun! With Alan Carr on documentary series, Alan's Adventures with Agatha Christie, Channel 4.

Dreda's Black History Month short story about the remarkable Althea McNish was narrated on Amazon's Alexa by Sir Trevor MacDonald. Ryan and Dreda both performed a specially commissioned monologue on the ground-breaking SkyArts50 on Sky TV. She was a judge on the Women's Prize, Discoveries initiative for new writers, 2025.

Dreda has been a guest on many radio shows and presented BBC Radio 4's flagship books programme, Open Book. She has written in a number of leading newspapers including The Guardian and was thrilled to be named one of Britain's 50 Remarkable Women by Lady Geek in association with Nokia. She is a Trustee of The Royal Literary Fund and an ambassador for The Reading Agency.

Some of their books are currently in development as TV and film adaptations.

Dreda's parents are from the beautiful Caribbean island of Grenada. Her name, Dreda, is Irish and pronounced with a long vowel ee sound in the middle!

Printed in Dunstable, United Kingdom

77350297R00298